NATIONAL BESTSELLER · INDIE NEXT PICK

"A clever novel about exes reconnecting . . . Do not underestimate McCauley's witty insights or his ability to make middle-aged, sexless companionship seem wildly appealing."
—*PEOPLE* MAGAZINE (BOOK OF THE WEEK)

"*My Ex-Life* is a pleasure of the deepest sort—it's a wise, ruefully funny, and ultimately touching exploration of midlife melancholy and unexpected second chances. Stephen McCauley is a wonderful writer, and this may be his best book yet."
—TOM PERROTTA, BESTSELLING AUTHOR OF *MRS. FLETCHER*

"McCauley delights with intimately, often hilariously observed characters and a winking wit that lets plenty of honest tenderness shine through. Readers will love spending time in these pages."
—*BOOKLIST* (STARRED REVIEW)

"A gin and tonic for the soul." **—*KIRKUS REVIEWS***

"A charming slice of life about former spouses (one gay, one straight) on the other side of fifty who have been kicked around by life but find purpose when they reconnect in a seaside Massachusetts town. Laughs included."
—*ENTERTAINMENT WEEKLY*

A BEST BOOK OF THE YEAR —NPR, SHELF AWARENESS

Praise for *My Ex-Life*

"McCauley fits neatly alongside Tom Perrotta and Maria Semple in the category of 'Novelists You'd Most Like to Drive Across the Country With.'"
                                        —*The New York Times Book Review*

"*My Ex-Life* is a pleasure of the deepest sort—it's a wise, ruefully funny, and ultimately touching exploration of midlife melancholy and unexpected second chances. Stephen McCauley is a wonderful writer, and this may be his best book yet."
                                        —Tom Perrotta, bestselling author of *Mrs. Fletcher*

"*My Ex-Life* is Steve McCauley's best novel so far—and that's saying a lot. For those of us who devoured his previous books and eagerly awaited another, *My Ex-Life* is cause for celebration. McCauley's trademark wit and cultural commentary is all here, as is a cast of smart, complicated, heart-sore characters. I love the nuanced portrayal of the friendship between David and Julie, the couple at the heart of the book—a divorced pair who reconnect after an absence of many years and find a way to build a mature and honest relationship on the foundation of the affection, and even the mistakes, of their shared past. You're going to love *My Ex-Life*."
                                        —Anita Diamant, author of *The Boston Girl* and *The Red Tent*

"This wonderful novel has its finger on the pulse of the present, but the questions it asks—about family and the ineluctable past and the strange, sustaining grace of friendship—are as timeless as the elegance and craft of its prose. Stephen McCauley is a master, one of our wisest and funniest observers of American life."
                                        —Garth Greenwell, author of *What Belongs to You*

"Before you read *My Ex-Life*, make sure the person you sleep with is willing to be woken constantly by your laughter. Stephen McCauley writes sparkling, graceful, witty prose with an ease and fluency that seems like sleight-of-hand. If I were the kind of reader who highlighted brilliant passages, the whole entire book would be underlined."

—Katherine Heiny, author of *Standard Deviation*

"From the first page of *My Ex-Life*, I was sending Stephen McCauley mental valentines and figurative fan notes, thanking him for this delicious, smart, funny novel, its endearing characters, and his wry, bighearted cynicism. Oh, if all books could be like this one!"

—Elinor Lipman, author of *On Turpentine Lane*

"*My Ex-Life* is a rich, yet delicate ragout of wonderfully vivid characters, hilarious dialogue, and spot-on cultural criticism. It satisfies on every level." —Richard Russo, bestselling author of *Everybody's Fool*

"One of the best books, as far as I'm concerned, this year is *My Ex-Life* by Stephen McCauley. It is quirky and funny and beautifully observed."

—Jane Green on NBC's *Today Show*

"Interesting. And complicated. And hilarious."

—Seija Rankin, *Entertainment Weekly*

"A clever novel about exes reconnecting . . . Do not underestimate McCauley's witty insights or his ability to make middle-aged, sexless companionship seem wildly appealing."

—*People* magazine (Book of the Week)

"I didn't know how much I needed a laugh until I began reading Stephen McCauley's new novel, *My Ex-Life*. This is the kind of witty, sparkling, sharp novel for which the verb 'chortle' was invented. . . . Like the best of comic fiction writers—I'm thinking, in particular, of the immortal Laurie Colwin—McCauley draws his readers into reflecting on some of the big questions (sexuality, mortality, failure) with the lure of laughter."

—Maureen Corrigan, NPR's *Fresh Air*

"A charming slice of life about former spouses (one gay, one straight) on the other side of fifty who have been kicked around by life but find purpose when they reconnect in a seaside Massachusetts town. Laughs included."   —*Entertainment Weekly*

"Everything you've heard (or read) about *My Ex-Life*, the acclaimed new novel by Stephen McCauley (of *The Object of My Affection* fame) is true; it's subtly wicked-funny and insightful."   —*Baltimore OUTloud*

"With *My Ex-Life*, a heartwarming comedy of manners about second chances and starting afresh, [McCauley] has pretty much outdone himself. . . . McCauley fires off witticisms like a tennis ace practicing serves. . . . In the vein of inveterate beguilers like Laurie Colwin, Elinor Lipman, and Maria Semple, McCauley is warm but snappy, light but smart—and just plain enjoyable."   —*NPR*

"Warm, very funny, and observant . . . In his adroit and affecting new novel, *My Ex-Life*, [McCauley] revisits the emotional territory of that first novel: the special closeness that may arise between a gay man and a straight woman."   —*San Francisco Chronicle*

"Funny, heartfelt, and utterly winning."   —*Southern Living*

"Divorce is the great reuniter in Stephen McCauley's sharp, laugh-out-loud novel."   —*Martha Stewart Living*

"McCauley delights with intimately, often hilariously observed characters and a winking wit that lets plenty of honest tenderness shine through. Readers will love spending time in these pages."
                                                    —*Booklist* (starred review)

"Summer reads don't get much sweeter than this novel. . . . McCauley charmingly juggles an assortment of funny, believable characters . . . as each, in their different ways, find their way home."   —*The Seattle Times*

"His writing is an absolute delight. . . . It's one of those stories I love so much because it's about the idea of who we surround ourselves with, the family we create, and all the different kinds of relationships we have in our lives and how wonderful and frustrating and heartbreaking and absurd they can be." —WAMC's *The Roundtable*

"Gentle, wise . . . This lovely novel . . . shows how, with some loving help, you can reset your life." —WBUR's *The ARTery*

"It's hard to convey the sheer joy of reading McCauley's effervescent, penetrating prose that can be simultaneously hilarious and heartbreaking." —*The Bay Area Reporter*

"McCauley has a remarkable talent for telling a story filled with insights into human behavior and laced with plenty of humor."

—*Shelf Awareness*

"This comedy of manners is a summery confection tinged with awareness of a coming autumn." —*Publishers Weekly*

"Captivating . . . McCauley [presents] wonderfully distinctive and detailed people who are smart and funny. The observational aspects of the novel are so vivid that you are likely to race through the book in a few sittings." —*Connecticut Post*

"Sardonic, wry, and ceaselessly funny as it may be, *My Ex-Life* genuinely surprises as it progresses, accumulating tenderness, warmth, and complexity, and providing some latitude for modest growth and underplayed epiphanies to all its vivid characters—even the most jaded, narcissistic, and rapacious." —*Almanac Weekly*

"Reading *My Ex-Life* sometimes feels like a long and especially brilliant *New York Times* 'Modern Love' installment, full of modern twists and turns. But it's more than that. It's a provocative search for the essence of home—a village, a house, a community, a comingling of souls with certain affinities that somehow find each other and are fortunate enough to recognize what they have." —*Wicked Local*

"A tender, strikingly 'true' story that is warm, clear, and nuanced." —*Library Journal*

"McCauley's effervescent prose is full of wit and wisdom on every topic—college application essays, Airbnb operation, weed addiction, live porn websites, and, most of all, people. . . . A gin and tonic for the soul." —*Kirkus Reviews*

"Together, this oddball group proves that a family can be a pot-smoking mom, a moody teen, and Mom's gay ex-husband." —Brit + Co

"A smart, fun novel . . . McCauley . . . describes the characters' evolving relationships with wit and warmth." —*AARP Magazine*

"You can recognize great writers in their minor characters. For every inspiring Elizabeth Bennet, there's a devious Caroline Bingley, and for every devastating Mr. Darcy, there's an unfortunate Mr. Collins. Stephen McCauley belongs to an elite club of authors who create such memorable supporting roles, and in his latest, *My Ex-Life*, he serves up a narcissistic San Francisco real estate agent, a bitter, tourist-town shopkeeper, and an exotic next-door philanderer, to name just three." —*Chronogram*

"Many readers will see aspects of their own lives reflected in these pages." —*BookPage*

"Nothing is more satisfying . . . than what can be aptly described as a plain, old-fashioned 'good read,' especially one as well-written as *My Ex-Life* from skillful storyteller and bestselling author Stephen McCauley." —Lambda Literary

My Ex-Life

Also by Stephen McCauley

My Ex-Life

Stephen McCauley

FLATIRON
BOOKS
NEW YORK

MY EX-LIFE. Copyright © 2018 by Stephen McCauley. All rights reserved. Printed in the United States of America. For information, address Flatiron Books, 175 Fifth Avenue, New York, N.Y. 10010.

www.flatironbooks.com

The Library of Congress has cataloged the hardcover edition as follows:

Names: McCauley, Stephen, author.
Title: My ex-life / Stephen McCauley.
Description: First edition. | New York : Flatiron Books, 2018.
Identifiers: LCCN 2017060580 | ISBN 9781250122438 (hardcover) |
    ISBN 9781250122421 (ebook)
Classification: LCC PS3563.C33757 M9 2018 | DDC 813'.54—dc23
LC record available at https://lccn.loc.gov/2017060580

ISBN 978-1-250-12244-5 (trade paperback)

Our books may be purchased in bulk for promotional, educational, or business use. Please contact your local bookseller or the Macmillan Corporate and Premium Sales Department at 1-800-221-7945, extension 5442, or by email at MacmillanSpecialMarkets@macmillan.com.

First Flatiron Books Paperback Edition: May 2019

10 9 8 7 6 5 4 3 2 1

To Denise Shannon and Denise Roy,

with gratitude for your invaluable support and advice

My Ex-Life

No, it was not the happiest moment of David Hedges's life. Soren, his partner of five years, had left him, he'd gotten fat, and somewhere in the midst of that, he'd woken up one day and realized he was no longer in his twenties. Or his forties. The last person he expected to hear from was Julie Fiske.

He and Julie had a history, albeit an ancient and complicated one. They hadn't seen each other in almost thirty years, hadn't spoken in more than twenty, and David assumed that their story, like a few other things in his life—his desire to visit Petra; his vow to study piano; his sexual relevance—had ended. This didn't diminish her importance to him. His memories of her lingered, faded by the years in flattering ways. In his mind, they were still best friends. He hoped the separation had boosted her image of him as well. He knew he was best appreciated in small doses and at great distances, a fact that bothered him less than he suspected it should.

He heard of Julie Fiske infrequently through a few mutual friends and an occasional late-night computer perusal when he was feeling maudlin. *Oh, Julie.* He'd pieced together scraps and had come to the conclusion that she had a happy life—a husband (her second), a teenaged daughter, a large house on the ocean north of Boston. She taught art at a private school for kids with learning problems, not what she'd imagined for herself in her younger incarnation, but who was he to judge? It appeared things had finally gone well for her. He was delighted. There had been years when he worried that she'd been set on a path of bad choices and bad luck by the mistake of her brief, misguided first marriage.

To him.

They'd been in touch sporadically for a while after the divorce, and then she'd met and eventually married Henry Bell, an investment adviser David had had the pleasure of never meeting. David wasn't good at making money with money, and he was suspicious of people who were, especially when they did it with other people's money, an activity he equated with plagiarism. More recently, Henry had turned restaurateur, probably a midlife bid for low-level glamour. He hoped Julie was happy with Henry while hoping she still had a special place in her heart for him.

Over the years, David had thought of trying to see her when he went east to visit family, but he'd never followed through. Having moved as far away as the continent would allow, it seemed easiest to leave three thousand miles between them. The period of life they'd shared was his ex-life, and he was resigned to leave it at that. In the wake of Soren's departure, he'd come to realize he was racking up a number of ex-lives he could look back on with varying degrees of happiness, disappointment, and disapproval. What was less clear was whether or not he had a viable life ahead of him.

And then one day during that season of his aggrieved discontent, he received a phone call from Julie Fiske that changed everything.

1

Julie touched the pocket of her white shirt. Yes, the joint was still there, and no, she wasn't going to smoke it. She'd given up pot, and thank god for that. Life was so much more clear and simple without it. Henry had told her he wanted to discuss something when he dropped off Mandy tonight, and since Henry rarely discussed anything—was, she finally saw, incapable of discussion in the ordinary sense of the word—she interpreted the comment as a threat and had spent the afternoon under a cloud of foreboding. She needed to be sharp for whatever was coming.

She took a seat on the steps at the back of the house, clutching a bag with half a dozen muffins in it, and waited for Henry's car to pull into the drive. The muffins were for Carol, the woman Henry had left her for. Naturally, Carol was younger. Julie knew only one man who'd betrayed his marriage for a woman older than his wife, and it was overstating it to say she *knew* Prince Charles.

A soft breeze was blowing up from the ocean, bringing with it the smell of salt and seaweed. From the steps where she was sitting, she could see the harbor and the shadowy lobster boats tugging on their moorings and the yellow lights starting to come on in the awful restaurants along the shore. It was funny how you could love a view, even while recognizing it as a cliché vista of the New England coastline. She'd been ambivalent about the town of Beauport itself at the start—so small, so provincial—but had overlooked all that because she loved (she loved!) the house. She eventually came to appreciate Beauport's obvious charms, although they were tinged with loneliness since Henry had left. Dumped her, but who was counting? It was important not to turn bitter.

At this point, it was hard to know how she felt about the marriage ending. She was too exhausted. They'd met almost twenty-two years ago, and while Julie had expected to spend the rest of her life with Henry, when she looked back with honesty and clarity—a rare and depressing combination—she saw that cracks had started to appear in the foundation about a decade earlier. These were hairline fractures she'd chosen to ignore: Henry's vague but persistent disapproval of her; his pervasive air of dissatisfaction; his decision to switch careers in his late forties to *run a restaurant*. Even his support of Mitt Romney had had an aura of aggression toward her, a how-do-you-like-that? quality she'd sensed but had been unable to label at the time.

Now they had a signed separation agreement and were inching toward the final act. The divorce was uncontested, they'd used a mediator, and so far, everyone was behaving like an adult. In Henry's case, a petulant, self-centered adult, but that made it emotionally easier to let go, even if she feared it might make it more complicated practically.

She knew that if she'd dragged in an antagonistic lawyer, she would have done better, but Henry was struggling financially, he was her daughter's father, and she'd always loathed people who exploited accidents and errors and alienated affections for profit. She was determined not to be one. It was one thing to hate someone for falling out of love with you, but another to attempt to turn it into an economic windfall. She'd been adamant about that in her divorce from David Hedges, against the advice of her mother. But there had been no property then, and there hadn't been a child. *I'm sorry, David.*

She was getting what she wanted most. Mandy would continue to live with her until she went to college—this crucial final year of high school when they could bond, with, hopefully, the cloud of unfinished marital business dispersed—and Julie would buy Henry out of the house. They'd agreed on a closing date in the middle of August. With the help of an ultra-organized friend at Crawford School, she'd actually sent in the paperwork to apply for the mortgage. The value of the house had more than doubled since they'd bought it, but years earlier, she'd paid off the joint mortgage they'd had with the money she'd inherited from her mother. What she now owed Henry—essentially, one quarter of the value quoted by a real estate agent—was daunting but not prohibitive.

She had confidence it would all work out. Shallow confidence, admittedly. It was similar to her sureness that she understood the specifics of the civil war in Syria—yes, but one pointed question and it all unraveled.

She'd been warned by friends who'd been through divorce that as the summer wearied on, she should expect Henry to grow less reasonable. Hopefully, tonight was not the beginning of this phase. He'd recently discovered that she'd started renting out rooms through Airbnb, despite her efforts at hiding it from him, so she had to be on best behavior. It was June 6; far from wearying on, the summer technically had not yet begun.

She pulled out the joint. Anxiously waiting for Henry to berate her wasn't doing anyone any good, and since she'd stopped smoking pot, it mattered less if she occasionally got stoned. Her slips were meaningless, parenthetical. Rain was predicted for tomorrow, so why not enjoy the lovely evening in a calm frame of mind? Weather was a useful excuse for so many things in life. Like air, there was always some of it, even if the quality varied from day to day. She lit and inhaled, and warmth flowed over her. The blue lights strung along the wharf that jutted into the harbor below sparkled and she could hear the faint, dreamy sounds of a piano from somewhere in the neighborhood, one of those thin, aimless, New Age chord progressions that the magic of marijuana transformed into Chopin. It was a shame pot did that thing to your memory, because everything else it did was so pleasant.

What she liked least about Carol was that she was essentially sympathetic. It would have been so much easier if Henry had left her for someone loathsome. Carol was small and anxious to please. She'd been so silently apologetic about their situation, Julie had wanted to hug her and tell her it was fine, even though, of course, it wasn't. There were lots of things Julie wanted to tell Carol: pink was not her color (pink was not anyone's color); the ponytail stuck through the baseball cap did not suit her; most of all, she was too good for Henry. Even Julie had probably been too good for Henry, but it had taken a while to realize that and some days, she still wasn't sure.

Naturally, if she said any of that, it would come out wrong, so instead she'd started sending small, inconsequential gifts back with Henry when he came around to pick up or drop off Mandy. Two weeks ago, it had been a jar of fig jam she'd picked up at a farmers' market. Mandy had reported that Carol liked figs, although she'd made it sound—as so much of what Mandy said these days sounded—like an insult. "She eats *figs*."

Tonight, muffins.

She took another hit of pot and heard someone calling her name. "Julie? Are you home?" Probably Tracy, the woman who'd arrived with her husband the night before. They were from . . . well, somewhere anyway, and were in Beauport for a wedding.

"Be right there," Julie called.

She tamped out the joint and was about to toss it into the trash when she thought better of it and slipped it into a fake rock she'd bought for extra keys (even though she never locked the doors) and kept tucked against the foundation. Knowing it was there would help her not smoke it.

As soon as she entered the house, she felt more at ease. She'd fallen in love with the place as soon as she saw it, a rambling nineteenth-century residence that allegedly had been built by a sea captain and added onto over the years with the exuberant eccentricity that appealed to her aesthetic. Every house in town claimed a connection to a sea captain, but this house was plopped on top of a hill, cherry-on-a-cupcake style, and was impressive enough to make the claim plausible. The woodwork, the stained glass panels, the graceful curve of the staircase, the built-in cabinets—so cozy and ship-like—the heavy porcelain doorknobs, and the wavy, blistered windowpanes that had survived blizzards and hurricanes and the baseballs and bad tempers of generations of residents. There were far too many rooms, a selling point when they'd bought it in the early, optimistic days of their marriage, a burden as time went on, and—as of three months ago when a colleague at school had persuaded her to rent rooms online because "everyone" was doing it—the source of an essential secondary-income stream. Once everything was settled, it would be the supplement she needed to cover bills and a few luxury items like—oh, food, for example.

When people showed an appreciation for the house as they checked in, she immediately liked them. One such person was Raymond Cross, the musician who'd checked in in April. But then, there had been so many things she'd liked about Raymond, it was hard to know where to begin. And best not to begin at all since she had no reason to believe she'd see him again. No matter how much she'd like to.

She found Tracy in the living room, lifting the seat cushion of a chair. Was she looking for quarters?

"Everything all right?" Julie asked.

Tracy turned, neither startled nor embarrassed. "I was looking to see if the other side was less stained. I guess you might as well leave it like this." She smiled, as if she'd complimented Julie's taste, showing off dazzling teeth, which, in Julie's heightened condition, reminded her of subway tiles. Nice hair, though. Blond, shampoo-commercial shiny, and snipped at the jawline in a way that suggested she was shopping for an identity at the hair salon.

"It's mostly family that uses the living room anyway," Julie hinted.

"I can see why. There's not enough light in here to read or do much of anything." Tracy had a cheerful voice that was completely out of sync with her comments, no doubt a sign of emotional disconnect. "Please," Tracy gestured. "Take a seat, won't you?"

Julie tried not to look insulted. After all, it was still her house.

"I'm fine standing," Julie said.

Tracy looked around the room, her eyes melting with empathy. "It is hard to find a place to sit with all this furniture you've got crammed in here, isn't it? How about we sit on this old sofa thing?"

The furniture in question was a 1950s teak daybed Julie had picked up for seventy-five dollars at a flea market in Rowley. Yes, it could stand to be reupholstered, but even in its current state she could easily get five hundred from a dealer she knew in Cambridge. And why sofa *thing*?

"I don't want to be rude, Tracy, but I'm waiting for my daughter to get dropped off. Her father and I have something important to discuss."

"Believe me," she said, "I won't take up more than a minute. I can see you're completely overwhelmed.'"

When Tracy and her husband got out of their spotless car wheeling identical black suitcases and wearing what appeared to be pressed jeans, Julie's eye had twitched. When everything looks perfectly right about a person, there's usually something significantly wrong. They were probably in their early thirties, that awkward age when people still believe they matter and that life is going to go their way. They'd stopped Julie this morning and asked if she knew a good place to run, preferably "a nice eleven-mile loop." Who ran that much, and why such an annoyingly random yet specific number?

"What did you want to talk about?" Julie asked, and then, fearing her tone might have been too harsh, she sat beside Tracy on the daybed.

"Isn't that more comfortable?" Tracy asked. She actually touched Julie's knee. "Did you read my profile when I made the booking?"

"I didn't study it closely." The line between understatement and lie was usefully blurry.

"That's all right. Jerry and I are professional personal organizers. We're the ones who coined the term 'messology.'"

"I'm afraid I'm not familiar with it," Julie said. She hated that everything had to be broken down into categories with cute labels, no doubt, in this case, as part of a branding scheme. A brand seemed to be more valuable than an actual talent these days, although the two things were connected somehow. It was true that given Tracy's spotless appearance and unflappable cheer, it was easier to think of her as a brand than as a person. Maybe it was the pot, but in this light, she did look like one of those bobble-headed dolls with her round eyes and her perfect hairdo.

"I'd be happy to work with you on one corner of a room in exchange for a free night. We've done some amazing work with people like you."

This was an accusation, one made in the superior tones of a religious fanatic, but it's always compelling to have someone tell you about yourself, even when it's something you'd rather not hear. "People like me?" Julie asked. "I'm not sure I follow you."

"I know it looks normal to you, but from where I sit, the signs are clear. We've developed a scale of the four stages of pre-hoarding. We call it the ABCD Scale. Aggressive Acquirer, Binge Buyer, Compulsive Collector, and Deluged Debtor. Jerry and I were discussing you in bed last night, and we think you're only at A, but what comes after A, Julie?"

A car pulled into the driveway. She did not need Henry to walk in on this conversation.

"I'm going to assume that's a rhetorical question," she said.

Tracy put her manicured hand on Julie's knee again. "I know it's tempting to get defensive, but is it worth it? When we see patients get defensive about their Aggressive Acquiring, we worry they're about to enter the next level."

Julie stood, trying to control her anger. She wanted to remind Tracy that she wasn't a patient and that there was no way she and her husband could insult their way into a free night. But remembering the threat of negative online reviews, she said, "I really appreciate your offer. It's so considerate, I'll gladly give you a fifty-dollar credit for your next stay." As she was leaving the room, she turned and said, "And it's a daybed, Tracy. A Danish modern daybed, not a sofa *thing*."

Henry was standing on the gravel driveway, surveying the back of the house disapprovingly. Seersucker shorts. Ridiculous at his age, but attractive on his newly defined thighs. Carol had issues with exercise that she was obviously passing on to Henry. Despite a desire to burst into tears—she was not a hoarder, barely a slob, just busy—Julie gave her most merry wave. Hopefully not one of those I'm-stoned-so-everything's-rosy waves. She headed down the steps carefully as Mandy emerged from the car with a thud, as if she'd dropped from a wall, and Opal bounded out after her. Opal ran over to Julie and began leaping up, at least to the extent that she could with her one hind leg. She growled in frustration, poor thing, and then raced around the yard frantically, barking. *Home, home, home, I'm home.*

With the joyless resignation that defined so many of her actions these days, Mandy lumbered to the trunk and pulled out her duffel bag.

"I thought you were going to have something done about those gutters," Henry said.

Julie looked back at the house. Henry had tossed out orders last time she'd talked with him. Naturally, she'd forgotten.

"I'm working on it," Julie said.

Mandy clomped over to Julie and planted a kiss on her cheek. A crumb tossed in her direction, but such a welcome one. "Nice *perfume,* Mom," she whispered.

It was getting harder to tell herself that Mandy knew nothing about her pot habit since, in the past year, it seemed as if Mandy knew more about most things while caring less about everything. Another reason to be glad she'd stopped smoking.

As soon as Mandy was inside, Julie tried to grab the advantage. She presented the oily bag to Henry. "A little something for Carol," she said. "Carrot muffins. I know she's big on vegetables."

He held up his hands as if she'd pointed a gun at him. "That's one of the things we need to talk about," he said. "No more gifts. It makes her feel terrible you're being so nice to her."

"Would it help if I included a nasty note?"

"You know what you're doing, so let's cut the comedy act."

Like a lot of people who have no sense of humor and take themselves entirely seriously, Henry assumed everyone else was playing it for laughs. Oddly, she'd been attracted to Henry's earnestness when she first met him, probably a reaction to David, who'd been compulsively ironic. The second husband was often a reaction to the first, just as Obama had been a reaction to Bush or—more appropriately in this case—Reagan had been a reaction to Carter. Henry had had the looks of an ordinary man you'd see grilling hamburgers in an ordinary backyard, a man you could imagine expounding too long on a topic of interest to no one, a contrast to David's lean angularity and floppy hair that had made him look, in certain lights, like a dashing minor character in a British miniseries about university life. Those less interesting qualities of Henry's had made her feel secure and, no doubt, a little more interesting herself. Henry had found her offbeat because she'd never worn makeup. Now he had Carol, who, according to Mandy, had a makeup mirror with multiple settings including one called "Home Lighting Situations." Julie had home-lighting situations, too, but they were blown bulbs, frayed cords, and trouble finding the circuit breakers.

She tossed the bag with the muffins onto the porch. "Fine. Was there anything else?"

He scanned the backyard in a way that made Julie nervous. She suddenly wished she hadn't smoked the joint after all.

"I had a call from Richard the other day," he said.

"Am I supposed to know who that is?"

Henry pointed to the hedge surrounding the property and indicated the house on the other side with his chin. "Amira's husband," he said.

"Oh, *that* Richard." Like most wealthy men who were married to gorgeous, much younger women, Richard's name was less relevant than his bank account. Julie and Amira were friends, at least to the extent that Amira was capable of having friendships with women. It helped that Julie provided less competition for male attention than Opal. She waited for Henry to say more, with a sick feeling growing in her stomach.

"He's interested in the house," Henry said. There was disingenuous enthusiasm in his voice, as if he really thought she'd be happy to hear this. *Good news! The tumor is malignant!*

"He has a house," Julie said. "According to Amira, he has several. And this house isn't for sale, so how is that relevant?"

"What do you need this monstrosity for? It's going to be a weight around your neck, trying to keep up with the bills and repairs. When Mandy goes off to college, you'll be rattling around in an empty house with the roof falling in."

"The roof is sound." That was true. The rest of what he'd said was up for grabs. It was important not to show that she was beginning to panic; Henry, like all cowards, had a knack for smelling blood in the water. "We have a deal, Henry. We've signed an agreement. I've submitted paperwork for the mortgage. Once we pass papers and finalize the divorce, you won't have to worry about the weights

I have around my neck. You'll be free, and frankly, so will I. As for Richard, he can buy some other historic house to knock down."

Henry shook his head with a combination of pity and disapproval, a variation on his prevailing attitude toward her since the glow had worn off their relationship and all the things that had charmed him about her began to annoy him. He'd been losing his hair for years, and recently, Carol had persuaded him to shave his head, a move that gave him a more solid and confident appearance. Specifically, he seemed more confident that he'd been justified in leaving her.

"I'm making sacrifices here, Julie. I need the money for the restaurant and Richard's offering more than we discussed. A hundred thousand more. Cash, no contingencies, no inspection."

"We did more than discuss it, we made an agreement. We have legal papers."

She could see his eyes wandering. This was what she'd come to realize about Henry, that he didn't listen when other people talked, just waited for them to stop talking so he could make his next point.

"The papers can be changed. And don't forget, the house is only one part of our agreement."

The summer was officially wearying on. The piano she'd heard earlier started up again, but this time it sounded jangly and jarring. Six months after she and Henry had moved into the house, she'd discovered she was pregnant. The place was bound up in her mind with Mandy and all the hopes they'd had for a happy life. She'd never known Mandy anywhere else, and if she lost the house, she'd be losing a connection to her daughter. She was stung by the realization that Henry had no nostalgic associations and saw the place primarily as a pawn.

"I don't like the direction Mandy's headed," he said. "She's evasive, she's cranky and surly. She comes over for the weekend and she doesn't even want to watch TV with us."

She didn't like the direction Mandy was headed in either, although it was hard to pinpoint a reason. She wasn't depressed, but she rarely exhibited anything like happiness. Her grades were holding steady, but somewhere in the mediocre range. She'd occasionally fly into a rage and stomp around the house, not caring if the guests heard her. There was something heavy about Mandy, like the muffins Henry had just rejected.

"So your concern is she's not interested in *House Hunters* and cooking competitions? You should spend a little more time with her peers. They're all like that. And you don't think your moving out might have hurt her?"

He pondered this briefly and then brought down the hammer. "Possibly, but she sees that I'm happy."

Julie had been happy for three days in April, when Raymond Cross had stayed at the house. But somehow, that brief respite had made her realize how numb she felt so much of the time. Maybe how numb she'd felt for years.

"I'm worried about college," he said. "I asked her what you and she were doing about it, and I got a vague response about a friend whose parents supposedly told her she doesn't have to go if she doesn't want."

"She's going to college," Julie said. "She took the SATs a couple of weeks ago. We'll know her scores in July. In the meantime, I'll get even more organized about it when my teaching's done."

"Really? Not too busy renting rooms and ignoring the up-keep on this place and forgetting to pay the bills? Those half-assed college visits earlier this spring?"

He moved his hands to his hips and glared at her for a moment across the twilit yard, once the scene of quiet evenings when she and Henry had sat side by side in Adirondack chairs and discussed their good fortune. She looked to the chairs, all too appropriately going to rot under the pine tree at the edge of the lawn. The contempt she could take, but when his face softened, something inside her dropped. She could smell trouble of a more serious kind on the breeze.

"Can we continue this inside?" he said.

As they walked in, Julie toggled between hoping he wouldn't notice all the dog shit on the lawn and wishing he'd step in it.

She indicated the sofa thing.

"Please," she said. "Take a seat."

"Thanks," he said. "I figured I could since it's still my house."

Henry plopped down wearily and she sat in a chair opposite him. "Have you noticed," she said, "that I've done a lot of tidying up in here?" Sometimes, if you plant a suggestion in someone's mind, they see what you want them to see.

He looked around doubtfully. "Still going to flea markets, I gather." He frowned and turned on a light. Or tried to. Home Lighting Situation #1.

"First of all," he said, "this isn't a fight. We're talking about what's best for our daughter."

The reasonable tone was clearly meant to allay hysteria. She felt as if a clamp was tightening in her throat.

"Please get to the point," she squeaked.

Again he cast a disapproving look with contempt in his eyes. "We have better schools where I'm living now."

She stood. "No!" Perhaps she said it too loudly; there was a creaking of floorboards from above, the room where the messologists were. "Absolutely not."

"Better schools, better counselors, more motivated students. A better place for her senior year."

"No. It's not part of the discussion."

"If you really expect to get primary custody, if you expect me to take peanuts for the house, maybe it needs to be. Have you thought of that? She needs rigor in her life and it's obvious she's not getting it here, especially with a lot of strangers tromping in and out."

"She's meeting people from all over the world," she said. "It's educational." It wasn't clear how changing sheets for a guest from Amsterdam was more educational than changing them for someone from New Hampshire, but there was no need to go into that. Newly bald Henry looked especially stern and steely in the dim light of the room. "I don't suppose you've even discussed this with Carol."

"As a matter of fact, it was her suggestion. She wants to get Mandy on a study schedule and take her out jogging with her."

After all the effort Julie had put into her little gifts. After trying to be so damned understanding for the past year and a half. What can you expect from someone who eats *figs*.

"If you had a shred of decency, Henry, you'd find Carol help for her fitness obsession instead of encouraging it and trying to drag your daughter into grade anxiety and body dysmorphia."

And then, in a depressingly reasonable tone, he said, "Come on, Julie. Admit it, you don't have a plan for college here."

"Actually, Dad, we do."

Julie turned. Mandy was standing in the doorway from the hall. She was wearing the same overalls and long-sleeved jersey she'd been wearing earlier, but had put on a woolen watch cap. Because it was so cold? Opal was beside her, looking up at her with the eager adoration Julie was no longer permitted to express to her daughter.

Henry's mouth was pursed in doubt. "Oh, really? And were you planning to tell me?"

"Mom contacted her first husband."

"What's he got to do with this?"

"He has a college-counseling business," Mandy went on. "We've been working together for a couple of weeks, talking schools and essays."

Julie was appalled by the audacity of this lie but said nothing.

A couple of months ago, Mandy had come across boxes of records and books of David's that were moldering in the basement. Julie had had no idea they were down there or why she had ended up with them in the first place. The boxes were a time capsule of a previous life she thought she'd let go of decades earlier.

"Who's David Hedges?" Mandy had asked, reading the name from inside one of the books.

When Mandy was ten, Julie had told her she'd been married before. Why not? But until that moment, Mandy had never seemed especially interested in the details, not that Julie had been eager to discuss them. As Mandy was flipping through the albums of Jane Birkin and Françoise Hardy and the other French singers David had introduced her to, Julie had felt an unexpected surge of nostalgia.

"The man I was married to briefly a million years ago," she'd said.

"Oh, right. Why'd you divorce?"

"That's a long story. We decided we were better as friends than husband and wife."

Mandy had nodded, looked through the records and books, and then, in a nonchalant way, said, "Gay?"

There was something galling about the fact that Mandy had apparently surmised in ten seconds what it had taken Julie years to figure out. She acknowledged that he was.

"We lost touch after your father and I met. He lives in California. I was thinking of him the other day." And then, as ghosts started to rise from the cartons, she said, "We had a little dog named Oliver with a tiny body and huge ears," and launched into a description of their pet and their apartment. Mandy had listened with unusual interest.

Mandy had taken the records and a few of the books up to her room along with the suitcase-like record player she'd found in some closet. She'd been listening to the records that weren't too warped, the singers' voices frail and melancholic, even when singing ostensibly happy songs. Julie had been out on the lawn one evening at dusk and Françoise Hardy's voice had come pouring down from the third floor, singing a heartbreakingly innocent song about friendship she'd recorded at age eighteen. The music had filled Julie with yearnings, partly for David and the imperfect life they'd been living back then, but mostly for the life she'd believed she would have. For the faith she'd had in possibilities.

Obviously, Mandy had done some investigating on her own.

"I thought he was in San Francisco," Henry said. "Appropriately enough."

Henry had enjoyed deriding David from the outset, reminding Julie that he was more of a man than David had been, whatever that meant. Men's obsessions with their own masculinity were embarrassingly effeminate. His jealousy of David had been ridiculous, but it was true that she'd always felt closer to David in an inexplicable way than she'd ever felt to Henry. At one time, she and Henry had been ardent lovers, they'd been companions for more than twenty years, and they'd been loving, cooperative parents, but she couldn't claim they'd been friends in the way she and David had been. It was a question of small matters: Henry never laughed about the same things she did; he'd never lain at the opposite end of the sofa and read whole novels to her; never sat up in bed and explained the virtues of Nicole Croisille's breathy delivery and Mistinguett's enduring appeal. He'd never opened up a world for her. He'd never even understood why she loved dogs.

"We're working on the phone and through email, Dad."

Mandy had moved closer to Julie's chair, and Julie felt a conspiratorial closeness she hadn't felt since Mandy was thirteen. She put her arm around Mandy's waist. "He charges a fortune for his service," Julie said. And then, to add something else that was not, technically, a lie: "We haven't gone over the specifics, but I know he'll agree to do it as a favor."

Henry stood up from the sofa thing and leaned back to relieve his spine. He and Carol loved showing off how much pain and irreparable joint damage their fitness cost them. "Is there some reason you didn't mention this when I brought it up earlier?"

"The thing is, Dad, we're telling you now."

"Just for the record," Henry said as Julie was walking him to his car, "I don't entirely believe that, but it'll be easy enough to check on whether you're getting anywhere. I want her to complete the common app and have a plausible list of colleges she plans to apply to by the date of the closing. That's August fourteenth."

It irritated her that the date had iconic status for him.

"If she doesn't, we're going back to mediation. I refuse to sacrifice everything."

"Wow," she said. "We've gotten to actual threats."

"Call me when you hear about the mortgage. If you get turned down, we need to start negotiating with Richard."

Julie was still buoyed by Mandy's use of "we" even if it had been folded into a lie. As she walked up the staircase to the third floor, she heard music, one of those Juliette Gréco songs that made you think of foggy docks and dark nights. It was warmer up here under the roof, and it smelled of tar and sunbaked wood.

When Mandy opened her bedroom door, the conspiratorial affection she'd shown earlier seemed to have evaporated. Probably it was too much to hope it would last.

"That's such a beautiful record," Julie said. "It makes me happy you're listening to this music."

"I'm not really. I like the way the scratches sound."

Surely there was something appealing in this, too?

"As you can probably guess," Julie said, "I have a lot of questions."

"I know, Mom, but you don't have a lot of time." She reached into the pocket of her overalls and handed Julie a scrap of notebook paper with a number on it. "You should call him tomorrow."

2

"Lorraine told me you did a great job on her daughter's college applications, David. She said you have a patented system."

"Patented in the loosest sense of the word." A more accurate description might be "applied OCD."

"Well, if you can help her, I don't think you'll have any problems with Nancy. She's been gifted since she was tiny."

The speaker was one Janine Rollins, a lawyer. Her husband and Nancy's father was a successful real estate developer, a term that, in San Francisco, had been a redundancy for well over a decade. Janine, Nancy, and David were sitting at the long library table in the dining room of David's rented carriage house. This was where he'd been meeting clients to discuss plans for their children's higher education for over fifteen years. On special occasions, he'd served meals at this table, but the surface and the room itself were so spotless, no one would have guessed it.

Nancy was still tiny, a small-boned girl with a mass of hair that fell from a center part and created a teepee of sorts around her face. She had the disturbing pallor David had come to recognize as a sign of either genetic illness or an unhealthy familiarity with Harry Potter. It was hard to imagine Janine as her mother. She was dressed in a conservative, perfectly tailored business suit and high heels, a popular and confusing combination of mixed wardrobe messages.

David had rarely worked with a parent who did not describe her child as "gifted." Usually it had to do with the parent's own identification with the title, if not quite the content, of Alice Miller's *The Drama of the Gifted Child,* a book as frequently invoked as it is misunderstood.

"She's been self-sufficient since she was two and spends most of her time writing as it is. Isn't that so, Nancy?"

Nancy shrugged. She'd said almost nothing since she and her mother arrived. David suspected it was not a question of timidity but a mixture of resentment and early-onset ennui over the fact that her time was being spent on this unnecessary outing.

"Are you interested in schools that have strong writing programs?" David asked her.

"She doesn't need that," her mother said. "She's written three novels already."

"Actually, I've written four," Nancy said. She had the uninflected, metallic voice of a robot in a low-budget sci-fi movie from the 1950s, a genre David was especially fond of. "I have two series. The Orgon Cascades and the Wreath of Mornia Glenn. I'm more interested in business so I can market my work and the merchandise I'm planning."

David found her use of "market" and "merchandise" upsetting. Like "investment portfolio" and "colonoscopy," they were terms that didn't sound right coming from the mouth of a sixteen-year-old.

Nancy reached into her backpack and handed him a spreadsheet with schools ranked according to criteria she'd listed on a separate page. "This might help you," she said, as if the whole project was for his benefit. Considering the fees he planned to charge her parents, he wasn't in complete disagreement.

At the end of their session, he handed Nancy a plastic folder with his logo printed on it and his standard (if not quite patented) questionnaires and timetables neatly tucked inside. *The Seven Steps to Your Future.* Really, there just as easily could have been four or even three, but he'd found that as parents became increasingly hysterical about the college application process, it helped to give their kids more to do. Last year there had been six steps. He was considering upping it to an even dozen for next year. By the time he retired, he'd be measuring it in miles. He'd actually had parents contact him to ask if there was anything their kids in grammar school should be doing to get ready for applying to college. "Looking for sane parents" was what he wanted to tell them.

Janine gave him her hand and complimented him on the light and views from the dining room. He thanked her, as if he'd had anything to do with them. From the bank of windows behind the table, you could see in the far distance the Bay Bridge and the soulless glass mistake of the Rincon tower, all bathed in the winsome glow that's typical of San Francisco light and, come to think of it, San Franciscans as well.

As David ushered them out the front door, Janine's heels click-ing on the hardwood, Janine said, "If you ever decide to sell this place, promise you'll tell me first. I've always admired the prop-erty when we drove past and wondered who owned the carriage house."

"I'm afraid I rent," he said. "The landlady lives in the main house. She's owned it for decades."

There was brief pause in which Janine absorbed this informa-tion, and David saw his stock sink. At some point, the idea of being a renter past the age of thirty had become shameful and unwhole-some, like living with one's mother into one's forties. He watched as Janine scanned the obsessively tidy living room and then—a sharp contrast—his own recently acquired weight and taut shirt.

"That's brilliant," she said, once she'd recovered. "Free to pick up and leave anytime. So unencumbered." She rested a hand on Nancy's back, either a subconscious acknowledgment of her own encumbrances or an attempt to get her daughter out of rented property as quickly as possible.

David's business was one he created out of the teaching and school counseling jobs that had formed the earlier part of his working life. It was a job he enjoyed and, based on the success of his clients and the frequency with which they referred their friends, one he was good at. He liked the editorial challenges, and it made him feel his professional life had progressed along a logi-cal path, versus his personal life, which had followed a more cir-cuitous route.

His title was "independent, full-service college counselor." He was paid to help the offspring of moneyed San Franciscans (a deep pool) select schools, organize visits, edit and structure essays, and get their applications in on time. He enjoyed the work—although there were moments when he tired of reading about saintly grand-parents and/or cancer—but he was secretly baffled by the intensity with which parents approached what was, ultimately, a straight-forward process.

While he was paid for *The Seven* (and counting) *Steps*, he thought of his true mission as helping his teenaged clients gain a realistic understanding of who they were and what they could achieve in life once they stepped away from their parents' self-aggrandizing fantasies of them. Their parents had been so insis-tent about instilling self-esteem, they'd fallen into the trap of telling their kids they could do anything. Unfortunately, almost everyone interprets doing "anything" as doing the same three or four glamorous and impressive things—going to Harvard, retiring before ever working, giving an Oscar acceptance speech, and be-coming the next Mark Zuckerberg, except hot. When it becomes clear, as it inevitably must, that those goals are out of reach, a lot of kids have a crisis of faith. David saw it as his job to make them appreciate themselves as they are, limitations and all.

David had nothing against self-esteem. After all, he'd spent tens of thousands of dollars over the years trying to buy some from an assortment of psychologists and therapists. It's just that he didn't believe it was something one should be given by one's parents in childhood; rather, it was something one should earn by talking about one's parents and childhood in therapy. He thought of the attainment of self-esteem as similar to aging with dignity—impossible but worth striving for nonetheless.

The questions he asked his clients to respond to had little to do with academics. On the whole, he'd found this area the most obvious but least helpful in getting to know them. He liked to think of his questionnaires as the Myers-Briggs personality test that that estimable mother-daughter team would have composed if they'd been your nosy gay neighbors. *What was your best birthday party and why? What were you wearing the last time you were happy? If asked to turn off your phone for eight hours, would your reaction be "I'm free!" or "I'm freaking out!"? Cake or potato chips? Do you know the difference between deciduous and coniferous trees? Without looking it up?*

The Seven Steps themselves were a good deal more mundane, but as a result, he'd become adept at setting up timelines and deadlines. He'd learned that it didn't matter so much what you told kids to do as long as you gave them a date to do it by.

Shortly after Janine and her prolific daughter left, David went for a walk to get some exercise and—its opposite—some cookies. As he was on the return leg, he received a call from Renata Miller. She was the mother of a former client, and they'd become friends over the past few years.

"You sound winded," she said. "What are you doing?"

"Walking."

"If you're trying to prove you're a better person than me, you win."

"I'm trying to lose weight." This was not strictly true, but it was an excuse fewer and fewer people questioned. Since Soren had left him about six months earlier, he'd gained over fifteen pounds, largely thanks to San Francisco's excellent bakeries and Thai restaurants with twenty-four-hour delivery. "Where are you?" he asked. There was traffic and a police siren in the background.

"Driving from an open house in North Beach. 'Restful retreat.'"

"No windows, I gather."

"I think there was one or two," she said.

"You're obviously not the listing agent."

Renata was another successful real estate agent who'd made a name for herself by representing a select number of high-quality, aesthetically unspoiled properties. It was a career she'd stumbled into after giving up her aspirations to act. She'd acquired many of the archetypical characteristics of high-end real estate agents, which, it turned out, were not so different from those of actresses—tooth whitening, Botox, expensive clothes, a taste for younger men, and a resentment of younger women.

"I went to look at the place for you," she said.

"Terribly thoughtful," David said. "But I have a long-term lease on the last good deal in San Francisco, remember?" Increasingly, David's low rent—the result of having a rich and eccentric landlady—had become one of the most interesting things about him in the real-estate-obsessed city.

There was a pause, and then she said, "I'm not far from you, and I need to put my feet up. I could be there in twenty minutes."

"If you want, but I don't have any food in the house. I'm dieting."

"It's all right, I'm fasting."

When he arrived home, he immediately began to throw magazines and newspapers around the living room so it would look more lived in. Renata took a dim view of David's increased tidiness since Soren's departure.

His business line rang, but he didn't recognize the out-of-state number, so he didn't pick up. No message.

Renata arrived half an hour later, complaining of traffic and parking problems. She was carrying her phone, a briefcase, and what appeared to be an expensive leather handbag. She looked around the room and tossed all of her accoutrements on the sofa.

"I'd love a drink," she said. "White wine if you have it."

"I thought you were fasting."

"I didn't ask for food. Anyway, they had sandwiches at the open house, if you can imagine anything more grotesque. I took a few for the office, and I was so frustrated with the traffic, I ate a couple before I knew what I was doing."

David led her into the kitchen, and as he uncorked the wine she stood leaning against the counter, surveying the appliances with the cash-register glance he'd noticed on all real estate agents. She opened a cabinet, one in which, to David's horror, the boxes, cans, and bottles were lined up perfectly by height.

They took their wine into the living room, and Renata dropped herself onto the sofa, removed her shoes, and arranged her long legs to their best advantage. She was an attractive woman with— despite her cosmetic adjustments—a casual nonchalance about her wardrobe. She wore expensive clothes but always looked as if she'd been in a rush putting them on. Someone else might have looked ragged with a blouse partly untucked or a clip coming loose from her hair, but those details gave Renata a world-weary glamour, like the former mistress of a French politician. She'd had Teddy—the son David had helped get into Tufts—when she was almost forty, and this, against all odds, added to her allure as well.

She checked her phone and then flung it aside with a sigh. All the details of her life seemed to frustrate or disappoint Renata. "What are your summer plans?" she asked.

"I might go on a wilderness backpacking trip for a month or so."

"Very funny. You should plan something. You're too settled into this house. It's not healthy."

"I'm not sure why settled is unhealthy. I prefer to think of it as stable."

"It's always a matter of resignation."

"You include your settled marriage in that?"

"Leonard and I stay together out of mutual antipathy, which is a different matter entirely. We despise each other enough to keep our marriage passionate. And yes, screaming at each other does count as passion."

Shortly after David met Renata, she took him out for coffee, ostensibly to describe her expectations for her son's education. Instead, she went on at great length about an affair she'd had years earlier with Paolo, an Italian airline pilot. David had the feeling she thought gossiping was the sort of thing one did with a gay male friend, and since she'd been in San Francisco acting and real estate circles for decades, she might have learned from experience. The story did have the well-polished veneer of a tale edited over the course of multiple retellings. It was as if she was offering him credentials to excuse what might otherwise have been assumed was, god forbid, a faithful marriage to a man most viewed as unappealing. Apparently, she and the pilot had met in a variety of luxury hotels whenever Alitalia did them both the favor of putting him behind the controls of a San Francisco–bound 767. Despite

Renata's claims of a genuine emotional connection to Paolo, what she mostly discussed with David were the brands of the toiletries in the bathrooms of their expensive hotel rooms and the exotic beauty of his uncircumcised penis. He hadn't heard anything about a more recent lover, leading him to believe she had none or, if she did, he had neither access to stellar hotels nor a foreskin.

Although Renata's mood was frequently a variation on her distracted crankiness of today, there was something about her frazzled energy that David found exciting. Her mind was always racing, and her body seemed to be set at a high temperature, releasing the scent of a signature Bottega Veneta perfume mixed with sweat. She could be so acerbic about other people, David remained in rapt anticipation of finding out what she found acceptable about him. When she'd had a few too many chardonnays, she liked to tell him that whether he knew it or not, he was almost certainly bisexual. He was insulted by these comments about his sexuality, mainly because she seemed to think he'd find them complimentary. He'd never mentioned having been married; he no longer considered his brief, youthful marriage to Julie Fiske or his earlier relationships with women evidence of bisexuality any more than he considered his weeklong trip to Prague in the 1990s evidence of Czech citizenship.

"What are you paying for this place?" Renata asked. She took another sip of the wine and puckered disapprovingly.

When David mentioned his rent, a sum Renata knew already, she said, "That's ridiculous. I hope you're not assuming it will last forever."

"No more than I'm assuming I will. And as a matter of fact, it will last for another five years, according to the terms of my lease."

"Your landlady has been a saint to you, David." She put down the wine with a formality that suggested she wasn't going to pick it up again. "I've heard a rumor that she's been talking with brokers."

This announcement, which David had heard before from Renata, had lost its power to throw him into a panic. Even so, it was unwelcome news. "You're not one of those brokers, are you?"

"I'm your friend, David."

"That's true, but it's not an answer."

"She contacted *me*. What was I supposed to say?"

He looked at her more closely. The conversation had entered new territory, and suddenly he saw malevolence in her unlined face. "As a friend, 'no' might have been a good place to start."

"And then what? She goes to the next name on the list, the property sells, and I lose the commission. As my friend, I doubt you'd want that to happen."

Part of what David found exhilarating about Renata was her ability to justify all her actions, not exactly an admirable quality, but, like anything done with conviction, compelling.

She leaned down and took up the wineglass with a resigned, almost disgusted expression. She and her husband were wine connoisseurs, which is to say, incipient alcoholics with money. "Anyway, she seems resolved to go through with it this time. Since you love this place so much, you must know the kind of enthusiasm it will excite. And since she's been so good to you all these years, I know you won't raise a fuss about the lease."

"At least you came to tell me in person," he said. "That shows character."

"If I wanted to show character, I'd stop getting my face injected. I came because you're a friend. Also to extend an invitation. Leonard's having some people over next week, and we'd love if you came."

"I'm not big on Leonard's friends."

"Leonard doesn't have friends. He has financial opportunities wearing socks. There'll be a lot of spoiled couples with spoiled children unqualified to get into the schools they're willing to pay you to help get them into."

"If you think this makes up for anything," he said, "you're mistaken."

Leonard was a pugnacious, excessively homely man who'd made a significant fortune for himself. He had a conviction in his own importance that made him seem, well, important. David had worked with a handful of families referred to him by Leonard and Renata, and with this house news, he was going to need to increase his client base in a major way.

Renata gathered up her things and stood, dangling her shoes from her fingers. David ushered her to the door.

"Maybe you *should* go on a hiking trip," she said. "Preferably in a car. It would take your mind off things. When you get back we'll find something for you to buy. Or rent, if you must. I know your landlady would like to have the place sold and be out of here by August thirty-first. Just so you have a deadline."

Upon hearing the word "deadline," David felt blood rush to his face, making him feel hot and chilled simultaneously. He was being treated like one of his high school–aged clients. Across the walkway to the main house, he could see his landlady talking with a crew of painters who had arrived two days earlier. A clue he had missed.

Despite the conversation, he kissed Renata. "You'd better put your shoes on or you'll wreck your stockings."

"It's charming of you to think I'm wearing them," she said.

David closed the door behind her, intending to call his friends at a Thai restaurant, but his business line was ringing again, a call from that same unfamiliar number.

3

D avid?"

The voice was tentative, but he recognized it immediately. He felt a strange grip of panic, assuming she could only be calling after all these years with bad news. He cleared his throat, and managed a raspy, "Julie!"

"Did I wake you?"

"No, no," he said, appalled at the idea. He'd been raised by a mother who believed that sleeping was suspect behavior, more shameful than alcoholism and compulsive gambling, two things about which the dear woman had known a lot. It was one of the few beliefs in her Italian and Catholic ideology that had left an imprint. "It's only four in the afternoon," he said.

"Oh? Oh, right, the time difference." She said it dismissively, as if it was an annoyance, and David felt an unexpected throb of affection. Julie had always been bad with time zones and directions and dates. He sympathized with her annoyance; he'd grown up in Rhode Island, and despite having lived in San Francisco for twenty years, he still considered East Coast time the real time and everything else irritating rebelliousness.

"I know you don't like to admit to sleeping," she said.

"I'm flattered you remember," he said.

"I remember a lot."

"In that case, I'm flattered you called."

"Don't be—I've forgotten a lot, too."

He saw Julie as she was the last time he'd seen her, a slim young woman with a love of white shirts and gray men's pants she ordered by the half-dozen from some utilitarian catalog and wore with enough conviction to make them unexpectedly sexy and chic. She'd kept her hair long in a casually nondescript way and spent money on presents for people she barely knew. She'd had muddled plans to become an illustrator or a graphic designer, plans that were constantly derailed by an inability to stick to one thing for long. She'd had the misfortune of being talented and capable in many areas without being expert in any of them. This, he'd noted, makes one interesting when young but usually, when middle-aged, disappointed. Or a teacher.

Back then, she'd made resolutions and broke them within the hour, started projects and left them unfinished. Those were the traits that had endeared her to David and made him want to fix things for her. His desire to be helpful was one he'd naïvely mistaken for lust back when he was less resolved about his sexual leanings, just as, years later when he was more resolved, he'd mistaken lust for affection, admiration, and even love. He and Julie had lived together in New York on the Upper West Side for more than two years and had been married for less than one.

"You must be shocked to hear from me," she said.

"I was at first, but I got over it quickly. Now I'm in the delighted phase." This was true. Her voice brought him back to a time in his life when the real estate news he'd just received would have been an upsetting inconvenience rather than a crisis. "Why did we fall off?"

"I think it had to do with the fact that one day we were supposedly in love and married and then, suddenly, we weren't either."

"I guess that will do it. And then," he added, a mild attempt at self-defense, "you remarried."

"Me and my marriages. Some people never learn."

"Is everything all right?"

"Oh, god, David. You don't think I'd call after all this time just because something's wrong, do you?"

That seemed like the most logical explanation, but he said, "I was just making sure."

"Good."

Having cleared this up, she started to cry.

David had reached the point in midlife at which he'd grown used to hearing friends burst into tears for reasons both personal and global or for no apparent reason at all. He made his way into the kitchen of the carriage house and started a pot of tea. It was unlikely this would be a short conversation.

"Do you remember those singers you used to play all the time?" she asked. "The French ones with the delicate voices? Do you still listen to them?"

"Sometimes," he said. "Although I think you may have ended up with most of the records."

"My daughter found them recently and started playing them."

He was beginning to understand why she'd called. "The past came flooding back on a tide of Jacques Prévert?"

"Something like that. They made me miss you. Not the marriage. I mean our friendship. I guess I'm in need of a friend."

He was taken aback by something in her voice as she said this, a sad, wistful quality that had always gotten to him in the past. Although his sexual preference had been for men for decades (his entire life if you included a few crucial years when he'd been in denial about the obvious), he'd always found it easier to feel protective of and affectionate toward women, possibly because underneath it all, he knew he was incapable of giving himself to them fully. The reason he'd been so open toward Soren for five years was because, underneath it all, he'd known that Soren was incapable of giving himself fully to anyone.

"I miss you, too," he said.

"I know you well enough to know you wouldn't say that unless you didn't mean it."

"But in this case, I do mean it. I'm more earnest and less skinny these days, both signs of aging, I've been told. I often think about those walks we used to take along Riverside Drive."

"At a certain point, it was easier than being in the apartment together."

"Yes, but they were still wonderful. All that gray water and granite, the low skies."

"Another way of saying there was always a cloud hanging over our heads," she said.

"I suppose. But as I recall, neither one of us was big on the sun."

They lapsed into reminiscences of people they'd known all those years ago and Oliver, the neighbor's sickly dog they'd adopted and had seen through to his death. He was the only dog David had ever lived with, and losing him had been part of the tumble of losses that had come at the end of their relationship. As the least personal, it was the easiest one to discuss now. Julie mentioned her teaching job and told David she was running an "informal B and B" out of her house. He thought it was best not to press for details on this. "Informal" probably meant "illegal." After another fifteen minutes, the conversation began to feel like one in which they were talking around something.

"I get the feeling," he said, "that there's something you're not telling me."

"That goes without saying, don't you think?"

"We have to get to it eventually."

"It's a favor," she said.

"That goes without saying, too. And I love feeling useful."

She hesitated, and he sensed she was calculating how much to reveal. "My daughter's a junior in high school," she said. "She needs help with colleges."

He was thrilled. After all this time, he really could be useful to dear Julie. But after talking for a few more minutes, he realized he was hearing only part of the problem.

4

Mandy was sitting on her bed while her friend Lindsay sat on the floor with her face buried in her phone and her back propped up against the mattress.

"So what's he like?" Lindsay asked.

"How should I know?"

"You just told me you've been working together for two weeks."

"I told you I told that to my father. Which has nothing to do with reality." She'd also explained to Lindsay about doing a search on David Hedges; that probably hadn't registered either. "There's a big difference between you and me," Mandy said, although it was beginning to seem as if there were many differences. "Neither one of us listens to other people, but I fake it better. You should work on that, it comes in handy."

Lindsay went back to her phone, where, Mandy knew, she was watching videos from one of the vloggers she followed. No doubt someone talking about makeup or Starbucks. Either that or she was rereading messages from Brett, a senior boy whose distinctive traits were playing football and being a Christian. Meaning that everyone wanted him but no one got him. Especially not Lindsay. The mere fact that he was paying attention to Lindsay had boosted Lindsay's status at school. Mandy had a sense that they wouldn't be hanging out for much longer, and this made her want to push her friend away all the faster, just to get it over with.

Lindsay and her family had lived next door to Mandy when they were growing up. Their friendship had always seemed like a matter of proximity and convenience, but then again, wasn't that the basis for most sibling relationships, too? After Lindsay's family moved to the other side of town, they still hung out, but less frequently and always with a feeling that they were killing time until a better offer came along.

Ever since ten days ago when Craig Crespo had stopped Mandy on the street and asked her if she needed a ride home in his van, Lindsay's relationship with Brett had seemed especially insignificant, and Mandy's friendship with Lindsay had been even more frustrating. It would have been nice to talk with Lindsay about what had happened with Craig—as he'd told her to call him—about his vague mention of "coming to work for him," but she knew that she shouldn't. Lindsay wouldn't approve (would be jealous, in other words) and would tell her incredibly bland and nosy mother. There would be phone calls and questions, and Mandy would end up humiliated, all before anything had actually happened. Lindsay considered herself a "romantic," which meant she was a Disney princess who'd read her mother's copy of *Fifty Shades of Grey.*

"But why did you bring up your mother's ex in the first place? They divorced so long ago."

"It's obvious my mother needs help. Who else am I going to bring up? Craig Crespo?"

At the mention of his name, Lindsay touched her neck. "But you don't even like your mother."

There was something about this comment that made Mandy want to cry. Lindsay wasn't stupid. Her grades were better than Mandy's, and she was always getting prizes for writing boring essays on politically correct topics even though her parents had creepy political views. How could she not read between the lines of Mandy's complaints about her mother and know that she was frustrated with her because she *did* love her and wanted her to get her life on track so that she could go off to college without worrying that her mother would fall apart completely?

It was now weird to Mandy that she'd never been interested in her mother's first marriage. But ever since she'd found the boxes in the basement and her mother had started talking about it, she'd been fascinated. Her mother and David had lived in a huge apartment on the upper floor of a building in New York they were subletting for practically nothing. Mandy loved the descriptions of it and felt as if she could see it all—the vast spaces, the crumbling ceilings, the little sinks in every bedroom, and, best of all, the tiny maid's room behind the kitchen that no one ever went into. That would be the room she'd want. A perfect, private hiding place.

When her mother talked about these details, she got a dreamy faraway look in her eyes, different from when she was stoned. She missed David Hedges. She'd even gotten teary when she talked about the dog they'd owned, and Mandy understood then why all three dogs they'd had since she was a baby had had names starting with O. As if they were descendants of that original mutt.

And then there was the photograph that had fallen out of a book: her mother and a skinny guy that had to be David sitting on a park bench with their arms around each other's shoulders and the dog her mother had described sitting between them like a small child. She'd seen pictures of her mother young before, but never from this period in her life and never looking so defiantly happy. She hadn't shown it to her mother for fear it would induce a pot-fueled weeping fit. She'd been keeping it in a pocket in her overalls.

Last weekend when she was staying at the horrible townhouse Carol and her father lived in—pale blue wall-to-wall carpeting—and overheard her father talking about selling the house to Amira's husband, she knew she had to do something.

"You know what, Lindsay?" she said now. "You need to get a clue."

"You can be a real bitch sometimes," Lindsay said without glancing up from her phone.

"Really? I was hoping it was all the time. But thanks."

Mandy picked up the book she was reading, one of the mildewed ones she'd found in the basement. It was a paperback about a village in England. The whole thing was like Beauport—a lot of petty people gossiping and fighting about who to invite to a tea party. It was probably meant to be funny, but it was funniest if you pretended it was supposed to be serious, the way everyone in Beauport was hilarious because they took themselves so seriously. She'd found a whole set of these books and was reading her way through them.

As for David, she'd finally received an email from him this morning.

> Dear Mandy, Your mother and I spoke a few days ago. It sounds as if you and I are going to be working on college applications. I hope you're as excited about this as I am. Your mother and I are old friends, so it will be a pleasure to get to know you. Send me a few good times to set up a first call. This is going to be fun!
> Best wishes, David

The whole thing struck her as dishonest, which was a disappointment. She'd expected more of an ally, someone who'd treat her like an equal or at least like an adult. Was he really "excited" to be working with her for free? As for "old friends," did he think her mother hadn't told her they'd been married?

She went back to the novel and read another few pages. What she loved about these books was that you knew the little crises that weren't even problems would turn out fine before the end of a few chapters, unlike, say, her own life, which she felt instinctively was headed toward a cliff.

She heard someone downstairs calling her mother. There were three guest rooms on the second floor and one closet-size room on the ground floor. Her mother had fixed this up "for an emergency, in case I overbook." You could view this as sensible, but also as proof that her mother knew the probability of her screwing something up was high. She and her mother had moved up to the third floor once they started the Airbnb thing.

Usually, the people staying in the house crept around, somewhere between family and thieves who'd just broken in. Even though they were paying to stay, they tended to be sheepish, as if her mother was doing them a huge favor by letting them pay a hundred bucks a night for a stale muffin and a bed with an old mattress.

The woman called for Julie again.

"Aren't you going to see what she wants?" Lindsay asked.

"It's not my problem."

"Is she the one with the cute husband?"

Mandy hated the word "cute" unless it was applied to puppies and infants. There was something sleazy about the woman's husband—the slicked-back hair, the loafers without socks. He was handsome, but calling him "cute" was just a way to make him seem less dangerous and sexy. Why couldn't Lindsay just say she was excited and terrified by him? If Mandy was going to talk about Craig Crespo honestly, that's how she'd describe her feelings toward him.

Mr. Crespo was probably in his late twenties. He ran one of those geek-in-a-van businesses and showed up at the high school once or twice a week when there was a computer glitch that needed to be fixed. About five seconds after he pulled into the school lot, word had spread through an invisible network of gossip and social media. It was like when there was a natural disaster or a mass shooting somewhere: people instantly *knew*. It didn't take much to figure out that everyone was in love with him, whether they realized it or not. The boys either bragged about knowing him, like he was their amazingly cool older brother, or talked him down because their girlfriends had crushes on him. There was no shortage of rumors: he'd been in Afghanistan; he'd been in jail; he carried a gun; he was gay; he'd been seen making out with Mrs. Mullen, the married history teacher; he lived with his mother.

Mandy hadn't paid much attention to him, mostly because she figured she was the kind of person Mr. Crespo wouldn't notice. But he wasn't easy to ignore. When he stopped to ask her if she needed a ride home, she knew that wasn't what he was really asking her. But what he *was* asking wasn't clear, so her instinct had been to say no and keep walking. She'd sensed danger, the way she had when she'd spotted a coyote around one of the quarries in the woods above town and just knew it was rabid. But in the case of Craig, she'd also known she was being offered an opportunity, one that probably wouldn't come again. And most of all, she'd been noticed by someone who mattered, a big *fuck you* to everyone who ignored her. She'd shrugged, surprised at her own ability to be nonchalant, and had gotten in. She'd been only two blocks from home, so it was a short ride, and aside from his random mention of a job, they'd said nothing.

The woman downstairs called for Julie again. Mandy got up off the bed and opened her door. "My mother's not home!" she shouted.

"What's that?"

"My mother isn't *home*."

"I think she forgot to leave us *towels*."

"If I'm gone more than five minutes," Mandy told Lindsay, "come looking for me."

She'd bumped into this woman earlier in the day and she'd treated Mandy as if they were sisters, asking her where she'd bought her overalls. As if it was any of her business or, based on what she was wearing, she'd be caught dead in them. Did she really believe Mandy would fall for the fake friend routine?

There were two weird things about renting out rooms in the house, one being that they were doing it at all, and the other being that no matter what anyone complained about, you could keep them quiet by offering more towels. Mandy had discovered this by accident. One morning some woman was making hideous faces and complaining to her that the coffee was "like ice." Really? That cold? As a goof, Mandy had apologized and asked her if she'd like more towels. Problem solved. A week later, some old guy from Ohio had told her that the windows had rattled all night and kept him awake. "So sorry," Mandy had said. "Can I get you more towels?" She'd never heard another word about the windows, and he'd even written a positive review, highlighting the "big fluffy towels."

Mandy stomped down the stairs. The woman in the hall was staring up at her with a totally phony smile.

"How many *towels* do you need?" Mandy asked.

"Just four or five. Put them on the bed, okay? I'm going out to the shops."

Mandy had persuaded her mother to keep the sheets and towels in one of the closets at the far end of the hall that locked, which was a good thing because otherwise they'd have been wiped out within hours. She got the towels and added a couple of facecloths for good measure. The door to the woman's room—"the Window Seat Room"; her mother was literal when it came to naming the rooms—was ajar. When she knocked, it swung open. The shower was running. She put the towels on the bed. The bathroom door was open and steam was billowing up over the shower curtain.

"They're on the bed," she yelled.

The curtain opened a sliver and a man's head popped out, the husband. Dark and handsome, not cute at all. "Where's Beth?" he said.

"She asked for towels and went out. I left them on the bed."

He wiped soapsuds off his face. "Just put them on the toilet. I don't want to get the floor wet."

This was a bad idea and she knew it, but, as with a lot of bad ideas—saying yes when Mr. Crespo asked her if she wanted a ride—she was pulled into it by an urge to find out what would happen that was stronger than the urge to listen to the voice telling her not to.

She carried the towels into the steamy bathroom that smelled of Irish Spring soap and set them on the toilet.

When she turned to leave, the shower curtain was open wider, as she'd somehow known it would be. There was something about having been given that ride with Craig and the way he'd looked at her across the seat—like he was trying to flatter her with condescension—that made her feel bolder. It had to do with her own power, but she hadn't sorted it out yet. Step one was finding out she had power, step two was figuring out how to use it. The man had his head thrown back, rinsing shampoo out of his hair but really showing off his body and the fact that he had an erection.

She swung the door shut as she ran out. As she pounded up the stairs, she had an uneasy sense that she was being chased, even though she knew she wasn't. She slammed the door to her bedroom so loudly that Lindsay actually looked up from her phone.

"Mission accomplished?"

"Pretty much."

"You look weird. What happened?"

"Nothing happened! What do you think happened? I was gone two minutes. Do you think I got raped?"

Lindsay frowned and starting putting her things into her backpack. "I have to get home."

"Why? You said you could stay until dinner."

"Yeah, well, I changed my mind."

"Are you seeing Brett?" Even to Mandy's own ears she sounded like a jealous girlfriend.

"Why do you care, Mandy? And as a matter of fact, yes."

She had such a strong, sudden desire for Lindsay to stay with her, she apologized, but that sounded weird, too. She listened to Lindsay's footsteps as she went down the two flights of stairs. When it was clear she'd left, uneasiness crept along Mandy's spine. She and the sleaze were alone in the house now.

She didn't understand why she was always making mistakes or why she got angry at her mother for screwing up. Craig had driven past her a few times since that afternoon, but he'd always had another adult in the car with him. And then today he'd sent her a private message on Facebook, telling her he was going to be around school next week and to wait for him behind the abandoned IGA for a ride home on Thursday, and even though she got that dangerous feeling again and had replied "maybe," she knew it was a definite yes.

It was like a date. When she thought about it, she felt the way she'd felt on a roller coaster at Six Flags—like she was going to explode from happiness and, at the same time, throw up.

She bolted her door and sat down at her computer.

Dear David, Thank you for writing. I am excited about working together. I really do need help with the college thing, not to mention everything else in my life. Ha ha, just kidding. You really should come visit us. Our rooms are cheap! (Free.) It would make everything easier. And my mother wants you to come but won't say so to you.

Mandy

She hit Send before she had time to think about it. She returned to the paperback, but she had trouble concentrating, and it didn't seem as funny as it had half an hour earlier.

5

As per usual, the weather report was apocalyptic.

"Some of these thunderstorms could be severe with wind gusts over 50 miles per hour and the potential for flash flooding. The good news is that tomorrow will be much cooler, and the tornado warning has been downgraded to a tornado watch for most of Essex County."

Julie didn't have the stomach for environmental crises tonight. It was after seven and the mortgage broker had sent her an email yesterday promising her he'd have news for her by tonight. She kept looking down at her phone to make sure she had service and had the ringer on. How late did these people stay in their offices?

There was a distant rumble of thunder. Tornado watch? That was the *good* news? Oh, well, extreme weather had become so commonplace that complaining about it was as pointless and boring as decrying public use of cell phones and the banality of reality TV.

She shut off the television and checked her phone again.

The refrigerator opened with a rattle of bottles. Mandy was in her room, so this had to be Natasha, the wan poet who'd moved into the Street-View Room two days ago. She'd allegedly checked in to have "a long talk with my muse," but so far she seemed primarily to be in discussion with Julie's refrigerator. She'd been pilfering yogurt and bagels and juice at all hours since the moment of her arrival. Julie was going to have to clarify what she meant when she told guests to make themselves at home.

In the wake of Tracy's ABCD admonitions and with gathering anxiety about her own financial pressures and Henry's threats, she'd started reading a blog by a woman who offered advice to Airbnb hosts. The author, Sandra, owned a "majestic Victorian mansion" in southern New Hampshire in which she'd been renting rooms for over a decade. She claimed to have put two daughters through college with her earnings. Another claim was that taking her advice could up your revenues by 25 percent and hiring her for an in-person consultation would double your income. Her online advice struck Julie as eccentric at best (she seemed to have an obsession with toss pillows and advocated an approach to hospitality that sounded like passive aggression raised to an art form), but her apparent success was hard to argue with. Julie was determined to get serious about this business and call her for a home visit.

"Never offer a good deal" was one of her pronouncements. Earlier in the day, Julie had received a reservation request for an older woman from Virginia who was coming to Beauport for a month to visit her son and daughter-in-law. The daughter-in-law had sent the request. Given the length of the stay and Mrs. Grayson's age, Julie considered offering a substantial discount. Then, emboldened by Sandra's blog, she'd given a price that she considered slightly criminal. The one-word response to this proposal had been "fine." Mrs. Grayson was arriving in two weeks, and the several thousand dollars had already been sent to Julie's PayPal account.

There was more thunder. Opal would be inconsolable even if the storm passed quickly. A wind gust blew a branch against the side of the house with a crack and Natasha gave a surprised cry. As Julie was getting up to make sure she was all right, her phone rang.

"Julie, this is Charles Phillips. About the mortgage."

She froze. "So good to hear from you," she said. Although she'd been waiting for this call all day, she suddenly had a bad feeling about it and wanted to put if off just a little longer. "Working late?"

"I apologize for calling at this hour, but we had a busy day. Are you having storms up there?"

"Not yet, although it sounds as if they're on the way. The weather is so unpredictable and crazy these days, you never know."

"Oh? Actually, I think thunderstorms at this time of year are pretty normal."

She interpreted the comment to mean he was a climate denier and therefore a Republican. She started to pace around the living room, waiting to get through the obligatory small talk. She'd met with Charles twice. He was probably in his mid-thirties and seemed to be overcompensating for his boyishness by wearing excessive amounts of cologne and treating her with cool professionalism that bordered on rudeness. She'd never felt he truly looked at her; his glance always missed her when he was talking with her, as if he was afraid of eye contact. She'd found herself adjusting her body so she'd enter his line of vision.

"I hope you have good news for me, Charles," she said, halfway thinking that saying this would make it more likely he'd tell her what she wanted to hear.

Instead, it made him pause for a few seconds. Finally, he said, "I'm afraid I don't. Your application has been turned down."

She fell back into a chair. Panic was not, she knew, a helpful response, but it was what she was feeling. She wished she had a more expansive technical vocabulary to ask follow-up questions, but the best she could manage was a barely audible, "Why?" dragged out to two syllables.

"I hope you remember, this isn't my decision. Just my job to deliver the bad news."

Things went downhill from there. Her credit rating was outside the acceptable range due to some credit card debt and a home equity loan, both of which she'd let slide longer than she should have, although she'd cleared them up in the end. He hauled out the financial crisis of 2008 and tighter regulations. "And, frankly, they didn't like your income."

Only someone who'd taken a vow of genteel poverty would *like* her income, but it wasn't insignificant, and, as she pointed out to him, she had an excellent benefits package.

"That's nice for you, I'm sure." Papers rustled in his shiny office, and then: "We've also learned that you're doing short-term rentals at the house. A lot of mortgage companies frown on that."

There was more thunder and wind, as if everything were conspiring against her. She was tempted to point out that she hadn't discussed that on her application, but there was no need.

"You didn't mention that. Not on the application and not to your insurance company either. It's a problem."

"I must have forgotten. How did they find out?"

Again there was an ominous silence. Clearly this was not the right question.

"Eventually," he said, "everything comes into the open."

"You can't be saying there's nothing I can do."

"Of course not. There's always *something* you can do." The tone in which he made this pronouncement reminded her of conversations she'd had with doctors after her mother had been diagnosed with lung cancer. There was always another option for treatment, another protocol, another expensive experimental drug. In the end, none of them had done more than prolong and intensify the agony. "You might, for example, go to someone who specializes in high-risk loans. You'll be paying at least triple the interest, but it's possible they'd take you on."

She heard drops begin to spatter against the windows and did a quick mental calculation of her retirement account and what she had in it. Within seconds, the rain was coming down so hard, it was cascading off the roof and the fallen gutter in a silvery sheet.

"If there's anything else I can do for you," he said, more cheerful now that he was done with her, "please don't hesitate to call."

She felt as if she were being swallowed up by the sofa and by her own anxiety. The lights were flickering as they often did in Beauport in storms. "I should go check on the windows," she said. "It's pouring. Of course, after the mild, snowless, totally weird, bizarre, scary winter, we need the water."

But she knew she needed so much more than that.

6

Renata and Leonard Miller lived in a shingled house hidden behind gates and gardens in a sequestered enclave on Russian Hill. It wasn't a large house, but its charms and location made it almost shockingly valuable. Renata was forever trying to persuade Leonard to sell it and buy a small condo in a nearby building famous for having appeared in *Vertigo*. Or so she claimed. Sometimes, David wondered if her telling him about her desire to sell was merely an excuse to flaunt the value of their real estate. It gave David a peculiar sense of satisfaction that his landlord's property, the place he was being evicted from thanks partly to Renata, was probably worth double.

Leonard let him into the house the night of their cocktail party. There was an awkward moment when it wasn't clear if they were going to shake hands or hug. The result was a standoff that ended when he handed Leonard the obligatory bottle of wine. Leonard did him the courtesy of accepting it without reading the label, the way you might avoid looking at a stain on someone's shirt or a mole on their lip.

His courtesy did not extend to avoiding a glance at David himself. "It's been a while since I've seen you," he said. Because this was accompanied by a disapproving scan of his body, David assumed it was a covert comment on his weight. Not that Leonard was one to judge.

"About six months," David said, and returned the harsh assessment.

Leonard was one of those highly successful men who gets expensive haircuts and manicures and has a tailor who makes outcalls. He treated his pudgy body with the worshipful coddling usually lavished upon a vintage sports car or an overfed cat.

"Can you believe Teddy's graduating next year?" Leonard said. "He's thriving. What he's learning, I couldn't tell you."

"I believe his major is American Studies."

"Yeah, but is he taking history, politics, law? As far as I can tell, the only American he's studying is Teddy Miller. To hell with it. He's getting a diploma. Have I thanked you for talking him into Tufts?"

Leonard had been fixated on his son going to Yale, probably in fulfillment of some class aspirations of his own. He'd initially blamed David for Teddy deciding against the school, conveniently skipping over the matter of the school deciding against Teddy.

"I don't remember any thank-you notes," David said.

"Don't hold your breath." Leonard put a condescending hand on David's shoulder. "We paid you enough."

"Not really. You still have an outstanding balance."

With heterosexual men like Leonard, it was important not to concede an inch of ground or within minutes they'd be asking your opinion of paint colors and Anderson Cooper.

Leonard laughed and called David a shark in an approving way that made it clear they'd had their requisite exchange and wouldn't have to speak again for the rest of the evening.

The first floor of the house had been professionally decorated and therefore had the strange cohesion that makes a space beautiful and serene but gives it the air of being uninhabited. David wandered to the far side of the room where a small fireplace had been converted to gas, the genetically modified version of a fireplace. Standing there was a couple Renata had referred to David. Joyce and Louis were a physically imposing pair; both were extremely thin, but Joyce was tall and her husband short. She had the melancholy, elongated beauty of a Modigliani, while he had the compact boyishness of a high school wrestler. Her way of being empathic was always to appear sad.

"David," Joyce said sorrowfully, as if they were at a funeral and he was the deceased's next of kin. "We didn't expect to see you here."

"I was an afterthought," he said.

"No, no. Don't say that. It's just that . . ."

"I was kidding. How's Hallie?"

"The important thing is," she said mournfully, "we don't blame you one bit."

"I appreciate that. For what, by the way?"

"She wants to drop out."

David nodded. He was surprised to learn she'd lasted two semesters. "I did try to talk her out of Indiana. Anyway, a lot of kids feel that way their first year."

"You mean the ones you advise." Joyce nodded with mordant forgiveness for David's failures.

"I meant kids in general. I'm sure she'll feel better next year."

"I'm sure she will," Joyce said. She was connected in an amorphous way to the world of dance and in a more concrete way to a father who'd founded an investment house. Louis was an architect who worked for a firm that designed austere buildings that seemed an extension of his barren affect. "I think it says a lot about you that you came tonight."

"It wasn't such a hardship," David said. "Free food and drink, after all."

"No, but I mean . . . considering."

He was about to ask for clarification, but none was needed when he saw Soren walk into the living room with his new paramour. Renata was between them, her arms looped between theirs—a low-rent Jeanne Moreau to this plebian Jules and Jim. It was a surprise, but not exactly a shock. David had seen Soren three times since he'd left, always in the company of Porter, his surgeon-lover. They'd carried on with civility.

"Oh, you mean them," David said. "It's fine. There's no animosity between us."

This wasn't true, but at that moment, most of David's anger was directed at Renata. She could have told him they were coming so he could have stayed at home or attempted to lose three pounds before venturing out. She was wearing a pretty camel's hair jacket buttoned incorrectly, and was making a pained, apologetic face. The three of them arrived at the faux fireplace and introductions were made. Joyce bid Soren a chilly hello—so thoughtful of her—but once she heard Porter was a thoracic surgeon, she looked at him with reverential wonder, and warmed up to his younger companion.

"It was such a nice surprise to hear Leonard had invited Porter," Renata said, a blatant attempt to explain the situation to David.

Porter described a development project Leonard had him investing in. He made a jokey comment about the fact that "with my luck, I'll probably lose my shirt." This fell flat; he was too attractive and accomplished to pull off self-deprecation.

Porter was probably in his mid-sixties. He was a meticulous man in the hygienic way surgeons and military officers often are, and he gave off a scent of limes and sandalwood. Everything about him appeared well designed, from his haircut to his sleek leather shoes. Although he and David had technically been rivals and David had lost to him, he nonetheless felt a kinship with Porter. David was probably a decade younger, but in the presence of not-quite-forty Soren, they were the same age. It was as if they were colleagues and he had passed on to Porter the duties of mentoring an interesting but difficult student. The duties, to a great extent, involved finances. That seemed right. There are certain things in life you must expect to pay for—electricity, dry cleaning, sushi. Past the age of fifty, a younger lover with a perfect ass must, realistically, be added to the list. While Soren's departure had knocked David into a whirlpool of depression, he couldn't blame him for having gone with someone in a far stronger position to support him.

As for Soren, he seemed rakishly amused by the encounter. He winked at David and adjusted the collar of his shirt. "Hi, sweetie," he said, his standard term of endearment for him. The role of the person who's left a relationship is to show that he still cares and feels fondly for the person he abandoned, while the role of the abandoned is to show that he has no feelings whatsoever.

"I hope you're not too upset about your landlady selling the house," Soren said.

"I'm upset that word about it has gotten around so quickly."

Soren's face showed a shadow of sorrowful disapproval. "Nothing lasts forever," he said.

"I'm learning that," David said. "It's lucky Porter has such a terrific house."

"Thank you," Porter said. Unfortunately, he was a man without malice, which made him hard to dislike. "I don't know how Soren talked me into believing we need a bigger place."

"I'm sure Renata could help you with that," David said.

"They called *me*," Renata said.

"Apparently that's the pattern," David said. "Your phone must be ringing off the hook."

"That's a dated expression, David, and if you're not nice, I'll bring Leonard over to join the conversation."

Joyce muttered a few mournful words of condolence about David losing his rental, and Louis spoke for the first time, tonelessly describing the way he'd redesign the carriage house and break the main residence into five or six luxury condos. He and Joyce had come to David's place to discuss their daughter's essay, the first draft of which had included the memorable sentence: *"One of my educational goals is to move away from my parents."*

"Admittedly, it needs a lot of work," Soren said. "But it would be a shame to break up the main house. You could make the carriage house into two units and get enough rent for each to have the property pay for itself. The main house would be a great place to hold parties."

"I can't imagine I'll ever know enough people to fill those rooms," Porter said. "But the light and views are wild from that second floor."

David took a cocktail in a martini glass from a passing tray and sipped. "Wild" was such an incongruously beatnik word to come from such an established person. Then he had a flash of understanding.

"Oh," he said, and finished off the drink. "From the second floor." He looked at Renata, but she refused to meet his gaze, a clear indication that his suspicions were correct. Soren gave David one of his sly smiles and shrugged, as close to an apology as he was likely to get.

"You wouldn't, would you?" David asked.

"Let's face it, sweetie, someone's going to."

"But there are so many others you could afford."

Porter looked genuinely confused. "Renata said you were planning to move anyway. No?"

Throughout his life, David had admired people who could work themselves into a rage over perceived injustices being done to them, blindly lashing out and reveling in the role of victim.

Unfortunately, he was not one of those people. If he couldn't be angry, he could at least make a stab at self-respect by pretending to be. He tossed a few caustic remarks in the general direction of Renata and Soren but began to feel the approach of panic, as if he was on a train that only he knew was about to derail.

He sauntered to a bathroom off a hallway behind the living room, but once inside, he made the mistake of looking in the mirror. He hurried into Renata's office, a small, tidy room with a view of the Bay Bridge prettily muffled by a frame of bougain-villea. The room was dark, making the view that much more sparkling, the thrusting lights of the bridge and the water blur-ring into one glittering impression. It was precisely the kind of view people crave and pay good money for, mostly, David sus-pected, because it tricks you into believing you're lucky, privi-leged, and maybe even happy. It was a variation on the view from David's bedroom, where it had tricked him into believing for a couple of decades that he belonged and had a home in this city.

As he turned from the window, he bumped against Renata's computer. The screen lit up the desk and the view dimmed, and he saw a stack of papers in a manila folder with his name on it. In-side were listing sheets of apartments that Renata apparently thought were in his price range. At the very least, it was a flatter-ing misconception. None was affordable in anything other than a lurid fantasy of his financial position. Five years of paying to keep Soren happy had depleted his savings to a shocking degree. Even so, as he basked in the coziness of self-pity, he felt a wave of sadness about Soren's departure lapping at his feet, bringing in with it the detritus of regret for missed opportunities that would never be presented to him again.

The computer screen went dark and the view of the bridge lit up again, and he found himself floating once more above the expensive, unstable landscape, apart from it and utterly inessential.

The familiar view brought him back to an evening shortly after Soren had left, an evening when everything—moving on, staying put—had seemed pointless and impossible. There had been tears and phone calls, some expensive vodka he'd found in the freezer, and, most embarrassing of all, a small quantity of the pills he'd been stockpiling to circumvent an announced diagnosis of Alzheimer's or the imminent start of an ecological implosion. He'd woken up twelve hours later, less groggy than he'd felt after taking melatonin. Still, his assumptions about his control of his own behavior had been badly shaken.

Sitting at Renata's desk, he tried to summon up a combination of people and places from his past that might gel into a vision of home for him or at least a safe harbor that felt like a place where he belonged. Mostly, he saw a blur of faces of former lovers race through his mind as fleetingly as he'd encouraged them to race though his life.

And then he paused on an image of Julie Fiske and felt more at ease. He saw the damp gray of the Upper West Side and felt the wind from the Hudson in late afternoon and heard the yapping of the small dog he and Julie had adopted. Objectively, it was the most tenuous and ill-conceived relationship of his life, but thoughts of it filled him with a sense of calm and belonging.

It was after nine on the East Coast, and if the weather app on his phone was to be believed, they were having thunderstorms. He'd been missing summer thunderstorms for decades. Mandy had, after all, invited him. A vacation would do him good, give him time to get his thoughts together, research his rights as a tenant, stall the sale of the house in a way that might prove unproductive but would at least be satisfyingly spiteful. All thousands of miles from his troubles and humiliations.

He dialed Julie's phone.

7

About ten minutes after the storm knocked out the electricity, and while Julie was still lighting candles and choking on the panic induced by the mortgage mess, she decided that her mother, dead for more than a decade, wouldn't forgive her if she sold her jewelry but that she, Julie, could live with the guilt.

A week before she died, her mother had grabbed Julie's hand and made her vow that she'd never sell this part of her inheritance. "Some of it, the Cartier pieces, came from your grandmother, but your father gave me most of it. It's worth hundreds of thousands, sweetheart, but its real value is as a reminder of how much your father adored me. Swear you'll cherish it."

Julie, who'd always felt like an interloper in her parents' hermetically sealed marriage, didn't need a reminder of the way her father had worshiped his wife, but she'd said she'd always keep it.

"No, Julie," her mother had insisted. "Look at me and promise me you'll never sell it."

What choice did she have but to look her mother in the eyes and promise?

It was highly unlikely the collection was worth what her mother thought it was worth, but if she could get even a hundred thousand and combine it with her retirement account, she'd be close.

The front door opened and Amira appeared in the living room, her hair dripping. Her beige silk blouse had gone transparent from the rain.

"You scared me," Julie said.

"I'm such a selfish bitch, I sometimes scare myself," Amira said. "And I do not call a town civilization when the lights go out every time it rains. You'd think my husband could afford a generator. You don't mind if I sit, do you?"

Almost the last person Julie wanted to see an hour after Charles Phillips's call. She'd been avoiding Amira since Henry had told her about her husband's offer on the house. It was hard to know where she stood on any issue since she deflected everything with outrageous comments about herself, the truthfulness of them impossible to discern.

She did, however, have a childish fear of thunderstorms that Julie found touching, and her showing up like this probably meant Richard was out of town.

"Take a seat," Julie said. "I'm just about done here."

"Do the inmates all have candles?"

"Inmates" was Amira's name for the guests Julie took in, a sadly accurate one in the case of Natasha and a few others. Amira had names for lots of things: "The Horror of Little Shops" for the downtown of Beauport; "Les Miserables" for the wives who lived in the neighborhood, wore holiday-themed sweaters, and exchanged amusing repartee about finding their husbands physically repulsive. The "Anonymous Alcoholics" were the interchangeable husbands of Les Miserables who talked anecdotally about drinking and their teen years. If she had a nickname for Julie, Julie was in no rush to learn what it was.

"I brought up lanterns. Hopefully the lights will go on soon." Hesitantly, Julie said, "Is Richard at home?"

"He's the kind of man who is at home everywhere, which in this case means Berlin or maybe Tokyo. Who can remember?"

The exact nature of Richard's work was unclear to Julie, mostly because Amira claimed not to know it. It involved consulting with multinational corporations and required frequent trips to foreign capitals. "I am lonely when he leaves," Amira had said more than once, always adding after a significant pause, "but not for long." Julie wanted to think he was a "good man" who was offering beneficial political or environmental support, but his elusive personality and wealth made it more likely that he was involved in nefarious activity and was part of the problem. His attempt to buy her house out from under her confirmed this suspicion.

Amira curled up on the sofa like a frightened girl, and Julie was torn between wanting to lash out at her and wanting to comfort her and dry her beautiful hair.

"If I was with a lover," Amira said, "I would be enjoying the storm, but all the men here are horrible. What's-his-name came over the other day to sell me his garbage marijuana, wearing this old T-shirt that smelled of sweat. I said to him, 'You do not come to a married lady's house dressed like that. Please, have a little respect and manners.'"

Julie nodded. This was a reference to Granger, the twenty-eight-year-old who supplied Amira with pot. Granger was from Hammond, the town that abutted Beauport on a rocky cape north of Boston. Despite the proximity, Hammond was a more rough and real place than Beauport, home to a once-thriving fishing industry that had fallen on hard times, as had most industries in the country. Granger affected a rough and real appearance of his own—skinny black jeans and ratty T-shirts, long hair under a bandana, no matter what the weather—but he was allegedly from one of the old families in Hammond, the ones with bankrupt claims to class superiority.

"It's probably a good thing to have some boundaries with him," Julie said. "You don't want him getting the wrong idea."

"No, I do not. You are right. The last time, after I had sex with him, he asked to borrow my car. I could not believe it. Do I look like Zipcar?"

No, she did not. Although she was Eastern European (either Hungarian or Bulgarian; Julie was afraid that asking for clarification at this late date would be insulting), what Amira did look like, especially in the flickering candlelight and occasional flashes of lightning, was a young, thin version of one of those Italian movie stars from the 1960s. She was olive-skinned and raven-haired and exuded sexual energy and heat just walking into a room. Meeting Amira, Julie had finally understood what people talked about when they talked about pheromones. Her accented English was one of six languages she spoke fluently, an indication that she had hidden reserves of intelligence. What else she had hidden remained to be seen.

"You're so lucky you have your clarinet-player lover," she said to Julie. "When is he coming back?"

In a fit of bad judgment, Julie had told Amira about the weekend in April she'd spent with Raymond Cross, or, more accurately—since he'd rented a room in the house—that he'd spent with her. Either way, it was obvious she hadn't paid much attention.

"He plays the saxophone," Julie said. "He's not my lover, and I don't know that he's ever coming back."

And yet, yesterday he'd emailed her a link to a piece of music he thought she'd like. He did this from time to time and occasionally sent her a sweet, noncommittal text message saying he hoped she was doing well.

"Don't be so technical," Amira said. "He will come back. You'll see."

"I'm not planning on it. I'm not even sure I want it. I have a lot to worry about right now without adding one more thing. I'm almost certain he's married."

"Of course he's married," Amira scoffed. "Why else would he have slept with you?"

Julie was insulted by this comment despite the fact that it aligned precisely with her own theory about Raymond's interest.

"When he does come back," she went on, "turn off all the lights and use candles. The house is prettier when you can see less of it."

This struck Julie as an appropriate segue. "It is, isn't it?" she said. "With the lights on, it's a horror."

"I have been telling you this for two years. You always defend it."

"No, you're right. In all likelihood I am the only person who'd want this ruin of a house."

"Don't forget," Amira said, "the land is worth a fortune."

Julie was appalled. "Yes, for those who want to tear down the house and dig a swimming pool."

"You have to admit, it would be nice in the summer instead of the ugly, rocky beaches in this town."

Julie leaped off her chair. "Let me tell you something, Amira. It wouldn't be nice for me. To be thrown out of my house, to lose everything. I'm going to buy this house. I'll have to sell my mother's jewelry and do some other things I didn't plan on doing, but I'm going to put together the money. So you and Richard can just scrap your plans for a pool party anytime in the near future."

Amira stared at her with amazement. "I am surprised you have such passion," she said. "You are not as uninteresting as you like to pretend."

Funny, Julie had spent hours with Amira pretending to be interesting. "I thought we were friends."

Amira stood and threw her arms around Julie. Her hair smelled of lemons, expensive lemons. "You're my only friend in this town. You're like my mother." Not how Julie viewed herself, but if it helped her case, so be it. "Henry is the one who came to us."

"Henry?"

"He showed up in his short pants. American men all want to be children forever. He told us you might not get a mortgage, and he wanted to give us the first chance to buy."

"So Richard's not interested in buying the house?"

"Don't be foolish," Amira said. "Of course he is. I would try to talk him out of it, but I have weak influence and no moral center. You just have to buy it first."

Julie's phone vibrated in her pocket, and she saw it was David. Before she could say hello, he was asking her if he was calling too late, in a rushed, anxious voice.

"No, not at all. Are you all right?"

"Do I sound funny? I've just had an upset here, nothing too major."

"I'm sorry." She was tempted to tell him about her own upset. Misery does love company, but no one likes to have theirs trumped, and she hadn't quite sorted through the significance of this latest insight into Henry's betrayal. "Have you heard from Mandy?"

"I have. It's why I'm calling. She sent me an email. Short, but nice. She mentioned it might be easier to do the work if I was there. It got me thinking. It's been so long, and I have a couple of weeks, open—well, relatively open—and there are cheap flights now. Cheap as long as you don't eat, drink, have luggage, use the bathroom, or need a place to sit. What if I came? Just for a little visit. Help her. Finally see you after all these years. A week or ten days."

"Are you sure you're all right, David? You sound wound up." It gave her a sudden feeling of tenderness to be able to recognize his mood.

"I'm at a cocktail party and I had a drink. It went to my head, which I guess is the whole point. It looks as if there are dozens of inns in that town, so maybe if you could recommend one."

Amira was on the sofa, texting with someone. It was impossible to imagine it was her husband, and since she didn't seem to care much for women in general, it was safe to assume it was one of her alleged lovers. It was convenient to think of Amira as a friend, but she couldn't be counted on. Not that David had been so reliable, but she'd never doubted his intentions. "I wouldn't let you stay in one of those places," she said. "That's out of the question. When were you thinking about coming?"

This question was enough to make Amira put down her phone and peer at Julie in the flickering light.

"I was thinking maybe as soon as I could get a flight," David said. "Sometime in the next few days?"

"Let me know when you make your reservations." Suddenly, this struck her as an answer to a prayer she hadn't uttered because, after all, she didn't pray. There always had been a calm, gentle quality to David that she'd found endearing and comforting. It had been a buffer against the chaos of the city they'd lived in together and her own tendency to overreact to world events and letters from her mother. He'd been thin to the point of appearing frail in certain lights, but he'd stood up for her with a ferocity that had consistently taken her by surprise. There were things she'd have to tell him, of course. Or more specifically, one thing, but she didn't need to worry about that now. "David," she said. "We might not like each other as much as we used to."

"I doubt that's true, dear," he said. "But we're certain to like each other more than we did at the end. Are you having storms?"

"We were. They seem to be passing out to sea."

When she'd hung up, Amira asked if this was the clarinet-playing lover.

"Saxophone," Julie said. "And no, it's my ex-husband."

"From when?"

"We were married almost thirty years ago. But not for long."

"I'm so jealous of all your exes," Amira said. "It's embarrassing having a stable marriage, even if I did marry for money. Are you still in love with him?"

"I scarcely know him anymore. He's gay."

"Oh, that's wonderful. The gay ones all love me. I have no idea why. I'll have a party for you both. He can help you buy the house and fix Mandy. He'll be your savior."

With eerie synchronicity, the lights flickered on just as Amira uttered the last word. Julie wanted to protest that she didn't need a savior, but she knew that wasn't true.

8

Somewhere over the Sierras, David felt California beginning to fade. He was heading away from his troubles and toward Julie's relatively well-ordered life. In a house she owned, not a rented space. It was clear she was dealing with her own complications, but perhaps they could help each other out in ways they hadn't been able to all those years ago.

He'd taken a red-eye, and already, less than an hour into the flight, the lights were off and passengers were huddled under blankets, attempting to sleep or, if medicated, sleeping. It had taken him a few days to get reservations and get organized. He'd left keys to his apartment with his friend Michael and had asked him to check in once or twice while he was gone.

As for Renata, she'd called at least a dozen times since the party, and he'd refused to pick up or listen to her messages. He'd sent her an email saying he was going to visit a friend on the East Coast and would let her know when he got back.

It had been too long since his last trip east. Six years earlier, he'd returned for his mother's funeral. He hadn't seen her much after he'd moved west—he lived too far for frequent visits, and she was always tremendously busy—but they'd spoken on the phone almost daily. She had a sweet attachment to him that stopped just short of wanting to know much of what he was actually doing. "I know you don't want to tell me anything about your life," she'd say hopefully, "but I'm glad you're finally happy." She'd made frequent trips to casinos in Connecticut where she ate a lot of shrimp and lost small sums of money that eventually added up to her net worth. His father had died when his mother was in her early sixties, and she'd experienced one of those second acts common to widows of her generation. She'd had freedom for the first time in her life and reveled in travel, drinking, and gambling with other newly liberated widows. These friendships were far more agreeable and intimate than most of their marriages had been.

After she died, David had keenly felt the loss of her and of family in general. He had one brother, a computer programmer who lived in North Carolina. He'd never forgiven David for divorcing Julie, even after David had assured him it had been a mutual decision. "You should have done the right thing and stayed with her," he'd said, a theory that alternated with a contradictory theory that he should have "done the right thing" by never marrying her in the first place, given what should have been obvious to him about his sexual interests. Religion came into his opinions. He was married to a pretty woman who used the expression "the Lord" in a disturbing number of sentences, and was homeschooling their three kids, always a red flag. He didn't envision having a rapprochement with Decker too much in advance of one or the other's deathbed. He was, essentially, without a family.

At some point in the flight, he fell asleep. When he woke up, it was early morning. The cabin smelled of coffee. Sunlight seemed to loosen the tongue of the young woman in yoga pants sitting next to him, who, earlier in the flight, had been watching cooking shows on her screen with don't-talk-to-me intensity. When David asked her now why she was going to Boston, she announced that she was visiting her fiancé. The word "fiancé" was emphasized in a pointed way, as if she was trying to let him know that any dirty-old-man attempts at hitting on her were doomed to fail. He'd noticed that since acquiring gray hairs and gaining weight, he was more often assumed to be heterosexual, specifically a straight man with a predatory job like selling life insurance policies. To heighten the confusion, he told her he was traveling to see his ex-wife. "We haven't seen each other in more than twenty-five years," he said.

Naturally, this was of absolutely no interest to her.

"And," she followed up, "today is my twenty-ninth birthday."

"The summer solstice," he said. It was June 21 or 22, wasn't it? Hard to believe Julie's first call had been only two and a half weeks ago. "Happy birthday."

When the flight attendant asked her if she'd like a coffee, she proudly told him she was pregnant and trying to cut down. "Heartburn," she said.

"Congratulations on the baby," David said. "By the way, that's the reason my ex and I got married, too."

"That's not why we're getting married. It's *because* we're getting married."

He saw his mistake immediately, apologized, and agreed that that was different.

"Why did you get *divorced*?" she asked. The hostile tone suggested the question was punishment for his earlier assumption.

"It's a long story." He was about to get into the tangled weeds of sexuality and who knew what when—that would also reassure her that he wasn't about to start pressing his knee against hers—but he wasn't sufficiently alert to make a coherent narrative out of a chronology that involved so much denial and so many deceptions.

"And she got custody of the baby?"

"Sadly," he said, "she had a miscarriage." When he realized this wasn't something a pregnant woman would want to hear, he added, "As I said, that was almost thirty years ago. That kind of thing happened more often then," as if he was discussing the 1840s. Sometimes, it felt as if it was that long ago. Two months earlier, David had had his license renewed, and when he filled in the year of his birth on the form, it had had an antique look to him, the way the dates of the First World War had looked to him when he was a child.

Both he and Julie had been surprised by the pregnancy, which had come after they'd been living together for two years without making any commitments to each other. It had felt like fate was intervening, and they'd decided to go in the direction they were being led. They married. A few months later, Julie lost the baby.

David rarely focused on his thwarted desires to be a father, but it was true that he'd chosen careers that put him in a mentor role with young people. Sometimes, when he thought about what might have been or imagined the adult their child would now be, he had pangs of disappointment. His neighbor in yoga pants was roughly the age their child would have been. This thought filled him with tenderness toward her, and he turned and smiled warmly. The look was misinterpreted, and the young woman immediately plugged in earphones and went back to her private little screen.

The drive to Beauport, according to the GPS in his rented car, would take an hour. The morning air was warm and humid. There was already a torpid heaviness that reminded him of his sunburned childhood summers on the beaches of Rhode Island and the seductive, medicinal smell of Sea & Ski suntan lotion. He was driving against the rush-hour traffic headed to Boston, and going against the grain gave him a feeling of freedom. It had been such a good idea to come.

Eventually, the urban sprawl thinned out and gave way to open fields and patches of pine trees and woods beside the highway. You had to cross a bridge to get to Beauport. A tidal river flowed far below the road, the water running swiftly as the tide either came or went. Everything below was sodden green, the trees, the marsh grasses, even the water itself. Once over the bridge, he passed along a road overhung with oaks and scruffy maples. A cool breeze that smelled of briny rot blew in. Suddenly, he was in the center of the village, all shingled buildings painted the washed-out colors of laundry left on the line for too many days. The ocean was at the end of the street, a vast field of blue dotted with bright lobster boats that looked so authentic and appealing, they might have been placed there by the tourist board.

As directed by the GPS, he turned up a hill that rose steeply above the town. In the rearview mirror he saw the village below, miniaturized and charming, like the invented setting of a children's game or one of those paintings that seduce with vain, cheesy nostalgia.

He pulled into the driveway of a large yellow clapboard house he recognized from Julie's online listing. Although barely recognized. It loomed above the houses around it with turrets and porches and ornamentation that bridged the architectural gap between Queen Anne and Carpenter Gothic. It was a hodgepodge on which nothing looked precisely right, but which, taken as a whole, exuded the chaotic appeal of a cheerful drunk welcoming you, martini in hand. *Come on in! Have a cocktail. Don't mind the mess.*

The website had undersold the size of the house and, to a much greater extent, its weatherworn condition. There were shingles missing along one side and a piece of gutter hanging from an upper floor. The porch railings looked as if they were having trouble supporting their own weight, never mind that of someone who might lean against them.

Oh, Julie.

The fat tires of the rented car crunched on the gravel as he drove it. The whole property was surrounded by a high, untended privet hedge, and as he stepped out he was overwhelmed by the cloying, slightly repulsive smell of the flowers, reminiscent of wax, vanilla, and semen.

He was stretching and trying to get his bearings when a woman of indeterminate age (sixty-three, he determined) stepped onto one of the small decks on the second floor. She was wearing a beige pantsuit, which, in the harsh morning light, made her look like a nude mannequin.

"No one's come with the extension cord for the air conditioner," she called down.

"I'm sorry?" David said.

"The extension cord. We've been waiting for half an hour and still nothing."

"I'll check on it," he said.

"Half an hour. Yesterday it was the same thing with the pillows."

The door behind her opened and a man came onto the deck and grasped at the unsteady railing. He was almost identical in height and size and was wearing a darker version of the same outfit. He had on big eyeglasses, unflattering but helpful in making a distinction. "You're going to 'check on it'?" he asked.

"That's what I just said."

"I'd think you could do more than 'check on it.' It's stifling, and we've been waiting over an hour."

"I thought it was half an hour."

"One is as bad as the other," the man growled.

"Not really," David said. "One's twice as bad as the other. Isn't that why you doubled the wait time? And please don't lean on that railing. It's primarily ornamental."

"That seems to be true of a lot in this house—the lamps, the bathroom fan."

David gazed around the backyard. There was an atmosphere of decline, characterized by a pair of peeling Adirondack chairs leaning haplessly against each other near a pine tree. He felt as if he'd stepped onto a stage in the middle of an underfunded play and, for reasons he couldn't figure out, was finding it relatively easy to ad-lib the lines.

The Seven Steps to Julie's Future would clearly involve a lot of carpentry. He wondered how much he could get done in ten days.

"You're not being hospitable," the faux-nude woman called down.

"I respond well to reasonable requests," David said.

A dog that had been barking inside the house pushed open a screen door and sprang out. It was a small thing, black and tan, a shrunken variation on a terrier with the tall ears of a German shepherd. It made its way down the back steps in a series of lopsided hops. A tripod missing a back leg, but dealing with the challenge with more stoic determination than David could typically summon to deal with a hangover. It bounded over to him and leaped up giddily.

"Sit," he told her calmly, and apparently relieved at being given an order, she settled onto the lawn with a lolling tongue.

"Opal!" It was Julie's voice coming from inside the house. "I hope you didn't go out."

"She can't control the dog," the woman on the balcony called down.

Some combination of the chaos and the worrying condition of the house began to grate on David. "She's perfectly tame," he snapped. "I wish everyone was as well-mannered as she is."

"I can't wait to write my review of this place," the man said.

Right-wingers, David thought.

Julie stepped onto the porch off the back of the house. She gave a cry of surprise and checked her watch. "I thought you were getting here at eleven tonight," she said.

Upon seeing her, David had the strange sensation of being in his former life, but with the players distorted by funhouse mirrors.

"No. Eleven a.m. I took a red-eye. As you'll notice once I get closer."

While it was sometimes shocking to see the physical ravages of time, David was just as often amazed by how unchanged people were, in an essential way. Not from decade to decade, but from birth to death. Julie's face, in the morning light, had the yesterday's-dessert look he'd grown accustomed to seeing in his peers and his mirror—everything a little melted, fallen, and shiny—but she had the same long, straight hair and the same demeanor of addled sweetness, most apparent in her bemused and slightly wary smile. She had on work pants and a white shirt, an outfit she'd adapted from the androgynous gamine singers they'd listened to together and had, apparently, been wearing for all these decades. The clothes emphasized her height and unchanged slenderness, and for a moment David had the feeling he was seeing her emerge from a store she'd stepped into to buy a pack of gum while he waited on the sidewalk. He found his bags in the vast trunk of the car and set them on the gravel.

"Let me help you with your stuff," Julie said and came down the steps.

"How about helping us?" the woman above shouted.

Julie had her back to the upstairs deck. She rolled her eyes and gave a concealed wave of her hand, dismissing them.

"We've been waiting almost two hours," the man said.

"This is my ex-husband," Julie said. With, David thought, a little pride. "I told you he was coming today."

"Yes, but you told us he'd be helping out, and we haven't seen any evidence of that."

David went to Julie and hugged her. Her back felt bonier than he remembered.

"They're in the room I was going to give you," she said.

"I don't mind at all."

"You might once you see where you're going."

Opal began circling their feet, a distant herding instinct kicking in. The couple once again made a disparaging comment about the dog. David assured them everything was fine. "Let me worry about the dog," he said. "I'll bring your cord up in a few minutes."

When the couple had retreated, David draped his arm around Julie's shoulder. He pulled the suitcase behind him as they made their way to the house, and Julie rested her head against him.

"You smell good," she said.

"It's the upholstery in the rental car. They spray it with something to make it smell new."

"If only it were that easy," Julie said.

9

How had she screwed up the time of his arrival? The answer was obvious and was yet another example of why it was important to have given up pot, even if she had had a little parenthetical slip over the past day or two to stave off anxiety. She'd made an appointment to have Sandra, the Airbnb consultant, come this afternoon before David landed. So she thought. She'd timed it specifically so that in his eyes, she wouldn't seem desperate and on the verge of losing everything. First impressions matter.

As she led him into the kitchen, she decided to call and cancel the appointment. Sandra was a little testy on the phone, but as long as she rescheduled for a time after David's departure, she couldn't object too much.

"I have to make a quick call," she said. "There's lemonade in the fridge. I'll be back in a minute."

"Great cabinets," he said. He opened one but closed it quickly, probably appalled at the lack of order.

She went into the living room and found her phone. She hadn't expected David to be so filled out, a polite way of saying he had a slight paunch and had lost the lean boyishness she remembered as his defining physical trait. So much the better. It made her less self-conscious about her own exhausted appearance. She'd been fearing that—having come out and moved to California all those years ago— he'd be trim, sunny, and immaculately groomed, like one of the deans at Crawford School, an impeccable gay man in his fifties who used the word "spectacular" too often. No worries there.

Sandra answered her call instantly. "This is Sandra. Good morning. I hope you're having a successful day." She had a high pixie voice Julie found piercing.

"Hi, Sandra, this is Julie Fiske."

"I know that. You're in my phone, Julie. All my clients are in my phone." How did she manage to sound so bright this early? "I'll be seeing you in a few hours, Julie."

"The thing is," Julie said, "something's come up, and I was hoping we could reschedule."

"Nope," she chirped without a pause. "Sorry to dash your hopes, but we made the plan almost a week ago, and I've arranged my day around it. I'm in Manchester-by-the-Sea, 7.8 miles from you, doing another consultation right now. If you cancel, I'll be at your door at the appointed time to pick up what you owe. In cash for cancellations."

"I'm not canceling, exactly. Rebooking. Sometimes things come up."

"If you're in the emergency room, naturally, I'll only bill a cancellation fee of 50 percent of the balance due."

"I'm not sure what to say . . ."

"Then I'll decide for you, Julie." The high spirits had evaporated. "I'll be there at two-thirty, as arranged days and days ago. And FYI, I'm never late."

The call was terminated. In the kitchen, David was dumping milk down the drain.

"It had curdled," he said. "Everything all right?"

"I'm afraid I made a plan to have an Airbnb consultant look at the house this afternoon. I tried to cancel, but it didn't go well."

"I promise to stay out of your way," he said. "Why is she coming?"

"To help me make more money off the rentals. My expenses are about to go up. I'm buying the house from Henry in August." She felt a spasm of panic as she said this, but it passed, like a cramp in your calf. "That's the goal anyway. Unless my rich neighbors end up buying it behind my back."

She brought him into the living room and watched as he took in the décor in a calculated way. Seeing it from his eyes, and knowing his fondness for order, she saw more clutter than she was used to seeing and noticed that there was a small water stain on the ceiling near one of the windows. "It needs a little organizing, I know," she said. "Is it worse than you were expecting?"

He put down his suitcase and hugged her. "The house makes me happy. I know it needs work, but it's exactly the kind of place I imagined you living in. A little out of control, but totally appealing. It's perfect for you."

This was the confirmation she needed that her plans weren't completely insane. As for "out of control," there was no point in trying to pretend it was otherwise, and besides, he'd meant it as a compliment.

The minuscule Cabinet Room, in which she was guiltily putting him, was between the kitchen and the living room. When she opened the door, David burst out laughing. "You chose the best possible name," he said. He flopped down on the bed, still laughing. The move was so youthful, she was transported back thirty years, and joined him, sprawling across the chenille bedspread, grinning.

"I have people booked into the other rooms," she said. "I'm sorry."

"No, no. It's perfect. I can't tell you how much I love it." And then, suddenly serious, he sat up and said, "I'm not here for the room, you know that. I'm here to help out with Mandy and whatever else you want. But mainly, I'm here to see you. This hasn't been the best year of my life, so I have selfish motives, too. I had to get away from San Francisco for a while. When I called you from that party, I was in a panic."

"I thought so. I heard it in your voice. You'll tell me about it?"

"Eventually, of course. But give me a chance to make a good first impression."

After all these years, they still had a lot in common.

As she helped him unpack his neatly laundered shirts and folded pants and watched him put them in the dresser beside his bed (too big for the room), she explained about the bathroom. It was across the hall, tucked under the staircase in what had once been a closet. "Anyone can use it, but no one does. On the listing, I call it a 'bathroom-with-privacy.'"

"Clever feint," he said. "People prefer privacy with their bathrooms."

She took his socks out of the suitcase and, remembering how he preferred to store them, rolled them into a ball. She was aware of how small and warm the room was and how close they were standing. There was nothing sexual in the proximity, nothing that stirred her in that way, but it was impossible not to flash back on all the private things they'd known about each other (his fondness for epically bad movies, his love of the subway, the freckle above his penis) and the stored images of the way their younger bodies had felt and tasted and moved together. They'd never be lovers again, but a ghost of what had once been between them hovered somewhere in the room.

There were other ghosts, too. In anticipation of David's arrival, she'd tossed restlessly throughout the preceding night, worrying about how she'd get around to having the discussion with him that was the one big, unfinished piece of business in her life.

"At some point," she said, "we'll have to recap some of the past, don't you think?"

He closed the dresser drawer, leaned against it, and rolled his sleeves up his forearms. She'd always found his forearms sexy although now she realized there was nothing special about them. "I'm not here for very long," he said. "Maybe we should let things come up when they do, without planning ahead too much. If that's all right?"

It was a welcome reprieve.

10

They had lunch, and after they'd finished, David sat on the front porch with Opal at his feet, waiting for the arrival of the Airbnb consultant, trying to make a mental list of everything he needed to do around the house.

He'd asked for a salad, part of a resolution he'd announced to "eat healthy," everyone's favorite euphemism for "lose weight." Julie had pulled all the vegetables out of the refrigerator, and the two of them had stood at the counter, washing and chopping. All the greens had had the weary look of food that had been bought with good intentions, then abandoned in favor of takeout pizza. He was going to have to go shopping with her soon and take over the cooking. He'd been the cook the entire time he and Julie had lived together, and it would be odd to have her serve him now.

Maybe it was the jet lag, but he was finding it impossible to prioritize tasks, something he usually found easy to do. There were so many. The most urgent need was the most selfish—declutter the cabinet he was sleeping in.

He pulled a little notebook out of his pocket and started to jot down items. When he gazed out at the street, he saw a woman passing by on the sidewalk, swinging a straw bag in an extravagant way. She was wearing tight white pants that came down to the middle of her calves, and even from a distance she gave off an aura of money and sex that seemed out of place in this town. This had to be the rich neighbor Julie had mentioned, the one whose husband either was or wasn't trying to buy Julie's house.

She caught his eye, waved, and strolled up the walk to the house.

"I didn't think you were coming until later in the week!" she called out, as if they were old pals. David reeled in Opal's leash. "Yes, hold that terrible dog so I can give you a hug."

"You must be Amira," David said as she bounced up the stairs and threw herself against him. She smelled strongly of a dense perfume that seemed to be an amalgam of the best scents from the most intimate parts of the body. Or perhaps it was just her natural odor.

She reached up, undid a button on his shirt, stood on her toes, and peered inside. Some glamorous women, he'd noted, seem to think the concept of personal space does not apply to gay men. Unfortunately, few glamorous men do. "I thought you would be hairier," she said. "And fatter. My husband waxes his back to be more attractive. Does he think I care how he looks?"

"I wouldn't know."

"Everyone knows I married him for money. I didn't think he'd move me up to this horrible, depressing prison. It is like death to be here." This pronouncement seemed to cheer her up. "We're going to have fun with you this summer. I'll have a big, hideously boring cocktail party. It will make me less depressed to be around Les Miserables and the Anonymous Alcoholics."

"You don't look depressed. You look extremely beautiful." When in doubt, compliment, in this case, truthfully. She was wearing a tight green T-shirt made from a stretchy material that clung to her body and showed off her small, perfect breasts and slender waist more clearly than if she'd been topless. On the shirt, printed in an elegantly simple font, was the adage, FUCK YOU. "Besides, I'm only here for a little over a week."

"That's not nearly enough time to solve all of Julie's problems. I predict you'll be here all summer. I would love to say more, but I'm meeting a potential lover at the hideous beach, so I have to hurry."

She waved and headed off, but as she was halfway down the hill, she called out, "David! David!"

He went out to the sidewalk, carrying Opal. "Yes?"

"You have to be careful with Mandy."

"Why is that?" he asked. The sun was in his eyes and he had to shield them to see her.

"She is one of those girls who thinks she is ugly and will let men take advantage of her. She is going to end up crying on the steps of the library at midnight if you don't help. That would be no good because there is only room for one of us. Cheers!"

Clearly, this self-absorbed showboater was not a reliable witness. And yet somehow he sensed that her comments about Mandy were valid. When he sat down again and took out his notebook and looked at his to-do list, he crossed out what he'd written and scrawled "Mandy" across the top of the page.

11

Craig had sent a text saying he'd meet her in the parking lot of the old IGA at two o'clock, but it was getting close to three and there was still no sign of him. Mandy had her sneakers off and was juggling with them to trick herself into believing she wasn't paying attention to the time. Not working.

The IGA had closed its doors less than a year ago, but it already had a postapocalyptic look, as if it had been abandoned for decades. The parking lot was littered with paper and the cracked hot top was sprouting weeds.

It was a humid afternoon and the air was sticky. David Hedges was showing up today and even though she was looking forward to having him in the house, she didn't want to be there until he'd settled in and he and her mother had said their hellos and cried or fought or whatever they needed to do.

She let one sneaker fall to the ground and, for the hell of it, tossed the other toward the Dumpster. Just her luck, it went in. As she was hobbling to retrieve it, Craig's van pulled around the side of the building. She felt a nervous thrill. He stopped next to her and leaned out. He had his curly hair pushed off his face with a yellow headband, a look that actually worked on him.

"I didn't think you'd still be here," he said.

"Really? How come you came?"

"How come you stayed?"

"No life," she said. "I have to get something. It'll only take a second."

She felt awkward climbing into the Dumpster but had an inkling he'd like her more if she cared less about his opinion of her. She found her sneaker on top of some contractor bags and empty Dunkin' Donuts cups. She tried to climb out as athletically as she could. She did care about his opinion of her. Of course.

Craig was shaking his head and smiling. "Looks like you've done that before," he said.

"It's one of my many interesting hobbies."

"Yeah? Maybe you'll tell me about the others."

It was clear that one of his hobbies was making pretty much everything he said sound like it had a whole buffet of meanings. Take your pick, but most sounded sketchy. The way he paused before saying "others" and then raised his eyebrows?

"I'm headed up to the water tower," he said. "It's cooler up there. Are you getting in?"

She had the same feeling she had whenever he spoke to her—like a warning signal was flashing in her head, red blue red blue red blue. She ignored it and opened the door.

"Don't forget your seat belt," he said.

"You're not wearing yours."

"I trust my own driving. A girl your age shouldn't trust any-one."

She knew this was true, but it was reassuring that he'd at least pointed it out. The back of the van was full of cables and computer parts from an earlier decade.

"So what are you doing with yourself now that school is out?" he asked.

"I've got a summer job," she said, hoping he wouldn't ask for more details. The name of the store was so humiliating—Beachy Keen—she had trouble saying it out loud, even to her mother. "It's called Beach something" was as much as she'd been able to get out.

"Working retail at one of the junk shops on Perry Neck?" he asked. "Minimum wage?"

Foolishly, she hadn't asked the owner how much she'd be mak-ing. It had seemed rude. Mandy had wandered into a few shops out on the Neck and Elaine Guild was the first owner to offer her twenty hours a week. "And wear something beachy," Elaine had said. So far, Mandy had worked two shifts and had worn her usual overalls, explaining that these were what she wore to the beach.

"Something like that," she said.

"You're wasting your talents," he said. "You could be making a lot more."

She was so happy to hear he thought she had talents, she didn't want to jinx the conversation by asking for details.

"Everyone says you were in the army," she said, trying to change the subject and maybe learn something concrete about him, something no one else knew for sure, despite all the speculation.

"I saw you change the topic," he said. "Don't worry, we'll get back to it. And who's everyone? Those snarky little friends of yours?"

"I don't have all that many friends."

"Don't say that like it's a bad thing. Neither do I. Your school is full of girls walking around in designer clothes and ten pounds of makeup, all trying way too hard."

"I'm not sure how designer the clothes are," she said. "Don't forget, it's public school."

"One of the things I like about you is you're not trying."

She was eager to know what some of the other things he liked were, but she didn't want to push her luck. "Why try when you know you'll never succeed?" she said. As a fallback position, self-criticism probably wasn't great, but it was reliable.

"I can tell you're smarter than all of them."

"I'm not so sure," she said. "They're too smart to get in this van with you."

"I wouldn't ask them."

He turned off the main road and started the climb up to the hills above town. The woods up here were dotted with scruffy pines and abandoned granite quarries. The water tower was at the highest point in town, and the van's engine strained as they went up the steep road. It seemed right that he drove a clunker. It was reassuring. She didn't like slick people, like that sleazy husband who'd shown himself to her in the bathroom. As bad as it was, the fact that he and his wife presented themselves as so perfect made it worse. She'd seen the wife again before they checked out, and she'd felt bad for her. She knew more about her husband than the woman did herself. It had made her want to cry as she watched them getting into their car like a happy couple.

The water tower was a favorite hangout of teenagers because it was remote and felt dangerous—the surrounding woods had been an encampment for outcast settlers centuries ago, and the quarries were filled with icy spring water that was rumored to be bottomless. From the side-view mirror, she could see the ocean falling off behind them and the crescent of the shops and restaurants on Perry Neck.

"So were you in the military?" she asked.

"That's what they say."

"Oh, come on. Is it really so hard to answer even one question?" She was surprised she'd said something so blunt, but having done so, she was encouraged to say more. "It's not like I asked for your Social Security number."

He rattled off a string of digits so automatically, she knew it had to be his actual number. He winked at her and said, "I was in Afghanistan for two years."

"Is that where you learned computers?"

"That's where I learned to mind my own business." The engine bucked and he shifted to a lower gear. "I get the feeling you're a girl who already knows how to keep secrets."

It had been drilled into her since birth that unless it was uttered by one of her parents while both of them were present, the word "secret" was radioactive. It probably shouldn't have been a compliment, but it felt like one.

"I don't have any secrets to keep."

He winked at her again, the first really unattractive thing she'd seen him do. "I don't know about that. I'd say you've got one now."

He pulled onto a dirt track that led off the road and parked in the shadow of the water tower. He yanked up the emergency brake and leaned his back against the door with his elbow out the window. He grinned, expecting something, though she had no idea what.

From here, there was what her father would call a "big view." The restaurant he and his business partner owned three towns away also had a "big view." Unfortunately, what it didn't have was "good food." The water below was a dark sprawling blue that seemed to go on forever. Lobster boats were headed into the harbor after a day of hauling traps. There was something sad about the small boats and the men who made a living off them. In her lifetime, this profession would probably become extinct, and the lobstermen had to know this, too. A lot of things would become extinct in her lifetime—frogs, rain, winter, lobsters, humans. Humans would definitely be the least tragic loss.

Craig reached into a cooler behind the front seat, and as he stretched, she smelled his sweat. His T-shirt lifted and exposed the taut, smooth skin around the waistband of his pants. He had smooth and tanned arms, too, one of the things she'd heard girls swooning about at school and had, therefore, decided to find unattractive. Up close, there wasn't much of anything unattractive about Craig Crespo. His long, curly hair, held back in the headband, was greasy, but even this made him look natural and comfortable with himself. He had a face that was technically ugly with a lot of big features fighting each other for attention. But when you put it together, all that imperfection added up to a weird beauty that she recognized as being "hot," a word she hated when unrelated to weather but that was the only one appropriate in this case.

He twisted the cap off the beer. "I'd offer you one," he said, "but the drinking age in this state is nineteen."

"It's twenty-one pretty much everywhere."

"In that case, do you want one?"

The smell of the hops was skunky but appealing, a little like her mother's pot. On top of that, the van was getting warm, and she was thirsty. But she'd only had a few sips of beer a few times, and she needed to be in control. "I'm good," she said.

She'd never thought about a physical type she was attracted to. It had always seemed irrelevant since she imagined it would be more practical to wait until someone was attracted to her and then invest her energy in convincing herself she liked his looks and personality. That appeared to be the definition of "happy marriage." But Craig was probably everyone's type. There was that dark, flawless skin, the long hair, the arms that were muscular but not overblown. The way he stretched back and exposed his stomach wasn't asking her to admire him, more like telling her she could if she wanted.

"So why did you move back to Hammond after the army?" she asked.

Naturally, he didn't answer. He touched one of the straps of her overalls and said, "So why do you always wear overalls?"

She felt herself grow hot and start to tremble. Another warning signal flashed, but while everyone else was gossiping about Craig, he'd been looking at her at least enough to know what she always wore. That was currency.

"They're comfortable," she said.

He smirked. He had nice teeth, which, for some reason, made her feel safer. How likely was it that mass murderers flossed?

"You know what else they are?" he asked.

"All cotton?"

"Easy to take off."

The shadow of the tower had moved and the sun was now blazing against the side of the van, and even though the windows were rolled down, it was getting stifling. She hoped she wasn't sweating too much. She felt her lips twitching with nerves, but she took some consolation in remembering that her public-speaking teacher had said stage fright is less obvious to the audience than the performer thinks.

"Actually," she said, "they're pretty hard to get off."

"Yeah?" He set the beer bottle on the dashboard and it rocked. As he leaned toward her and shifted his body, the seat beneath him creaked, an intimate sound in the silent van. She knew it was something she'd remember for days. He reached out and, without touching her body, fiddled with the hooks on her straps. The bib of her overalls fell to her waist. She had on a jersey and underneath that, a tight, sleeveless T-shirt, so it wasn't as if it was a big deal. Still, she felt naked.

"That wasn't hard at all," he said.

"Now what?" she asked.

"You tell me."

Instead of waiting for an answer, he leaned in and slipped his hand behind her neck and pulled her head closer to him and kissed her on the lips. His lips were chapped and warm, but his tongue, which he almost immediately worked into her mouth, was cool. She knew there was something sloppy about his move, even though she'd never been kissed before. Like he was doing it for a reason other than because he liked her.

"You taste like beer," she said.

"I wonder why. You know what you taste like? Bubble gum."

"I don't chew gum. I stopped when I got braces at twelve."

"I didn't mean it literally. I meant you taste like a teenager."

"That's creepy."

"Are you surprised? Don't you think I'm a little creepy? You don't have to answer. But I'm not going to try anything, so don't worry."

He kissed her again, but not as long and deep this time. He leaned back against the window with the beer bottle in his hand.

"I'm not worried," she said.

"Good," he said. "Because I am."

"About what?"

"My investments."

He finished the beer without taking his eyes off her and threw the bottle out the window. It hit the ground and bounced. This struck her as the worst thing he'd done all afternoon. Worse than keeping her waiting, kissing her, or saying she tasted like a teenager. She got out of the van, picked it up, went to his window, and handed it to him.

"I don't recycle," he said.

"You should start."

He took the bottle. "Yes, ma'am."

When she got back into the van, he started the engine. She

couldn't tell if he was annoyed with her or pleased, but either way, she was glad she'd done it. It made her feel more like they were equals, even though she knew they weren't.

"I'm going to message you about doing some work for me this summer," he said.

"I told you . . ."

"Yeah, the job. I remember. Believe me, this is way better. More fun, and you'd make a ton of money."

"Doing what?"

"Just being you. That's the best part. Wouldn't it be nice to get paid for just being you?"

She felt that there was something wrong with this turn in the conversation, but she didn't know what.

He released the emergency brake. "If anyone asks you, remember, nothing happened today."

It was a ridiculous thing to say. Who would ask her? And more to the point, something definitely had happened.

12

As Julie was cleaning up after lunch, she heard a car pull into the drive and called to David. He came inside, and they went to the window above the sink to watch Sandra's arrival. The car was one of those small, oddly shaped boxes that seem designed for grabbing attention more than practicality, like asymmetrical hemlines. Sandra emerged from it slowly. She was a large woman, probably six feet tall, and so big-boned, it was hard to imagine her fitting into the little sedan. This was not what Julie had been expecting, based on her dainty voice.

She was wearing a floral skirt that came to just above her ankles and a silky peach top. Her pixie hairdo struck Julie as odd on someone so large. When she opened the hatchback on the car, Julie saw stacks of cartons, yellowed newspapers, and shopping bags stuffed with more paper. Definitely a B—at least—on the ABCD Scale.

"Isn't this a lovely house," she enthused as Julie led her in. "And the location. My goodness. You can't beat the location. We call this a 'million-dollar location' in the trade. You'll always have guests clamoring to stay, with a location like this. If I had a location like this, I'd be driving a Mercedes. I'm going to help you make a lot of money, Julie Fiske, so isn't it good I didn't allow you to cancel? And as I told you when we made the appointment *days* ago, I prefer to be paid the balance owed me for the consultation in full, immediately upon arrival."

Since this had been mentioned three times during that phone call, Julie had a check ready and handed it to Sandra. She caught a whiff of powder as Sandra took the check and began to settle down at the kitchen table. She removed papers and a clipboard, a tin of Altoids, and a large thermos from her bag. Also, paper clips, pens, a bottle of Wite-Out, and a stapler. She stamped PAID on a bill and clipped the check to it, all the while asking who David was and what he was doing here. "I thought you said your husband had moved out."

"David's an old friend. He's staying for a week to help with a few things."

Sandra looked up from her paperwork and examined David over the top of a pair of half-glasses. "Isn't that nice. Are we giving him a discount, Julie?"

"He's a friend, as I said."

"And if you were running a shop, would you let 'friends' come in and walk out with half the merchandise? If you ran a car dealership, would you let him come in and drive off the lot in a new Mercedes?"

"I'd prefer a Tesla," David said.

"I'm glad you think it's funny, David, but business is business and as I understand it, Julie is desperate."

"I'm not sure I said I was desperate."

"You didn't have to. I've got eyes." Changing her tone again, she said, "And isn't this a quirky kitchen! Dark, outdated, practically depressing by today's standards, but quirky. Remember, Julie, 'quirky' is one of those subjective terms you can use on your owner page to describe anything. We'll get to the owner page later."

She took a drink from her thermos and made careful piles of papers.

After all, "desperate" might be the most accurate if least flattering way to describe her situation. There was something a little off about Sandra, the high, childlike voice and hulking body, the swift shifts in tone. But Julie was clinging to hopes, even if she suspected Sandra was selling snake oil. Maybe she was just quirky. "I'm grateful you came," Julie said warily, trying to convince herself that she was.

"Gratitude doesn't come into it. When my guests tell me they're grateful to me for sharing my lovely Victorian mansion, I remind them that gratitude is free and my rooms are not. You remember that, too, David."

"Duly noted," he said. He was leaning against the sink and raised his eyes at Julie, more amused than insulted.

"Good. And I'd love a tall glass of water," Sandra said. "With crushed ice and a slice of lemon."

Julie eyed Sandra's thermos, but went to get a glass.

"You're making a mistake already, Julie. You're going to get so much out of this consultation, I can tell you right now." Sandra chuckled, though without much humor. "I should have charged you more."

The three-hundred-dollar fee had struck Julie as plenty high already.

"To ask for a glass of water is reasonable, but to specify the size of the glass is not. To ask for ice that's crushed is ridiculous, and the lemon slice crosses the line completely." She'd finished arranging the papers in front of her, checked the watch buried in the flesh of her wrist, and noted the time on the corner of a page. "You're eager to please, Julie. It's touching."

Sandra had oddly small eyes, but Julie felt for a moment that she was seeing through her.

"You never refuse a guest anything, Julie. You apologize and offer them an alternative. An unlikely alternative. 'Gee, Sandra, I'm so sorry, but I'm fresh out of lemons and crushed ice. I have some carrots, if you'd like one of those in your tap water.' 'Gee, Sandra, I don't have any memory-foam mattress covers right at this moment. Can I offer you a beach towel?' You see the point?"

"Isn't it better to make them happy?" David said.

Sandra lowered her glasses and gazed at him. "Making people happy is the psychotherapist's job. And last time I checked, there are no guarantees on the outcome there, despite paying her $175 per hour for six months." She took another drink. "'Oh, I've got all the answers, Sandra. Write me another check, Sandra. I can save your marriage, Sandra. Just another two grand, Sandra.'"

She gave them each a stack of papers. These turned out to be carefully organized checklists of items for the rooms, ranging from lighting and cleanliness to hand sanitizers and, of course, toss pillows. Each one was ranked from one to five. You couldn't fault her on professionalism.

There was a whole new layer to the economy that was made up of rogue businesses like room rentals and car services and pop-up trucks, businesses made possible by the internet and social media. Julie supposed it was a good thing—people were making money and providing services; David's career fell into this category somewhere—but it was hard to imagine they'd exist if there was a robust manufacturing sector or strong, respected labor unions. Sometimes Julie wondered if these enterprises weren't just ways to keep people busy and distracted while villains dismantled the middle class.

"We'll start in the living room," Sandra said, pushing herself up from the table wearily. "Is he coming along?"

"I'd like to, if you don't mind," David said. "I'm sure I'll find it interesting."

Maybe that was true, but Julie knew he was going along to protect her. It had been a long time since she'd felt protected, and for a moment, she thought she might weep.

"I don't mind," Sandra said. She took a long drink from her thermos. "But if I find you're trying to piggyback off Julie for a freebie, I'm sending you a bill. I'll need your address later. Let's get this show going."

As she walked past, Julie got a whiff of something acrid mixed in with Sandra's powdery smell. Gin? She glanced at the thermos.

Sandra's main point was that the living room needed less of everything. Less furniture, fewer books, end tables, and footstools.

Fewer scatter rugs that people could trip on and fewer small items. "Some of them like to steal small things. You never accuse them, you sit in wait until you catch them in the act. Then you pounce."

Predictably, the one thing Sandra advised more of was toss pillows.

"I'd like to see four or five times the number you currently have. It doesn't look as if you've been reading the blog closely, Julie. You can pick them up for pennies at bargain stores, thrift shops, even pharmacies."

"Won't that make the room look cluttered?" David asked.

Sandra sighed and shook her head in disapproval. "People associate toss pillows with well-run short-term rentals. Nothing makes a room, a whole house, more welcoming and relaxing. You literally cannot have too many. And if you have a sofa you don't want anyone to sit on—probably not a problem here—you add even more. You create a welcoming atmosphere, but in practical terms, the sofa is impossible to use. I don't see any hand sanitizers here."

"In the living room?" David asked.

"We have a lot of opinions for someone who isn't paying rent, don't we? People want germ-free environments, David. They don't want to stay in someone's house and think about all the DNA and fecal matter on every surface. You put out a bunch of hand sanitizers and they plant a suggestion that everything is clean. End of story. I'm sorry, Julie, but I can only give this room a three. And to be honest, that's generous."

As the tour went on, Sandra became more persistent and, if not quite hostile, less and less friendly. "Ever hear of a vacuum cleaner, Julie?" she asked at one point.

At the bottom of the staircase, David pulled her aside and let Sandra get ahead of them. "Are you sure this is a good idea?" he said. "I think she might have some problems with anger management."

"I was thinking alcohol," Julie whispered. "I'm getting a smell of gin from that thermos."

"You could call it off. I don't see much good coming out of this."

"I doubt she'd give a refund, and she does have some advice."

"All I'm hearing is pillows and feces. If you're worried about telling her to leave, I'm happy to do it for you."

"Let's just finish."

In the bedrooms, Sandra tested mattresses, chairs, and lamps. She made note of the number of hangers in each closet, and scolded Julie about the absence of toss pillows on the beds.

"Do you hear people through the walls?" she asked.

Julie looked at David and then back at Sandra. "Sometimes, I suppose. Some voices."

"No, Julie, I mean do you *hear* people. Couples."

The suggestive tone—part revulsion, part drunken titillation— made Julie uncomfortable. "It hasn't been a problem."

"Then you must not have been paying attention. I went to an entire seminar on this topic at our annual convention. It's a huge problem nationwide. You're letting people into your space. I'm doing a post on it soon, all the ways you can make your home as inappropriate for sexual activity as possible, to discourage people before it starts. Heavy valances and window curtains, potpourris in the bedrooms, floral slipcovers on the chairs, quilted bedspreads."

David stepped forward and put a hand on Sandra's shoulder. "We appreciate this," he said, "but I think we get the general idea."

"I came to do a job, and I plan to finish it," she said. She turned to Julie and said, "Where do you sleep?"

"Third floor," Julie said. "My daughter and I have rooms there, but we don't rent on the top floor, so it's not relevant."

"Everything's relevant," she said. "I'm going up."

The staircase got hotter and stuffier as they ascended. At the sound of footsteps, Opal, who was locked in Julie's bedroom, began to bark and scratch at the door. "Probably best not to open that door," Julie said. "If you don't mind."

"You don't need to tell me! I'm not a dog person," Sandra growled.

She opened the door to Mandy's bedroom and grunted with disapproval. "This the daughter's room?" She made heavy slashes on her papers.

"Are we done?" David asked.

This was not, apparently, the right question. "Some of us are never done, David. Do you know who runs the majority of these businesses? Single women. Women who are single because they were left by their husbands, even though they tried to do everything they could to save the goddamn marriage. So to make ends meet, you let a parade of strangers traipse through the house, stealing your ashtrays and leaving everything else filthy. And god forbid you should be in the kitchen having a snack when one of them comes in and thinks it's her duty to give you a lecture on carbohydrates. As if I care.

"And then you have to tell your friends how much you love

having people stay with you, how fascinating it is to meet these people from all over the world even though the people who rent from you instead of springing for a hotel room are pretty much carbon copies of each other, no matter what stamp they've got on their passports."

"We're going downstairs now, Sandra," David said. "I'll follow you."

"What's the matter? Can't handle what I'm saying? Well, don't forget, she's the one who called me because she's lost her husband and is about to lose her daughter and the house. And I don't care if you like it or not, I'm going to send my report. I follow through on my promises. But let me give you a little preview, Julie.

"This isn't going to work for you. You're not cut out for it. The place is a mess, you're letting people stay here for free, there are about four toss pillows in the whole house, and if you think I didn't see that joint in the ashtray on that shelf behind the sofa, you're wrong. This kind of scene brings down the whole industry. So get rid of the dog and the freeloaders, and bail. You're not cut out for this."

13

It was turning out to be a much longer day than David had expected. It felt as if he'd left San Francisco weeks ago. After escorting Sandra to her car and making sure she didn't plow through the hedge on her way out, he walked into the house and called, "That was memorable. I'm ready for a nap. Or some of whatever it was she had in that thermos."

But when he walked into the hallway, he saw that Julie was crouched against the wall by the staircase with her head buried in her knees. He was alarmed by the fact that she didn't look up, and then he realized she was crying. The nap was off the table. He slid down onto the floor next to her and put his arm around her. "She was drunk," he said. "And I can't imagine she'd be a lot more credible if she was sober."

She shook her head and David felt her hair brush his face. There was, he saw, gray mixed in, something that had escaped his earlier scrutiny. Even more touching, it was obvious she colored it. She who'd always criticized her mother for coloring her hair, who'd always eschewed makeup and asserted she'd never do anything to hide her age. What an easy promise to make when age had seemed like someone else's problem.

He hugged her to his side, and was transported back to another, similar moment almost thirty years earlier when he'd returned home from a school trip to Washington, D.C., and had found her curled in a ball, sobbing. It was a moment that had haunted him for many years. He hadn't been used to seeing such raw, undisguised pain, although in the years that followed, he'd see more of it from stricken young men and their mourning families and friends. He'd had a sense back then of what had happened as soon as he saw her, but it had taken almost an hour of coaxing before she said that she'd lost the baby, and in the moments that followed, all their assumptions about their future had begun to fray.

"I can't believe you're taking this so seriously," he said now. "I was hoping to start turning this into an amusing anecdote before dinner."

She waved this off, newly bereft. He leaned down and kissed the top of her head. He remembered it, all at once, as a gesture that had always calmed her down, as it often quiets infants and dogs. The sudden tenderness he felt toward her shook him because it brought back a time when this closeness would have led somewhere it clearly was not going to lead now.

When Julie had composed herself, she sat up and shook back her hair. "The problem is," she said, "she's right. She's awful, but she's right. This is never going to work out. And even if it does, it's never going to be enough."

"Enough for what?"

"There's a lot I haven't told you," she said.

"That's a good thing," he said. "Between that and what I haven't told you, we won't run out of things to say. I gather Mandy's education is the tip of the iceberg?"

"Considering the climate, that metaphor will be completely obsolete soon."

"That's a yes?" he asked.

"That's a yes."

She took him out to a relatively private spot in the backyard where the decrepit Adirondack chairs were roosting between an old barn she was using for storage and the immense pine tree. The ground was fragrant with fallen pine needles.

"I'll be right back," she said. He watched as she went to the side of the house, rummaged around near the foundation, and returned with a stone. There was nothing promising in this.

She sat in the chair next to him, slid aside the bottom of the rock, and pulled out a joint. "Don't judge me," she said. "I stopped smoking a while ago, but I keep a little around to prove to myself I don't need it." She flicked a small red lighter, and inhaled. "Anyway, it makes me more honest."

David thought of smoking pot as a habit people outgrew in their late twenties, possibly because that was when he'd stopped smoking it. It was an assumption that made no sense since he knew scores of gray-haired potheads in San Francisco, but he'd put it down to the place. Over the years, he'd noticed that while alcoholics were, on the whole, a lot less appealing than potheads, they rarely made claims that drinking gave them special powers; regular marijuana users alleged that everything from their lovemaking to their deductive reasoning was improved by being stoned. Maybe there was some truth in that.

"Do you think it would make me a better listener?" he asked.

She handed him the joint. "It's worth a try."

He took a hit of pot and immediately felt himself slide into a remotely familiar pocket of warmth tinged with euphoria. The humid late-afternoon air was soothing, and he had a brief moment of believing this trip was the best move he'd made in ages, icebergs and all.

Then Julie began talking. Mandy, the house, the money. Henry's attempt to sell to the rich neighbor. Henry's late-in-life change to the restaurant business. A rejected mortgage application and a plan to sell her dreadful mother's allegedly valuable jewelry. His own situation, which had seemed so dire back in San Francisco, looked relatively simple from this new vantage point. Unless maybe that was the pot talking.

"If I were you," she said, "I'd get on my computer and book the next flight back to San Francisco. This whole vessel is sinking."

"No you wouldn't," he said. "And there isn't much waiting for me back there. I'm familiar with sinking vessels myself."

She was going to have to come up with $250,000 by the middle of August, and Mandy had to have a credible plan for college. The Seven Steps to Julie Fiske's Future was beginning to look like a much steeper climb than he'd anticipated. And that wasn't even taking into consideration Amira's theory of Mandy and the library.

"You've got two months," he said. "I'll sit down tomorrow and make a plan, and we'll work through as much of it as we can while I'm here to get you started."

The pot and the heat had made him sleepy but certain he was in exactly the right place.

14

The next morning, he woke with a gasp, as if he was being suffocated. Over the course of the night, he'd managed to entangle himself in the sheets of the single bed so thoroughly he was practically mummified. Had he gotten up in the middle of the night and trekked to the bathroom? He couldn't remember. Then it came to him—the weed. That seductive layer of fog between reality and consciousness of reality. He'd have to be sure to stay away from it. He'd have to try to get Julie to give it up. Or at least admit that she hadn't already done so.

The house was quiet, but somewhere in the distance, he heard a lawn mower chewing through grass. It triggered memories of his largely unhappy childhood in a gruff suburb outside of Providence where lawn mowing—along with, and somehow related to, car washing and alcoholism—had been a competitive sport. He saw his father, the tall, scowling owner of a hardware store, standing in the kitchen knocking back a glass of whiskey and rattling ice and announcing he was going out to "cut the fucking grass." He hadn't thought of him in ages. This was one of his few happy memories of him.

The lawn mower roared until there was a loud clunk of blade against stone, a shouted curse, and then quiet. David opened his eyes and gazed around the room, not exactly a taxing experience. The one window was almost flush with the privet hedge and the overpowering scent of the flowers filled the air. Still, he hadn't been lying to Julie when he said he loved the room; it felt like a small but significant corner of the house, just as he hoped to play a small but meaningful role in her life. How long she'd be able to keep the house was another matter.

As he was contemplating staggering across the hall to the bathroom-with-privacy, he heard from above the sounds of creaking and muffled pants, followed by a few lazy grunts. He recalled Sandra's warnings. Unfortunately, he had nothing to throw against the ceiling. It had to be the jumpsuited couple from yesterday consummating their relationship. Julie had told him they were religious fundamentalists and had bumper stickers on their car imprinted with the numbers of New Testament verses. Once decoded, these gaudy Public Displays of Religion usually translated to tiresome condemnations of some aspect of his life, which made it even less appealing to listen to them enjoying theirs. He wasn't sure why, but he was mildly repulsed by the thought of religiously devout people of any faith, age, or gender combination copulating. He realized this was intolerant, but he took some comfort in reminding himself that they felt the same way about him, and at least he had no desire to restrict their civil rights.

A few minutes later, when he'd come back from the bathroom, the noise had stopped. Above the sound of footsteps, he heard the man say in clear tones, "Well then you clean it up, goddammit."

This, he decided, was the mission statement for his visit. Even at this early hour and with a mild pot-over, he felt more energized than overwhelmed by the challenge. It was a chance to make up for his mistakes of decades ago. Antrim, the man who'd been the catalyst for the end of his and Julie's marriage, had appeared in his stoned dreams last night, gawky and young. David hadn't thought of him in years, and it had been disconcerting to have a visit of sorts from a man who'd disappeared from his life after turning it upside down.

There was a small desk wedged against the foot of the bed, and he set up his laptop on the wobbly surface. This room, like much of the house, was cluttered, but given the minute size, it made even less sense here than elsewhere. What was the purpose of the tiny end tables in this room and the chair jammed into a dark corner or even the ornate frame for the single bed that took up too much space?

His email inbox was as cluttered as the room, most alarmingly with coupons from a company that specialized in clothes for "men of substance." Were these being sent to him because he'd complained about having gained weight in a few emails or because some fishing expedition had calculated the caloric content of the take-out orders he'd made over the past six months and drawn their own conclusions? Either way, the sight of them made him furious at Soren for having abandoned him, not exactly because living with him had been such a great pleasure but because living without him had been such a hunger-igniting trial.

There were emails from several clients and one from Renata. Sooner or later, he was going to have to confront that reality.

Dear David: When I told Soren you'd gone east for a while, he said it might be to visit your ex-wife. Excuse me? After all this time, you never had the decency to tell me you had been married? To a woman? And you dare to play the victim here? Contact me immediately! Porter and Soren want to close on the house as soon as possible. I know you don't want to complicate things for your landlady who's been so absurdly generous to you all these years.

He deleted the message immediately. Let her stew.

One of the client emails was from the son of a prominent artist in Sausalito. He was a dark, intense boy who was on Step Five of his path to the future—The Personal Essay. He was applying to Brown, Harvard, and Princeton. He'd told David that he planned to drop out after his first semester, but felt that dropping out of an Ivy League university would look more impressive. He had a point: in the world of outlier gaming and software that interested him, rejecting Harvard had more cachet than graduating from it.

"*Growing up,*" his essay began, "*my father encouraged my brothers and me to piss in the kitchen sink when my mother wasn't home.*"

David was stopped cold. This was either the worst opening sentence he'd read or the most brilliant. About 90 percent of the essays his clients wrote began with mention of a grandparent or cancer. According to admission directors he'd dealt with, these rarely got read. They were all so similar it was impossible to plow through them without having the brain freeze. In this case, it was impossible to imagine the person who wouldn't read on, even if it was because he was appalled.

The rest of the essay was about the passionate hatred for each other his parents shared and how it defined their marriage, which had endured for twenty-three years and was still going strong. Ashton made only a few direct references to himself (holding his baby brother up at the kitchen sink, for example, so the infant could urinate into it), but by the end, David had such a rich sense of him, it was as if he was there in the tiny room, speaking with him.

"This is genius," David wrote to him. "No one is going to ignore it, but let me talk to a few people to get a sense of how many will be appalled. I think we should apply to a few other schools as well so you'll have a wider range to reject out of hand."

He was about to close down his laptop when he thought again about Renata's email. What was it she'd said? He went to his trash folder and reread it. ". . . Complicate things for your landlady." He hit the Reply button and wrote: "I can't tell you how much I appreciate this message, dearest Renata. You'll hear from me soon."

He checked the time. It was much too early to call his friend Michael in San Francisco, especially since he didn't have anything salacious to report. Salacious reports formed the bulk of their conversations.

He wrote him an email. "Listen, Michael, call me when you wake up. You know how you've always said you love my carriage house? Wouldn't you love to vacation there for a little while?"

He rummaged through the pockets of his corduroy pants and found the little notebook he'd been scribbling in yesterday.

The Seven Steps to Julie Fiske's Happy, Henry-Free Future, he typed into his laptop. Boy, was that optimistic.

1) *Mandy—Common App, tests, essay prep, feelings about library(?)*
2) *Declutter house, repair and repaint living room ceiling, buy more toss pillows (optional), room rates increased (excepting mine)*
3) *Yard work and related outdoor decay and pandemonium*
4) *Pot Problem*

Mercifully, there was a soft knock on his door before he got to Finances. He reached behind him to open it, and the door swung in and banged against the bed. Mandy (it was obviously she) stood there, arms folded against her chest, grinning in a way that was straddling sardonic and shy. She looked younger than some of the kids her age David had worked with, something about her round face and flushed cheeks (a contrast to Julie's pale, narrow face) and the overalls she was wearing. Or maybe "coveralls" was a better way to describe them since she seemed intent on covering up her body. On closer inspection, there was something sorrowful in her face that made her appear more mature. David was drawn to sadness in teenagers, which he took to be a sign of intelligence. What teenager with half a brain looking at the condition of the planet they were set to inherit wouldn't be bereft?

He made the extremely short trip from chair to door and hugged her. "It's nice to finally meet you," he said. "I'm sorry I conked out so early yesterday. I took an overnight flight and was up most of the night before."

"That's okay. It's probably good to get as much sleep as possible." He couldn't tell if this was a general statement or a recommendation to rest up for what was ahead. "Can we get something out of the way? I'm not sure what I should call you. Mr. Hedges? Uncle David?"

He was impressed and unnerved by the blunt maturity of her desire to clear this up. She had dark hair, although its color looked a little too dark and uniform to be natural. It was cut into a short bob that—along with the overalls and a long-sleeved flannel shirt—gave her the look of Louise Brooks unconvincingly playing a farm girl. It seemed unlikely he'd be able to get away with false cheer or optimism.

"I think 'David' is probably best, don't you? 'Mr. Hedges' is too formal and 'uncle' might undercut your respect for me professionally."

She looked over his shoulder at the rickety desk and narrow bed and smiled. "This room already did that."

"Should I complain to the management?"

"You can try," she said. "But you should read some of the online reviews before you expect too much satisfaction."

He'd read some of the online reviews in bed the night before.

He'd rarely seen such eloquent or frequent uses of the words "eccentric," "lumpy," and "dust."

"I'm totally satisfied," he said. "I like small spaces. I'm going to be a very comfortable corpse."

When he told her he thought they should start working on her applications that morning, she said she had to leave for her job at a store downtown.

"Can I walk you there?" he asked. "I'll take Opal along. I wouldn't mind some fresh air and a better view of downtown." What he really meant was a better look at her state of mind.

It was still early, but the sun was warm and he felt the summer heat starting to build under the unrelenting sunlight, something that rarely happened in San Francisco. He did love the oddball, erratic climate of that city, a feature that made up for a disappointing dearth of trees on the streets. Tourists were beginning to appear on the sidewalks of Beauport, walking tentatively in clusters and stopping to gaze into shop windows as if they were desperate to find something, anything, they could buy. He liked the fleeting glimpses of the harbor between shops and restaurants; the views had an intimate appeal that made you feel you were being embraced by the scenery rather than being asked to stand in awe of it.

Mandy proved to be an affable tour guide who knew more about the history of the town than he'd expected. When he complimented her knowledge, she said, "They drill it into us in school, so we'll have civic pride. They leave out the racism and anti-Semitism."

"They usually do."

Opal appeared to be a celebrity of sorts, probably because of her disability. People are vastly more tolerant of deformities in animals than in humans, he'd noted. Animals are generally assumed to be blameless and thus forgivable, while humans are assumed to be complicit in their own tragedies. How else could you explain the right-wing attitude toward health care, poverty, and prison? Mandy had a sweet rapport with the dog, although she kept her under tight control when they passed other people.

Opal's personality resembled that of a twelve-year-old who didn't quite believe herself to be lovable and was therefore always testing the strength of her parents' affection. Her backward glances toward Mandy were eager, her enormous ears alert on her small body, as if she was the one walking them, and she wanted to make sure they approved of her choice of direction. "Come on," she seemed to be saying. "I've got something really cool to show you."

If Opal was leading them on a hike, the destination was apparently something called Kenneth's Kitchen. Most of the other shop windows were stuffed with oddball trinkets and gift items— one definition of "gift" apparently being "useless, unattractive article made by child labor"—that looked as if the store owners had merely dumped a carton of goods behind the glass. Little figurines were piled on top of one another and partly hidden under pillows, throws, and the ever-popular, utterly useless woven basket. Kenneth's window, on the other hand, contained an artfully arranged selection of colorful flatware, pottery turned with Japanese delicacy and refinement, and boxes of crackers and jams that must have been chosen for the beauty of their packaging and the way the colors coordinated with the pottery. Kenneth, one had to assume, was not heterosexual.

Opal sat on the sidewalk out front, craning her neck to look inside.

"The owner gives her treats when he sees us out here. He's a nightmare, but he likes dogs, which is a good sign."

After a few minutes, a small man emerged holding something in his hands. "Please don't pretend you're not expecting a snack," he said. "We're beyond that charade."

He spoke in the tone of fond annoyance one often uses when speaking to pets, but it wasn't clear to David if he was addressing Opal or Mandy. Either way, he held out his hand, and Opal snatched a biscuit off his palm and chewed voraciously.

"You know," he said, this time addressing Mandy directly, "it wouldn't hurt to come in and actually make a purchase. She obviously enjoys them."

"I don't have a lot of money," Mandy said. "They're expensive."

"Yes, they are, so you might consider the cost to me next time you drag the dog down here."

"I'm happy to pay," David said, reaching for his wallet.

"I *gave* the biscuit to the dog," he said. "I'm not out here panhandling."

His voice had a sharp edge and what David took to be the traces of a southern accent.

"I didn't suggest you were. What I meant was, I'd love to buy a bag of whatever that was."

Kenneth gave him a look that was either withering or approving and in either case involved a head-to-toe sweep of his body.

David guessed him to be in his late thirties or early forties, but boyishness still clung to him, as it often does to men with good hair or unresolved relationships with their fathers. He was tidily dressed in short pants and a green polo shirt, and he wore around his neck a lanyard with a heavy set of keys attached, a little like a gym teacher or an obstreperous camp counselor.

David followed him into the store. Kenneth's step had the slight roll of someone who wants to make sure his ass is being observed. Walking into the store was like entering a cool, fragrant aquarium; the floor, walls, and ceiling were all Atlantic blue, and the back wall was glass and opened to the harbor.

"It's beautiful in here," David said. "You've done a great job."

"Thank you for noticing. I did it all myself. Naturally, it's not appreciated."

"I'm sorry to hear that. Is business slow?"

"I discuss my income with my accountant and my husband."

The last word was uttered with an emphasis that sounded like a rebuke, as if David had made a pass. This was the second time in two days that a pass he hadn't made had been rejected. Kenneth handed him a small box with the name of the dog biscuits hand-lettered on the front: CAREY'S CANINE COOKIES.

"They're artisanal," he said. In David's experience, this usually meant an overpriced, undercapitalized product that goes out of production in less than a year. "And vegan."

"I'm sure Opal will appreciate that."

Kenneth mentioned the price defiantly, as if expecting a shocked reaction. David handed him his credit card, thinking that he'd have to find a way to take them as a tax deduction.

"Are you the uncle or something?" Kenneth asked.

"More the something. I'm an old friend of Mandy's mother. Do you know her?"

"I know she owns that *house* on the top of the hill." David was impressed by the menace Kenneth was able to cram into that single word. "She must have enough rooms up there to do short-term rentals if she wanted to."

"I'm sure there's a lot of that in town," David said, trying to be noncommittal. Short-term rentals were still controversial in San Francisco, but no doubt Soren would find a way to rent out the carriage house for six thousand dollars a week once David had cleared out and the papers were signed.

"Some people feel there's too much of it," Kenneth said. "Are you and Julie good friends?"

David paused, not knowing how much of her personal life Julie spread around; but since Kenneth had mentioned he had a husband, David thought he might put himself in a better light by indicating he'd once been capable of intimacy. He wasn't sure why he wanted to put himself in a better light. Kenneth struck him as one of those hyper-capable men who turn difficult at the drop of a crumb and mask their insecurities by demanding to be treated like little princes. Still, there was something attractive in his narrow body and nicely shaped legs, and he had a promising hint in his eyes that the meticulously pressed clothes, bossy attitude, and Zen window display were compensating for an insatiable need to be dominated. Vigorously. Probably there was some panic thrown in about aging, too, despite the husband. It was obvious Kenneth had had the misfortune of having been pretty for most of his youth.

"Julie and I were married," David said.

Kenneth handed him back his credit card and evaluated him again. "Briefly?"

"Briefly."

He fiddled with tissue paper and raffia and handed David an artfully composed bag, the keys around his neck jangling. "Nice meeting you. Come back soon." David was surprised to find himself stirred by the invitation, although quickly deflated when Kenneth added, "Those cookies go on half-price sale tomorrow."

After the cool of the store, the sidewalk was even warmer. Opal was tied to a parking meter, and Mandy was leaning into the window of a dusty van. As the van pulled off, David got a glimpse of a profile: male, curly long hair, definitely not a high school student.

"A friend?" he asked Mandy.

"Someone who does work at the school. How much did you pay for those biscuits?"

"They're cookies. And considering the price, I plan to eat them myself. Sorry, Opal."

"I think Kenneth likes you," Mandy said. "Can you tell?"

"I didn't see any sign of that," David said, although he had sensed something flirtatious in the antagonism. "Besides, he's not available. He's married." It wouldn't have been appropriate to add that this usually makes a person more available.

They walked out onto Perry Neck, a spit of land that stuck out into the harbor. The narrow streets were lined with shingled buildings that had probably once been fishing shacks and now sold cheap jewelry and T-shirts and ice cream and other items that one buys only while on vacation and rarely looks at afterward. David found this accumulation of junk inherently depressing, especially when combined with the paintings for sale in the galleries. To a great extent, these depicted Beauport in an idealized fashion, which is to say, without all the commercialization and trinkets and sad art galleries.

"Which is the store you work at?" David asked.

"It's up there a little. I'd rather you didn't see it."

"Why is that?"

"It has a humiliating name and sells a lot of embarrassing stuff. Plus the owner might be out front in resort wear and sunglasses. The only good thing is, I get time to read."

She reached into a pocket on the leg of her overalls and pulled out a copy of one of E. F. Benson's Mapp and Lucia novels. David recognized the battered paperback as one of his own from decades earlier. He knew the crease on the cover and the circular stain from a coffee cup that had been either his or Julie's. It was the third volume in the series, *Lucia in London*. He flipped through it and handed it back to Mandy, swamped with nostalgia and tenderness: he'd read these books, all six of them, aloud to Julie in the living room of their apartment and in bed over the course of the first year they'd known each other. "Did you read the first two?" he asked.

"I think so. I didn't pay much attention to the order."

"I loved these books once upon a time," he said. "Your mother did, too."

"I love them now."

David found it reassuring to hear teenagers tell him they shared his interests. It made them seem more emotionally stable, and made him feel less out of touch. He stopped walking and gave her a hug. "I think we're going to get along well," he said.

"Are you sure? This girl I know, sort of a friend, told me I can be a real bitch." She said this in a way that suggested she was genuinely concerned about it.

"I'm sure she meant it as a compliment. You don't want to be late for your humiliating job."

He watched her lope down the street, certain that Amira must have been wrong in her estimation of her, but as he walked up the hill to Julie's house, he was unable to shake the image of the man with the curly hair driving off in his van.

15

Over the next two days, Mandy pleaded that she was too busy with her job and too tired in the evenings to focus on college applications. "But I'm only here for another six days," David said, to which she replied, "You can change your reservation and stay longer."

This response was so immediate and had been made with such conviction, he suspected she was delaying their work to encourage him to remain.

The suspicion was confirmed when, on the morning of his third day, he returned from the "bathroom-with-privacy" to find his old, musty copy of *Queen Lucia* on the foot of his bed, the first in the series of E.F. Benson novels Mandy had been reading. Apparently, Mandy had waited until he was out of the room, sneaked in, and left it there.

He lay back against the headboard and opened to the first

yellowed page. *"Though the sun was hot on this July morning, Mrs. Lucas preferred to cover the half mile that lay between the station and her house on her own brisk feet . . ."*

"Brisk feet!" he said aloud. The expression brought the fierce, petty Lucia to life and made him laugh. He read on, remembering even before he got to it that the real reason for her walking was to *"cause one of those little thrills of pleasant excitement and conjectural exercise which supplied Riseholme with its emotional daily bread."* There was something ridiculous and irresistible in "conjectural exercise" and "emotional daily bread." It was encouraging to think that Mandy, despite access to video games and social media, could appreciate this.

He was transported back to the village of Riseholme and, simultaneously, the living room of the sprawling, rent-controlled apartment he and Julie had shared in New York and the worn sofa they'd collapsed on each evening so he could read aloud to her from these novels. It was telling that some of the happiest times they'd had together had revolved around these fey, campy books, but they'd been genuinely happy hours and romantic in their own way. He had a longing to share this with her again that was so strong, he would have rushed upstairs at that moment to do so if he hadn't seen her leave for school an hour earlier. He read a few more pages, trying to recall the voices he'd used for the characters all those years ago and the particular passages that Julie had especially loved. How many volumes could he read to her in the little time he had here?

It turned hotter that afternoon, and he sweated heavily as he carried furniture out of his room and into the barn behind the house. The barn appeared to be a structurally sound storehouse of rejected items Julie had bought at yard sales and flea markets—pot buys, or PBs, as she called them. Items of questionable taste and value that had looked too interesting to pass up when she was high, too damaged or ugly to bring into the house once she'd come down, too full of "potential" to get rid of entirely. Like everyone he'd met who shopped for secondhand castoffs, Julie clung to the belief that much of it was of great value to some mythic (and apparently wealthy) collector of these very items. No doubt pot clouded one's judgment, but as a gateway drug to hoarding, it couldn't compare to *Antiques Roadshow*.

As he was sorting through a box of kitschy ashtrays and some plates printed with boomerangs, trying to decide if Julie would notice if he brought the whole lot to the recycling center, he realized that his own life had been full of PBs, too, even though he didn't smoke or go to yard sales. There was that eight-hundred-dollar juicer he'd bought online and was briefly convinced would change his life, the massively expensive Swedish mattress he thought would forestall aging. Probably the move to San Francisco had been an impulsive pot buy. And when you came down to it, hadn't Soren himself been a PB? Handsome, garrulous, and flushed with the magic-hour glow of youth right before it sinks below the horizon, he'd been too tempting to pass up. Instead of admitting his mistakes, David had tried to build a whole life around them. Maybe the ashtrays weren't the only things that needed to be hauled to the recycling center.

His phone rang. His friend Michael, returning his call at last.

"Tell me," Michael commanded with gruff seriousness. "Anything to report?"

"Not in the way you mean," David said. He sat on an overstuffed chair in the hot, far reaches of the barn, releasing a cloud of dust into the shafts of sunlight. "Unless you've developed a sudden erotic interest in housecleaning and minor home repair."

"Thanks, I'll pass. I had enough of that in my previous incarnation."

Michael lived in an apartment a few blocks from David's carriage house. He was seven years older than David, but because he'd come out in his late fifties, he was still, in many respects, an adolescent. "Anything to report" meant sexual encounters. Most of what Michael said either referred to sexual encounters directly or sounded as if they did, even something as banal as, "I just had a delicious *hamburger.*"

Michael was from Cincinnati. He'd spent the bulk of his life married to his childhood sweetheart, raising two beloved daughters, and working at a law firm doing estate planning for wealthy Ohioans. Then, after a cancer scare, he'd accepted what he'd been trying to deny for decades, had come out, retired early, and moved to the city of his dreams of liberation around the time of the second Obama inauguration. Extricating himself from his previous life had cost him dearly. He could only afford a tiny one-bedroom that was largely subterranean, but because he felt free to live without apology for the first time, he inhabited his own microclimate of blue skies and balmy breezes. He referred to his apartment as the Penthouse and the name seemed to express his sincere feelings about the place.

David and Michael frequently talked about how much they had in common, by which they meant that they'd slept with a surprising number of the same people. This was the source of conversations that were lewd in content but nostalgic in tone, largely because they were aware of the ways in which their erotic options were rapidly changing. They'd both entered the "daddy" category, but Michael was on the cusp of the "paying customer" category.

"There must be some homosexuals there," Michael said. "Lonely, desperate for attention."

David knew he had to toss Michael a scrap if he wanted him to agree to his proposal. "There is one," he said, surprised at how happy he was to mention Kenneth, even obliquely.

"Aha. I knew it."

"He has a kitchen store and a husband."

"A married shopkeeper? How wonderful. I'm sure there's a private storage area behind the cash register. You'll have to tell me everything once you've sealed the deal."

"I wouldn't hold my breath on that. I've got too much to do around here to chase down distractions."

"The whole trip is a distraction, David. When are you coming back?"

"Saturday, supposedly, but I'm beginning to wonder. There's a lot to do here, and I haven't even started working with the daughter. Julie stands to lose everything she cares about unless I can help her pull a few things together. In the meantime, I'm getting worried about the Palace." (Michael's name for the carriage house.) "Renata is trying to hustle me out, and I'm afraid she might go in and riffle through my things."

"I see, I see. And find the porn and sex toys?"

"The file cabinets in my dining room. They've got tons of information about clients' grades and test scores and psychological profiles. Most tantalizing to her, there are financial records. I wouldn't put it past her to start collecting phone numbers."

"Surely you locked everything."

"If you think that would stop her, you don't know much about Renata."

"I know we've met three times, and she still has no idea who I am."

Michael was easily wounded by perceived slights.

"I must have told her where you live," David said. Like men who literally don't see older women, Renata had a blind spot for anyone who was connected to unappealing housing. "You'd be doing me a huge favor if you moved in while I'm out here. Refuse to let her in if she knocks or brings my ex and his meal ticket around."

"How is he affording it, anyway? I thought doctors were supposed to be swamped with malpractice insurance bills."

"Rumor has it he invented a piece of metal that's used in open-heart surgery and he earns royalties every time someone's chest is sawed open. Rumor also has it he's a genius with investing, although his arrangement with Soren calls that into question. Will you help me out?"

"Leave the Penthouse with a suitcase and a bag of groceries? I don't know. What's in it for me?"

David had been prepared for this reluctance. If he was going to be away from San Francisco for longer than he'd planned, and it was becoming clear that he was, he didn't want his place sitting empty. The idea of Renata and possibly Soren and company wandering through was disturbing. And recent revelations about Renata's machinations made the idea of her breaking into his files entirely plausible.

"I'm going to tell you a secret," David said. "If you use a photo of the Palace on your Grindr profile, you can pretty much have your pick of anyone you want. If you can't be young and beautiful—and we both know that, at this point, those are off the table for us—the next best thing is to show off valuable real estate. How do you think I got Soren? Just remain vague on ownership and let them in through the kitchen so they can see the expensive espresso machine. I drink tea, but I got it to impress my clients."

"I don't know how to use it."

"It won't come to that."

There was a promising silence in which David knew Michael was weighing the pros and cons.

"You do realize I'll go through all your drawers looking for incriminating evidence."

"It's not called incriminating evidence anymore, Michael. It's called social media. And you're welcome to search anything you like. Do you think you could move in today?"

"If it's really that urgent, I suppose so. The kitchen door, you said?"

David was relieved as soon as they hung up. Now he had to persuade Julie to let him stay on so he could cancel his return flight.

16

Julie was happy that school was ending in a few days. She'd be able to concentrate on getting her money together for the house, talk to the benefits people at school about her retirement account, and oversee Mandy's progress. And then there was the weather. The grounds and facilities at Crawford School were famously beautiful, but the buildings were not much better air-conditioned than her own house. David hadn't complained, but the Cabinet Room was especially problematic. It would be wrong to seal off its one window with an air-conditioning unit, and the room was so tiny, it would get too cold too quickly anyway. David had bought a vintage fan for the night table and claimed it was comfortable. She had AC in her own window, but in solidarity, she'd decided not to use it.

She'd opened all the other windows and was lying on her bed, trying to catch an early-evening breeze as the tide was turning.

She was tempted to go out to the backyard and take a hit of pot. That always made the heat seem tropical and languid instead of insufferable and polluted, and the sky outside her window was a majestic blend of magenta and ocher. But that would mean walking down two flights of stairs and then climbing back up, and she didn't have the energy for that.

As she was driving home from work, she'd made a stop in Essex and dropped off the box of her mother's jewelry with a woman who ran estate sales. Julie had met Pamela Kern a dozen or more times at sales she was running in nearby towns, and they'd struck up a friendship, albeit one that had proved to be site-specific. The time they'd met for dinner had been awkward; Pamela was a picky eater with multiple food intolerances and allergies that she seemed, based on her behavior, to blame on the waitstaff. She'd made an ambiguously derogatory comment about Elizabeth Warren and had given Julie the name of a man who came to your house to detail-clean your car. So much for a friendship.

But she had integrity about her work and knew every dealer in furniture, jewelry, rare books, and ephemera in New England. As Julie opened the lined box for her, she felt as if she was displaying buried treasure. A trace of her mother's perfume ("Jicky by Guerlain, dear, the first modern perfume. Cheap scent is for amateurs") wafted into the room, so faint more than a decade after her death, Pamela might not have noticed it, but to Julie it was instantly recognizable. She felt as if her mother had caught her doing the one thing she'd promised her she would never do.

Julie didn't wear jewelry (or perfume, cheap or otherwise) and found these rings and diamond watches and encrusted broaches gaudy and even embarrassing. They recalled her mother's fondness for status and her attention to style, things Julie had rejected early on. Her mother had worn these to faculty parties and when she spoke at academic conferences, all to make sure no one mistook her for another dowdy professor. Some of the pieces her mother had inherited looked almost Victorian in their ornate opulence, but most of the bracelets and rings her father had bought were sleek, influenced by the Art Deco design aesthetic her mother had worshipped, even though her subject was Renaissance poetry.

Pamela had held up a silver pendant covered in stones that somehow evoked both New York in the 1930s and Tamara de Lempicka's Paris and eyed it lustfully. "This jewelry is wonderful. Are you sure you want to part with it?"

"It took me a lot longer to bring the stuff in than I thought it would, but now I'm sure."

"It's hard because you loved her so much." Pamela nodded, no doubt having been through all this before with many other people.

"No," Julie said. "Because I didn't. I promised her I'd never sell it, and because we didn't like each other all that much, I know she wouldn't forgive me. But I've hit a few speed bumps I didn't foresee. When it comes to things I want to hang on to, this is low on the list."

Pamela looked at her pointedly. "What's high on the list?"

"My daughter and my house."

Pamela had cataloged everything, given Julie a receipt, and promised she'd have an estimate for her. "Probably in a couple of weeks," she said. "Three at the most. I'll get multiple estimates from a range of specialists. It will take a while to authenticate some of it."

Julie had been hoping to hear sooner than that, but it was important not to seem desperate, especially when you were. "Any guesses on value?"

Pamela had winked in a way that seemed carefully rehearsed. "I've learned to never guess."

The one saving grace of the day was that a few minutes earlier, she'd received a text message from Raymond Cross, her clarinetist, as Amira would say, even though he wasn't hers and didn't play the clarinet. Hope it's cooler by the ocean than it is here. That had been all, but it had been enough to lift her spirits. Briefly.

She heard footsteps on the stairs and David appeared in her doorway, smiling in that way he often did—not to express his own happiness, she'd come to realize, so much as to encourage hers.

He entered the room and sat on the foot of her bed. "It's warm up here," he said. "Why don't you turn on the air conditioner?"

"I don't like it all that much. It's like sleeping in a refrigerator, when you think about it. You should use it for your room."

"I'm happy with the fan."

"I'll take you at your word," she said. "Even though I don't believe you. I got a call from the older woman who's coming for a few weeks. She's arriving tonight, and she asked if she could get a cab at the train station. I told her I'd pick her up. Hold dinner until I get back?"

"Unless you're planning to charge her, I wouldn't admit to

Sandra you're offering shuttle service now. Want me to come with you, in case she turns out to be a killer?"

"I'd love that. A little welcoming committee. I feel bad for her, and I have no idea why. Today was the first time we actually spoke."

"Speaking of train stations . . ." David showed her the paperback book he'd been holding against his leg. "I started rereading it." He opened to the first page and read aloud the first loopy sentence.

"'Brisk feet!'" Julie cried.

"Exactly," David said. "I had the same reaction."

"I missed Lucia," she said. "She's so horrible and endearing. Where did you get it?"

"Mandy has been reading them. She put this on my bed. A small, sweet thing to have done."

Julie was mortified to learn that she'd missed this about Mandy. It made her wonder what else she was missing, for surely there had to be something.

"Read on," Julie said.

By the end of the second page, he'd stretched himself out at the opposite end of the bed with his free hand casually massaging her foot. The cozy, hilariously nasty world of the novel was just as it had been when they'd left it thirty years ago, just as it had been when it was written. Reentering it now made Julie immensely happy, even if more aware of how much had changed in her own life. When, after ten minutes, he stopped, she asked him to please read to the end of the chapter. She knew something amusing was going to happen with the guru, but she couldn't remember what, and David's voice had lulled her into the happy dream world of the past—both the characters' and theirs.

"We can get to it later," he said. "I came up to ask a favor. And don't say no or yes before you give it some thought."

She studied his face for a moment. He had an eager look, and she knew that what he was about to ask wasn't so much a favor as permission to do her one.

"I need to be out of San Francisco for a little longer than I thought. It's all about the place I'm living. If I could stay here for an extra week or two, it would be a big help to me."

What he meant, obviously, was that it would be a big help to her. If his place was being sold, he'd be better off there, looking for somewhere else to live. Still, he'd been in Beauport four days, and she hated thinking that his time with them was running out already.

"I'd only agree if you move upstairs to a bigger room when one opens up," she said.

"Out of the question. I love that room, and since I've spent the last thirty-six hours fixing it up, there's no way I'd move. Do we have a deal?"

"As long as you don't try to pay."

"I don't like the room that much, believe me."

She felt her back starting to sweat. The longer he stayed in Beauport, the more likely it was that "things would come up," and more specifically, one thing.

"I know you're staying partly because you feel bad about everything that happened all those years ago," she said. "But we both made mistakes."

"I know that," he said.

No, she thought. *Not really.*

He got up off the bed and turned on the air conditioner. "And you don't have to leave this off just because I don't have one in my room. And don't look so surprised—I know you better than you think."

But she knew that that wasn't true either.

17

Julie recognized Mrs. Grayson as soon as she stepped off the train, even though she'd had no idea what, precisely, to expect. The daily commuters were confidently and purposefully returning home, while she was arriving like a well-fed refugee. She was a short pillow of a woman wearing a flowered dress and, despite the temperature, a cardigan draped over her shoulders. Probably in her eighties, although it was hard to tell with someone like this, someone who seemed to be out of another era and had probably looked exactly the same since turning fifty.

"That must be her," she said to David.

Beauport was the last stop on this line, and as the train emptied out, the conductor set Mrs. Grayson's suitcase on the ground and handed her a shopping bag with a hideous yellow stuffed animal sticking out.

"I'm surprised she's not wearing white gloves," David said.

"Don't tease. Poor thing. Those shoes." They were an ecru variation on nurse's shoes, and one look at them told Julie she'd bought them from a catalog that targeted the elderly with cheaply made, overpriced clothing and accessories whose main virtue was the ease of getting in and out of them. She looked so out of place and so alone, Julie strode down the platform and, without thinking, put her arms around her.

"Mrs. Grayson, welcome. I'm Julie Fiske. We're so happy you're here. I hope you're going to like your room."

She appeared slightly disoriented by all the attention, but recovered quickly. Her face was powdered but damp, and there was a little smudge of makeup on her collar. "You were awfully nice to meet me. It's been a long day, but I could have taken a cab to the house."

"I think it's best to be met. And we're only a couple of minutes from here." She took the handle of Mrs. Grayson's suitcase and wheeled it behind her as they walked toward David. "We were happy to come. This is David, a friend of mine."

"Do you have everything?" David asked.

"I travel light. A good thing since I had to wait at the train station in Boston for almost two hours."

As they were getting into the car, outrage boiled up in Julie. Mrs. Grayson's son and daughter-in-law—baby or no baby—should have been here or, for that matter, gone to Logan to meet her plane. Given their impressive address, they could have sprung for a driver from the airport if they were too busy. Julie asked her if she was planning to have dinner with her son that night.

"No, no. They're too busy feeding the baby and getting him to sleep. I'm here to help if they need me, not get in their way. They said they'd call in the morning and arrange a good time for me to come in the afternoon."

Julie looked at David, but he was focused on the road. She could tell from the traces of a smile around his eyes he was planning something critical to say once they were alone, but she wouldn't have it. It wasn't as if she'd been such an attentive daughter herself, but then, her mother had been the opposite of this gentle, gracious woman. "In that case, I hope you'll have dinner with us," she said. "David always makes more than enough." It wouldn't do to explain her relationship to David; Julie was sure she'd wouldn't understand or, if she did, approve.

She appeared to be embarrassed by the invitation. "You're kind, but I couldn't. I bought a cheese sandwich at the station, and I'll have that in my room."

Another heartbreakingly lonely scene appeared in Julie's mind. Couldn't she at least have bought herself roast beef? The only consolation was that she'd given her the Room in Back Room, the best in the house.

"Isn't it lovely," she said as Julie showed her in and put her suitcase on a footstool beside the bed. "So many lovely knickknacks."

When Julie walked into the kitchen to help David cook, she said, "I can tell from the look on your face you've been practicing an ironic southern accent, but don't try it or I'll start to cry."

"But I have her down so well," he said. "I was hoping to conduct the entire dinner conversation in her style."

"No. It will make me miserable."

"In that case, I'll wait. Is this your first crush on one of the paying guests?"

"I plead the Fifth."

18

It was obvious to Mandy that Elaine Guild hated her and regretted hiring her at Beachy Keen. She had a million variations on disapproving glances and sighs, and she used them daily. She was practically frantic about making sure that Mandy was busy all the time, even though it wasn't clear what she herself was doing in her crowded little office all day except complaining to assorted friends on the phone.

Yesterday, Elaine had brought in a feather duster and a big piece of orange felt-like material that Mandy had seen advertised on infomercials. "When it's not busy," Elaine had said, "you should be dusting the merchandise. And carefully, Mandy. It's fragile."

Somehow, none of this would have bothered her as much if Elaine had at least been old, but she'd seen her license lying on her desk, and she was thirty-nine. Not young, but too young to be such a crank.

Mandy had been working at the store for over a week, and so far it had never been busy, which meant she could look forward to spending massive amounts of time doing what she was doing right now—walking around waving the feather duster, pretending to keep the shelves clean.

The merchandise at Beachy Keen ran the gamut from practical to pathetic. The practical items you could easily buy almost anywhere else for half the price: low, webbed beach chairs, sun hats, dark glasses, flip-flops. CVS was less than a mile away, had a better selection of these items, and had started running sales the minute the temperature climbed above sixty. Then there was jewelry made out of lacquered shells and what was alleged to be "genuine beach glass" but was really broken bottles that had been processed for a few days in giant drums of sand and water in Kansas or some other landlocked state. When Mandy had asked why they didn't just use the real thing, Elaine had snapped that since everyone was too PC to litter, there wasn't enough of it on the beaches anymore. There were bottles and jars filled with different-colored sand that Elaine had labeled "beach art." Incomprehensibly, these were among the best-selling items in the store. They were ugly, and although Elaine had put a sign on their shelf alleging they had been made by "sand artists," Mandy had seen the boxes they'd come in, clearly indicating they'd been mass-produced in Bangladesh.

Mandy took her duster and wandered over to the most radioactive area in the store—the shelves for this summer's "Signature Item." Signature or not, the Beach Trees were definitely the most pointless items in the store. They were spindly trees made out of toxic synthetic material that had on the ends of the branches tiny beach chairs and umbrellas and sunglasses and fake seashells instead of leaves. When Elaine had hired Mandy, she'd shown them to her proudly and told her they were going to fly off the shelves. She'd gotten a good price on them by agreeing to a nonreturnable deal with the distributor. "I can't tell you how excited I am about these," Elaine had said in a moment of enthusiastic bonding before she realized how much she distrusted Mandy. Mandy saw now that she should have forced out a "me, too!"

So far, Mandy had sold about ten Beach Trees, and one person had come back to complain that the "leaves" had fallen off five minutes after she walked out the door.

Elaine's office was directly across from the shelves with the Signature Item, probably so she could make sure no one stole them. As if that would be a problem. Mandy heard her voice through the closed door, talking in her manic way. From what she could make out, she was complaining with another store-owner about slow business. But when she heard "Airbnb" clearly and more than once, she stepped closer to the office.

"Exactly. And why else would so many cities be trying to legislate against it? Exactly. If they're too cheap to pay for a hotel room, they're not likely to shop downtown. How many people have signed?"

As Mandy was stepping back, the door to Elaine's office opened, and Elaine stood there, holding the phone pressed against her chest. "Can I help you with something, *Mandy*?"

"I was dusting. The Beach Trees. Like you asked."

Elaine wasn't buying that, but it was partly true, and she had no way of proving it wasn't.

"I'm guessing you didn't make the quota today."

"I tried," Mandy said. This was true, humiliating as it was. Elaine had set a goal of selling fifteen Beach Trees a day. "I sold one and had serious interest from two other people. They said they'd come back tomorrow."

Elaine was boring into her with her eyes. She was a pretty woman, another reason Mandy couldn't understand her moodiness.

"Why don't you take off now," she said. "I was planning to close early anyway. The town is *dead*. And, Mandy, if you're not going to wear something beachy, can you at least wear something less depressing than those *overalls*?"

These were the longest days of the year, and despite Elaine's comments about the lack of tourists in town, the streets were jammed with people. It was true that at this time of afternoon people tended to forage for crap they could eat, not crap to clutter up their houses. Mandy looked up and down the main street as she almost always did now, wondering if Craig Crespo would drive by. He was one of those people who appeared out of nowhere, as he had a couple of days ago, pulling up beside her, leaning out and saying, "Did you get fired yet? Ready to work for me?" and then driving off before she had a chance to respond.

Tonight, no sign of him. She had a feeling Elaine wouldn't keep her through the summer, assuming the store didn't fold before August. It was just like her to blame Airbnb for slow business when it was obviously the crazy merchandise and inflated prices.

Mandy thought that a lot of Elaine's stress and discontent had to do with her husband. He'd come into the store one afternoon. He was athletic, clean-cut, and handsome, like someone who'd had Olympic ambitions when he was in high school but had dislocated a shoulder at exactly the wrong moment. He was in "sales," whatever that meant, and there was something in the restless, flirty way he'd been with Mandy that made her think it was only a matter of time before Elaine found out he'd had an affair with a babysitter in town. They didn't have any kids, and Mandy was positive that had been his decision, not Elaine's.

When she got home, David and her mother were sitting on the front porch in rocking chairs and he was reading aloud to her from the book she'd left on his bed. Her mother had her eyes closed and was grinning as she listened, and looked so relaxed, Mandy felt she'd actually done something right for once in her stupid life. By her calculations, David was scheduled to leave in two days, but there was no sign of that happening.

When David spotted her, he put the book down and stood up. "I've been waiting for you. No excuses. We have to get started tonight. We're running out of time."

"You could stay on a little longer," Mandy said. She knew she sounded too eager, but maybe he'd be flattered.

"He is staying on," Julie said. "But since we don't know for how long, you'd better get to work. Everything takes longer than you think."

"Your plan worked, Mandy."

"What plan?"

"Stalling, refusing to settle down, leaving that book in my room.

I have to stay until we get to the end. Let's go inside. And, Julie, no listening in. Maybe take Opal for a walk?"

Mandy had been dreading this moment, even though she was the one who'd invited him to Beauport. She felt somehow that all her weaknesses and flaws were going to be exposed as they discussed college, her lack of direction, and her shameful absence of talent, which was maybe the thing she liked least about herself. But sooner or later, she was going to have to face it.

She followed him into the cool, dark dining room. There were only stained-glass windows here, high up on one paneled wall and facing the hedge. It was always shadowy and quiet. He'd set up papers and folders on the table, all of which looked surprisingly official to her, considering how informal he was when they talked and how she'd only seen him in his beat-up corduroys and long-sleeved blue or white shirts with the cuffs rolled up. Tonight it was blue.

He handed her a folder that was labeled THE SEVEN STEPS TO YOUR FUTURE, with her name below in marker.

"Seven steps?" she said. "How long is this going to take?"

"We won't do it all at once. Mostly that's just so I can charge my clients more money, which obviously isn't an issue here."

"You aren't sorry you came, are you?"

"No, of course not." He looked so surprised as he said it, she trusted he was being honest. "I've loved being here."

"Why?" She had a burning need to know.

"Among other things, I've lost four pounds. Your mother has been dragging me on long walks after dinner. And it's given me a feeling of purpose, which isn't something I realized I needed so badly until I got here."

She studied him as he said this. She knew she'd been around adult men who didn't have children, but she wasn't sure who they were. Even Amira's husband supposedly had children from another marriage stashed away somewhere. Craig didn't have kids as far as she knew, but then, he didn't come off as an adult either. Maybe childlessness was what made David feel purposeless. If he needed a mission in the form of a needy child to take care of, he had his hands full with her mother.

"I appreciate your interest in me," he said, "but we're here to talk about you. For starters, why don't you tell me what you like least about high school?"

"The bottom of the incredibly long list? Probably the gossip—in person, online, social media."

"Funny," he said. "I love gossip. I like hearing about people's lives. It's what I like best about my job. If I had my life to do over again—which I'm guessing is unlikely—I'd study psychology."

Something came into her head that she'd been mulling over for days without fully realizing it. Before she could stop herself, she said, "If you had your life to live over again, would you still ask Mom to marry you?"

He took off his round reading glasses and studied her face. "That's a complicated question."

"Because you're gay?"

"I suppose that's the main reason, yes."

She reached into the pocket on the leg of her overalls and pulled out the old photo of her mother and David and their dog that she'd found months ago. She looked at it briefly. She'd grown more attached to the photo since she'd found it and she really wanted the happy, free look on her mother's face to count for something. If he said no, that he wouldn't have married her, it would negate the whole thing. She slid the photo across the table to him. He put his glasses back on and studied it for a moment as his face softened.

"I see your point," he said as he passed it back to her. "We had a lot of happy times, and no, I wouldn't trade them. So I guess the answer is yes, I would. Does that make you feel better?"

She fell back into her chair as if she'd been relieved of a great weight. "I think she might have a secret boyfriend."

"Good for her. I hope she does. What about you? Do you have a secret boyfriend?"

He asked it casually, as if he was setting a trap. She figured it was best to change the subject.

"To be clear, my mother hasn't said anything about it, but one weekend when I came back from my father's, she seemed a little different. Like she was happier but trying not to show it."

"Maybe you're not as averse to gossip as you claim."

"Maybe. Which step are we on now?" she asked.

"We're farther along than you think. I work stealthily." He took out some more papers from his folders and said, "Your grades are decent."

"Meaning not great?"

"I think you know that. We'll hear in a few weeks about your SAT scores. That should give us a better idea of appropriate schools." He closed up his computer and put away his glasses. She was surprised the interview seemed to be at an end. For some reason, it disappointed her. She felt she'd let him down. "You know this means a lot to your mother, don't you?"

"I think it means more to my father."

"If you mean he cares about your education more than she does, you're wrong. They're still a united front on that point. If you mean your father is scrutinizing Julie to see how much you get done this summer, you're right. I need you to care about this, Mandy, for everyone's sake."

"I went to look at schools with my mother," she said, although even to her own ears it had a tragic ring. They'd spent a weekend dragging through a series of campus visits, the specific campuses chosen because they could cram them all into two days of driving around New England. The awful part was, she did care about it, more than he could know, more than she liked to admit to herself. The hardest part was imagining that any decent colleges would care about her. She had a terrible urge to please him, to get his approval, but for some reason, it's always easier to get a person's disapproval. "Don't give up on me," she said.

"Don't worry about that," he said. "I give up on myself much more quickly than I do other people." He handed her a sheet of paper with three questions on it. "These are from the application for University of Chicago. I'm not expecting you'll apply there, but they have notoriously creative essay questions on their application. I'd like you to try responding to one of these, and then we'll look at it together and start there. Does that sound good?"

Tell us about the relationship between you and your arch-nemesis, real or imagined.

Dog and cat. Coffee and tea. Everyone knows there are two types of people in the world. What are they?

What is Square One and can you really go back to it?

"They're not easy," she said.

"That's pretty much the point," he said. "I'd recommend choosing the one that leaps out at you without giving it too much thought. If you can come up with something good, we can adapt it for the common app essay. Their questions are a little more bland and straightforward."

"Bland and straightforward is more my style," she said.

"It's not, but you don't realize it yet. I'm making omelets for dinner. They should be ready in about an hour. Maybe you could jot down a few words while waiting. Beginning is the hardest part."

As she was almost at the staircase up to the second floor, he said, "You never answered me about whether or not you have a boyfriend." This was a question she assumed she'd successfully dodged. She hoped she wasn't blushing. "I thought maybe the guy with curly hair you were talking to in a van the second day I was here was one."

"I don't have a boyfriend," she said. The idea that Craig was anyone's boyfriend, was capable of being a real boyfriend, struck her as ridiculous. On the other hand, he had made out with her in the front seat of the van. It wasn't as if that didn't mean anything. And so she added, "Not really."

"That's usually an evasive way of saying yes. If you ever want to talk about it, you know which minuscule room you can find me in. I don't want you to end up crying on the steps of the library at midnight."

Once she'd made it to the top floor of the house, she took out her phone and texted Craig.

Hey it's Mandy. Just making sure you haven't done any more littering.

She spent the next ten minutes staring at the phone, but there was no response. Then, right before she was called down to dinner: Ready to come work for me?

She wished she could take back the stupid comment she'd made to David. *Not really.* Yes, really, she really had no boyfriend. But at least she had someone's interest.

Not yet, she wrote back. But I'm thinking about it.

19

Julie had always believed that even if it's the big, unexpected events (good and bad) that make life memorable and occasionally exciting, it's the small, predictable routines that hold life together and make it worth living. By the end of David's first week in Beauport, they had an established routine. She wasn't yet sure if it was enough to hold her life together, but at the very least, it made it a lot easier to wait for Pamela's estimate on the jewelry.

David cooked dinner in the early evening, using ingredients she'd shopped for, and the three of them—if Mandy wasn't working at the store—ate at the dining room table (with candles!) and then cleaned up together. Mandy didn't even grumble about doing the dishes. They'd fallen into this pattern easily and spontaneously, and suddenly they felt like a reasonably happy, if slightly dysfunctional, family.

Poor Mrs. Grayson—who spent more time waiting to be sum-

moned by her son and his wife than she spent in their company—
had no idea what to make of the arrangement and was too discreet
to ask for clarification. She grinned whenever she saw them all
together, commented on the weather, and wandered off to the
porch to sit and await a phone call. She must have known David
was sleeping in the tiny room off the hall, but probably didn't know
how to process the information.

David referred to her as "the long-suffering southern belle"
and felt there was passive-aggression in her stoic refusal to complain about the way she was being treated even though she made
damn sure everyone knew she was being ignored. Julie had
dropped her objection to his credible imitation of her Virginia
accent and accurate mimicry of the loud stage whisper she
spoke in, as if she was afraid to disturb anyone but was determined to be heard. He was being a little mean, but not cruel, and
Julie could see his point. No doubt, she'd idealized Mrs. Grayson.
She could laugh with him but preferred to play the role of dutiful
surrogate daughter to compensate for the way Mrs. Grayson was
being treated by her real family.

After dinner, she and David took Opal along the Atlantic
Pathway on walks that cut across the cliffs above the ocean. It was
something she'd insisted on once she understood he was wrestling
with his own demons and seemed to be making an effort at getting into better shape. Sometimes, to her surprise, they held
hands as they walked. One of them would reach for the other, and
they'd amble along talking about old friends and past adventures
and memorable moments from their time with Oliver, the long-
gone mutt who'd died as they held him. The time they thought

they'd lost him in Riverside Park, the time he'd opened a drawer and chewed up a pair of socks. She supposed David found their touching as comforting and uncomplicated as she did. She hoped so.

They never talked about her pregnancy or his friendship with Antrim, and everything that had happened in their final months. She was grateful for that.

When they got back to the house, they'd stretch out at opposite ends of the sofa thing in the living room, and he'd read aloud from *Queen Lucia* until one or the other of them fell asleep.

It was on one of their walks, on an evening when the sky was still light at nine o'clock, that he asked her if she'd looked into other options, in case she wasn't able to come up with the money in time to buy the house from Henry. Naturally, she had thought about this, had even spent a Saturday evening perusing real estate listings, had gone to two open houses, but the question stung her. She'd been counting on him as an ally, and merely bringing it up felt like a small but deep betrayal. She dropped his hand and froze on the path.

"Why would you even ask that?" she said.

"Not to upset you, that's for sure," he said. "I mean as a Plan B to have in your back pocket."

"I don't want a Plan B. I want to make this work. I have over one hundred fifty thousand in retirement savings, and I hope the jewelry will make up the rest."

She wanted to think he was judging her unfairly, but in the evening light and with the breeze blowing in from the ocean, he looked kind and concerned. "But you'll have to pay penalties on that if you take it out and you'll have no reserves."

"I'll build them up again. I'll keep renting rooms and put money aside. I have good job security." She wished she hadn't taken a few hits of pot when they started the walk, not because having done so impaired her perceptions, but because she knew that to him, she must look like someone with impaired perceptions. "With the way the real estate market is going in this state, the house could be worth two million by the time I'm in my seventies. At that point, when I'm too gone to care, I can sell and go into a nice little assisted living facility."

"What worries me," he said, "is that Henry might be trying to undermine you. Have you ever thought that it might have been him who told the mortgage broker you were doing short-term rentals?"

This was a suspicion she'd ruled out shortly after she'd heard the bad news from Charles Phillips. Henry, she told David, was capable of being selfish and unkind, but she couldn't bring herself to believe he was that cruel.

"But what if it wasn't a matter of cruelty?" David asked. "What if it's desperation? In that case, he's probably going to try to keep putting up roadblocks, right to the end. You can't afford to assume anything. I made that mistake. I assumed I'd always have my deal-of-the-century in San Francisco, when I should have been making backup plans."

She attended a final faculty meeting at school the next day, and as she was driving home from it, she found herself pulling off the highway and heading for Henry's restaurant.

You could see it from the off-ramp, a wooden building that looked something like an overgrown fishing shack and something like every other suburban restaurant in the world, floating in the middle of a vast parking lot. The fact that it was so close to the highway and that the back looked out to the green of salt marshes and, in the distance, the ocean, had made it seem like a surefire investment. And for a while, it had been. A short while.

There were only a few cars in the lot, to be expected in mid-afternoon. Julie arranged herself in her mirror before getting out. Not that it mattered how she looked for Henry, but weirdly, now that they were divorcing, now that it truly didn't matter any-more, she cared more about her appearance than she ever had when they were together. This was one of the many things that should have tipped her off about the marriage but hadn't. She'd viewed their invisibility to each other, the annoyed glances she'd occasionally spot coming her way, the almost implausibly child-ish way she'd sometimes make faces at Henry when he turned his back, as a quirky, shared dynamic that held them together. The way alcoholism held some couples together or religion or affec-tion for a sports team. Since moving to Boston all those years ago to teach at Crawford, she'd lost count of the number of couples she'd met whose relationships appeared to revolve around wor-ship of the Red Sox, a neurotic obsession that involved T-shirts and hats and bumper stickers.

The interior of the restaurant was gloomy, which was odd con-sidering the massive windows that looked out to the marsh. Per-haps the dimness was for the best, because the carpet was grimy and the whole place smelled faintly of grease and fish and whatever cleaners were being used to hide same. Dark paneling? Paint it, Julie had suggested. Brighten it up. But Henry had an all-or-nothing attitude toward fixing the place that perfectly mirrored his all-or-nothing attitude toward her.

There were two tables occupied by the windows, one by a solo male diner reading something on his phone, the other by a gray-haired, silent couple who might as well have been on their phones. What meal was this for these people? Lunch? Dinner? There had never been anything wrong with the food Julie had eaten here, but the problem was, there had never been anything right, either. Like so many restaurants in this part of the world, the dishes were unmemorable; after dinners Julie had had at the restaurant (and she'd had many in the years after Henry had purchased it), she'd forget she'd eaten by the time she got home and wonder what she was going to scrape together for a meal.

It was well over a year since Julie had been here. Since then, the place seemed to have fallen into a depression of sorts. There was an air of defeat. The stale smells, the heavy, outdated rock maple tables, the heavy, outdated patrons silently and (one had to assume) joylessly eating. Inconveniently, the place made her feel bad for Henry, just as she was trying to steel her resolve to confront him. Maybe it was better to attempt the confrontation over the phone.

She turned to go, but as she was leaving, Henry came out from his office in back.

"A little early for dinner, isn't it?" he asked.

"Not really," she said. "I'm almost at the early-bird-special stage of life." He said nothing, as if he was agreeing with her—how dare he?—so she said, "I do think you should paint the paneling, Henry. It would brighten things up. At this time of day especially."

"I'm not going to do a paint job right before I renovate the whole place. And I'm guessing that's not what you came here to talk about."

"No, obviously not."

They sat at the bar, another grim affair, brightened only by TV screens. Julie remembered a time when sitting in a bar or restaurant, taking a cab or an airplane, waiting in line at the grocery store did not involve watching TV. But those memories were vague. She imagined the renovation of the place would, inevitably, involve more TVs. The bartender was one of the dour, bloated ex-athletes in his early thirties Henry typically hired. Henry liked being associated with their competitor pasts and was unthreatened by their gone-to-seed presents. He handed them beers.

Always begin with the good news. "I wanted to tell you that Mandy has been making great progress on the college front."

"Really? And how do you define 'great progress'?"

"She's started working on her essays, and David has set up a whole seven-step plan for her. An action plan." This was a phrase she'd heard somewhere.

"And you're overseeing all this, along with everything else?"

"David came to work with her, so we're overseeing it together."

"He's here? Staying at the house?"

"Of course he's staying at the house. Why wouldn't he be?"

Henry took another drink from his bottle and put it down on the bar. He asked the bartender something about inventory and told him he'd like him to use the new cleaner on the chrome cases. This was all said in the tone of a boss, a move toward establishing further dominance over her. It was clear he was jealous and mildly upset that David was in the house. That made her happy even while she recognized it as petty, impotent happiness.

When he spoke again, he'd lost some of his energetic righteousness. "I know you think I'm trying to make your life miserable, but I'm not. I'm just trying to make mine better. I'm trying to move forward. And if your idea of moving forward is hanging out with some guy you shouldn't have married in the first place, go right ahead. You're not a bad-looking woman, Julie."

"Gee, I'd almost forgotten what a suave flatterer you are."

"You could be dating if you wanted."

The word "dating" struck her as absurdly adolescent, but still, the image of Raymond Cross passed through her mind. He had texted her again yesterday. He hadn't asked her for a date, but he'd said more than he'd said in his other texts, specifically, that he wanted to see her again.

"Have you been trying to undermine me, Henry?"

"If you expect an answer to that, you'll have to be more specific."

"I know Richard didn't come to you asking about the house. You went to him and told him it was for sale, or would be when I was unable to get the money together."

"How's that going, by the way?"

David's question about Henry's involvement in the mortgage proceedings came roaring back. "It was going better before you made sure I didn't get the mortgage. Before you let the broker know I have a few people staying at the house once in a while."

He looked at the TV and said, "So you did get turned down?"

"Stop drooling," she said. "It doesn't look good in a restaurant. Whether I got turned down or not, I'm buying the house. I have a Plan B."

"Oh, really? Is David Hedges giving you the money? Tell him he'd better hurry. You've only got another month and a half until our deadline." And then, as if he regretted all his harsh words, he put his hand on her forearm and looked into her eyes. It was fascinating that someone whose touch had once thrilled her could now make her skin crawl. It was like waking up one day and discovering that chocolate actually doesn't taste good after all. "My suggestion is to get a life, Julie. I can tell you from personal experience, it feels really good."

She yanked her arm from his hand, reached into her bag, and pulled out a few bills and some loose change that had been rattling around on the bottom. She spilled them onto the bar. "That should cover the beer," she said. "And I have a life, Henry. I have a perfectly nice life. And since you're the one who brought up dating, you'll be happy to hear, I have a lover, too. And on August fourteenth, I'll have the house."

20

Raymond was most definitely not her lover. But . . .

Good day, Miss Julie, he'd texted her yesterday. Guess what? Will be in your area again. Beverly Music Tent. Late July. Just to let you know.

How nonchalantly she'd responded and how anti-nonchalant she'd felt. That's exciting. Good venue! Should I reserve a room for you? Reserve a room. Sandra would be proud.

I have to be closer. They're putting us up in a hotel. Motel? I'll have some free time. I'd love to see you again.

He had arrived in early April. She'd recently begun renting rooms. She hadn't heard him pull into the drive, hadn't heard him knock on the door. She'd been upstairs and remembered that she'd left a kettle on in the kitchen and had run downstairs barefoot, and there he was, standing in the front hallway. She'd brushed the hair off her face and said she'd be right back, burned herself when she moved the kettle, and went into the hall again sucking her thumb. When she met his gaze, she felt something pass between them. It had been so long since she'd felt this kind of instant attraction and had felt it reciprocated, she tried to talk herself into believing she must be deluded. But even then, right at the start, she'd known she wasn't. When she tried to describe to herself what it was, the best she was able to come up with was a look of recognition. *Ah, you! You've come at last.*

He was tall and lean—a morning jogger, she'd later find out—and he had thin hair pulled back into a ponytail that looked absolutely natural on him, neither hipster nor hippie. He was wearing a T-shirt and cargo shorts, a pair of nerdy black eyeglasses, and beat-up sandals. He was part of a jazz ensemble that was playing at the Reese Music Hall in the middle of town that weekend, and he was carrying a canvas backpack and a saxophone case. She judged him to be her own age, or somewhere in that unfashionable district.

"This house is fantastic," he said.

"Do you think so? It needs a little work, but . . ."

"No, it's terrific. The staircase, the woodwork? I almost stayed at a motel. I'm glad I found you at the last minute."

So am I, she didn't say.

He had a way of looking at her with what she took to be intense compassion. As if he understood that she was dealing with a lot, was out of her depth, in over her head, and yet wasn't judging her. Maybe she was reading too much into it and his eyeglass prescription was merely out-of-date. She showed him to his room and asked about the performances at the hall. They were doing one each of the next two nights and then a matinee on Sunday. "You're welcome to stay as late as you want on Sunday. There's no one coming into your room on Monday. Where are the others in the group?"

Two lived close enough to drive and the rest were staying at a hotel in Hammond. He wasn't one of the long-term members of the group but was filling in for the usual saxophonist, who'd been sick. "I'm the outsider, but they were desperate," he said. Naturally, she found this attractive, too. It made her feel closer to him, as if she and he had more of a connection already than he had with the people he played with. He lived in western Connecticut, not so far, but not close enough to drive home every night. He wasn't wearing a wedding ring, she noticed, but it seemed implausible that he was single. She told him to make himself at home and please tell her if he needed anything, her standard welcome, but for the first time since she'd been doing this, she meant it.

Musicians had always been mysterious to her. They looked like everyone else (leaving aside Mick Jagger) but they had within them an ability to produce sounds that cut straight to your emotions and could break your heart or make you soar.

Mandy was off at Henry's that weekend and although Julie had planned to go for a long walk, she decided instead to bake cookies. She wanted to be in a room he might happen into and she couldn't think of anything else that would take as much time. Half an hour later, he did come into the kitchen and ask her directions to the concert hall.

"Can I make you a sandwich?" she asked, and he told her, to her surprise, that although he usually ate after a performance, he wouldn't mind a little something.

"Do you go to many concerts?" he asked.

She rarely went. She'd intend to go when she saw a list of upcoming events and then, unless someone else got the tickets, she'd forget. "I don't go as often as I'd like," she said.

"It's too convenient," he said. "Most people don't go out to things unless it's inconvenient and they have to plan ahead. You'd think it would be the opposite."

She handed him a turkey sandwich and sat at the table with him, watching him eat.

"I'll leave a couple of tickets for you at the box office," he said. "In case you want to go. But no pressure. It's the least I can do, seeing as this is such a good deal."

After he'd left, she puttered around the house, nervously trying to decide if it would look too eager to go or rude to stay home. She called a couple of friends, but no one was interested. The concert hall itself was beautiful and a source of local pride. The events held there were another matter. "Experimental jazz? You can't be serious."

In the end, she showered and changed and walked to the hall. The entire wall behind the stage was an immense window from which you could see the ocean washing against the rocky shore and, if you were lucky, the sunset. The ensemble apparently had a small cult following who came from all over to see them. They knew what they were in for. Julie hadn't given much thought to it. The performance involved a lot of improvised noise. When someone scraped his chair on the floor or dropped a block of wood or quacked, the faithful followers laughed and applauded appreciatively. There were references and inside jokes she was missing entirely. It was like watching a Japanese film without subtitles. A noisy Japanese film.

Somewhere toward the middle, Raymond played a solo. It had started off as disjointed as everything else she'd heard that night, but gradually evolved into a lush melodic line that touched her in an inexplicable way and almost brought tears to her eyes. The rest of the audience seemed uninterested in, even bored by, what she considered the only truly musical moment of the entire concert.

She walked home trying to figure out what to say about the concert. It would be too obvious and embarrassing to say she only liked his performance, since that was about 2 percent of the whole.

She arranged herself on a chair in the living room, somewhere he'd be likely to see her. But of course, he'd go out afterward for dinner or drinks. She'd taken a few hits of pot on the walk home and after fifteen minutes, she fell asleep. She was woken up by the front door. He came into the living room and sat across from her.

"I should have warned you," he said. He spoke softly, almost in a whisper, as if he was worried he'd wake up another guest. But there were none. They were alone in the creaking house with a light April wind blowing against the windows.

"About what?" she whispered back.

"It's an acquired taste. It took me a long time to acquire it, and I'm still on the fence."

"I liked what you played," she said softly. "I was carried away by it. I don't know if you could see, but the light behind you during that solo was beautiful. A cold, cobalt-blue sky."

"A bit of luck, I guess. Like finding you," he said, gesturing to the room.

She wanted to tell him that no one else was in the house, so there was no need to keep talking at that volume, but it would, she feared, sound too loaded. Like the other musicians, he was wearing a tuxedo, but wearing it ironically. The neck was too big and he still had on the sandals. She found this endearing.

"I was hoping you'd like it," he said. And then, not flirting but simply stating a fact, he said, "I played it for you. When I saw you'd come, I wanted to give you a few bars you'd enjoy."

"How did you know my tastes so well?" she asked. "We only talked for ten minutes or so."

"That's when you find out everything you need to know about a person. The rest is embellishment, to fill in the gaps. Don't you think?"

In a sense, she did. It was what she'd felt the minute she saw him, as if she knew everything she needed to know. She wanted some of the embellishment but was certain it would include details she'd rather not know. A wife, children, those kinds of details.

They chatted for a few more minutes in the dim yellow glow of the living room, and then he said she must be tired after trying to stay awake through the whole concert. He got up and shut off the lights in the dining room and kitchen, a small kindness that felt so spontaneous, she almost swooned. It had all the comforting familiarity of a long-term relationship mixed with the excitement of the new and unknowable.

They walked up the main staircase together and then, in front of his room, he opened his door and whispered, "Good night, Julie."

"Good night," she said.

If she'd turned then, nothing, she was sure, would have happened. But she'd waited maybe three seconds, during which they held eye contact and everything that followed was decided. He took her hand, and they went into his room.

When he left on Sunday afternoon, she waved cheerfully from the porch, and then went into the house and wept with a mix of gratitude and loneliness.

And soon, he was coming back.

21

"I suppose you thought I was joking when I said I'd be opening drawers and cabinets," Michael's email read. "I've learned quite a lot about you I didn't know before."

David hadn't thought Michael was joking. Having lived most of his life with secrets, Michael was now committed to absolute truth; when he said something, he meant it. What surprised him most was that Michael had found anything of interest. As far as he could remember, he'd never hidden any of his exploits from Michael; occasionally, he'd exaggerated them. It was July 3, and Michael had been in the carriage house for almost two weeks, had blocked Renata from entering twice, and had even learned to use the espresso machine with the help of a young visitor who (of course) turned out to be a barista.

David took another bite of the expensive dog biscuit, the only dessert he was allowing himself these days. And considering the lack of moisture and sandy texture, he preferred to think of it as desert. Tasteless as they were, they had a hardy, punitive appeal to him—satisfaction and punishment for it all in one compact package. It was fortunate Opal had refused to touch them.

Michael's email continued:

I found some interesting papers in the unlocked file cabinet in your bedroom. You never told me you had a lease. And a long-term one at that! I had assumed some eccentric verbal agreement with the nutty landlady. It has my lawyerly brain churning. I see a potential windfall for you and a commission for me. Call! When are you returning?

He wrote back:

I don't know what your lawyerly brain is cooking up, but I'm not litigious. The landlady was good to me for so many years, I couldn't possibly cause trouble. And I'm not sure about returning. I'm loving Beauport so I'm in no rush. Sitting at my spacious desk looking at the Atlantic.

Well, he was looking *toward* the Atlantic. No need to say he was in a coffin-size room with a view of a privet hedge. It was true that he was in no rush to leave; he'd returned his rental car two days ago and hadn't bothered to book another westbound flight since he'd canceled two already. He was measuring his contentment in inverse proportion to his weight. He eyed the dog biscuits but resisted. If he stayed another month, he'd have to buy new clothes.

After removing half the furniture that had been in the room, he had enough floor space to do a desultory round of calisthenics each morning. And then there were the marathon walks he and Julie took nightly, which seemed to have become the center of his days. She was extending these to cover more and more ground, an act of kindness to him.

His waistline was not the only improvement.

Since taking the recommendations on changing their Airbnb profile Sandra had sent in her hostile written report ("Raise your rates and block off some dates so it at least appears to be a desirable property"), they'd had significantly more inquiries. Two days ago, an enthusiastic (about everything) couple had moved into the Window Seat Room for a week, and last night, a florid middle-aged woman named Mona had settled into the Street-View Room.

The latter had arrived with one overflowing bag that had been stuffed with clothes rather than packed in an organized way. She claimed she was scouting apartments to buy or rent, but David hadn't seen her since she'd checked in.

Mona was a certain type of woman that Beauport attracted, a type that appeared to have been blown to this easternmost point of land on a tide of misfortune. Like Mona, many had obviously been beauties in an earlier phase of their lives but now gave the impression of having been badly used by life in general and by men in particular. David suspected Mona's overstuffed bag had a few prescription bottles in it. Barbiturates, naturally. To be fair, David himself had been blown here by misfortune. Happily, with Julie's help, he was turning it around.

As for Mandy, he hadn't given up, but he wasn't wildly optimistic about her college plans. After their initial meeting, she hadn't seemed eager to get together and answer his questions, investigate websites of colleges he'd mentioned, or struggle through a few attempts at essays. She was clearly bright and had an instinct for reading people that was unusual in kids her age, but her grades and lack of activities meant it was going to be difficult getting her into a decent school. Usually, David could find a toehold with even an unpromising student from which he could begin to build a case—a summer internship that could be made to sound interesting, a poem that had been published in the school literary journal, even a Twitter account that showed some wit and an expansive awareness of the world. He hadn't found any logical starting point for Mandy.

After pressing her on her interests, she admitted, sheepishly, that she was interested in studying psychology. "And I was before you brought it up," she made clear. "Unfortunately, I'm probably too screwed up to go into it."

He assured her that being screwed up was practically one of the requirements for studying psychology, but even there, it was hard to pinpoint what her particular problems were.

They'd compiled a list of an even dozen schools—four reaches, four targets, and four safeties. Privately, David was beginning to think that the target schools—Carlton College, Farmingdale State, Providence College among them—were more like reaches. As for Smith, Wellesley, and Sarah Lawrence, there was no point in even trying. Not that he was going to tell her that just yet.

She'd been quick to make a stab at an essay, and the opening paragraph had had some quirky potential:

"For a long time, I thought Clara Dunston was my arch-nemesis. It wasn't until she'd been bullied online and taken out of school that I realized I thought that because we were a lot alike."

After that, it drifted into essay clichés about lessons learned that clearly, from his experience of her, she hadn't learned at all. Honesty in these essays was what counted most (a stunning admission about peeing in the kitchen sink, for example), and aside from a few exceptions, it was what he had the most difficulty coaxing from his young clients. At least Mandy was educable, and Massachusetts had a few good state schools. It was hard to know what Henry was expecting for her, although his impression was that he mostly wanted to use her as a bargaining chip in the divorce.

Would he, he wondered, have been a selfless parent himself, always choosing what was best for his child no matter what kind of sacrifice was involved? It was easy for David to believe so since now he would never be tested. The truth was, once he'd gotten over the shock and the sadness of Julie's miscarriage, he'd been relieved. It wasn't until the past decade that a more insistent disappointment gnawed at him when he thought about the child who'd never been. Eventually he and Julie would have divorced anyway, but they'd have figured out a way to form an eccentric little family. Probably not unlike the eccentric arrangement they were forming this summer. Unlike Mandy, their child would have been in her late twenties by now, so they would have weathered (or not) this rough adolescent period.

One maudlin night after Soren had left him and he'd had too many glasses of bad wine, he'd started writing an explanation of what had happened to their relationship and how things had gone wrong. It wasn't exactly a journal entry (he'd had an aversion to keeping journals since reading one he'd kept in college and discovering it was mostly lies) and it wasn't a note to himself. After writing a full page, he realized what he'd been composing, in his addled state, was a letter to his adult daughter. (He and Julie had never known the sex of their baby, but he'd always imagined a girl.) A letter explaining himself to someone whose connection to him could not be broken by the arrival of a better offer. Since then, he'd occasionally found himself addressing this imaginary person and even filling in a few details of her life. She played the piano reasonably well; she was married to an honest man of modest means; she didn't like to cook, but occasionally baked bread.

"How can you sit in this horrible closet with that noisy fan?"

Amira was standing in his doorway. He rarely closed the door since doing so made the room seem even smaller. She looked radiant in cork sandals and a short yellow sundress that screamed, "I'm not wearing panties."

"I'm doing some work," he said, "and having a snack. Would you like one?"

She came into the room and looked around with a mixture of dread and disapproval. "So ugly," she said. She reached into the proffered bag and bit into a biscuit. "But these are wonderful!"

David was disappointed by this reaction; he was hoping to shock her. "I'm glad you like them."

"Yes, if I have another one, I'll throw up. I'm not a bulimic, but if it happens, I usually don't mind."

She had, as Julie had predicted, wandered into the house a few times since he'd been there, made outrageous statements, and settled into a chair somewhere, pouting. Despite her intrusiveness and a general attitude that suggested she was performing for a large audience of appreciative fans and appalled prudes, there was a sympathetic, childlike quality about her that was irresistible. When the topic of Julie's house came up, she usually turned vague, but it was difficult to know if this was because she was planning a coup or because she was an inveterate tease.

As David watched her take a seat on the edge of his bed in her provocative sundress (no, she was not wearing panties and yes, she did wax), it occurred to him that she was, in her own way, not unlike Mona and the other lost ladies of Beauport, blown east to this rocky spit of land, next stop open ocean. True, in her case, it was into the safe haven of a rich husband who would provide a buffer between her beauty and a world that was eager to exploit her for it, but the open ocean was right at the end of the street if Richard suddenly tired of her antics.

"You're making the house nicer," she said. "I was not hit by a dust storm when I came in."

"That's my goal," David said. "And speaking of which, I'm planning to move some furniture out of a few of the other rooms and into the barn. Do you know anyone who could help me?"

"Of course," she said. "I am a wonderful resource for everything. I will send you my pot dealer. He does for me whatever I tell him."

"That's convenient," David said. "How did you manage to enslave him?"

"The only way possible," she said. "I figured out what he wants and then I never give it to him."

David assumed this was a reference to what she was endeavoring to not conceal under her sundress, but when he asked for clarification, she said, "He wants praise. It's what everyone wants."

"I suppose that's true," David said.

"Don't pay him more than twenty dollars an hour. He did some work for me and he works like he fucks—lazy. He has a long penis but it is thin. Do you prefer them long or thick?"

"To be honest," David said, "I'm mainly interested in my own."

"Oh, that's no fun. You're as bad as a straight man. I thought I could complain with you about my husband's thing."

"I'd prefer you didn't." He enjoyed listening to discussions, no matter how lurid, about a person's extracurricular sex life, but discussions of the sexual activity of married or long-partnered couples struck him as related to discussions of medical problems and bodily functions and made him cringe. To change the subject he said, "What about the party you claimed you were going to have? As far as I know, we haven't received any invitations."

"What's the rush? You will probably stay forever."

"I'm afraid this room is too small for me for forever."

"There are other rooms in the house," she said. "And the disgusting barn. But we'll have the party next week anyway."

As soon as she mentioned his staying on, he recognized it as something he'd thought about previously, in a fleeting way. He felt strangely detached from San Francisco, as if a wire that had connected him to the West Coast had been snipped. He hadn't brought this up with Julie, but then again, he hadn't fully acknowledged it to himself until this moment. "Forever" seemed like the wrong word, but then again, he was approaching the age at which "forever" was only a matter of a few decades.

She stood and smoothed down her dress. "I hope you're helping Julie steal the house from my husband. I'd love a pool, but I'd much rather see him disappointed. Please walk me out? I hate running into the inmates. They resent me for being allowed to leave the institution while they remain confined in their cells."

He walked her to her gate. Her house was carefully hidden behind hedges and evergreens, and he'd yet to set eyes on this fabled dwelling. As he was returning to Julie's house, a car pulled into the drive, and a woman dressed in a tailored summer suit stepped out. Not their typical clientele, and as far as he knew, there was no room at the inn for walk-ins.

"You must be David," she said, and stuck out her hand. "Pamela Kern. Julie's told me all about you." He supposed from this that she assumed he'd heard about her as well, but if so, he didn't remember. "Not all, of course, but the essential biographical details. I'm impressed the two of you have remained friends. Julie needs friends."

She was an energetic woman, and between the fast talk and the incredibly spotless car, it seemed certain she was in sales of some kind.

"I'm afraid Julie isn't home," he said. "She should be back in an hour or two."

"I should have checked first. I should have called. To be honest, I wanted to tell her in person, but now I'm relieved she's not here. It's not good news. Not bad news exactly, just disappointing."

She hit a button on her keychain and the trunk popped open. She handed David a large Hermès shopping bag. When he felt the weight of it, he had a sense of what this was about. "Her mother's jewelry?" he asked.

"There are some lovely pieces in there. I'm tempted by some of them myself. I'm sure there are a lot of memories attached to many of them. In the end, that's usually the greatest value there is to the things we inherit."

The meaning of this was abundantly clear. "Would you like to come in?" he asked.

"I'm afraid I can't. I have two potential clients who want estimates on the contents of their mothers' houses. It's always mothers' houses. The women invariably outlive the husbands. It's revenge. People think I'm in the business of antiques, but really I'm in the business of death. I get called shortly after the family calls the funeral director."

"So the jewelry . . ."

"There's an itemized list in the bag. It's not nothing, but it's about a tenth of what Julie was told, or what she was hoping. That's the way it usually is with jewelry. The Cartiers are rarely by Cartier. That's the way it is with everything, come to think of it. You'd be amazed at the number of people who plan to put a child through college with a couple of pre-Columbian artifacts great-great-uncle so-and-so sneaked back in his luggage from a dig in Peru in 1920. I can usually get more for an original-in-box *Star Wars* action figure."

David took the bag to his room and opened up the itemized list. When he read the grand total at the bottom of the fourth page, he sat at his desk and gazed out the window at the hedge. It seemed to be even closer than it had been a few minutes ago. No, as Pamela had said, it wasn't nothing, but it was so far from what Julie would need to get the house, it counted as mere frosting.

"I wish I had some pre-Columbian artifacts of my own to sell," he said to himself. Or perhaps not quite to himself. To that nameless, imaginary adult daughter, to assure her that he'd help out her mother if he could. They were all in it together.

The orange Hermès shopping bag with the box of dashed hopes inside seemed to be in flames on his bed. If he had any possibilities of his own, he'd hide it from Julie for a few days, but he had nothing of great value to sell. It was probably best to climb up to her room and leave it on her bed and let her discover it in private when she returned from the grocery store.

On the landing on the second floor, an idea came to him. He went back to his room, slid the bag into the suitcase under his bed, and called Michael. It was always a mistake to underestimate lawyerly minds, and although it was true he hated litigious people as a rule, that didn't mean his behavior couldn't be hypocritical.

22

Classes were over for the summer, but twenty-five years of teaching had made Julie an early riser, even when she'd stayed up late the night before or had, possibly, had a hit of pot out in the yard at some point in the evening. She usually got up at six, which gave her enough time to make David a pot of the strong black tea he'd been drinking for as long as she'd known him. "Thank you," he'd say every morning when she set it before him, as if she'd given him an elaborate present. In fact, she felt as if she was the one who'd received a gift by having him there.

After they'd eaten, they laid out the defrosted muffins and pieces of fruit, items Sandra had recommended they refer to as the "breakfast buffet." "Never cut up the fruit," she'd written on her blog. "People are much more likely to eat it." And then, proudly: "The apples and oranges I set out typically sit there for so long, I have to throw them out!"

Mrs. Grayson rarely showed her face before ten, and Julie left out bread for her, since she seemed to subsist largely on white toast with the crusts cut off and other pale food.

"Isn't it a lovely morning?" she said to Julie today. She was sitting at the end of the dining room table, daintily buttering toast, cardigan carefully draped.

"A little warm," Julie said, "but after last winter, I suppose we shouldn't complain."

Last winter had been mild, but complaining about New England winters was the only truly safe topic of conversation with guests. Accurate or not, it offended no one. Accuracy was beside the point lately anyway. Among a certain segment of the population, acknowledging the existence of scientific data was considered unpatriotic, akin to acknowledging the existence of gun violence unless perpetrated by Muslims or racism that didn't involve a white person losing a job to a person of color.

It was the Fourth of July, and Julie was certain that Mrs. Grayson's son and daughter-in-law would be having a cookout or party of some kind. Surely they intended to invite her. Her son and his wife lived on the opposite side of town—the "gold coast"—in an enormous house built out onto the rocks. Julie, along with everyone else in town, knew the house; it was that large and imposing, built in an epic style Julie thought of as Late Hedge Fund. There had to be eight bedrooms, which meant a dozen bathrooms, which begged the question: Why was she staying here? Her son's house surely had extra bedrooms and probably whole wings.

"Is your son doing anything special for the holiday?" Julie asked.

"They're having some people over. I wasn't going to go, but they gave the au pair the day off, and they said I could take care of the baby. He's the dearest little thing. They let me see him for almost ten minutes yesterday."

The wording suggested she was usually led into a room where the baby was sleeping before being hauled out sixty seconds later.

"Are you and your brother doing anything?" Although Julie had introduced him as "friend" and referred to him as such, Mrs. Grayson sometimes called David her "brother," other times her "companion," other times her "guest." She'd considered clarifying once and for all with "my ex-husband" but she suspected that would only confuse the issue.

"You must be proud of your son," Julie said, fishing for more outrageous information. "He's done so well."

"I sure am proud of him," Mrs. Grayson said. She clutched her throat. "I just hope he's a little bit proud of me."

This was so heartfelt, Julie felt unsettled. She sat at the table and put her hand on Mrs. Grayson's. "Of course he is. Why wouldn't he be?"

"It's different with boys," Mrs. Grayson said. "Once they get married, everything changes. You're lucky you have a girl. She'll always be your devoted daughter."

Daughter-in-law issues. That explained her exile to this house on the other side of town. An hour later, when Mrs. Grayson was out on the front porch reading a large-print edition of *Reader's Digest,* a black SUV pulled up to the curb. Mrs. Grayson waved and gathered her things. A stern woman sat in the front seat texting while Mrs. Grayson climbed in and then pulled away without any apparent conversation. It was unclear if this was the daughter-in-law or the driver, but either way, David's long-suffering southern belle was getting no respect.

Julie's mother had wanted a proud, devoted daughter, too, but one devoted to her reputation and legacy as a scholar, not to her as a good parent. "Anyone can be a good parent," she'd once told Julie. "It's hardly a talent."

In the last couple of decades of her life, her mother had been in contact mostly through letters, ones she'd insisted Julie hang on to. "I'm not suggesting they'll be worth much," she'd said, "but if a biographer contacts you, it would be ideal to have them all in one place."

Her mother, who'd been an apparently well-known scholar at Yale and an authority on fifteenth-century poetry, had always assumed someone would write about her, although given her claims that she was hated in her field, it wasn't clear why she assumed that. Her letters were full of criticism of Julie, often phrased in ways that justified her own choices and child-rearing decisions and crafted with a formality that seemed intended for publication. They were in a big plastic container in the basement, safe from the destructive forces of water and air, just as her mother would have wanted. Every once in a while, when Julie was feeling masochistic or was, inexplicably, missing her mother, she'd look at them. It had only recently occurred to her—with horror—that Mandy, with her love of digging things out of the basement, might have seen them, too.

"I feel terrible your learning disability wasn't diagnosed earlier," her mother had written. "We took you to many specialists, but of course in those days, there was considerably less literature on the matter. If there had been, you might have been able to pursue the academic career your father and I had always planned for you instead of the roundelay of sad marriages and pointless drifting that your life has been. And just to reassure you, darling, we were always proud of the way we accepted the reality of who you are, even though it was so far from what we'd hoped."

Mixed in with these assaults were comments that she had to know would be of no interest to Julie: "Your father and I attended a lecture by Nadine Sanderson. It was riddled with factual errors about Renaissance poetry and simple historical details. The fact that the audience seemed to appreciate her talk is more a comment on the current state of academia than on her skills. When she came up to me afterwards to praise my work and practically kiss my hand, I was embarrassed. I know she wanted me—someone she has idolized and emulated for decades—to heap praise on her. I told her I had rarely seen a speaker use the microphone more effectively, letting her interpret the comment as she wished. In attendance were . . ."

Her mother's popularity with students at Yale had always been a source of confusion for Julie. Was she kinder to them than to her own daughter? Did she actually love them more, meaning perhaps that they were more lovable? Back when they were married, David had explained that undergraduates often mistake condescension and sarcasm for pedagogy, a comforting thought that hadn't comforted her.

As Julie was clearing off food from the "breakfast buffet," she realized she had it all wrong—she didn't see Mrs. Grayson as an idealized mother figure, but as a possible future version of herself, alone, melancholy, and trying to put the best face on the slight, grudging interest of her child. Mandy's devotion wasn't a given, and why should it be? What had she given Mandy to be proud of?

She went to David's room. He was sitting at his desk with his computer open.

"Do you realize," he said, "that since we raised the rates, inquiries about the rooms have increased almost 50 percent? Hiring that lunatic was a brilliant decision, my dear. We should have her back for a cocktail. If we raise our prices again, we'll have to build an addition."

She wanted to play along with him, but she was afraid she'd lose her resolve if she didn't bring it up right now. "I want you to help me with something," she said.

"You sound serious."

The way he said it made it clear he thought she wasn't. "I am, David. I hate to ask another favor, but I can't do this on my own."

That got his attention. He opened the desk drawer and took out a sheet of paper with "The Seven Steps to Julie Fiske's Happy Henry-Free Future" printed across the top. He handed it to her. "My guess is we've arrived at Step Number Four."

This was labeled simply "Pot Problem."

"You're always right. I stopped completely six months ago, but as you know, I still smoke a few times a week. I keep telling myself that since it's not addictive, it can't matter that I'm hooked."

"That sounds logical."

"It sounds even more so when you're stoned. The worst thing is, Mandy knows. She won't come out and say it, so I talk myself into believing it doesn't matter, but it does. On some level, she's probably ashamed of me."

"I'm not giving you drug tests," he said. "If that's the help you were thinking about."

"I have to get rid of it," she said. "All of it."

"How much is there?"

While it was undeniable that pot had deteriorated her memory, there was one exception: she remembered every cupboard and closet and hidden ashtray and outdoor fake rock and—relics from a past civilization—plastic film canisters in which she'd stashed joints or buds or a few loose crumbs. It took them almost half an hour to gather it all in a glass bowl. A weird Easter egg hunt that David seemed to find entertaining. "Did you have pot stashed all over the apartment when we lived together?" he asked.

"Of course not. I came to it late in life. If I had been smoking then, I wouldn't have hidden it from you." As if there weren't things each of them had kept hidden from the other?

"I hate to admit it," David said, "but looking at this all piled up in the bowl makes me want to roll a joint. Should we give it to Amira? Or better yet, sell it to her?"

Julie considered this for a moment. It was tempting, but Amira would chide her for being a prude and they'd end up high within ten minutes.

"I think we should go out and toss it into the ocean," she said.

"A grand gesture. I approve."

She went to get Opal while David emptied all the pot into a

brown paper sandwich bag. By eleven, they were walking along the Atlantic Pathway. It was usually windy there, but today the air was still and the water sparkled as it often did in the morning. It was going to be another hot day. They left the path and scrambled along the rocks that jutted into the water until they were as far out as they could get, with the ocean sloshing and sucking at the seaweed that clung to the boulders below. David took the bag out of the pocket of his corduroys and handed it to her. She shrugged and, trying to make it look less consequential and difficult than it felt, dumped the contents into the water. They watched as a swell came in and pulled it under.

"That's that," he said.

"I doubt it, but it's a start."

They lay back on the rocks in the sun, and within minutes, she felt herself growing sleepy. David reached over and took her hand and squeezed it. Sun-drugged, she dozed off for a few minutes, and when she woke up, he was still holding her hand.

"Good nap?" he said.

"Brief." She felt as if she was swimming up to the surface of consciousness, but the heat was making it slow, heavy work. From their perch, they could see the rocky beach near the center of town where they were constructing a tower of wooden pallets for the Fourth of July bonfire.

"I'm going to do my best to make sure it all works out," he said. "The house, Mandy. I'm going to try."

This supposedly optimistic sentence made it clear he was having doubts. They were a month and a few days from the closing, and everything was still up in the air. Why had she been so resistant to a Plan B? She still hadn't heard back from Pamela, and while she wanted to think that the silence meant she was gathering up a variety of enthusiastic bids for the jewelry, she was beginning to wonder. And still, the water was so calm, and David's hand was reassuring.

"You're losing weight," she said.

"I know. It's because you're making me take all these walks. The fact that there are no Thai restaurants in town doesn't hurt either. Sometimes city living is too convenient."

"I think you should come back every Fourth so we can do this."

"You might be remarried sooner than you think."

"There's not too much that gives me more pleasure than knowing I will never remarry." This was the truth. It was like having money in the bank, not that she knew a whole lot about that. With her eyes closed and her face turned up to the sun, she said, "I slept with one of the guests."

"Thank god Sandra didn't know that. Anyone I've met?"

"A saxophonist. He's coming back in a couple of weeks. Not to stay at the house."

He squeezed her hand again. "I can't wait to hear all about it. Does he have a friend for me?"

"He probably has a wife."

"Ah, well. Not exactly what I had in mind."

Because it was so warm and because they weren't looking at each other, and because she'd just mentioned Raymond and had therefore made selfish motives seem less likely, she asked, "Is it ever what you have in mind? Women, I mean."

"No, dear. Not since you. Men are just a better fit for me. I suspect it's like finding the proper key to sing in; it just feels right. Which is odd since on the whole, I like women better as people and attribute most of what's wrong with the world to the stupidity and reckless behavior of men."

Although it meant inching closer to their past, she said, "Did you ever see Antrim again?"

He propped himself up on his elbow, looking at her, and pulled aside a strand of her hair that had blown onto her lips. "I didn't. We lost touch after the field trip to Washington. I've never tried looking him up, mostly for fear I'd find out he died."

"I liked him so much," Julie said. It was a peculiar thing to say, considering the role he'd played in their lives. But she'd been a little in love with Antrim. Once she got some distance, she decided he and David had been perfect for each other. But timing is everything, and in that, they were both unlucky.

"I liked him, too," David said. "So much. But not enough to justify hurting you." He leaned down and kissed her lightly on her mouth. "Mandy told me she thinks you have a secret boyfriend."

"Apparently, she knows about everything."

And yet, she had the nagging fear that the one thing she didn't know about was how to take care of herself.

23

The door to Beachy Keen opened, letting in a gust of steam heat, and two identical women entered. There was a 90 percent chance that *Nice and cool* would be the first words Mandy heard.

"Isn't it nice and cool in here," one woman said to Mandy. "You're lucky you get to work in the air-conditioning all day."

Instead of being on vacation like you? Mandy felt like asking. She smiled and told them she *was* lucky. Predictably, the women headed for the "sand art." The one who'd spoken held a bottle up to the other and said, "Isn't this lovely!"

Her friend mopped at her face and said, "You'd better put that down if you know what's good for you. You go home with that thing and George will divorce you. Either that or you'll drop it and there goes twenty bucks."

"You have no imagination," the woman said, although she did put it down.

The real shock was that there was a George in the picture somewhere. The two women were so similar in appearance and outfits, Mandy had assumed they were a couple. Maybe they were twin sisters.

What astonished Mandy most about working on Perry Neck was that so many of the people who came in made the exact same comments, usually in the exact same tone of voice. Maybe that shouldn't have been so surprising considering that they all wore the same pastel clothes and had the same middle-aged-mom hairdos. The do that screamed, *I'm done.* If there was one benefit to working at Beachy Keen it was that she'd begun to appreciate that no matter how annoying and scattered her mother was, no matter how sadly sincere, she was at least original. If she walked into a store like this, her first comment would have been, "Let's leave."

As for men, they were few and far between in the shop. When they did come in, they wandered around with glum expressions and, if asked by a wife or girlfriend their opinion of something, grunted and then were told they were "no fun."

Mandy heard Elaine rustling papers in the back office, a reminder that she'd better swing into action. Now that they were in the second week of July and summer was in full swing, there were more customers. But Elaine still complained that she wasn't being aggressive enough as a salesperson.

"Those are one of our biggest sellers," Mandy said. This was the line she'd been instructed to use when someone showed interest in anything and then put it down. More often than not, it worked.

Hearing that a lot of other people wanted to spend twenty dollars on a worthless bottle of sand made it all the more desirable when, clearly, it should have made it less so.

"Did you hear that, Beth? It's one of their biggest sellers."

Beth gave the bottles more serious consideration. "George will still kill you if you bring it home."

"Oh, you're no fun." She turned to Mandy, grinning that unique tourist grin that implied everyone was supposed to be happy they were on vacation. "I should have left her at home. She's no fun, is she?"

Mandy mostly wanted to get back to her notebook. She was starting to rewrite her college essay since David had praised her pages about Clara Dunston in a way that made it clear he hated it. She'd decided to switch from the nemesis question to the one about two different types of people. She'd start off saying she thought she and Clara were Cat and Dog but ended up realizing they were runts from the same litter.

"I'm not sure," Mandy said. "I don't know her."

The women appeared offended by what Mandy considered a simple statement of fact, huffed, and walked out.

Elaine came out of her office and went to the shop window. She followed the women with her eyes as they went into the next air-conditioned nightmare. Without turning to look at Mandy, she said, "If you'd tried harder, Mandy, you could have made a sale. They just went into Sunbrella, and I guaran*tee* they'll come out with a bag."

"I told her it was one of the bestsellers," Mandy said.

"Yes, but you didn't sound excited when you said it. You didn't sound enthused. Could we add a little energy and enthusiasm here?"

"I'm sorry," Mandy said.

She was, too, at least in the sense that she could see Elaine was winding up for something, and she wasn't much in the mood for a big confrontation today. If she was a failure at a job as idiotic as this one, it was proof that applying to colleges, never mind attending, was hopeless.

Elaine turned away from the window to continue her rant. She was wearing a pair of sunglasses and a straw hat. These didn't make her look "beachy" so much as "crazy."

"When the other one said the thing about the husband . . ."

"I think that was Beth," Mandy said.

"Thank you. I'll store away that *vital information*."

Elaine usually got testy when she'd been doing the books or when she'd come back from lunch with one of the other storeowners. She was skinny and high-strung like those women on TV who rarely eat and sneak bottles of wine into the trash in the morning. Mandy supposed the storeowners complained to one another about business and their pathetic employees. Also about short-term rentals. It was clear from the snippets she'd overheard that there was a group organized to try to limit or regulate them.

The tone Elaine had used to burn Mandy with "vital information" was a combination of sarcasm and anger. Mandy had dubbed it "sarcanger." The more time she spent in her little office calculating receipts and complaining about Airbnb, the sarcangrier she became.

"When she made the comment about the husband, you should

have directed her to the Beach Trees. You should have said, 'Maybe your husband would like one of our Beach Trees. They're our *Signature Item* this summer and they're *incredibly* popular with *men.*'"

Mandy said nothing. What was there to say? Despite the uptick in business, sales of the Beach Trees had not improved.

"And I'll tell you something else, *Mandy,*" Elaine said. She uttered her name dripping with sarcanger. "You're not a team player. You're wearing overalls and a flannel shirt. Who wears *a flannel shirt* to the *beach*? You have an *attitude.*"

Technically speaking, didn't everyone have an attitude?

"You don't have anything to say for yourself? You can't help me understand why sales have been down this year over last year at this time by 42 percent?"

"The economy?" Mandy asked.

"You don't think it has anything to do with the fact that you're working here this year versus last year when Lizzy Croft worked here?"

Lizzy Croft's name came up frequently. She was a salesperson of almost mythic proportions who'd managed to sell out last year's Signature Item—the T-Bag, some combination of T-shirt and tote bag—before the middle of August. Elaine had a picture of her on her desk, sitting behind the counter wearing a floral sundress, beaming. She'd gone on to a local business college, blah blah.

"No theories?" Elaine said.

"Do you really want me to tell you?" Mandy asked.

Maybe she'd sounded more serious than she intended, but Elaine actually reeled back as if Mandy had thrown something at her. "Oh, indeed I do. I'm *all ears.*"

Mandy recalled some of the things David had said about her essay in prompting her to rewrite. Too cluttered. Too crowded. She needed to edit and focus on a theme. She needed to be ruthlessly honest.

"I think there's too much in here," Mandy said. "It's hard to focus on any one thing because it's so crowded. It might help to edit. Like maybe put out two or three of every item instead of ten and fifteen. And to be honest, and I know you won't like this . . ."

"No, no. Go right ahead. It's only *my store*."

"To be honest, I've noticed that people don't really look at the Beach Trees. When I mention them to people and they do look, they avoid that side of the store. So maybe it would be good to choose a different Signature Item?"

"They *avoid* that side of the *store*? I don't think so, Mandy. I think you're making that up. You want to know what *I* think? I think they see a pouty, unenthusiastic girl dressed in *overalls* with an *attitude* and they walk out. Can you blame them?"

That stung. It was one thing for Elaine to be upset and angry, but this was personal. Boss or not, it only seemed right to her that she stick up for herself.

"The Beach Trees are ugly," she said. "No one is going to buy them because they're ugly and expensive."

Elaine composed herself and took off her sunglasses. This composure put Mandy on alert. She sensed that something bad was coming, and she had confirmation from David that she was a perceptive person.

"I'll tell you what's ugly, Mandy. What's ugly is your attitude.

And if there's one thing I can't stand, it's an attitude, not to mention an ugly attitude. You don't know what it's like to own a shop, do you? The responsibilities and the problems? The *debt*? At your age, you've had everything handed to you and you probably think it's always going to be that way. Well let me be the first to tell you, good luck with that, Miss Mandy."

Elaine looked at her with contempt and calmly adjusted the straps on her sundress.

"If you think I'm going to sit by and let an ugly attitude destroy my livelihood and my dreams, you have some growing up to do. I suggest you just pack up that notebook you're always scribbling in when you should be *dusting* and . . . go."

Mandy had done her best to follow this rant, but she was confused. "Do you mean for the afternoon or are you firing me?"

"You know something, Mandy, your life will be a lot better if you make a resolution today to stop playing the victim."

Mandy tried to process this piece of advice.

"So you mean I should come back tomorrow?"

"No, *Mandy*," she said, the sarcanger back in her voice. "That's precisely what I do *not* mean."

Mandy gathered from this that Elaine had just fired her, but for some reason didn't want to use those words. She wasn't sure how she was supposed to respond since she'd never been in a situation like this, so she began to do as told and gather up her things. There would be explaining to do at home, especially to her father, who'd let her know that having a summer job was important and part of the deal for spending the summer in Beauport. On top of that, she had planned to help her mother out since she gathered from what she'd overheard that she needed to put together a big lump of cash for the house.

As she packed up her belongings and put them into her backpack, she felt something she wouldn't have thought possible—a little pang of nostalgia for the store with all its useless and ugly clutter. It was dark and relatively small, and perched as it was over the rocks in the middle of Perry Neck, it had become, she realized, a refuge of sorts. The likelihood of anyone she knew walking in was approximately the same as her being nominated for a Grammy. No one who lived in Beauport ever went out to the Neck, let alone shopped there. Why hadn't she realized the unlikely appeal of the store sooner? Maybe she was doomed always to realize things only when it was too late.

As she was heading to the door, Elaine popped out of her office and leaned against the doorjamb.

"Mandy," she said. "I just want you to know, sweetheart, that I don't blame you for your behavior."

Mandy was about to point out that she'd just fired her for her behavior, but the "sweetheart" had come as such a shock, she forgot to say anything.

"I know you've had a rough couple of years with your parents divorcing and all that."

"They're not officially divorced yet."

"See, this is what I mean about your attitude, Mandy. I'm on your side, sweetie. Or I'm trying to be. Everyone knows your mother has *issues,* and that's not your fault."

She went into her office and returned with money in her hand. "Here. Have a decent lunch or something." She handed Mandy a twenty-dollar bill. "And please don't put me in the awkward position of asking me for a letter of recommendation. It's not going to happen."

Mandy looked at the money and then back at Elaine, but she was having trouble seeing her through tears. "I don't need any recommendations from you," she said. "Someone already offered me a job. And don't talk about my mother. She's a better person than you'll ever be. And I don't need your charity." She took the twenty and hurled it onto the floor.

At the door, she thought better of it, turned back and snatched up the rumpled bill. "But I'll take it," she said.

24

As soon as she stepped onto the street, Mandy had an urge to comment on the heat and humidity, just like every predictable customer that came into Beachy Keen. Unlike them, though, she had no one to say it to.

Cars were not allowed out on Perry Neck, but the streets were packed with sweating people staggering along with stupefied expressions and limp hair, as if they were waiting to be herded to some cooler, happier place. She let herself be swept along by the crowd for a little while, just beginning to accept the fact that she'd lost her job and probably with good reason. She'd had a bad attitude about the store even before she was hired. She never said anything insulting to any of the customers, but maybe her feelings showed through.

The only person who wouldn't freak out and start accusing her was David, but she couldn't call him. He had enough on his plate already, and he and her mother were going to a party at Amira's house this afternoon. She wondered if drunk David would be as supportive.

She broke away from the pack and headed off the Neck and toward the center of town. The Village Green, as Elaine had told her to call it because it sounded more quaint. Well, she had, even though the Village Green was more like a traffic island in the middle of two busy streets. There were a few benches there and a couple of planters that the garden club maintained annually until late August, at which point they gave up watering and let the geraniums and impatiens wither and die. There were a couple of suffering trees in the middle, too, so there was at least the hint of shade.

As she was halfway across the street to the green, she saw that Lindsay was sitting on a bench there with a girl on either side of her. She couldn't turn around because she'd get hit by a car, and besides, it would look too weird. With what seemed like telepathy, Lindsay looked up at that instant and made eye contact with her.

It was obvious why Lindsay never called her anymore and didn't answer her texts. The two other girls, both sitting up on the back of the bench, were popular. Lindsay was moving up the food chain. Michelle was a skinny blonde who was alleged to have "an amazing voice" and was treated like a reigning pop star whenever she sang at talent shows or in a school play. Mandy found her high, reedy vocals grating, but she did envy her ability to get up on stage and actually pull off a performance. Whether or not Michelle was a great singer, she had confidence, and when you came down to it, confidence might be the root of all talent. She had over ten thousand followers on Instagram, mostly because her family had vacationed in Lake Placid last summer, and Michelle had bumped into Lana Del Rey and her sister on the street and taken a series of photos with them that made it seem like they were best friends. Also because she was a vegan, even though at this moment she appeared to be eating frozen yogurt.

The other girl was Wallis. As far as Mandy could tell, her popularity was based on the fact that she had an unusual name and was going to transfer to Buckingham Browne & Nichols for her senior year, a school where Mindy Kaling and the actor from *Psycho* had gone. She too had confidence, not about any particular talent but the fact that she thought she was better than everyone else in general.

Lindsay waved, a little shyly, as Mandy stepped onto the green. All three girls were eating out of gigantic neon orange cups from the self-serve yogurt place around the corner. Michelle actually spoke to her. "Oh, Mandy. Great. You can take a picture of us. I want to get the sign for the candy store in the background."

As humiliating as it was to be asked to perform this service, it at least gave her something to do with her hands. As she was snapping the photo and Michelle and Wallis were draping themselves over the bench to look like models, she realized it was a lot less embarrassing to be on her side of the camera than in the middle of these two wannabes the way Lindsay was. She handed the camera back to Michelle. It was a Sony something or other that looked expensive, a toy she'd probably persuaded her parents to buy for her as an investment in her career in social media mediocrity.

"You should get some of this," Wallis said, holding up the cup. "The taro root is incredible."

"I'm not exactly hungry," Mandy said.

Michelle, who clearly had a complicated relationship with food, eyed her up and down suspiciously. "Aren't you broiling in those clothes?" she asked.

Mandy was still reeling from having been kicked out of the store by Elaine, and all of this struck her as irrelevant noise.

"I just got fired," she found herself replying.

Lindsay, who was the first person Mandy had told when she got the job—way back when it seemed like they were friends—looked genuinely concerned. Poor Lindsay. Mandy had always had trouble controlling her temper around her, so she understood why she'd stopped returning her calls. What she didn't understand was why she missed Lindsay more than she'd have guessed. "What are you going to do now?" she asked.

"Maybe your mother can hire you to make beds or something," Michelle said.

So Lindsay had told them about the room-rental thing, even though Mandy had sworn her to secrecy.

"I don't think that's going to happen," Mandy said. "I'm doing it for free anyway, why would she suddenly pay me?"

"So why did you get fired?" Lindsay said.

"No offense," Wallis said, "but it's not like it's the most unimaginable thing in the world, Mandy getting fired."

Mandy knew this was intended as a blow, but she didn't have the energy to be offended. "She said I have a bad attitude. I guess I do."

"What are you going to do about a job?" Lindsay said. "Your mother will kill you."

Lindsay's mother was more the killer type; she kept a 24/7 watch on her daughter and monitored her every online search and phone call. She spent more time on the school portal than the teachers and knew every assignment and test score before her daughter did.

"I have a couple of options," Mandy said.

"You should get an internship," Michelle said. "That's what we're doing. It looks a lot better on your CV for colleges."

Mandy wondered if the "we" included Lindsay. Last she'd heard, Lindsay was working for minimum wage at the day care center a few towns over that her mother managed. It wasn't exciting, but it was probably the perfect job for Lindsay since she claimed to be interested in education and had always been one of those girls who was destined to work with kids. It was impossible to imagine her doing anything else. People said she had a great understanding of children, but from what Mandy could tell, it was more that she had a great desire to remain one herself. Brett, Lindsay's so-called boyfriend, admired this immaturity and the baby voice Lindsay sometimes lapsed into. Red flags!

"What's your internship?" she asked Michelle. She might have asked Wallis, but wasn't all that interested.

"I'm working at the music festival. Since I'm planning to go to Berklee College of Music, it's great experience on my CV."

There was something embarrassing about the fact that Michelle had used the expression "CV" twice in the last few minutes. She could see Michelle sitting down at the kitchen table with her mother—a duplicate of Michelle, except worn, like a library copy of the Hunger Games trilogy—writing up this document and congratulating each other. Based on how she behaved in the audience of shows Michelle performed in, her mother was living through her daughter. At least Julie knew she and Mandy were different people.

The three-week chamber music festival had a national reputation. The concerts were considered "serious," a nice way of saying "boring."

"What do you do there?" Mandy asked.

"I work in the box office and sometimes in the gift shop."

"So it's kind of like working in a store except you don't get paid?"

"Wow," Wallis said. "You're really negative, Mandy."

She got up to throw away her yogurt cup, and Michelle handed her hers. Mandy saw that it was still half full. Like exactly half full, as if her portion had been sliced with a knife, right down the middle. Since the yogurt came from a self-serve place, why not just put less in to begin with?

Wallis turned to face them with her back against the trash barrel. She had an expression of cartoonish surprise on her face, eyes and mouth perfect circles, and she shook her hands as if she was trying to dry them. "Don't look now," she said, "but Craig Crespo's van is headed this way."

Mandy felt a thump in her chest. She wasn't sure if she was excited by this news or alarmed. She wasn't thrilled that he was going to see her with these girls since the only real compliment he'd ever paid her was saying that she wasn't like them.

"Whoever gets the best shot of him gets to post it," Michelle said.

"Where?" Mandy asked.

"There's a Craig Crespo hashtag on Instagram," Michelle said. "It's hilarious."

Mandy doubted it was. In fact, she doubted Michelle thought it was because the way she said "hilarious" made it sound a lot more like "exciting" in a sexual way. She also said it as a reproach to Mandy, like she couldn't possibly get how hilarious it was.

As the van approached, Wallis and Michelle got their phones ready. To Lindsay's credit, she didn't. Mandy had an urge to duck, but then she remembered that she'd long ago decided that if you were going to do something, it was better to look as if you were proud of what you were doing.

The van, which had once been white and was now a dusty shade of something else, sped past them and then, half a block away, stopped and began to back up. This produced a flurry of nervous excitement. Michelle and Wallis, who'd wandered to the edge of the green to get a photo, dashed back to the bench like children and pretended to be involved in their phones. The fact that Lindsay hadn't played along made Mandy realize that no matter how annoying she could be, there was a reason they'd once been friends.

Craig pulled up against the curb and stuck his head out, the headband a reminder of the afternoon they'd gone up to the water tower. "Hey, ladies," he said.

"Hey, gentleman," Wallis said in a surprisingly deep and mature way. It seemed like something she'd practiced and made it clear that she and the senior boy she'd dated last year had probably gone all the way.

This made Craig laugh. "You got *that* wrong."

There was a little more back and forth that Mandy felt completely excluded from. She checked out, mostly because she felt jealous and betrayed, like the time she'd spent with him in the van hadn't happened. Then, through the fog of laughter and cooing, she distinctly heard him say, "You want a ride, Mandy?"

Everything around her froze. Michelle and Wallis looked at her with disbelief that she suspected would quickly morph into some version of jealous anger. Lindsay was staring at her in slack-jawed wonder. When Mandy stood, Lindsay said quietly, "What are you *doing*, Mandy?"

"What?" Mandy said. "It's just a ride."

But as she opened the door and looked back at the expressions on the faces of the girls, she understood clearly that it was much, much more than that; it was a triumph.

25

This has nothing to do with a lawsuit," Michael said, "so you don't have to make the mandatory apologies about not being litigious before attempting to cash in. You have a lease, your landlady is selling, and you're getting kicked out. It's a buyout. They're as common as almond milk in this town. Even more so in New York. Someone there held out for seventeen million a few years back. Don't get your hopes up, dear; I'm not suggesting you're in the seven-figure league. San Francisco has good tenants' rights, but sadly, you're not in a wheelchair or in your late nineties."

"Some days I could pass for ninety, if that helps."

"I think you're looking at low six figures, assuming you let them know you're willing to play hardball."

This was an encouraging sum, already far better than David had been hoping. "Who pays it?" David asked.

"The landlady, of course. She's making millions. It's not as if it cuts into her profit in any meaningful way."

The whole idea still struck him as exploitive. After his land-lady had been reasonable about the rent for so many years, this was a betrayal. The only way he could justify it was by reminding himself that he wasn't using the money selfishly.

"How would you define 'hardball'?" he asked.

"You start off asking for an outrageous sum, and then you let them know you're willing to hold out and torpedo the deal until they make a decent counteroffer. It helps that Soren and the sur-geon want to close by the end of the summer. If they back out, the landlady has to go through relisting and having showings and all those unpleasant things she avoided by having the buyer handed to her."

That might be true, but what was less helpful was that Julie needed the money as soon as possible. David had no desire to tell Michael why he wanted the buyout or what he planned to do with it, but it was probably best to emphasize his own timeline now, be-fore Michael began investing energy in the project.

"I should let you know that I want to settle the matter as quickly as we can. Have you contacted Renata yet?"

"No, but I can't wait. She's dropped over a few more times; I act as if we're old friends, a sort of gaslight approach since I can tell she's scrambling to figure out who the hell I am and why I seem to know her. It's great fun. I make her espresso."

"I'm glad you're enjoying yourself. What's your commission?"

"I was joking when I mentioned that. I couldn't take a penny.

But if I were the sort of person who could, 30 percent would be standard."

"I'll keep that in mind. When can you get the ball rolling?"

"I have a letter written up, and if you tell me how to use the printer you've got here, I'll send it certified mail to Miss Renata this afternoon."

"Wouldn't it be easier to just go to the Penthouse and use your own?"

"I'm trying to make the most of every minute I have here. You were so right about boys and real estate. Last night . . ."

David did not want to hear the details of what Michael was doing in a place he still considered home. And in his own bed. Especially since he had nothing to contribute in response. He'd walked past Kenneth's store a few times, but business seemed to have picked up, and he didn't want to intrude. The one time he had gone in, there had been a high school student behind the counter, and he ended up buying more dog biscuits and leaving without asking about Kenneth.

"I hate to cut you off," David said, "but I have to go to a cocktail party."

"How 1950s. I suppose there's a lot of alcoholism in that town."

"It's a small town on the ocean with a commuter train to the city and a lot of tennis courts and churches. You do the math. Let me know when you hear back."

David mentioned none of this to Julie as they walked to Amira's house. It had been a few days since the woman had dropped off the jewelry. He was going to have to tell her the bad news soon, but if he could tell her something definite about the buyout, it would soften the blow. She'd been dealing with the benefits office at Crawford School about her retirement and had lined up closing out her accounts. There, too, she was ending up with less than she'd been expecting, thanks to penalty fees and taxes.

They cut through an opening in the privet hedge and walked up the driveway. Although the house had been completed only two years earlier, the yard was lush with the impeccable gardens and mature trees that money can install, full-grown and healthy, in an afternoon.

As for the house itself, it was a striking two-story glass box, a nice contrast to the heavy Victorian piles and dull, shingled Capes that David had begun to tire of. It was surrounded by soft lights that blended with the early evening glow to create an amber halo around the whole property.

"Impressive," he said.

"It's meant to be," Julie said. "But don't be too seduced by it. There was a beautiful house here from more or less the same period as mine. One day, I came from work and saw it had been extracted, like a bad tooth. If Henry has his way, Richard will do the same to mine, all for the sake of a pool. As if we don't have enough problems with the water table."

"Anything I should know about the guests in advance?" he asked.

"They'll probably assume we're a couple. And by their standards, we are. Most of them brag about sleeping in different rooms and not having had sex since the nineties."

The interior of the house was stark. What furniture there was was low and light in color with the crisp lines of starched shirts.

There was so much neutral fabric and glass and reflecting metal, all of it seemed to disappear before your eyes the longer you looked. There were more people than David had expected, but the central room was so open and expansive, it still felt airy and un-derpopulated. Given what he knew of Amira and her relationship to the town, he suspected most had come not out of friendship but to get a look at the décor.

David grabbed two glasses of wine from a passing tray and handed one to Julie. She refused it and went to hunt down Amira and her conniving husband. She seemed to be dealing with sobriety with uncomplaining stoicism, although he was noticing a little dis-traction creeping in around the edges. She seemed happiest when he was reading to her in the evening, both of them carried off to-gether to another time and place, which they entered through the window of *Queen Lucia*. They were more than halfway through the book and already debating what occurred in the next volume.

One of the most striking aspects of the gathered multitudes was that they'd parted, like the Red Sea in *The Ten Command-ments*, into two groups. In this case, segregated along strict gen-der lines, all of the men along one side of the room, the women off to the other. It could have been a dance at a junior high, mi-nus the expectations of hookups and the fears of pregnancy. The males were typical of the suburbanites David had grown up among—men who'd lost touch with their bodies a decade earlier, allowed themselves to be dressed by their wives, and grudgingly accepted being infantilized by spouses and children. The women's efforts at keeping themselves fit and groomed were clearly aimed at each other since they'd become as invisible to the men as the men were to them.

As he was surveying the crowd, trying to decide which side of the room to go to, he was approached by two smiling women who were probably in their early fifties. (Since turning fifty himself, years earlier, David had acquired mysteriously accurate abilities to evaluate the ages of others.) They introduced themselves as Maureen and Sheila. When David asked for clarification about who was who, one of them said, "Let's not go there. You won't remember anyway."

Good point. They were similar in terms of height (nondescript) and weight (healthily robust) and a slight blotchiness of complexion that one often saw in seaside communities where people tended to spend too much time sitting in the sun at midday and drinking wine at night. Michael's guess had hit the mark precisely. They were both beautiful women who radiated the athletic, alcoholic glamour of lady golfers. Their style of declining beauty, with its aura of decay, was as authentic as that of an eighteen-year-old supermodel, but, like the decaying beauty of Detroit, a good deal less marketable.

They assured David they knew all about him as an ex while at the same time asking pointed questions about how he got along with Julie's husband, an obvious attempt to sniff out the current status of his relationship with Julie. He deflected by asking them about themselves, clearly what they most wanted to discuss anyway.

They'd been friends since college. One was married and had lived in Beauport for decades, the other was recently widowed and had moved here to be closer to her old friend.

"Which is your husband?" he asked the married one.

She waved a hand toward the other side of the room and said, "He's over there. Take your pick. They're all pretty much the same. Sheila and I are much closer than me and whatshisname. Since men and women can marry and now gay couples, I wish they'd legalize friendship unions."

This would solve a lot of problems, he agreed, thinking that Julie had been right: in this crowd, their relationship was standard fare.

Maureen and Sheila had an established routine of quips and mild insults, one more dominant, the other the more frequent butt of jokes. All couples start off as Romeo and Juliet and end up as Laurel and Hardy.

When he asked them how they knew Amira, the married one said, "Everyone knows Amira. Naturally, she has no idea who we are."

"We're not male," the other said. "She can't abide women."

"And having been friends with each other for thirty years, we sympathize."

"Don't listen to her, David. Her misogyny goes back to her horrible mother."

"It's true," the other said. "My mother was awful. A real . . . oh, what's that word? The terrible one that begins with a 'C'?"

"Catholic?" David asked.

The two were delighted by this comeback (which also turned out to be true) and lapsed into companionable laughter. He could tell they would incorporate the line into their routine, probably as a bit they'd work out before the evening was over. They had an air of shared secrets about misguided drunken episodes from their past that probably counted as their fondest memories.

Once it was clear they'd run through everything they could possibly talk about, David excused himself and went to find Julie. He was distracted by the sight of the bartender, one of those people who is so good-looking he has an almost alien appearance that's as disconcerting as it is irresistible. David enjoyed the safety of flirting with this sort of person. The difference in age and looks was so great, there was no question of being taken seriously. It was like the time he and Michael had gone to an open house for a six-million-dollar apartment: it was so obvious they were out of their depth, no one resented them for their voyeurism.

Guthrie (naturally he couldn't have a simple name like "Bob") did him the kindness of responding with patient indulgence. While making a comment about the heat that might be interpreted as a crass double entendre, he felt the presence of someone behind him, and turned to see Kenneth from the kitchen store. He had his arms folded across his chest and a wineglass in one hand. In this light, and after gazing at Guthrie for five minutes, Kenneth's relatively normal good looks were a visual relief. He seemed spectacularly accessible and, relative to everyone else there, practically a friend.

"Greetings," David said. "I'm the almost-uncle of Mandy, who—"

"Yes," he said. "I know who you are. I hope I'm not interrupting a meaningful conversation."

"We were discussing vernal ponds," David said.

"Oh? I was under the impression you were discussing your interest in unobtainable men."

"Now, now. Guthrie and I are old buddies from high school."

"If I were you, I wouldn't admit to hanging around high schools." He paused, sipped, and suggested David follow him to the rooftop deck. "There are beautiful views and fewer distractions." With quiet and surprising sincerity, he added, "I'd love to show you."

David was flattered by this comment as one is always flattered by a show of kindness from an otherwise impossible person. He told Kenneth he'd noticed in walking past his store that it was often crowded. "I gather business has picked up."

"In sheer numbers of people, yes. Unfortunately, everyone is looking for a bargain. They're all Airbnb-ers."

"I see."

Kenneth was dressed in the same polo shirt and shorts outfit he'd been wearing in the store that first day they'd met, with the same set of keys dangling from a lanyard around his neck. As David followed him up a glass staircase to the roof, he enjoyed watching Kenneth's ascent, which, with its calculated rolling gait, seemed to have been learned from Marilyn Monroe.

The deck was almost the size of the footprint of the house and had unobstructed views of the harbor in one direction and the hills above town in the other. It was furnished with the stark, refined taste of the rooms below, with one enormous chaise longue in a corner, adding an Alice in Wonderland note of whimsy. Although Julie's house was right next door, the breeze here felt cooler, and the air smelled fresher.

There was a small group of people on the far side of the deck, sitting on an austere wooden bench and smoking cigarettes. One woman was brushing back her hair with her hand as she clasped the cigarette between two fingers and tilted her head to exhale. The gesture was rooted in 1930s notions of allure, but in the context of current attitudes toward cigarettes, it made her look slightly demented. It was hard to pull off these gestures since cigarettes had become more commonly associated with chemotherapy than with Lauren Bacall.

"Is your husband here tonight?" David asked.

"I don't have one."

"I'm sorry, I thought you mentioned a husband when I met you in the store."

"I did, but only because I wanted to let you know I'm gay."

A simple hello would have been sufficient, David didn't say. "I thought you were warning me off."

"I was hoping to encourage you."

David was charmed by the lack of guile. "I like that you cut to the chase."

"Taking age into consideration, I thought it was best."

"You're hardly old," David said.

"I was referring to your age, not mine."

David laughed at this, and then gazed at him with what he hoped was a serious, assertive look. "You don't have to work quite so hard with me, Kenneth. You have my full attention already." He moved a little closer to him, so their arms were brushing. The sky was heavy, and the breeze was picking up. A line of dark clouds was blowing in. "How well do you know Amira?" he asked.

"She comes into my store and buys a lot of things she probably never uses or eats."

David pointed at Julie's house, off to their right and looking, from this vantage point, like the unfortunately plain sister of a younger beauty. "Has she ever said anything to you about wanting to buy Julie's house?"

"I don't believe most of what she says, which makes her more entertaining."

From this, David gathered she'd discussed the issue with him, which probably meant she'd spread the word around town.

"You should invite me out one night," Kenneth said.

"I'm considering it," David said, "but I'm risk averse. I want to be sure you'll accept."

"It would depend on what you propose."

"How about a movie? Julie told me there's an eccentric movie theater in Hammond with sofas and end tables that shows subtitled foreign films."

"I have lowbrow tastes," Kenneth said. "In case that wasn't obvious. I consider reading and watching a movie two different and incompatible activities."

"A long beach walk?"

"I don't like sand."

"I don't either, now that you mention it. On top of that, it looks like it's going to start raining soon. We seem to be out of luck."

The sky looked increasingly dark and threatening and the little group of smokers had made their way down the dramatic staircase.

"I'm a good cook," Kenneth said. "I could invite you for dinner."

"That's kind," David said. "But I'm trying to lose weight."

"I've noticed. And don't worry, I didn't say there'd actually be food."

Without the preliminary warning of stray drops, it began to pour.

26

W hat are the odds," Craig said, "that the story of me pick-ing you up is going to spread through your school like an oil spill?"

"If you'd picked up one of them, it would have spread a lot faster. They'd have made sure of it."

What she meant, but didn't want to say directly, was that there was a fair amount of status involved in being picked up by him, and since Michelle and Wallis looked down on her, they weren't about to do her the favor of making sure their classmates knew.

"Those girls look like the types who'd faint if you farted in front of them," he said.

"I won't faint if you do, but I'd still rather you didn't."

Craig was wearing an olive-green T-shirt and it made his eyes look incredibly beautiful. She hadn't noticed before what a clear, light green they were and how they made sense of all the other heavy features of his face. The T-shirt wasn't exactly clean, and she could see sweat stains under the arms. Maybe he'd worn it to bring out his eyes. She hated vanity, but she was willing to overlook it in his case because his looks were so clearly one of the main things he had going for him. She could see in the slant of the early evening light coming in the windshield that he had a small scar on the right side of his jaw. She had an urge to reach out and touch it, but of course she didn't. It was odd to her that there were things about his face she hadn't noticed before. What else was she missing?

"So I just got fired from my job," she said.

He carefully negotiated a corner, while peering into the side mirror of the van, and turned onto the road to Hammond. The flashing red-and-blue warning lights went off in her head, but she ignored them. He said, "No big surprise there. You probably had a shitty attitude."

He'd made it sound like a compliment, so for the first time today, she was almost proud of having failed. "How'd you guess?"

"Why wouldn't you? You hated the idea of working there from the start."

She was sure she'd never told him this and the fact that he'd guessed it so accurately made her feel for a moment as if he knew her better than she knew herself. It was a strange feeling, because usually she thought she knew others better than they knew themselves.

"So now you'll have a lot more free time on your hands," he said. "Which is a good thing for me. Now you have no excuse for not working for me."

She had known this was coming, and even though there was something sketchy in the idea, right now it was nice to know somebody wanted her.

"I'm not exactly a computer wizard."

"I'm betting you're a fast learner."

They were heading along the ocean, and overhead, it looked as if there was going to be a rain shower. "I hate to be nosy," she said, "but are we headed someplace?"

"I'm taking you to my house to lock you up in the basement," he said.

If someone was actually going to do this, they probably wouldn't tell you first. And anyway, he'd kissed her, which meant they weren't complete strangers. "Coming from someone else," she said, "that might be a lot funnier."

"Here's what you don't realize: I'm the least scary person you know, Amanda."

She didn't think this was true, but he was, without question, the most interesting and exciting person she knew, and if there was something scary about him as well, it seemed like a fair trade-off. "Here's what *you* don't realize," she said. "My name's not 'Amanda.' Just 'Mandy.'"

She never talked about her name with anyone, except when she lost her temper and screamed at her mother about it, even though it wasn't entirely her mother's fault. But she felt like opening up to Craig because she knew somehow he'd get it and wouldn't hold it against her.

"I was named after a song by Barry Manilow. Ever hear of him?"

"Oh, yeah. My mother was a big fan. Used to go to his concerts at casinos with a bunch of other old ladies."

"Yeah, exactly."

"Kind of like Liberace but without the jewelry and the boys."

"I think there were probably a lot of boys. Anyway, one of his big hit songs was this incredibly lame ballad called 'Mandy,' and my father loved it and wanted to name me after it."

"At least it was a hit. Sing it for me."

"You don't think I memorized it, do you?"

He turned away from the road for a second, looked through her with his pretty eyes, and said, "Yeah, I do. I think your father used to sing it to you every night when he put you in bed and wanted you to go to sleep and you used to think it was the sweetest thing in the world and you'd cry and have a fit if he didn't sing it to his little girl because you loved the sound of his voice so much you couldn't go to sleep without it. Then he moved out and left you and your mom and it got all mixed up with how angry you felt toward him and now you bury your head under the pillow anytime he tries to serenade you."

This was such an eerily accurate description of her life and her childhood and her current feelings about her father, her head started to spin. She was literally dizzy.

"How did you know he left my mother?"

"It's written all over your face," he said. "Plus, don't forget, I have access to all the computers at your school."

"So you looked me up?"

"Maybe. Or maybe I'm just really good at guessing."

She knew, through gossip and by searching for his name online, that his father, a fisherman, had died about ten years earlier and that his mother, who'd worked for the food service at Hammond Junior High, had died more recently, both from lung cancer, according to the obituaries she'd read. There was something in Craig's snarky personality that made it impossible to imagine him having had a good relationship with his father. Probably the father had been jealous of his looks and had been a drunk. Drinking was a common enough problem in Hammond, and now heroin was becoming more of one. Probably Craig had been beaten. Maybe that was where he'd gotten the scar on his face. This thought made her want to reach across the seat and touch him, even though she had a low opinion of girls with rescue fantasies who were attracted to boys primarily because they wanted to save them from themselves.

They were driving past the tidal marshes behind Safe Haven Beach, and the air smelled salty. The sky was darker than before. As they crossed into Hammond, a fierce downpour started, as if a tap had been opened full. Craig swore and turned on his wipers. They slapped noisily from side to side without doing a whole lot besides making the windows even more streaked.

The downtown of Hammond had once been a thriving center for shopping with an emphasis on the practical. Not that Mandy had any actual memories of that, but she'd been told so many times by her mother and father as they drove through town about the great shoe store that had been *right there* and the old-fashioned hardware store that had sold *everything* (whatever that meant) that she felt as if she'd seen them. What she had seen growing up was the steep decline of the town, with half the stores empty and shut-

tered. Things had turned around again, but it was the opposite of
what it had been, with the most impractical stores imaginable—
florists whose most expensive arrangements were the ones with
the fewest flowers; bakeries that made fifteen loaves of bread so
they'd sell out daily—plus yoga studios and some expensive restaurants with pretentious names like "Twice" and "Parsnips" and
"Flaubert's." Craig drove through downtown quickly, the windshield wipers snapping.

Just beyond the downtown was a gritty little neighborhood
that stuck out into the harbor like a thumb, a thumb with dirt
under its nail. It could have been one of the nicer parts of town
and no doubt probably would be again one day, but there had been
a fishery out there that had dominated the neighborhood. It had
closed years ago, but the whole area still smelled of fish, especially
on humid days, when all those murdered cod took their revenge
and their smell rose out of the pavement like zombies.

They pulled into the driveway of a small turquoise house that,
like all of its neighbors, was surrounded by a chain link fence and,
like most of them, was sided in aluminum that had probably been
put on so long ago, it qualified as hip. Also in keeping with its
neighborhood, the house had a few religious statues in the front
yard. Since Mandy couldn't imagine Craig going out to hunt
down a bathtub Mary, she assumed they were holdovers from
his parents.

"Do you live here alone?" she asked.

He turned off the engine and the windshield wipers stopped
and the rain quickly made it impossible to look out.

"Since my mother died. I had to buy my sister out. Believe me, she and her husband didn't need the money, and they certainly didn't need the market value of the house. That's why it's always good to know people's secrets, Mandy."

She gathered from this that he'd held some threat over his sister's head to get her to agree to give him a good deal on the house. It should have made him seem like a thug, but Mandy took an instant dislike to his sister, based on nothing except the fact that Craig clearly didn't like her.

"I'm going to dash in and open the door. When I'm inside, you run in. I don't want you standing out there while I'm trying to get the door unlocked."

"I don't mind the rain," she said. "Anyway, it was just a downpour. It's letting up already."

"I don't like people knowing my business. Wait till I get in."

He dashed out into the rain and spent a minute negotiating the lock and then pushed the door open with his shoulder. He fell into the house, her cue.

The back door led into the kitchen, which is to say straight into the 1960s or some other decade well before she was born. It was all yellow-and-black tile, yellow floral wallpaper, and big yellow appliances. It was probably supposed to look cheerful, like one of those sitcom kitchens in shows that turn up on TV Land, but it looked sad. Retro was okay as an expensive design choice, but the real thing just looked old. And, case in point, too real. There were food smells, greasy, bacony smells that undoubtedly had been cooked into the tiles when Craig was a kid.

Craig was making feeble attempts at cleaning up the kitchen, tossing a few dirty dishes into the sink and closing some cabinets.

She was touched by the fact that he wanted to make a good impression on her, even if the effort was a failure. His green T-shirt was stained darker in places by the rain, and his hair was flattened against his head in front.

He went to the yellow refrigerator and took out a beer, and she sat down at the Formica kitchen table. There was a burn mark in the middle that had to have been there for decades. He hoisted himself up onto the counter near the sink and sat facing her, drinking the beer.

"Do you drink beer all the time or only when you're around me?" she asked.

"So Mandy got fired," he said. "Congratulations."

They were back to him not answering her questions.

"It's my major accomplishment for the week," she said. In that moment, for the first time, it somehow felt as if it was.

"How much were they paying you?"

She shrugged. "I'm not planning on buying any real estate."

He took another swallow from the bottle and wiped off his mouth with his hand. "I can't tell if you know how cute you are or if you don't and that's what makes you so cute."

Hearing this made her unaccountably happy, as if she was being told the thing she'd been waiting her whole life to hear, despite her wariness about that word. Weirder still, having heard it applied to her, she desperately wanted to hear it again.

He came over to where she was sitting and kissed her on the mouth—that cool, beery taste again. Looking at him as he stood near her, she saw that he was shorter than she'd realized. "You know you've got something all those little girls you hang out with haven't got and you know they're all too stuck up and busy post-ing their pictures of themselves and their little faces on their In-stagram accounts to realize it."

She almost felt as if she was going to start crying because once again, he'd guessed exactly what she thought to be true. Or hoped to be true.

He pulled her chair out from the table more and straddled her and actually sat on her lap, looking into her eyes. He was lighter than she thought he'd be, and she hoped he couldn't tell her legs were shaking.

"You know you're special, but you don't really know how. You've got a talent, but you've never known what it was. But guess what, Mandy? I do."

It didn't seem likely to her that this was true, but what if it was?

"And you know what else? I'm going to show you. And you're going to be making so much more money than you would have made all summer at that store, you won't believe it."

It seemed odd that making money had come into the equation so suddenly. It was pretty much the last thing she was interested in right now.

"And in case you were wondering," he said, "I'm not even going to touch you."

A funny thing to say since he was straddling her legs. This close to him, his eyes looked a little crazy, and she saw that he had long, almost feminine eyelashes. Probably his father had accused him of being "pretty."

He put his forearms on her shoulders and leaned in so their foreheads were touching and he started to sing "Mandy" to her.

He knew all the words and even though he had the tune a little off, he had a decent voice. *"You came and you gave without taking ... Oh Mandy."* Against all odds, it made her feel so calm, it was almost as if she was being lulled to sleep.

"Let's go downstairs," he said. "I want to show you something."

"So you really are going to chain me up in the basement?"

He pulled her up out of the chair. "There's only one way to find out, isn't there?"

Whenever she saw a movie in which a character was doing stupid or crazy things because they wanted to experience everything to find out about life, she was filled with wary admiration, mostly because they were brave enough to be irresponsible. For herself, she always thought there was a better approach to figuring out about life—like maybe using your imagination? Or, for that matter, Google. Usually, she backed away from the edge of dangerous experience and steep cliffs and took the cautious route home. Then she got angry at her parents for raising her to be a coward. As she stood in the greasy kitchen, she felt she had an opportunity to make up for all that.

He opened the door to the basement and flicked on the light. "You coming along?" he asked. It was fate that Craig had driven through town shortly after she got fired. Why else had she gotten in with him and let him drive her this far if not for the opportunity to be, for once, the fearless, irresponsible heroine of the story of her own life?

27

When Julie looked across Amira's living room and saw David and Kenneth descend the staircase, both wet and grinning, she felt a stab of jealousy. She wasn't sure why. If decades of separation hadn't killed their friendship, it was unlikely a date or a hookup with this man would. And yet, despite what she'd said to David earlier about couples, it was true that there were evenings when they were lying on the sofa and he was reading to her that she had a longing to curl up with him. Not to have sex—that was happily off the table—but to share a deeper physical intimacy.

When Kenneth had attached himself to a group of admiring women—customers no doubt—David wandered over to her.

"You look happy," Julie said.

"Pleasantly distracted but wet. I should head home and dry off. Ready to leave?"

"Very."

As they were headed to the door, Amira's husband intercepted them. "Not going so soon, are you?"

He was wearing light, fitted clothes and what appeared to be expensive leather sneakers. He kissed Julie on both cheeks, an affectation he'd picked up from Amira or perhaps his mysterious business excursions.

"I'm afraid David got caught in the rain," she said.

"But not you," he said. "You look more lovely than ever." He shook David's hand and said, "If I were a younger man, I couldn't be trusted living next door."

It was the privilege of wealthy men married to beautiful, younger women to flirt outrageously with women like her, women he would not, under any circumstances, touch. It was as close to insult as it was to compliment, but she appreciated it anyway.

Richard was a tall, imposing man. His long face was not unlined, but there was a taut perfection to his jawline that struck her as implausible on a man his age. Prior to learning about his interest in her house, Julie had developed a crush on him, probably because he appeared solid and unflappable. He made her feel he was on her side in his ruthless, right-wing way. It was, therefore, especially chilling to think of him as working against her behind her back, with Henry's assistance. It was impossible to imagine that he hadn't chosen to marry Amira as a decorative object, but Julie had noted an indulgent protectiveness he had toward her that she was convinced was born of love and made him a more sympathetic and interesting man.

She introduced David and added that he was her ex-husband.

"How could you possibly let a woman like Julie get away?" he asked.

The facile comment was to be expected, but Julie was pleased that he remembered her name. He was that imposing.

Richard asked David if he, like Julie, was "in the arts." He was a politician at heart. He remembered a few facts about people—possibly with the guide of sophisticated mnemonic devices he'd learned at mind-control seminars—and then hauled them out, not out of interest but to show off that he knew something about you.

Richard listened, or appeared to listen, as David explained his work. "I have two teenaged daughters," he said. "One's about to start applying to college. I'd love to put you in contact with her. She lives in Iowa with her mother, but she's coming here in late August for a week. Will you be around?"

"That's not clear," David said. "I'm helping Mandy with school, and helping Julie with the paperwork to buy the house from Henry."

Richard had no reaction to this comment but said in an unreadable way, "Henry is a good man. He just doesn't know how to take 'maybe' for an answer."

The rain had stopped, and the streets, when they stepped outside, were slick from the earlier downpour. After a few days of heat, the air smelled of damp earth and refreshed flowers. As she and David walked home, she said, "What do you think he meant when he said Henry can't take 'maybe' for an answer?"

"I'm not sure exactly, but considering the context, I'd say it has something to do with the house."

"It worries me that I haven't heard back from the woman who has my mother's jewelry. She said it wouldn't take more than three weeks and it's coming up on the third week."

"People always underestimate," he said.

"Maybe I should call."

He took her arm. "Give it another week," he said. "Whatever happens, we'll figure it out."

Even if his optimism wasn't convincing, his calm was catching. Why wouldn't she want to believe he could help her make things work out?

"I've added a new item to your Seven Steps," he said. "It's a big one. Ready? I think we should invite Henry and his girlfriend for dinner."

"I don't see that being a glittering success as a social event," Julie said.

"Probably not, but it might be useful. Make it for a few weeks from now. We'll have a better handle on the finances, and I'll have made more progress with Mandy. It will also force us to get through some of the earlier steps related to home repair."

"What happens when we get to Step Seven or Eight or whatever ends up being the last one? Is that when you leave?"

"I'd rather not think about that," he said. "I'm too happy waking up every morning and having you hand me a cup of tea. And we still have the rest of the Lucia series to get through."

As they turned into her yard, Julie thought she saw Mandy

hurrying into the house, but when they went into the living room, she was lying on the sofa with a book. "You worked late," Julie said.

Mandy looked up at her, flushed and surprised. "No. I've been home for over an hour."

It occurred to Julie that if she'd been stoned, she probably wouldn't have noticed Mandy sneaking in or would have doubted what she'd seen if she had. She was about to press the issue, but what was the point? Mandy had a right to her own privacy, didn't she? It didn't seem as if she could get into too much trouble between Beachy Keen and home.

28

Nancy, the budding novelist and upcoming senior in San Francisco with whom David was continuing to work, had shifted the focus of her application essay from her grandmother's cancer to her grandfather's heart attack. He'd found it nearly impossible to talk students out of writing about death and fatal illness. "It made my parents cry" was the usual defense of these predictable and typically uninsightful essays. Even the most pallid apparently led to floods of parental tears. Cynically, David sometimes wondered if the emotional reactions didn't have more to do with being reminded of pending tuition costs than any specific content.

If he couldn't talk kids out of writing about death, he at least insisted they open the work with a strong scene, something admissions committees would remember, even if they forgot everything else.

To her credit, Nancy had written a good one. One evening when he and Mandy were discussing the latest draft of her own attempt at an essay, he handed her a copy of Nancy's and asked her to read it aloud. She did so without stumbling and with a surprising amount of dramatic flair.

"As the ski lift sped up the California mountain," she read, *"the air around us grew colder and the wind blew stronger. I wrapped my cloak around me more tightly and brushed the crystal snowflakes from my eyes. When Grandfather leaned against me, clutching at his jacket, I thought he was trying to keep me warm. He had always been kind and protective. But as the wind grew colder and his weight against me got heavier, I sensed that something was wrong, and before we reached the top of the mountain, I knew he was dead. What I didn't know was what to do next.*

"That's a cliff-hanger paragraph," she said.

"Almost literally," he said. "Go on."

The essay described, in harrowing fashion, the decision Nancy faced about what to do at the top of the mountain, and how to signal to the operators that there was a problem, without doing something that might cause her grandfather's body to fall prey to gravity and be *"sucked from the lift and into the piles of deep, cloud-like snow beneath us."*

When Mandy came to the end, he asked her what she thought.

"It was a good story," she said. "It made me a little jealous that nothing like that happened to me."

"Consider yourself lucky. Anything else?"

She silently reread some of the essay and handed it back to him. "I like the story, but I'm not sure I believe it."

"Oh? Why not?"

"Some of the details are too weird. Like, who wears a cloak skiing? That and 'crystal snowflakes' sound like something out of a fantasy novel. And if your dead grandfather was leaning against you, wouldn't the snow look scary and forbidding instead of 'cloudlike'?"

As soon as he heard her critique, he realized that he'd been troubled by something in the essay without being able to pinpoint what it was. He looked at Mandy with new respect, wondering why, when she was such a careful reader, her grades in English were so uninspired.

When he wrote to Nancy with a few pointed questions, she admitted, without coaxing or concern, that although her grandfather had died at a ski resort in California, he had not been on a lift, and she had not been with him. She had no interest in skiing, she'd proudly informed him. When he'd been unable to talk Nancy into writing something more truthful, he'd appealed to her mother, Janine. Her response had been swift and definitive, although not in the way David would have guessed. "It's close enough to the truth," she'd written back. "She's writing about my father, and I have no plans to sue, if that's what worries you. Besides, it made me cry, and I assure you I don't cry easily."

He decided to let the matter slide.

As for the content of an essay his own imaginary daughter might have written, David liked to think she would have composed something meaningful about her gay father and the complicated, original arrangement her parents had constructed to give her a sense of family and continuity. The complicated, original arrangement would probably have ended up looking a lot like the life he'd been living with Mandy and Julie over the past few weeks. Unlike Janine, he hadn't wept when thinking about this, but to be fair, he'd come close.

While he waited for Michael to update him on the progress of the buyout negotiations, he and Julie worked around the outside of the house to create a few memorable vignettes that guests would focus on and thereby overlook the generally shabby appearance of the rest. David had been obsessed with the concept of outdoor rooms since reading the opening pages of *The Portrait of a Lady* in his early thirties. After searching through multiple closets, Julie had produced the key to a lock on the door of a garden shed behind the house. The inside proved to be a mausoleum for abandoned tools. "When did you last come in here?" he asked.

"I don't know exactly, but I have a feeling Mandy was in a papoose on my back."

They salvaged a lawn mower, some clippers, and a few other basics. He cut the grass and Julie weeded a few sadly neglected flower beds—these latter being testaments, he suspected, to a happier and more optimistic period of Julie's marriage to Henry. He spent one entire day trimming the privet hedge by hand with the rusty clippers they'd found, while Julie stood below, steadying the ladder for him and telling him about her favorite student at Crawford School, a neurotic girl with the unfortunate name Ankell Brightman. "Her mother couldn't decide between Angel and Kelly, either of which would have been bad enough, so she crammed them together and saddled her with that. Not that Mandy is happy with her name, either. It was Henry's idea."

"What was your choice? And I have to go up to the top rung to get the high branches, so make sure I don't topple over, if you would."

"I was considering Lucia," she said as he wobbled to the unsteady top of the stepladder. He looked down and saw that she'd turned away and was frowning. Mandy had loaned him the boxy old record player she'd found in the basement, and they'd stacked up a few of his old albums. Juliette Gréco was singing to the accompaniment of an accordion. It was an ostensibly cheerful song that now sounded haunting and sad. He and Julie had joked about naming their baby this, although they'd never made real plans. She seemed to regret making this reference, and before he could respond, she said, "Hurry up there, please. I have to go in to the bathroom."

They repainted the peeling Adirondack chairs and placed them on a durable carpet that had been in the barn. With a couple of wrought-iron tables, this created one of those charming spaces that everyone would comment on enthusiastically and no one would ever use.

The hanging gutters and wobbly porch railings proved—with the advice of a cluster of employees at the local hardware store—relatively easy fixes. He took paint chips from the outside of the house and brought them to a store owner in Hammond who was said to be able to match any color exactly, even taking into consideration sun damage and winter weathering. "On second thought,"

David said, "don't make them 100 percent accurate. I want someone to register the repainting, even if subconsciously."

The "someone" was Henry. He needed to be wooed, possibly asked for more time, depending on the outcome of the San Francisco buyout negotiations. He couldn't put off telling Julie about the jewelry much longer; the bag under his bed troubled him when he was working at his desk and was making it hard for him to sleep at night.

For help with the fixes, David hired Amira's pot dealer. Granger turned out to have the lean, long-haired brand of good looks that has been popular among a certain class of seaside families since James Taylor bought his property on Martha's Vineyard. He was helpful in a vain, nonchalant way that made David think Amira's assessment of him as a lover was probably accurate. Although he tended to be lackluster at painting and scraping the siding of the house and clearly didn't approve of deodorant, it was easy to be around him. After the house repairs, it came time to move out some of the furniture and rearrange what was left. Because David knew it would be difficult for Julie to deal with her precious yard-sale finds being sent into exile, he chose to do this piece of the job on a day when she would be out. Specifically, the day she was seeing her musician-lover at his hotel.

"He's not my lover," she insisted, but she'd spent an extravagantly long time getting ready, and when he'd hugged her as she was leaving, he felt like he was giving her his blessing. Was he jealous? Certainly not. It wouldn't make any sense for him to be jealous, besides which, it seemed likely that this man wasn't available enough to usurp David's place in the household.

Granger showed up at the house half an hour after Julie had left. He was especially adept at figuring out spatial relations at a glance and conceiving the best way to maneuver sofas and tables and loveseats to get them down narrow staircases and out nineteenth-century doorways.

"Did you ever work for a moving company?" David asked him as they were walking a red velvet sofa out of the front parlor.

He had not, but he informed David with languid stoner pride that he'd always had an uncanny ability to envision rooms and structures in vivid, 3-D detail. "It started after the first time I dropped acid."

Of course it had.

"Have you considered studying architecture?" David asked.

This suggestion was met with a look of appalled confusion. "Why would I pay a fortune for an education that's going to put me in a profession where I can't make as much money as I'm making now?"

It was a valid point, as far as it went. "You might not feel as drawn to selling pot when you get older. This would be something you could grow into."

"I don't have the talent to stand out. There's more status in being a really good dealer than in being a mediocre architect. Plus there are some great opportunities in Colorado for people in my field. I've been approached by a couple of headhunters to move out there."

A big reorganization of the economy was under way just below the surface. David had heard from a few former clients who'd moved to Colorado for agricultural ventures after graduation or development projects for resorts and entertainment complexes related to marijuana. Maybe Julie had decided to quit at exactly the wrong moment.

"Amira will miss you if you leave," he said.

Granger gave a fond, sly grin that might have been from recalling an adventure with her or might have been from dreaming about finally receiving her praise. "She's crazy," he said. "But not nearly as crazy as she'd like you to believe."

After several hours of moving and rearranging, the house had a more clear and refreshed look. He was pleased. He went around vacuuming, polishing furniture with one of those products that's credibly better for the environment because it's less effective as a cleaner, and replacing lightbulbs with new ones that supposedly lasted longer than he expected to live. He sat in the living room, awaiting Julie's return, growing more anxious as the time passed.

29

The room at the Marriott Courtyard was too aggressively air-conditioned, but they were under the covers. Her back was pressed against Raymond's chest, and his long arms were wrapped around her. There was a little pool of sweat cooling in her lower back. It felt now as if what they'd finished a few minutes earlier was just to get to this—cuddling.

"I was looking forward to that for so long," he said quietly. "You have no idea." He lifted her hair off her neck and blew on it lightly.

"I have, too," she said. "Thank you."

And yet she'd been anxious about meeting him in his hotel room. Partly because of the lighting. The several times they'd been together in her house that April weekend, she'd made sure the lights were low or nonexistent. The fact that he seemed to understand the necessity for this was one of the many things about him that had charmed her. It hadn't occurred to her until much later that he might have had his own reasons for wanting the lights off. He radiated complete confidence in his body, or maybe it was complete comfort and acceptance. He had a stringy, athletic physique, but he was in his late fifties and surely there were some features that had to trouble him just as the slackness of her upper arms and the crepey skin of her thighs troubled her. She'd always been thin, a genetic gift from her impossible mother, but there were downsides to that, too. She didn't spend a lot of time worrying about her aging appearance, but she had spent a few hours since meeting Raymond wishing that things were as full and firm as they'd been decades ago, that she'd been able to be at her best for him. Not that she'd cared much for her appearance back then, either.

Julie had never met a man in a hotel room before. She saw this as a gap in her résumé, an indication that she'd always been too steady and steadfast, too reliable, too cautious. She'd never cheated on a husband or the three boyfriends she'd had between David and Henry, even the one who had lived in Chicago and she only saw once every few months.

At the same time, there was something inherently sad about a hotel assignation. Two people meeting on middle ground that had nothing to do with either of their lives and had been designed to radiate pale neutrality. The perfect metaphor for this relationship, if it could even properly be called a relationship.

He was playing with a small orchestra that was backing up a singer at the North Shore Music Tent. The singer was Louise Lundy, a former soap opera star who sang a program of romantic ballads and up-tempo pop hits from the nineties that vaguely mimicked the drama of her life or the life of the character she'd played for twenty-five years on TV, not that anyone could tell the difference. Julie had looked her up on YouTube so she'd have something to talk about with Raymond. She didn't have a pleasant or appealing voice but she was able to hit notes and had great costumes, and much of her appeal was probably due to the fact that audiences were so surprised she could carry a tune, they were willing to ignore something as insignificant as quality. On the whole, Julie would have enjoyed it more than the experimental jazz concert. The touring company was paying for Raymond's hotel room for two nights. She wondered if he'd invite her back tomorrow afternoon.

She'd driven there trying to balance her excitement and anxiety. She'd texted Raymond from the parking lot, and he'd run down to the lobby to meet her. It had been a small, gallant gesture, the way turning out the kitchen lights had been that first night he arrived in Beauport. He put his arm around her waist and walked her back to his room.

"You've been getting sun!" he said enthusiastically, as if he'd harbored a memory of how she'd looked back in April.

She'd been plagued by an unanswered question, and had asked David if he thought she should ask him about his wife.

"What about his wife?" he'd said.

"If he has one, for starters. I'm sure he does, but if we don't say anything about it, it feels like we're pretending."

"Then you should," David had said. "But wait until after. And expect to feel upset even if you already know the answer."

Now was officially "after."

"We can raid the minibar," he said, "if you happen to be craving pretzels and Toblerone."

"I'm craving this," she said, and leaned back into him. "Tell me about the show."

She could tell he was thinking it over, carefully coming up with a diplomatic answer. "It's at the opposite end of the accessibility scale from what you saw in Beauport."

"I looked her up on YouTube."

"She draws a huge audience and gets huge applause. Ovations, even. I think people like standing as a way of convincing themselves they got their money's worth. She isn't great, but she's professional, which is a kind of greatness. It would be easy to condescend to it because, to be honest, there's a lot that's embarrassing. But it makes twelve hundred people happy every night, so who am I to judge? Some of the happiness spills over to the orchestra. You feel as if you've done a good deed in a world that's falling apart."

She loved that he felt this way. Increasingly, she found it hard to trust or respect anyone who thought the world was heading in a positive direction. He was undoubtedly a gentle, accepting father. Unlike Henry, who'd always worried that showering Mandy with too much approval would make her spoiled and unproductive.

"Doesn't she have her own band?"

"She travels with a quartet. They pick up the other musicians in whatever city they're playing. It's a lot cheaper than having a whole entourage traveling with you. The money all goes into the lighting and promotion."

It was such a small and irrelevant piece of information, but she loved hearing it. It was one of the things she'd always liked most about being in a relationship, all that new knowledge you gleaned from the other person.

"Lighting does matter," she said. He had, thoughtfully, closed the drapes and left on only one light in a corner of the room.

She took one of his hands in hers, both because it made her feel closer to him and because it was starting to stray from her ribs to the flesh on her stomach.

She wasn't sure how she wanted to bring it up. She'd been thinking about it all day, trying to come up with something that didn't sound clingy or accusatory. She decided to just come out with it.

"I assume," she said, and managed to keep her tone as neutral as the carpeting. "I assume you're married."

He must have known this moment would come eventually, but he lay still and silent for a moment and then kissed the back of her neck. "Why do you assume that?"

"Because why wouldn't you be?"

"There are probably a million and one reasons why I wouldn't be. Musicians are notoriously self-absorbed. Also perennially broke. We're temperamental and moody. Prone to heavy drinking and drug abuse."

"You don't seem to be any of those things."

"I'm not. Which maybe explains why I'm married."

Of course she'd known this was the answer she'd hear, but having heard it, she felt as if she'd just lost something, even if it was something she'd known all along was a fantasy. *Expect to feel upset.*

"Tell me something about her," Julie said.

He rotated her body so she was facing him. He had a kind and sad look in his eyes. "Are you sure you wouldn't rather I talk about you?"

"God no. I know all about me and there's nothing of interest to say."

His face changed, as if a cloud had passed overhead and thrown him into shadow; he darkened. But it was too late to turn back now.

"We've known each other since high school," he said. "As corny and unbelievable as that seems."

"I don't think it's either. I think it's wonderful." She hadn't kept in touch with anyone she'd known in high school. The less said about that humiliating period, the better. This information about his marriage was consistent with what she took to be his steady, reliable, loyal personality. Inconveniently, it made her like him more.

"And you still love her." She made it a statement so he wouldn't think she was asking him to deny it.

"Very much."

She wanted to wriggle out of his arms, but she knew it would make her feel even worse to flee, to be seen as needing to flee.

"Is the length of time you've been together a factor?" she asked.

"In my being here with you?"

"In infidelity in general."

He laughed softly. "There is no infidelity in general. You're the only other woman I've been with in many years. Not since we separated for a while back in the nineties."

She loved and hated hearing this; it made her feel both more special and more guilty.

"You do believe me, don't you?" he said.

"I don't have any reason not to. Except that I'm not the kind of woman a faithful man would cheat on his wife with."

"Oh? Who is?"

"I can't offhand think of any twenty-four-year-old Pilates instructors by name, but you see what I mean."

He sat on the edge of the bed, and she propped herself up on her elbows. She watched his long, sinewy back as he scratched at his scalp and then redid the elastic band around his ponytail. "In addition to being beautiful—and please don't attempt to wedge in self-assault—there's something incredibly endearing about you."

"Endearing" was such a soft word, but at least easier to accept than "sexy" would have been.

"I think one of the things that made you so attractive to me as soon as I saw you is that you looked lonely. Don't get me wrong, it's not that I prey on lonely women, it's just that I've been lonely myself for the past nine years. It made me feel as if we were kindred spirits."

As soon as he said it, she realized that this was one of the things that had attracted her to him. He was the one outsider member of his jazz group, he didn't stay with the others, he didn't even care for the music they played. But there was more—a neediness in his eyes, not for sex so much as companionship. For talk, a proffered turkey sandwich. She supposed he was talking about the loneliness of travel, but the way he'd turned serious, the fact that he was still facing away from her, made her think it was something else. She reached out and touched his back. "What is it, Raymond?"

"She's sick." He said it in the matter-of-fact way of someone who'd been dealing with a problem for nine years.

"I'm . . ."

"She has MS."

Julie had grown used to hearing people announce they had cancer and then, after a long, painful tunnel of horrors, very often announce that they had come out the other side. But this? The specificity and special darkness of the disease overwhelmed her. There was no "other side." She felt weak.

"I'm so sorry," she said.

"Thank you. I am, too. It's just how it is, and you get used to everything, but it's incredibly lonely. More so for her, of course. You drop into a different world where people only see you as that. When I play, I go so deeply into the music, even if it's a pop song I hate, I'm outside of myself. I forget. That's how I felt when I walked into your house. It was immediate."

She now saw some of the texts he'd sent her or some of his responses to hers in a completely different context. Talk later, dealing with minor crisis. Or: Some people here at the moment. Or: At appointment, will call later. He told her more about the onset and course of the disease—more than she wanted to know, but considering all his family had been through, listening was the least she could do. There was the reaction of their three kids, the youngest in her midtwenties, the cast of home health-care workers that came and went, the doctors. Finally, there was this, said without tears or bitterness, just a terrible sincerity: "If I could be the one sick, not her, I would be. Without giving it a thought."

She inched closer to him and took his hand again and thanked him for telling her. The room was even colder and although she'd been grateful that the drapes were drawn and the lights off, she wished now that it wasn't quite so chilly and dark. She wound her fingers through his and squeezed, but as she did so, she recognized that there was something different about the way they were touching. Having this new information—which might have made her question his decency for being here—made her more certain of the fact that he was a good man. A good man she could never see again.

He turned so he was looking into her eyes with the kindness she'd come to appreciate.

"I want you to know something, Julie," he said. "This meant a lot to me. We've only spent a total of a few hours together, but in my mind, I've been with you much more often than that."

They both knew he was saying goodbye.

At the door to the room as she was leaving, he pulled her into his arms and hugged her tightly. It was a loving embrace, but there wasn't anything sexual in it. He kissed her anyway and then said, "One other thing. You don't seem as lonely as you did. I felt that as soon as I saw you in the lobby."

"I've been getting more sun," she said.

"No, something else."

She realized that he was right; she didn't feel as alone. She would have said it was because of him, because he'd made her feel seen for the first time in years, relevant, hopeful in an inchoate way. But now that this was over, now that he had moved to a remote part of her life even though he was standing in front of her, she didn't feel defeated or alone.

"I have someone helping me out," she said. "My first husband, actually."

She saw something in his eyes that she wanted to believe was hurt. "Love of your life?"

"No, it isn't like that. Just a very good friend. Unfortunately, he'll be leaving soon."

Raymond's room had a view, meaning that instead of facing the highway, it looked out to the back where there was a parking lot and, beyond it, a tidal marsh thick with tall grasses, beginning to look overgrown now that they were past the middle of July. When she stepped outside, the air was cooler and the sun was low, slanting into the marsh. It felt suddenly as if they were on the waning side of summer. He'd tried to walk her down, but she'd asked him not to. It was better to say goodbye in the darkness of his room. When she got to her car, she looked up and thought she saw a ghostly silhouette of him in his window, although the glass was reflecting back the late afternoon sunlight.

She got into the car and hit her steering wheel repeatedly. Shit. Shit shit shit shit.

She unlocked the glove compartment, where she'd hidden a joint far in the back, behind the registration papers and insurance. A form of insurance unto itself. Surely she'd earned it this once. She pushed in the lighter on the dash and looked up again at the window. If he'd been there a moment ago, he'd withdrawn. So that was that.

The lighter popped out and she grabbed it, but before she

touched it to the end of the joint, she fell back into her seat. How dare she? How fucking dare she? This wasn't her tragedy. Not even close. She could drive away, back to her house where she had someone waiting for her, not a husband, not a lover, but a friend, even if the friend was yet another person who'd soon be leaving her.

She tossed the joint out the window and started the car.

Halfway home, Pamela called her about the jewelry.

30

David was in the living room reading a massively long novel he'd rescued from the far reaches of a bookcase. The record player was on a table near him, and he was listening on repeat to a 45 of Jane Birkin singing "Fuir le Bonheur." As he saw it, it was a song about fleeing happiness for fear that it won't last forever and therefore getting a jump on the disappointment. To move on to other things preemptively. Yes, he'd done that throughout his life, either physically or emotionally, and this time he was determined not to make the same mistake.

He checked his watch again. Apparently, Julie's visit with the musician was going well. She'd been gone almost four hours. What stamina!

As for the novel, it had been famous in the 1950s and concerned a doctor's surfeit of ambition and lack of money. David remembered reading a *Reader's Digest* abridgment of it as a child that had boiled it down from 800 pages to 150, including illustrations. Reading this baggier version filled him with nostalgia of the safest kind, that is, a longing to reminisce about a period of his life he had no desire to return to.

He heard the screen door slam, and Julie came into the living room looking more tired and agitated than pleased about her meeting. She flung herself on the sofa opposite him without acknowledging or seeming to have noticed the changes he'd made in the room. How was that possible? At least 40 percent of the furniture had been removed, the sofas had been rearranged, and all the new light had created a warm glow. He thought it best not to mention her meeting with the musician until she brought it up. Instead, he showed her the novel and asked her if she'd read it.

"Did you find it in the house?" she asked. "If so, the answer is probably no."

"It sold millions of copies in the 1950s and was made into a famous movie," he said. "But today the author is known primarily for his elaborate recipe for roasting a turkey."

"I'll keep that in mind come November."

"My point being," he said, "it's not always your greatest accomplishments that are most remembered, although at eight hundred pages, this accomplishment might have been too great."

Judging that sufficient time had passed, he asked her if she noticed anything different about the room. She stood and made a tour, running her hand along the backs of chairs and the edges of tables. She wandered into the front parlor and the dining room, and returned looking more upset than before. In a tone so harsh it caused Opal to leap to the floor and head to another room, she said, "Put it all back."

"You don't like the way it looks?"

"What does that have to do with it?"

"Everything, I'd think."

"Not everything, David. For the time being, it's still my house, remember? It might not be for much longer, but at the moment, it's my home. You can't come in and tear everything apart like this."

"We talked about it," he said. "You agreed to let me make some changes. I just moved it out to the barn. It's not like I tore anything apart or sold it off."

"No. What would be the point of selling it?" she asked. "I'm sure it's all worth nothing. And please turn off the record. I can't stand to hear that song one more time."

"You used to like it," he said.

"I used to like Mel Gibson, too."

He got up and lifted the needle off the record and the room became eerily silent, without the sound of a passing car or a creak of floor from above.

"Pamela called me as I was driving home from my afternoon at the Marriott Courtyard," she said. "She wondered why I hadn't contacted her with a decision about whether or not I still wanted to sell, given the estimates. In addition to feeling humiliated by the actual value, I felt like a child who's so fragile she has to be protected from bad news. I'm guessing that's why you didn't say anything. But I'm not a child, and you should have let me know. It was cruel not to."

He'd been hoping to delay the bad news about the jewelry until he had a definite response from Michael about the buyout. Now he saw that he'd delayed too long and had compounded the problem. He thought he'd learned his lesson about secrets long ago—as tempting as they were, they never remained secret forever, and they never made life easier in the long run.

"Did you bury it in the backyard?" she asked.

"Under my bed. I was going to tell you."

"When? As the moving van was arriving?"

"Sit down," he said. "I want to talk with you about something."

"I'm tired of people telling me to sit down. I'm just fine standing, thank you."

Having said that, she sat on the sofa opposite him, arms folded, waiting.

"A friend of mine in San Francisco, a lawyer—a retired lawyer, to be exact—has been trying to get my landlady to buy me out of my lease so she can sell the place I've been renting for the past twenty years without the encumbrance of me in it. Since my ex is moving in, it's especially important to get me out. The property is selling for millions, so if it works out, which he's confident it will, it will be a substantial amount of money. More than enough to help you out."

While he hadn't expected her to fall to her knees in relief and gratitude, he hadn't expected her looks of puzzled annoyance, as if he'd said something completely insane.

"You don't think I'd take money from you, do you?"

"It's not as if I earned it," he said, "or even, to be perfectly honest, deserve it. It's a completely unexpected windfall I can live happily without. On top of that, I have selfish motives."

"If this has something to do with tax deductions, don't bother explaining the specifics."

"I want to propose something, but you have to promise me you'll say no if the idea doesn't appeal to you."

"I'm not promising anything until I've read the contract."

"That's so unlike you."

He began, growing in conviction as he spoke, describing the plans he'd been toying with for weeks now. Maybe since he'd first canceled his return flight to San Francisco or maybe, without knowing it, when he'd boarded the plane to Boston.

"It's time for me to relocate," he said. "It's not that I don't like San Francisco. Everyone likes San Francisco. It's just that, for whatever reasons, I've never felt at home there, less and less so as it's become the real estate capital of the planet. All those tech-savvy billionaire children in shiny cars. On top of that, most recently, it's associated in my mind with a series of mistakes and bad judgment calls on my part."

"And I'm not?"

"I'd like to think that the fact we've been getting along so well means we've moved past all that."

"So your relocation plan is to live in the Cabinet Room for the next thirty years?"

"I have some dignity," he said. "I've been spending a lot of time going in and out of the barn. It's in decent shape, as far as I can tell. The roof looks good, and it has plumbing. It would be a big project to turn it into a little house, but if my friend is right, there will be more than enough left over from the purchase to make changes. We could legally convert it into a condo and figure out a way to make it work financially once we get there. It would solve a lot of problems for both of us."

She still seemed doubtful, although not for herself.

"Beauport is the kind of place people move to when they're folding their tents," she said.

"Are you folding yours?"

"After this afternoon? Yes, I suppose I am."

"I'm sorry. Married?"

"I wish it were that simple. And I'm sorry, too. More than I care to admit." She looked around the room again as if she was reassessing the new arrangement of furniture. "You can't do this because you're trying to please me or because you feel bad for me or to make up for something that happened decades ago."

"I'm not."

"Because you're not the only one who made mistakes, David."

"I didn't assume I was, but I'm relieved to have confirmation that I wasn't."

She was pulling her hair back from her face, and in the now brighter lights of the room, he saw a hesitation in her eyes, or, perhaps, a longing to say more. She let her hair drop and her expression changed to one of docile gratitude. He got up and sat beside her.

"You don't really want me to put everything back, do you?" he asked.

"No, of course not. I don't even remember what was in here. But maybe we could go through the barn and retrieve a lamp or two to put back?"

"That's how trouble begins," he said.

"And this is how it ends?"

"I'm not ready to think about endings," he said. "But I'm ready to say that for the moment, this plan makes me very happy."

31

It had been almost a week since Mandy had received the email telling her her SAT scores were available online. At first she'd been tempted to look at them, the same way you were tempted to look at an accident on the highway, just to see how bad it was. But each day it got a little easier to resist going to the website to find out. The scores were somehow less relevant since she'd followed Craig into his basement more than a week ago. In a few days, probably they wouldn't matter to her at all, no matter how low they turned out to be. What she'd been doing at Craig's made it seem unlikely she'd even go to college, despite David's help.

Still, to please David, she was sitting at the table in her room with a fan blowing on her, making another stab at an essay.

Clara Dunston, my arch-nemesis and my soul mate, had her life ruined by social media and a glue gun.

The school that didn't read the rest of that paragraph was a school Mandy didn't want to go to anyway.

Clara had been a classmate who'd come to a bad turn in cyberspace, a lesson for Mandy, and one of the reasons why she stayed away from social media as much as she could. She knew she was the kind of person who didn't fare well in the world of competitive "friend" tallies and "likes" and displays of outfits and fifteen-second video clips you made with your talented BFF. Too bad Clara Dunston hadn't learned that lesson.

Mandy thought a lot of Clara's problems stemmed from her mother, one of those big, enthusiastic women who love baking and sewing and "crafting"—an awkward word that meant you took a lot of ugly scraps and used a glue gun to transform them into something equally ugly but wearable. These were homey activities that should have made a person seem clever and interesting but really made you seem like you belonged to a cult.

It didn't help that Clara's mother wore long skirts and blouses with ruffles, and it was even worse that she made clothes for her daughter that were shrunken-down mirror images.

Clara was good at a lot of things, but they were all the wrong things. She was a skilled musician, but she played the oboe. She knew how to use a sewing machine, but she used it to make vests out of old curtains. She was athletic, but her sport was throwing the shot put. She had beautiful hair, but she wore it in massive curls that looked as if she'd styled it with soup cans and then forgot to take out the cans. She had cats, which was fine, but she had eleven of them, which tipped into intervention territory.

Mandy had found her interesting, maybe because she was even

more of an outsider than she was herself. She and Clara could have learned a lot from each other. But if someone like Michelle, who had selfies posing with pop superstars, could afford to take on Clara as a mascot-like friend (not that she ever would), she, Mandy, could not. Aligning herself with Clara would magnify their problems instead of neutralizing them.

Clara's biggest mistake had been thinking she fit in. She was always posting pictures of her cats and videos of them doing things that she thought were cute but were not. Licking themselves in embarrassing places, stretching their fat bodies in the sun, climbing a weirdly elaborate carpet-covered structure her father had built that took up most of their living room. She'd been hounded for everything she did, even when it was something a cooler person would be applauded for.

One afternoon when Clara and Mandy were sitting on the sidelines during a gym class, Clara had excitedly told her she was starting a YouTube channel dedicated to pets and unusual fashion.

Mandy had turned to her in sad disbelief. "It's none of my business," she'd said, "but you might want to take a break from social media for a while."

"God," Clara had said, "you're not a very imaginative person."

Mandy wanted to tell her that some people—like the two of them—couldn't afford to be imaginative; some people had to lie low and duck for cover. The bullying just kept getting worse, until Clara's mother tried to organize a parents' group against it. But the problem there was that mothers didn't want to be associated with her any more than students wanted to be associated with her daughter.

In the end, Clara was taken out of school and the family moved away. That was a relief. Mandy had no idea what happened to her. She'd probably end up winning *Project Runway* one year and *America's Got Talent* the next. Or living on a compound in the South, sewing bonnets.

Either way, Mandy had used her as a role model of what not to do, and that was where she was headed with the essay when she got a text from Lindsay.

Do you know what's been going on?

Mandy hadn't heard from Lindsay since the day Craig had picked her up on the village green/traffic island, and she knew instinctively that whatever had been going on was not likely to be good for her.

Do I want to know?

No clue. But you SHOULD.

A few seconds later, Lindsay sent her a screenshot from Wallis's Instagram account. It was a photo of Mandy getting into Craig's van. It was a badly composed shot in profile, but it was unmistakably her with her overalls and haircut. Underneath the photo were the words NOT SLUT-SHAMING. JUST SAYING.

It was the middle of the afternoon and the room had that hot, attic-in-July stuffiness that she halfway liked, even if it sometimes made her so sleepy she had to take a nap. Maybe that was why she liked it. But when she saw the photo, she felt as if the walls of the hot room were closing in on her. She turned on her air conditioner, but it was so old, it didn't work well enough to make up for the high-pitched whining.

Am I supposed to care that a jealous bitch posted me doing something she wishes she was doing?

It's been shared 350 times!!!!! He's 27!!!

Mandy couldn't stop herself from texting back: Actually he's 28.

There was a long silence, and Mandy figured that Lindsay was trying to think through what it meant that Mandy knew this.

#1—only trying to help #2—fuck you

Mandy stretched out on the bed, a little stung by the harsh words, a little impressed that Lindsay had used the f-word since ordinarily it was the kind of thing she'd gasp or giggle about. Maybe Michelle and Wallis *were* good influences on her.

Among the many mysterious things Mandy had to think about was why—despite the content—she'd been so happy when she got a text from Lindsay after all this time. And why being with Craig, which you'd think would make her feel good, had started to make her feel lonelier when she was with other people. She officially had a secret life, but it turned out that having a secret life made you feel as if the people you spent most of your time with didn't know you at all because *they didn't know your secrets.*

On a whim, she texted: movie tonight?

The message came back as undeliverable. Lindsay had blocked her. That was unexpected. Now Lindsay was probably letting her new friends know she'd dumped her and sending them copies of their texts.

She started to sweat. She switched the fan to high so the hot air was blowing on her like a minor hurricane. It wasn't quite August and they'd already had eight days over ninety. They were predicting huge storms for tonight with microbursts, flash floods, and high wind gusts. This was not a good thing, but the idea of a violent shakeup of the atmosphere had its appeal. It was true she was fucking up all over the place, but the whole planet was so obviously fucked up, it probably mattered less. It was a pain walking up the hill to their house, but at least when Beauport was under water they'd still have dry ground.

She got up and went to the drawer of her desk and took out the money she'd made from Craig. Twelve hundred dollars, all in crisp hundreds he'd taken out of the ATM over the course of a few days. Technically, he was a horrible person, but actually, he wasn't a bad guy. She had more than enough to buy herself a few of the things she had been wanting for a while—a bright green bicycle she'd seen online; an orange ukulele in the window of a music store in Hammond; a new air conditioner for her room—but then she'd have to answer questions. Even minor purchases would set off warning bells, especially since her mother had, apparently, given up pot. She didn't know how she knew this—no one had told her—but she knew. She was more focused and alert. She didn't have that dopey grin all the time, and you had the feeling she remembered what you'd told her two minutes ago, even if you'd rather she didn't. It was a relief, but also annoying: was she suddenly supposed to send her flowers because she'd stopped a habit she shouldn't have had to begin with? But who was she to complain about anyone else's bad habits, considering her new summer job?

When she'd followed Craig into his basement ten days ago, she'd pretty much known she wouldn't find a scene out of a horror movie with people in cages or chained to the walls, but she hadn't 100 percent ruled it out. But it was just a basement and a lot less damp than the one in her own house. It was clear someone had started to renovate it by putting up framing and a few sheets of drywall. She imagined that Craig had begun the job and then had abandoned the project. Since then, she'd gotten a clear picture of the fact that he was full of ideas and ambitions for making money and fixing up the house and expanding his business, but he believed he deserved to skip over the drudgework it would take to get where he wanted to go. For example, she was the one who was doing all the actual labor on this business of his.

He led her into the half of the basement that had been partly completed. "I'm almost done with this room," he said when he noticed her looking around.

She nodded, but there were cobwebs on a bucket with tools in it and dust covering a jigsaw. It was touching that he thought she wouldn't notice.

He told her to take a seat at a desk in front of a computer with a lot of mismatched parts. Something he'd put together out of castoffs from various jobs. He rolled over another office chair and sat with his leg pressed against hers while he signed in to the computer and brought up a website.

Somehow, she'd known what he was going to show her, so when he did, it didn't come as a surprise or a shock. The website contained the usual lurid colors and cluttered graphics of every porn site she'd ever seen. He banged a few keys, entered some passwords (his password was a long string of zeroes, more indication of laziness), and then they were looking at a live feed of a woman sitting in front of her computer with a bed in the background covered in stuffed animals. Mandy was almost sure she'd never seen a site like this, but there was, nonetheless, something familiar about it, almost iconic: semi-naked woman with neck tattoo in funky bedroom.

"Why are we looking at this?" she asked, turning to Craig.

He put his hand on her thigh, a gesture that, against her better judgment, excited her. "I thought you'd find it interesting. I thought you were pretty much interested in everything."

"Some things more than others."

Still, she turned back to the computer. The woman was white, spectacularly regular-looking, not old or young. She was talking to a group of people who were typing messages to her. "Thanks, Todd52. Yeah, I just got it colored yesterday. Glad you like it. Hi Caveman. No, I move the little fuzzy friends when I go to sleep. Thanks Shrewd Dude. What do you want to see?" She had one of those flat accents that was hillbilly but also the way a lot of townies in Hammond talked. She had a rhinestone stud in one nostril and an uneven dye job. Looking at her, you could smell coffee and cigarettes. She had on a bra, but not the sexy kind, which Mandy guessed was what made it sexy to some of the people watching. Within a few minutes, Mandy felt as if she had been able to assess everything she needed to know.

The longer she watched, the more interested she became. Nothing about it was remotely seductive, and that made it fascinating. You could piece together this woman's whole life. She probably had a boyfriend or husband who was on the road a lot or maybe in the military. She almost definitely had one baby. It probably was best not to think about the stuffed animals, the "fuzzy friends," but Mandy loved how out of place and yet perfect they seemed in this picture. Of course she'd have a bad purple dye job, a nose piercing, a job doing porn, *and* a bed full of stuffed animals. Maybe she was broadcasting from her daughter's bedroom. There was something about this that was so real, it was heartbreaking. The pale skin, the heavy breasts. Mandy wanted to turn away from it and run and at the same time become a part of it. It was honest, versus the phony world of most of the girls at school who gave blow jobs and called it making love. There were no pretenses here. Yes, this woman was selling herself, but false advertising was not involved. You had to respect her for that.

Craig still had his leg pressed against hers, and she could smell his sweat and his beery breath. "What do you think?" he asked.

"I think that bra is coming off at some point, right?"

"Yeah, she said she's waiting for another hundred points and then she'll take it off."

"Frequent flyer points?"

"You can't give people money, so you buy points through the site and donate them, but it's the same thing. This way it's legal."

"Nice to know there are still some law-abiding citizens in this country." That was one her social-studies teacher's sayings. The teacher was a big right-winger and had these pat sayings that were supposed to be inspirational, but usually sounded like they were somewhere on the racist spectrum. The woman on screen probably also had a target goal for doing more than taking off her bra, and Mandy had zero interest in seeing that part of the show.

"I think I get the idea," she told Craig. "So this is the job offer?"

"I didn't say that. But you'd be good at it."

"I'm actually pretty shy."

"Actually, you're not, but you don't realize that yet. Plus, you understand people. That's the biggest part of it."

She did understand people. Not counting herself, of course.

"What's in it for you?" she asked.

He twisted in his chair and tossed his legs across her lap, like she was his girlfriend. "Money, obviously. Plus solving world hunger."

"What if I decide to run for president one day?"

"Then I make a lot more money. Anyway, it's all live so it's not like there are videos floating around online."

Everything in the world that was happening at any given moment was recorded, one way or the other. Every time you shopped at a mall or stopped at a traffic light or walked across a street, someone was recording it.

He hugged her around the waist and pulled her up and over to him so she was sitting on one of his thighs. If he told her he wanted her to call him "daddy," she was out of there.

"I'm not the type these guys expect on a site like this," she said.

"You're right. And that's why you'd have hundreds of guys following you right away. Plus, you're smart and you don't give a fuck."

Sleazy or not, Craig saw her in some way that no one else did. He saw her as the person she'd always felt she was inside but never got credit for being. She told him she'd think it over, which was another way of saying "yes" while pretending to herself she might say "no." Before the afternoon was out, she agreed that she'd chat with guys, but she absolutely would not take off anything.

He told her she could create a new name, something she'd wanted to do since her father had walked out on them. He made obvious suggestions—Crystal, Brandy, Amber, Madison—but she told him they sounded like a cross between a stripper and a New Age palm reader. She tried on a few names she'd always wished her parents had chosen for her—Jane, Emily, Lisa—but in the end she decided to call herself Muriel, since it sounded so completely inappropriate for the job. The men she chatted with, almost without exception, told her they found her name "hot." One shock among many. They probably would have liked "Mandy" even more.

So far, she'd done it seven times. Even though on the surface it was all about sex, it was, right below the surface, about something else entirely. She was pretty sure that something else was loneliness. It was amazing how much you could figure out about a guy from a few short messages. They ranged from the creeps whose heavy breathing you could hear even though they were typing, to those who wrote, "You're a slutty little bitch," and that kind of original thing. Some were probably equally awful but less obvious about it. "I'll bet you get good grades." You got the feeling they were probably old and out of shape, probably in unhappy marriages, maybe had lost their licenses because of a DUI. They sometimes made comments about the government or Hillary Clinton that made it obvious they were on the dark end of what her dad called the lunatic fringe, but in those cases, it was easy to justify that they were giving money to her instead of a group that blew up Planned Parenthood offices. She already had a handful of regulars who asked about her dog and wanted to know where she was planning to go to college, normal things like that. Even sweet things. She knew what kind of person these men wanted her to be from their tone, right from the start. It made her feel strong somehow, as if she was in control. It was confusing that way.

She hadn't shown off anything until the end of the second time she'd done it. Craig had told her it was up to her, she didn't have to do anything she didn't want to do. He left her on her own down there while he was upstairs or out on a call. That was his way of manipulating her. She saw through him, but it worked anyway.

Despite the fact that he was so great-looking and had to know it, Craig was insecure and clumsy. They'd made out a few more times, and once he'd put her hands on the crotch of his pants so she could feel the lumpy bulge of his penis. "Do you like that?" he asked.

The funny thing was, it sounded as if he really wanted to know, as if he wanted her to reassure him. She hadn't liked it or not liked it. As far as she was concerned, that part of him—while not irrelevant—was less interesting than everything else about him.

A lot of men told her they wanted to see her "tits." She hated the sound of that word more than the idea of showing them off. She told them that, expecting to lose viewers, but it had the opposite effect; a lot of these men wanted to be put in their places by someone other than their wives.

The men had the money, but she had what they wanted to buy. Clearly, hers was the stronger position.

She'd known she couldn't hold out forever, so she'd shown them what they wanted, but not, to her utter astonishment, shyly. Instead, she'd taken down the bib of her overalls and lifted off her T-shirt slowly, like a striptease, but with confidence. After spending seventeen years covering up her body to the best of her abilities and feeling vulnerable under her layers of heavy clothes anyway, she felt, pretty much for the first time, completely invulnerable. There was nothing to hide, nothing more to reveal. No matter what anyone typed, no matter what they said they'd like to do, no one could touch her.

And yet.

And yet, Lindsay's messages had made her feel even more apart from everyone than she usually did. The fan blowing in her face had started to annoy her, as if her skin was being sandblasted by the hot air. She turned it off and the room grew quiet. It was four in the afternoon, and the whole world seemed quiet. There was no breeze, and the tide was dead low. The smell of rotting seaweed and sulfurous mud would go away when the tide turned and a wind blew in, but that was hours away.

She went to Wallis's Instagram account. It was pretty much what she'd been expecting, a lot of stupid poses of her, intended to prove to the world how incredibly happy she was about being her. Some of them showed off almost as much as Mandy had shown in the basement, but in this context, it was somehow considered okay. "Empowering" was the word everyone used, even mothers.

When she got to the picture of herself getting into the van, she was shocked mainly by how bad the overalls looked on her. She'd thought she was covering up, but she was just drawing more attention to herself with them, a little like Clara with her homemade vests and skirts. The comments under the picture were what she expected. The only remotely clever one said: "Pretty sad, OVERALL." All the others just borrowed lines and phrases, as if being clever meant using the words of some other clever person instead of making up your own.

She closed the app and went to her laptop. Since she already felt she was at a weird low, she might as well know the worst and get it over with. She followed the links to the SAT scores, looked out the window, and then slowly turned back to the computer screen.

For a minute, the meaning of the numbers before her didn't register. When, after reading them a third time, they did, she unplugged her laptop and bounded down the stairs to show David.

32

Well, well, well, Renata's email read. So you've decided to play hardball. In case you're not familiar with that sports metaphor, I'm referring to your lawyering up and attempting to make a profit off a landlady who's been UNREASONABLY generous to you. Will do you the kindness of not saying what I think of "Michael Taylor's" hilariously implausible demand for a buyout. (Although I confess he does make an excellent espresso.) Even as an outrageous, irrelevant opening bid, it shows ignorance of the market and a complete lack of professionalism. And yes, David, I deal with these all the time, so I know what I'm talking about. Foolish me, spending hours trying to find you something affordable. That's over.

I do feel bad about the way a few things unfolded, so I'll secure you a check for 25K right now and we'll never mention any of it again. In return, you get back here and clear out ASAP. I know you're the world's most neurotically organized human, but it will take even you longer than you think to pack, and Porter and Soren want to start work on the house September 1st. Oh, by the way, did you see their engagement announcement on Facebook?

David deleted the email, as he'd been deleting the majority of the messages he received from Renata. The most insulting part of everything she'd written was the assumption that he spent his time looking at Facebook posts, the online equivalent of listening in on conversations in the checkout line. How dare she assume he didn't have better things to do with his time than read recipes and vacation updates?

The best part of the marriage news was that David felt no jealousy or envy or regret. If sadness about Soren's departure had been noise from another room that occasionally distracted him, he could no longer hear it. Three cheers. It was a small but happy victory. He felt secure and superior in his flawed and circumscribed arrangement with Julie. Loved, for one thing, and, maybe more important, able to be loving without the fear of betrayals and the complications and dirty laundry of sex. (That could—and hopefully would—be had elsewhere. Although he'd been busy trimming hedges and repairing gutters, he was getting antsy in that department.)

As for the rest of what she'd written, it was hard to know. The message was typical of Renata's bluster and self-aggrandizement, but it was undeniable that she knew San Francisco real estate. The research David had done into buyouts was inconclusive. It was possible that Michael was overstating the case with a lawyer's tendency to go for the jackpot. The 25K wasn't enough to change Julie's prospects, but at least it was better than nothing.

He closed his door and called Michael.

"Don't answer the email," he said. "She's clearly rattled, but she shouldn't be going around your lawyer. It's totally inappropriate. By the way, how was the shopkeeper?"

"He wasn't. We have a dinner date in a few days."

"Oh, a *dinner* date," he said in a pornographic drawl.

"I'm conflicted," David admitted. "I'd rather end up with twenty-five thousand than nothing."

"Cold feet are completely natural. Let me handle it. That's what I'm getting paid for."

In each communication David had with him, Michael had inched away from his refusals to accept a commission and closer to a demand of his fair share. The buyout hadn't yet been settled, but pieces of it were already getting chipped away. If negotiations went on much longer, Michael would probably expect half. Considering his role in the whole affair, that might be fair, but it wouldn't help Julie.

"The window of opportunity is narrowing, so we can't keep putting it off. Julie's closing on the house is coming up in three weeks. We need to settle this. She doesn't have a backup plan."

There was a silence on the other end, during which David realized his slip. He hadn't intended to tell Michael about his plans for the money, knowing he'd disapprove. When Michael spoke again, he was unusually cold.

"I thought this money was for your own real estate needs."

It's always best to come clean, especially when you're up against a deadline.

"In a sense, it is," David said. "My real estate needs have shifted east, that's all."

"You're not suggesting you're thinking of staying, are you?"

"It's not the kind of place I imagined myself ending up, nor is Julie the person I imagined ending up with, but I feel more at home here than I've felt anywhere in a very long time." And then, making what seemed like a major confession, he said, "I'm happy here."

"Feeling 'at home' lasts about as long as being 'in love,' which, in most cases lasts until the lights go on."

"If it helps, I'm not 'in love' in the way you mean. The lights you're referring to went on decades ago, so I'm making the decision in a brightly lit room."

"And what about me? You're just going to abandon me?"

David was taken aback by the naked hurt in his voice. "You'll come to visit."

"Never. And that's not what I'm talking about. I'm talking about you being my single friend who is as essentially lonely as I am. I suppose I'll have to go back to Cincinnati and move in with Louise again."

"I thought she was remarried."

"That marriage won't last. She still adores me. And your business? What happens to that?"

"More and more of it is done online anyway. On top of that, I have leads for six new clients here already through Julie's school. And I'm contacting all the private schools in the area about giving a seminar for parents. The East Coast is even more obsessed with education than the West Coast."

There was a knock on David's door, and when he called out "Come in," Michael, willing to abandon his resentment for salacious gossip, said, "Anyone with potential?"

"Not in the way you mean," he said. "I'll call tomorrow. See if you can make some progress with Renata."

He opened the door and found Mandy standing there and clutching her laptop with a sheepish expression.

"I wanted to show you something," she said.

He gestured to her and sat beside her on his bed. He had a strong suspicion about what was coming. The week before, three clients had sent him news of their SAT scores. He'd been tempted to ask Mandy about hers, but thought it best to let her tell him in her own time. He could tell from her faint and trembling smile as she pulled up the website that the scores were good. Still, it was a shock when she showed them to him and he saw just how good they were.

"Would you be insulted," he said, "if I told you I'm surprised?"

"A little, but I wouldn't believe you if you said you weren't."

33

"Her scores change everything," Julie said.

"A month ago," Henry said, "you were trying to convince me that test scores aren't as important as they used to be." He was driving with the phone hooked up to Bluetooth, giving his voice a welcome underwater quality.

"Even if that's true, these put her in the ninety-something percentile. It matters. Plus, she'll be a lot more confident when she goes back to school in the fall."

"You're suddenly the world's leading expert on tests and college applications," Henry said. "I wonder why that is?"

"Sarcasm doesn't suit you, Henry. You should go for direct, unveiled insults. They require less imagination."

She peered through the doorway into the dining room to see if anyone was in hearing range. David was sitting with Mrs. Grayson, showing her a map of Beauport and explaining where she and David walked each evening, a route that had grown to several miles. She cringed to think they might have overheard her bitter pronouncement.

Everything involving the intimacy of coupledom was either embarrassing or all-out humiliating when exposed to the light of day. The generic terms of endearment that were so comforting and reassuring in private (darling, sweetie, lovey) were cloying when overheard. Pet names were even worse. They tended toward the saccharine and too often simultaneously hinted at physical attributes or sexual practices and preferences that casual acquaintances didn't need to know. Stinky, Honeypot, Cuddles, Lumpy, Gumby. Horrifyingly, there was one Vietnamese-American teacher at her school whose husband (a generic WASP hybrid who wore boat shoes) called her Gookie. If it worked for them, it was really none of her business, but overhearing him call her this at a fund-raiser had made Julie view her colleague's marriage differently.

Public disputes were probably worst of all. They carried so much pent-up vitriol, you got an unwelcome glimpse into the historical context of the fight and learned tidbits you didn't want or need to know. "At least I don't use an entire roll of toilet paper every time I go to the bathroom." "How would you feel if *I* spent five hours a day looking at porn?" "She criticizes me for not washing my hair enough, but I have to look at her picking her nose whenever she's driving."

David looked up and winked at her, and she closed the door to the dining room.

"I'm sorry if I don't have as much *imagination* as you," Henry said too loudly. "I sometimes wonder where you get all your *imaginative* ideas."

This was typical of Henry's indirect accusations. In the past she'd felt too guilty about her smoking to do more than pretend she hadn't caught the reference. But now that she'd taken action, she felt the self-righteousness of recent converts to juice fasting and Zumba. In fact, she welcomed the insult; she'd been dying to tell people she'd given up pot but had worried that doing so would be an implicit admission that she'd had a problem. At last, an opportunity to brag.

"The connection is good. You don't have to shout. And if that's a reference to the fact that I occasionally took a hit of pot, you'll be happy to know I've stopped completely."

"Really? Interesting you'd quit after assuring me for so long that there was no need to since it wasn't a problem. I suppose David is helping you?"

One of the side effects of giving up smoking was much greater access to her anger. This was never more true than in her dealings with Henry. When she was driving or was out walking Opal, she had imaginary conversations with him in which she berated him for moving out, for not giving her another chance, for making Mandy's life so complicated, for dragging their neighbor into house negotiations, and, most of all, for making her purchase of the house that much more complicated. Less comforting was the fact that the increased anger probably meant an increased awareness of her sadness about his leaving. All that was piled on top of her disappointment about the way things had turned out with Raymond, although she'd never managed to drum up any anger toward him. *In my mind, I've been with you much more often than that.* The brilliant kindness of Raymond's comment was that it allowed her to think that she might, in his mind, still be with her from time to time. She found it easier to think of him as her "lover" now that she knew she'd never see him again.

"I called with an invitation," Julie said. "We thought it would be good for everyone if you and Carol had dinner with us."

"Who's the *us*? You and David?" She heard annoyance in his voice. Could it possibly, plausibly be jealousy?

"Yes, as a matter of fact. Do you have a problem with that?"

"None that I haven't expressed previously. What's the point of the dinner?"

"Show support for Mandy, celebrate her scores, all get on the same page about her college plans."

"If you think I have any interest in getting on the same page with David Hedges when it comes to making decisions about my daughter, you're sadly mistaken."

Although his words had obviously been intended to let her know that he considered David an irrelevant intruder in their lives, they made her feel, for the first time since Henry had skipped out on her, the subtle but significant power of being publicly connected to another person. Even if the nature of the connection was, at best, ambiguous.

"What about August fourth?" Julie asked.

"I'll see you a week or so later at the closing, assuming there is one."

"There will be," she said, trying to sound more confident than she felt. "But that's not about Mandy."

"I'll ask Carol and get back to you."

After she'd hung up, she went into the dining room. The map was still on the table, but David was in the kitchen. "I think we're in for a stretch of nice weather," she said to Mrs. Grayson. "Your son must have a swimming pool?"

When there was no response, she walked to the other side of the table and saw that Mrs. Grayson was holding a butter knife, but her eyes were closed. Julie froze. It was impossible to tell if she was breathing, and Julie was afraid to touch her.

"David!" she called. "Come in here."

Mrs. Grayson opened her eyes. Julie tried to cover the alarm she felt but was obviously unsuccessful. David dashed out and stood behind her with his hands on her shoulders.

"I must have dozed off," Mrs. Grayson said. "Are you all right, Julie? You didn't think I'd passed out, did you?"

"No, no, of course not," she said.

"She wondered if you'd like more toast," David said.

"Was I eating toast?"

"Let's you and me go out on the porch," Julie said. "It's a little warm in here."

To the best of Julie's knowledge, Sandra had never written about how to handle the death of a guest in her blog, but it might be worth double-checking.

34

Mandy was sitting in the back of the bus to Hammond, gazing out the window at the patches of woods alongside the road. It was another hot day. The trees looked as if they were ready to start dropping their leaves and give up, even though it was only the end of July. Unless maybe she was projecting some of her own feelings of weariness onto them.

Today, for the second day in a row, she'd put on a sleeveless T-shirt under her overalls. Seeing herself so covered up in that Instagram photo had unsettled her. Since she'd started showing off her body online, she'd begun to look at herself differently. She still didn't like what she saw in the mirror, but she'd at least begun to allow for the possibility that in this particular matter, her judgment could be wrong. There were men who were actually paying money to talk to her and to see her. It wasn't as if she valued their opinions, but they had to count for something. She felt as if she was walking a tightrope with a bizarre new confidence on one side and a bottomless pit of regret about what she was doing on the other. Either way, if she lost her balance and fell off, she'd be in over her head.

The news about the SAT scores had given her a thrill, but it had lasted for only a few days before she realized that they were abstract numbers that meant more to other people than they meant to her.

Sometimes she went home at night and claimed she was tired from work and lay curled on her bed, listening to music and clutching the purple stuffed elephant she'd dug out of the far reaches of her closet. Benny, a toy she thought she'd lost interest in more than five years ago. Fortunately, she hadn't thrown it away. She still didn't understand a word of the French songs she listened to (except for the frequent mention of "amour," of course, not that she *really* understood that), but now she felt that she understood the emotion in the singers' voices better, the intense longing to be changed or rescued by something, most likely by amour. She and David shared the record player, moving it between the living room and her bedroom, depending on who wanted it most. Sometimes, she cried, but she was never sure if it was about her own life or if it was a reaction to the manipulative music.

One of the weirder things about working in Craig's basement was that it had started to feel like a job. There were times she was supposed to arrive, specific hours she was expected to appear online and chat with the group of men who'd become—there was no other word for it—her fans. As with the job at Beachy Keen, her labor was making someone else more money than it made her. On top of that, she gave herself a lunch break every day and went for a walk around Hammond and got a sandwich at an Italian deli that was tucked into Craig's beat-up neighborhood.

The other consolation was the money, which she'd started keeping in an envelope taped to the back of her desk drawer. She still hadn't made any purchases, although she had talked to the guy in the hardware store about installing an air conditioner in her room one afternoon when no one was home "as a surprise for my mother." It was nice to walk into the high-end coffee shop in the middle of Beauport and order anything she wanted without worrying about the ridiculous prices. Also to leave the girl who worked behind the counter a big tip because clearly she had to work in a place that was always hot and in which the customers were constantly complaining. Yesterday, as she left her tip and waved goodbye, she'd almost started to cry. When she got outside, she realized it wasn't for the girl, but for herself. Even if the girl was sweating through her shifts and making less money than Mandy, she was still doing something that was honest, that didn't have to be hidden.

The most confusing thing of all was trying to figure out why she couldn't quit, even though she knew she should.

She could tell Craig was more attached to her or maybe more dependent upon her, and maybe that was part of it. Maybe he loved her a little. He sometimes called her "Sis." She tried not to think too much about what this meant. She chose to believe that it was a little like the way Rooster Cogburn called Mattie Ross "Little Sister" in *True Grit*, which remained her favorite book of all time. Her own feelings about him were tangled. Sometimes she wished he'd make out with her again—he hadn't for at least a week—hold her, maybe even do other things. Sometimes he seemed like an older brother she hung out with and took care of. There were heaps of laundry tossed next to the washing machine in the far corner of the basement, and she'd sorted it and run six loads through the machine over the course of a few days, folded and arranged it all in neat piles. He'd never thanked her, but it had given her satisfaction and the illusion that they had a halfway normal relationship of *some* kind.

She walked from the bus stop, down along the buildings where the fishing industry had once been thriving. A lot of them were closed, but they still blocked the view of the water. When she got to Craig's neighborhood, she was sweating lightly. The old woman who lived next door was out in her yard in her turquoise housedress, moving around pots that didn't have any plants in them.

"Hi, Daisy," she said. "What's the project today?"

"Same as always. Trying to keep up here."

"Do you want help moving anything?"

It was impossible even to guess how old she was, but she had the hump of an old lady, fingers that looked like claws, and a crazy bathrobe.

"Aren't you sweet to ask," she said. "I need to keep busy. We all need to keep busy." One of the clay pots she was holding fell out of her hand and smashed on the ground. She didn't seem surprised or upset. Maybe she hadn't noticed. "You going to help Craig? He's a good boy. His mother always worried he'd end up in prison or on the streets after she died. She'd be proud he has his own business. Whatever it is."

The way she'd paused before saying this last sentence, the way she'd looked away from Mandy when she did say it, made her think she knew something or at the very least had her suspicions. It made Mandy feel a little sick to her stomach.

"I have to get going," she said.

Craig was in the dining room, working on a laptop that had been lying around for weeks. A lot of what he did seemed to be the equivalent of doodling.

"You should open the windows sometime," she said. "It smells like bacon in here. All the time."

When he looked up, he shook his head and said, "I can't believe you're dressed like that again."

She looked down at herself. "Why not?"

"I don't like it."

"Okay. So?"

He got up from the table and took her by the upper arm and moved her so she was standing sideways to the ornate wooden mirror over the buffet. "Look from the side." He undid the bib of her overalls and let it fall to her waist. He pulled at the T-shirt and said, "You might as well be naked. I can see everything."

"I had the top up," she said. "I wasn't riding the bus like this."

He still had her arm and it was starting to hurt. She wrestled out of his grasp, and pulled up the top of her overalls. He was being a protective older brother, unless maybe he was being one of those controlling men she'd been warned about.

"I don't want you going around with your tits out," he said. "It makes you look like a slut."

"Think about what you just said, Craig. I mean, really, does it make any sense at all, considering the job *you gave me*?"

"And where would you be if I hadn't?" he said. "Making a few bucks an hour in some shop until they fired you?"

"I'd rather be!" she shouted.

"No, you wouldn't."

She saw that he was jealous of the attention he imagined she was getting on the bus (none, as a matter of fact). She knew it was unhealthy and probably part of his private craziness, but, undeniably, it made her feel special, despite the thousands of lectures about consent and abuse at school. Despite knowing she'd probably think about this moment later in the evening and curl up on her bed with Benny and cry.

"You're being a jerk!" she shouted.

"Really? Am I scaring you?"

"A little. Mainly you're making me want to leave."

"There's the door. I'm sure you've got a lot of other places to go. Practice for the intramural tennis team maybe?"

After years of privately deriding jock girls with their flushed complexions and boring talk of scores and workout routines and their faint smell of sweat and chlorine, she felt an intense pang of longing to be one of them. To be outside in the sun and the heavy, humid air doing something good for herself instead of being here doing no good for anyone. She had a crazy urge to tell him about her SAT scores, but she knew he'd turn them against her and make her see how meaningless it was to brag about them.

And then, suddenly, Craig's face changed again, and he smiled. "I'm sorry," he said. "Come here." He reached out and wrapped his arms around her and pulled her to him. His body felt so warm, it was as if he'd been lying in the sun for hours. His T-shirt smelled like greasy food, in a familiar, ordinary way. She relaxed against him and slowly moved her arms so they were on his waist.

"Remember what we talked about yesterday?" he asked. He said it quietly, just to her.

"The weather?"

"Yeah, the weather. Smart-ass." But he used his teasing voice that meant he was trying to be friendly and get her to do something. She shouldn't have been relieved that their fight was over, but she was.

What they'd talked about yesterday was a request from a regular, a man who described himself as "a successful businessman on Wall Street." This was laughable. If he was successful, what was he doing chatting with her in the middle of the day three times a week, sometimes for as long as a couple of hours? She was pretty sure a successful businessman on Wall Street wouldn't describe himself that way. More likely he was a blobby married guy whose wife had left him. He'd told her he had diabetes and was impotent as a result. Okay. The most shocking thing about what she was doing was that a lot of men talked to her about their illnesses. Diabetes was a common one. It was like they needed to confess; she was supposed to tell them it didn't matter to her, which, since she didn't know them and would never meet them, was true. She'd read up on a few of the diseases and asked them questions about their medications, which made them more grateful and generous. At this rate, she thought maybe she should start looking into nursing programs.

The alleged Wall Street guy had said he'd pay a lot if she agreed to do a private session with him so he could watch her do something to her boyfriend. The expression he'd used was "orally pleasure," a term so bizarrely polite, it sounded like something you'd say on TV to get around the censors.

"What if I don't have a boyfriend?" she'd said to him.

"That can't be true," he'd typed back, "and if it's a girlfriend, even better. You'd make a sick man happy, just to watch."

At first, she didn't tell Craig about this since it was asking for trouble. But then, as the day wore on, she'd felt an overwhelming desire to prove something to him—not that she was desirable or sexy or anything like that, just that she was a valuable employee. That she was doing a good job. Fuck you, Beachy Elaine.

His first question, of course, had been: "How much?"

When she'd told him, he hesitated and then said, "So do you want to?"

"No!" she'd said immediately. "I do not."

Craig had shrugged and walked away, but before she'd left in the afternoon, he'd said, "You know, if you really didn't want to do it, you wouldn't have told me. You do know that, don't you?"

She did know that. Or partly knew it. She'd heard girls at school talk about this with their friends, how it didn't count as anything, how it made it easy to get what they wanted from their boyfriends, how it was essentially gross but usually quick. They seemed proud of the fact that they did it, bragging that they were good at it while claiming they didn't enjoy it. That last part might or might not be true.

Now, standing in Craig's dining room, with her arms around his waist, he said, "So have you thought about it more?"

"About the weather?"

"Yeah, about the weather."

"A minute ago, you were complaining about my T-shirt, and now you want me to do this."

"What can I say? I'm a complicated guy."

This was true but probably he—unlike, Picasso, say, who they'd studied in art history—was complicated in a fundamentally uncomplicated way.

He moved so he was against her and his crotch was pressing hers. Unmistakable what was going on there, even for someone like her who was completely inexperienced in that department. She felt herself shake a little. She was afraid, not of him but of the part of herself that wasn't going to say no. The warning lights were flashing, but she was ignoring them yet again.

"Aw, come on, Mandy," he said. "The weather's fine."

He was right—it hadn't been "so bad," not that it had been good. It was a relief when it was over and it had become an experience she'd had, and was no longer one she was having or waiting to have. She'd spent a long time washing in the bathroom, and when she came out, Craig had sweetly offered to drive her back to Beauport. She turned him down because she wanted to be alone. She got on the bus and settled into the last row, watching the same scenery she'd watched a few hours earlier. But now it was different in the late-afternoon light, sadder and even more tired. A few weeks ago, it had seemed the days lasted long past dinner; it was still light when David and her mother returned from their walks. The change to shorter days had happened suddenly when she hadn't been paying attention. There were so many things she hadn't been paying attention to.

When she got home, she went into the living room, where her mother was watching the news. She sat on the sofa next to her and pressed her body against hers, the way she'd been curling up with her stuffed animal. Her mother put her arm around her and kissed her on the forehead. Before she even knew she was doing it, she said, "I know you stopped smoking pot, Mom."

Her mother stiffened against her, and then hugged her tighter without saying anything.

"I know it wasn't easy. I'm proud of you."

She felt her mother's chest rising and falling against her, as if she was taking in deep breaths. To help her out, she said, "I know you'll cry if you say anything, so really, you don't have to."

They sat like that for a while on the sofa, then her mother said, "David has a date tonight, so it's just you and me. We'll go in and fix something in a minute."

But when she added, "Let's watch the weather first," it was Mandy who burst into tears.

35

In terms of hills and ocean views, David had come to think of Beauport as San Francisco's smaller and less interesting sibling. Having had a brother who was better-looking and more athletic and entrepreneurial than he was, he'd developed a fondness for the lesser sibling, the appealing human equivalent of a halfway decent B-side. The town lacked the scenic grandeur of San Francisco, but it had its intimate charms and more manageable vistas that caught your eye as you turned a corner or appeared before you unexpectedly on the far side of a hedge or behind a walled garden. As he walked to Kenneth's house on the night of their dinner, he took in the views of the harbor with its fishing boats and rocky jetty with the possessive and slightly bored pride of a resident.

Except he wasn't officially a resident yet, and Michael was beginning to sound more doubtful about getting anything close to what he'd originally quoted as a buyout. "I could get whatever you want if you could seriously threaten to hold things up for a year or more, but as it is, you're too eager to settle it. The people in New York who got millions held out for over a decade."

There was logic in this, but David had begun to wonder if Michael's disapproval of his plans to relocate to Beauport and, especially, to live with Julie played into it. Michael had led him into the middle of this maze of legal negotiations, but it was looking as if one mention of what he intended to do with the money had led to abandonment. Michael had even begun to comment on the fact that Renata could be good company if you got her in the right mood. "She has a pretty racy past, and she loves talking about it. And you know how I love airline pilots and Italians."

If things did fall through, where did it leave him? When he pictured living in Beauport, he pictured living on the same property as Julie, wandering into each other's houses without knocking or planning, having breakfast with her and reading aloud to her in the evenings. Not being a stepparent to Mandy, but at least playing the role of one. They'd decided that he could wait to put a kitchen into the barn, and the two of them would use hers communally. He'd be there to help her welcome tenants and make beds when they left, the latter a task that he did with special flair and efficiency. His skill with hospital corners was finally being put to good use. If they had places on opposite sides of town, the sense of home vanished, and sharing a condo or small house was fraught with too much intimacy. Her house and barn offered the precise combination of qualities they needed.

No sane person would look upon living in San Francisco as a

bad idea. If Michael was right, he could hold out for a year for a large buyout and would be able to afford something decent for himself. Still, the idea made him feel like a failure and unaccountably lonely. He and Julie had worked through most of the Seven Steps he'd outlined for her happy future, but not all. It would be terrible to let her down by not delivering on the two most important— Mandy and the house.

Kenneth had sent him walking directions that included the admonishment: "Please follow these exactly, even if you think you know a better route." Kenneth's pushiness in this matter was more exciting evidence that he was probably a complete submissive elsewhere, assuming they got there. David made a stand for himself, tossed the directions, and took an alternate route. Within minutes, he was lost.

It was nearly twilight when he knocked on Kenneth's door. Beauport was full of small houses tucked behind other houses, garages renovated into rental units, and cottages planted into gardens. In that sense, too, it resembled San Francisco. Kenneth lived at the bottom of a set of concrete steps that cut through vines of Virginia creeper and wisteria.

Kenneth opened the door dressed in a starched short-sleeved shirt, a pair of navy-blue shorts, and red sneakers that seemed out of place with the rest of his outfit, not to mention his age. David handed him a bottle of wine and an absurdly expensive imported Italian soda. Kenneth scrutinized the soda and said, "Where did you buy this?"

David mentioned the store in Hammond, a pale imitation of Kenneth's Kitchen.

"They come into my shop, study my inventory, take *photos*, and then copy everything I do. I wish you wouldn't shop there."

"I felt bad about that, but since I was bringing it tonight, I didn't want to spoil the surprise. I suppose you know they have lower prices."

"More evidence they don't know what they're doing. If you overprice something by a little, people feel ripped off. If you overprice it by a lot, customers assume it must be superior and buy it by the case. Part of what they pay for is bragging rights to the obscene price."

"I'll remember that if I decide to go into retail. May I take a seat?"

The cottage was even smaller inside than it appeared from the walkway. It was one open room carefully furnished in blues and whites so it resembled the interior of Kenneth's store. The white cotton curtains were billowing in on a breeze in a way that was romantic but made the room seem smaller. The selling point of the place was its location: it backed up to a small pond with a cemetery on the opposite side. The view from the windows in that direction made the cottage feel completely private, almost as if it were a houseboat floating on the still surface of the water.

David took a seat on a small chair with a white slipcover. It was so close to the ground, his knees came up and he had to lean forward to balance.

"I have a suggestion," he said. It was something he'd thought about on the walk over and had rehearsed his choice of words. "It seems as if we've adopted trading sarcastic comments as a form of communication. I propose we try something else."

Kenneth was in the adjacent kitchen alcove opening the wine. "I'm afraid I don't have any board games, if that was what you had in mind."

"I was thinking more about swapping a few salient biographical details."

Kenneth handed him a glass and sat opposite. "The résumé approach to conversation? Where did I grow up, last book read, all that?"

"I don't see why not."

"I'm about halfway into *Great Expectations,* but don't ask me when I started because junior high was a long time ago."

"Noted. Let's move on. Politics?"

"I don't pay all that much attention, although I do vote. I'm heavily influenced by celebrity endorsements, assuming I like their music or movies."

"That seems reasonable, as long as Clint Eastwood isn't one of the celebrities."

Kenneth gave him a puzzled look. "Who?"

"Never mind. Maybe I should tell you what I do for work."

"You can if you want, but I already looked you up online. I'd send some of my nieces and nephews to you, but I'm guessing you don't specialize in underachieving public school students from rural Kentucky with alcoholic and occasionally abusive parents."

"It sounds rough. I'm sorry for them," David said, but what he really meant was that he was sorry for Kenneth and the struggles his comment necessarily implied. "Do you have a lot of nieces and nephews?"

"I've lost count, which is some indication."

There was a smell of food drifting in from the kitchen, specifically, the clean, starchy smell of rice. Given the appearance of Kenneth's person and his cottage, David was counting on an artfully presented dinner that was under-salted. And yet, the more they talked, the more clearly the conversation drifted into flirtation and significant glances. David had a sense that dinner would not be served anytime soon. When he asked Kenneth if he was a good cook, he shrugged in response and bounced his crossed leg. When he asked what he was serving, Kenneth looked at him over the rim of his wineglass and raised his eyebrows in response.

David stood up from the low chair with difficulty and led Kenneth to the side of the room with a bed. There was the smell of mud from the pond and the deep croaking of bullfrogs. A copy of *Architectural Digest* was open on a chair by the bed, and David was moved by the thought of Kenneth spending his evenings here alone, exhausted from work and reading up on the extravagant décor of country estates and rock-star penthouses.

He'd expected Kenneth to be a greedy and demanding lover, but, contrary to almost every other aspect of his personality, he turned clingy and affectionate as soon as they were sprawled out naked on the white sheets of the bed. At one point, he looked up at David and said, "Don't hurt me, okay?" David had assumed that that wasn't possible or, if possible, would have been welcomed. He assured him that he would go slowly. "No," he said. "I mean don't hurt me."

Most of David's recent sexual escapades had been with people who texted him on an as-needed basis, stopped by his carriage house, and rarely said more than the mandatory, perfunctory complaints about traffic and internet billionaires before leaving. He'd accepted these encounters as a practical solution to his simple human needs. These had changed over time but had not, to his great surprise, abated. If these encounters weren't as satisfying as he'd hoped, they at least weren't as depressing as they sounded in theory. He missed the warmth of greater intimacy, but, like reducing your sugar intake, you got used to it.

Kenneth's display of vulnerability touched him so deeply, he cupped his head in his hands, kissed his mouth, and assured him he wouldn't, all the while pushing aside the panic he felt at the implied responsibility he was accepting. Maybe he was growing up.

Over dinner, he learned that the cottage was rented and that the rent was modest. While everything Kenneth owned was carefully curated and spotlessly clean—the furniture, his clothes, the dishes, the bicycle leaning against a wall on the porch off the back—none of it was new and, on closer inspection, all of it showed signs of age. He'd noticed a small patch on the white bedsheet that Kenneth had sewn in expertly. He described himself as coming from "a long line of chain smokers and QVC shoppers." David imagined this meant a scarring coming-out experience and a difficult passage through high school.

On the subject of boyfriends, he was circumspect. "There are more people with drug problems around here than you'd guess," he said. It didn't take much reading between the lines of this and other comments to see that there had probably been heartache followed by a few arrangements with men already in relationships, the last refuge of those who were themselves unsuitable relationship material.

The food was, as David had suspected, a triumph of presentation: a molded pyramid of rice, a scoop of steamed vegetables, a fillet of flounder rolled into a tube and dusted with paprika.

As he was clearing the plates, Kenneth said, "I hear you're organizing your ex-wife's house."

"Really? Did Mandy come in and tell you that?"

"No, just local gossip. As for Mandy, I haven't seen her since she stopped working at that store."

David was distracted by the disappointment of the dessert that was set in front of him: a poached pear. It was something a caregiver would serve to an invalid wearing a bib. When he finally registered what Kenneth had told him, he said, "I don't know what you're talking about. She still works there."

"She most definitely does not. Elaine came into my shop the day she fired her and complained for an hour about her attitude. She was overcompensating. She felt bad about turning her out. After all that, she tried to talk me into giving her a job."

"Mandy never said anything to us."

"She was probably embarrassed. High school kids usually don't last more than a month at any store. They bounce from one to the next. Aren't you going to eat the pear?"

"When was this?"

"I don't know the date, but weeks ago."

It was hard to know what to make of this news, but he was unnerved by it. If Julie knew, she would have told him. Mandy was still going to work, so maybe she had replaced one retail job with another and, as Kenneth indicated, had been ashamed of having been fired. Probably it was best not to make a big deal of it. He could go to the store and ask a few questions before confronting Mandy.

His phone was vibrating in his pocket, but it seemed impolite to answer. Naturally, Kenneth, who seemed to notice everything, heard it. "You can get that if you want, as long as it's not a boyfriend."

It was Mandy. "David," she said. "Mom asked me to call you. Can you come back? Something's happened here. We need you."

36

Julie had held Mandy tighter, and smoothed down her hair as she cried quietly through the weather report. It was wrong or maybe morally impoverished to take advantage of your own daughter's unhappiness, but she'd felt such a thrill in being allowed to hold her like this after more than a year of Mandy's brushing off her affectionate advances, she'd had to revel in it just a bit, briefly ignoring the dark undercurrents.

"What is it?" she'd asked, after she'd turned off the TV. "Is everything all right?"

She'd felt Mandy shrug her shoulders against her and shake her head. She smelled of an unfamiliar soap, probably a product they used in the store. "Did something happen at work?"

Mandy hadn't said anything, just burrowed in closer to Julie. She knew she ought to be thinking more about what this meant, but she couldn't help wondering instead why Mandy had denied her the pleasure of this closeness for so long.

"You don't have to tell me if you don't want to," Julie had said, "but I wish you would."

Mandy had looked up at her, and through her tears, she'd seemed to be searching Julie's face, as if she was evaluating whether or not she could trust her. Julie had a million questions she wanted to ask, beginning with "You're not pregnant, are you?" but she'd thought it was best to say nothing and follow Mandy's lead. Besides, she'd never heard a word about any boys.

"I wish I made better choices sometimes," Mandy had said finally.

This was so open-ended and contained so many awful possibilities, Julie could barely get out: "About what?"

"My job." It was hard to know if she'd said this as a statement of fact or as a question, but either way, if this was what they were talking about, it had been such a huge relief that Julie sighed as she stroked Mandy's hair.

"You can always find something else. School starts in a month. If you want to take off a few weeks, I'm fine with that."

They'd gone into the kitchen and made a dinner from leftovers.

It wasn't until they were cleaning up that they heard a loud noise from above and a scuffle of feet. Maybe, Julie thought, it had been a mistake to let strangers into the house. Mandy had never objected loudly, but it was possible that she'd had unfortunate encounters with guests who'd been rude to her. After taking some of Sandra's suggestions and letting David play bad cop, it was turning out to be profitable, but if the whole venture made Mandy feel like a servant in her own house, she'd have to figure out something different.

The people in the room above the kitchen were from Quebec; Hélène and Philippe, a quiet couple who spent most of their time reading French novels on the porch and, in disbelief, showing her photos they'd taken of the food they'd been served at various restaurants in Beauport. A mound of cottage cheese, a slab of steamed fish, a ball of mashed potatoes. "It's all the same color," Hélène had said incredulously several times. "No color at all. Do you think they do it on purpose? Maybe it's an art project?" They didn't seem the types to be moving furniture at this hour of the night.

She heard panicked voices from above, and as she was about to investigate, Hélène appeared in the doorway, breathless.

"You need to come up," she said.

"Is Philippe all right?" Julie asked.

"Yes, he is fine. But the old woman, not really."

Mrs. Grayson was lying on her side on the floor of the hall. Her eyes were wide with fright, and she was clutching her cardigan to her chest. Not dead, Julie concluded with relief, but beyond that, hard to tell.

"Should I call 911?" Mandy asked, taking out her phone.

"Please," Julie said. "Call from her room." She sat down on the floor next to Mrs. Grayson and took her hand. "Don't worry about anything," she said. "Mandy's calling an ambulance. Hopefully they'll be here soon. Can you sit up?"

She could not, a discouraging sign.

"That's all right, dear," Julie said. "It's more comfortable lying down anyway. Let's see if we can put your head on my lap until someone comes."

Julie found the weight of her head against her thigh comforting. She saw from this angle that the dandelion-puff hairdo was designed to hide her shiny scalp. "Is your son's phone number written down somewhere?"

Mrs. Grayson looked pale and anxious, and she shook her head slowly. "I don't want to bother them," she croaked. Her speech was thick and slightly distorted, as if her tongue was in the way. "It was a dizzy spell."

"I'm sure they'd want to know," Julie said.

Mrs. Grayson gripped her arm. "No. Please."

Julie saw that Mrs. Grayson had wet herself. She reached down and discreetly arranged the loose material of her skirt until the stain was less obvious. Loss of dignity inevitably boiled down to being betrayed by the body in a way that recalls the helplessness of infancy. The carefully dry-cleaned beaded cardigans, the soft, white hair, the delicate tread on the steps, all had been undermined by a trickle of urine. Wasn't this the very thing that everyone feared? To be sick, stricken, among strangers? When the ambulance did come, Julie would need to go through Mrs. Grayson's purse looking for insurance cards; maybe she'd find the son's number then. She hoped she wouldn't find anything else—a flask or a stash of chocolate bars. Just thinking about it made Julie feel so lonely and sad, she was tempted to lie down next to Mrs. Grayson and put her arms around her.

When Mandy came back with a pillow, Julie told her to call David. "It might take a while for the ambulance to get here, and he'd want us to tell him what's going on."

Maybe that was true, but mostly, surrounded by the strangers who were staying in her house, she herself was beginning to feel stricken and abandoned and wanted him to be there with her.

37

The distraction of Mrs. Grayson's stroke was beginning to wane, as, fairly or unfairly, almost everything in life does, replaced by the human demands for shopping, cooking, and updates on celebrity divorces. She was still in the hospital, poor thing. She'd had a mild stroke but would recover her mobility in time. Her son had insisted on having her moved to Mass General in Boston and, when she was released, to a fancy rehab facility about forty-five minutes away. It was an irony that David had noted before: wealthy offspring who'd paid minimal attention to a parent when she was healthy spent vast sums on the best medical care when she got sick, especially if it guaranteed keeping them at a distance. Money is easier to dispense than affection, even for the most miserly.

Naturally, in his mind, David's imaginary daughter would have been attentive to him throughout her life, freely dispensing as much affection as he'd earned. In gratitude for her kindness, he'd off himself at the first signs of irremediable trouble and spare her the expense and boredom of overseeing the slow decline. Abrupt endings were problematic in movies but rarely—after the initial shock—in life. He thought about death as often as he thought about the period of his life before he'd been born, which is to say, close to never. His view of the subject was an Epicurean one: it was not an event he would experience, so why worry? It would be like spending hours trying to figure out what to wear for his date with Zac Efron.

Beachy Keen was housed in a shingled building that, like the majority of the buildings on the Neck, appeared to be tilting in response to the prevailing winds. The girl at the register was young, probably not more than fifteen, and decked out in heart-shaped sunglasses and a beach costume that seemed like an unintentional but nonetheless unwholesome reference to *Lolita*. She greeted David with cheerfulness that struck him as both rehearsed and genuine. Seeing this sunny girl with her broad grin, David found it impossible to imagine Mandy standing in her place, playing the same role. No wonder it hadn't worked out.

"If I can help you with anything," the girl chirped, "just let me know. My personal favorite item in the store is the Beach Tree. It's such a fun gift, they're flying off the shelves. They're our Signature Item!" She made this announcement with the reverence one might use to say "recipient of the Nobel Prize!" "And you're in luck because they're 70 percent off. Today only. Pretty great, right?"

David had a strong suspicion that "today only" was a variation on a lie, but he hoped he'd never return and have reason to find out the accuracy of his suspicion.

"I'll check them out later," he said. "I was hoping I might have a word with the owner, if she's in."

She cheerfully told him she'd check and stepped into an office in the back of the store. The owner strolled out, dressed for a Caribbean cruise, and shook his hand. She told him that she was delighted he'd come in, but that she had finished buying merchandise for the season.

"That's not why I'm here," he said, insulted that she thought he was a salesman hawking the kinds of trinkets the store stocked. Even worse was coming.

"Well, I'm not hiring now, either, so if that's . . ."

"It certainly is not. I'm a friend of Julie Fiske, Mandy's mother. I was hoping you could tell me a little about your experience with having Mandy work here."

The owner looked at the girl behind the counter and indicated with a gesture of her manicured hand that he should precede her into her office. There was no window in this dark alleyway of a room, but an air conditioner was turned on, blowing in chilled, unbeachy air.

"I don't like to talk about former employees in front of Trisha. She's very bright for her age, as you could probably see."

"She is extremely enthusiastic," David said, a fact he'd taken, in this context, as evidence of a lack of intelligence.

Elaine nodded and smiled. "She's a find. She came in one day and fell in love with our stock. She was looking for a gift for her mother's birthday. *She* and her mother are very close." There was an emphasis on this last bit of information that made David think it was a comment on Mandy's relationship with Julie. "I actually had to talk her into working for me. I pleaded with her. I needed someone different from *Mandy*."

The name clearly left a bitter taste in her mouth.

"I'm sorry that didn't work out," he said. "I'm helping her with her college applications, and it would be useful to understand why you let her go."

Further prompting was unnecessary. "If you take everything we said about little Trisha's personality, enthusiasm, and retail instincts and imagine the polar opposites, you'll have some idea of what Mandy was like as an employee. I think it's safe to say she was a complete disaster."

"I'm sorry to hear it," he said. He didn't doubt there had been problems, but considering how little was at stake here, "complete disaster" surely was inappropriate. "She spoke so highly of you and your merchandise."

"It would have been nice if she'd shared some of that supposed enthusiasm with the customers. Sales have shot up since I let her go."

"When was that, by the way?"

She produced the date instantly, the way one would produce the date of a marriage, birth, or release from prison. It struck David as almost alarmingly long ago.

"I suppose business must pick up at that time of year anyway, doesn't it?"

"When you have an employee with an attitude, it doesn't much matter what the date is. I don't blame her entirely. I didn't realize at the time I hired her that her mother was involved with Airbnb." If that was the tone she used to utter "Airbnb," how did she articulate "White Supremacist Movement"?

He decided it was best to turn officious. "Yes," he said. "Short-term rentals are becoming an important part of the tourism industry worldwide."

She eyed David and sipped from a lipstick-stained coffee cup with a sailboat on it.

"Oh, they certainly are. They bring in hordes of people who are used to shopping online for the lowest prices. At brick-and-mortar stores, they try to make deals, as if we're all used-car salesmen. On top of that, the Airbnb hosts are undermining the established B and B's who play by the rules, have standards, and are *members of the Chamber of Commerce*. And they make it ten times more difficult for legitimate, year-round, long-term tenants." She put down the coffee cup and looked at him as if she'd scored an irrefutable point. "I'm surprised your friend Kenneth didn't discuss this with you. He's helped craft a petition to regulate them in Beauport, assuming we can't ban them outright. I believe your friend Julie's house was listed in his evidentiary findings."

This was infuriating news. Kenneth had driven him home after Mandy's call, had come into the house and been helpful setting Mrs. Grayson up until the ambulance arrived. He'd poked around with what David had assumed was simple gay-male curiosity about the window treatments. Now he realized he was responsible for letting the enemy into their camp. No doubt, he'd been looking for code violations and more "evidentiary findings" (*please!*) for his report.

He heard the door open in the shop and the bustle of a few people entering. "It's nice and cool in here," a woman said. "You're lucky you get to work in air-conditioning all day."

"Aren't I?" Trisha enthused. "And I get to work surrounded all day by these incredible treasures you can't find anywhere else. If you want to know my personal favorite . . ."

No, it was ridiculous for Mandy to have even tried working here.

David stood, ready to make his escape. "Kenneth mentioned she's probably at a different store out here. Do you happen to know which one?"

"As far as I know, she hasn't been out on the Neck since the day she left here with her tail between her legs. I'd have heard from the storeowner if they were considering hiring her."

David thanked Elaine and said, "By the way, Mandy's SAT scores were extraordinary."

Elaine was already examining receipts. "I'm sure that will be of interest to someone," she said.

As he was walking home, wondering where it was Mandy went when she claimed to be going to her job, Michael called him.

"We're at a dead end," he said. "They're not budging past the twenty-five thousand, and I'm afraid the whole deal is going to collapse. Renata pointed out a few problems with your lease that make it less airtight than I thought. I confess, I'm probably not as up on California statutes as I should be. To her credit, she's begun looking again for something you can maybe afford. It turns out

I had her wrong all these years. She invited me to a party her husband is throwing next week. Since you won't be able to buy in Belle Reve or whatever that town is, let me know when I need to go back to my own apartment. Twenty-five thousand is better than nothing."

38

As soon as Mandy went into the dining room to work with David that afternoon, she sensed that something was wrong. He was on his computer when she sat down opposite him at the table, and he said "hello" (*hello?*) without looking up. While she waited for him to finish whatever it was he was doing, she calculated all the possibilities. One was that she just had a guilty conscience and was imagining things. If there was one value to the work she'd been doing for the last few weeks, aside from the questionable one of the money, it was that she'd become more confident than ever that she had a real talent for reading people and understanding their feelings.

The second possibility was that David was stressed because her father and Carol were coming for dinner tomorrow and he wanted to make sure everything went well.

Either of those things was an option, but there was something in the anger he was trying not to show that was clearly aimed at her. What did he know and how had he found out?

Worst of all, she hadn't been able to do the work he'd asked her to do. She'd tried. She'd completed her essay about Clara Dunston, but she knew it was weak. She'd tried taking the personality tests he'd given her, but had lost heart halfway through. Right now, it was hard enough to remember she'd had birthday parties without trying to recall a favorite one. She'd tried to organize her list of college choices they could present to her father over dinner, but that hadn't worked out either. All the online photos of the colleges showed a rainbow coalition of happy students working in labs and playing guitars and tossing around Frisbees. When they were shown gazing into computers, they were in libraries, not dank basements, and they were fully dressed. Everything made her feel depressed and angry. Deprangry. She couldn't get past the feeling that even though she had been equally deprangry at the start of the summer, she'd been a different person then. An unhappy, upset, inexperienced, untalented, unpopular person, true, but not a person who'd let herself be used, not someone who'd become a weird variation on a virgin whore. She'd been a *better* depressed and angry person.

Books about time travel annoyed her. If there was something about going backward or forward in time in the description of a novel, she put it down instantly. And yet, she'd become obsessed with the idea that she might go back and undo everything that had led her to this point.

She realized that she'd chosen the wrong essay prompt anyway. She should write about going back to Square One, but that would mean revealing everything about herself she had to hide.

When David finally looked up from his computer, he said, "Did you finish the essay?"

Reluctantly, she took out the two pages she'd printed out. He put on his glasses and read them, occasionally biting his lower lip. When he finished, he took off his glasses.

"What?" she asked.

"Do you remember when I showed you the essay about the ski lift? Do you remember how you critiqued it? Why don't you try doing that to your own." He handed her the pages.

It made her a little sick to look at them, but what choice did she have? "I love the first sentence, about the glue gun. I think it's fun."

"I agree, but there's a problem."

"The problem is, I love it too much, and it shows. It looks like I'm writing about this topic because I wanted to use that phrase more than discuss the topic itself."

"Good. Go on."

"And why am I writing about Clara Dunston when she's not the one applying? I meant to get around to making the essay about me, but I ran out of space."

He stuck his glasses on top of his head. "Oh, is that the reason you didn't get to yourself?"

"No, of course not. It's because I couldn't face writing about myself honestly, and I didn't want to lie. So I guess I'm half a fraud."

"I don't see it that way. But care to tell me why you can't face writing about yourself honestly?"

She tore the pages in half. Not dramatically, but slowly, because she knew they were useless. "Because I don't like myself a whole lot right now."

"Then start by trying to like yourself a little more," he said. "Cut yourself a little slack. I'd like another revision in two days. Do you have the rest of the work I gave you?"

Taking a page from Craig's Big Book of Behavior, she changed the subject. "Are you basically going to be moving in here?"

He slammed down the cover of his laptop. There were some things you'd just rather not see, and his anger was one.

"You were the one who contacted me and asked for my help. You were the one who suggested I visit. You know how much this dinner with your father means to Julie. You're the one going to college. I don't see why you've decided to let the ball drop at the worst possible second."

"Why are you screaming at me?" she shouted.

"You can tell I'm not happy, but I didn't raise my voice once. Accusing me of that is yet another way to change the subject."

She had a terrible feeling that she was going to start crying, something she was doing so often these days it was beginning to scare her. And, naturally, made her want to cry more. Somehow, it had all started out so innocently. She'd always had a fantasy that she had a boyfriend in another town, someone unconnected to her school, someone incredibly handsome and amazingly talented. She imagined herself showing up at a school event with him, proving to everyone who'd ignored or dismissed her that she was worth more than they'd supposed. She could see now how stupid it had been to think that Craig Crespo could ever be that person. She'd simply dug a deeper hole for herself.

If she was going to write about Square One—or write honestly about anything—she'd have to start somewhere. "Can I tell you something?" she asked quietly.

"You'll have to speak up," David said. "I can't hear you."

"Remember when you asked me if I had a boyfriend, and I said 'not really'?"

"I remember."

"Well, I sort of do. I mean, he's not a boyfriend, just someone I see. But he's a disappointing person."

"Disappointing in what way?"

"Maybe what I mean is I'm disappointed that I spend time with him. Maybe that's why I don't like myself so much. And I'm sorry I didn't do what you asked me," she said. "I promise I'll try."

He surprised her by reaching out and touching her face tenderly, and looking at her almost as if she were someone else, like maybe a nice girl who worked behind the counter at Beachy Keen.

"You asked about my plans," he said. "Your mother and I were waiting for a good time to discuss them with you. She and I talked about me staying and eventually fixing up the barn to live in, assuming I could figure out the financial details. Well, the details are not looking too good right now, so a lot of things are up in the air. But whatever happens, Mandy, you'll stay with your mother. Promise me that. At your age, your wishes have a lot of influence with judges."

Who knew what kind of deal her mother and David had going, but maybe the particulars didn't matter so much as long as they both had someone. Except now it sounded as if that was falling apart, too. "I want to stay with her," she said.

"And, Mandy," he said, "if you're disappointed with yourself for spending time with this guy, you should stop seeing him."

She went out to the porch and sat in the rocking chair she'd come to think of as Mrs. Grayson's. All the people who'd stopped at their house and spent a few nights were beginning to accumulate in her mind, like a needy mob demanding her attention and sympathy. The same was true for the foolish men she chatted with online, whose faces she never saw but whose personalities she knew so well. She'd always been a little frightened of mobs.

David was right: she should just stop. Of course she should, but something that looked so obvious and easy was, underneath it all, complicated. And if she stopped now, she didn't yet know where she'd be.

39

Over the course of cleaning out the house, David had come across photos of Henry at various stages of life and hair loss. He could imagine his mother saying of Henry that he had a "pleasant face," which is to say a look you couldn't find fault with. Although he wouldn't have admitted it to Julie, he felt no particular animosity toward Henry. It was true that his treatment of Julie had been unfair, but David's had hardly been exemplary. He'd had enough life experience to know that making assumptions about the relationships of others was like forming opinions of books you hadn't read: tempting, but pointless. On top of that, it always backfired.

Through little details Julie had tossed his way ("He's not exactly enlightened on some subjects" and "He grew up in a fairly conservative family"), he inferred that Henry was blandly homophobic. He was familiar with this type of man, since many of the successful fathers who hired him fell into that category. It wasn't that they believed he shouldn't have the same civil rights as everyone else, it was just that their body language and mildly condescending gazes conveyed the impression that they considered themselves inherently superior. They didn't want you to be unhappy, they were just convinced that in the grand scheme of things, your homosexual happiness counted for less than their heterosexual joy. David's brother, Decker, was one of these: he was fine with the fact that David had the right to vote, he just thought David should have the decency not to exercise it.

It was a question of masculinity, of course, but this made no sense to David since he'd come to believe that the libidinous excesses of gay men expressed male desire in its purest form. This made them more genuinely masculine than their heterosexual counterparts, even if they sometimes went overboard with eyebrow shaping and mid-century sofas. Children factored in, too. If you didn't have them, you were still human, but you were living a lame-duck life that mattered less. Although Decker had never expressed it in so many words, it was clear to David that he felt the fact that David had *almost* been a parent was proof that, as the Bible had made clear, he was not meant to live a full life. Among the many hypocrisies of the "religious" was the fact that they viewed god as omnipotent, but treated Him like a ventriloquist's dummy by putting their words and crackpot beliefs, prejudices, and unfounded biases into His mouth whenever it suited their purposes.

David had a mordant curiosity about Henry and a more eager one about Carol, whose photos were not to be found anywhere in the house. And yet, the day of the dinner, he'd woken up feeling as if a couple of social workers were coming to evaluate the household for an undisclosed purpose. His own purpose was to make enough of a case for the progress he and Mandy were making to take Henry aside and, man-to-man (or whatever), ask if he could hold off on the closing of the house for another few months. That might be enough time to go back to San Francisco and try some negotiations of his own with the landlady or seek some other options for Julie. He hadn't broken the bad news to Julie, but he could tell she knew something had happened.

Julie had told him that Henry and Carol would arrive promptly, and at exactly seven-thirty, as David was sliding a casserole dish into the oven, he heard tires crunching on the stones of the driveway.

"They're here," he called into the house.

"I told you they'd be on time," Julie called back. "They're just impossible."

When David looked out the window again, Henry was surveying the yard and the house with what he hoped was approval. He was better-looking than his photos suggested, a point that gave him an advantage, but that was neutralized by the fact he was wearing short pants and no-show ankle socks that were showing. The latter accessory was associated in David's mind with women who wear sun visors to play golf at restricted country clubs and men who depilate their legs for unknown reasons.

Carol, even from a distance, exuded the nervous eagerness for approval Julie had mentioned. She stepped out of the car and adjusted her light hair, brushed down her pink, scoop-necked jersey, and gestured to Henry to move the car closer to Julie's so it wouldn't be taking up two spaces. Clearly, she ruled Henry's life with her anxiety and punctuality. He was certain she had selected Henry's socks, especially since she was wearing them, too.

When Julie came into the kitchen, Carol was taking a large bouquet of flowers from the backseat with the care you might use to lift an invalid. "Oh, no," Julie said. "Flowers. And so many of them. Be sure to make a fuss about them; she spends half her time planting and weeding. Gardeners always make me feel morally inferior."

David put his hands on her shoulders. "She's not a better person because she grew some delphinium." In truth, he saw his own impatience for gardening as a character flaw on a par with his inability to memorize the names of constellations and his complete lack of interest in observing wild animals in their natural habitats.

"I hate that you tossed off 'delphinium' so easily," Julie said.

"If it's any consolation, I'm not sure that's what those are."

David went out with Julie to welcome them, realizing a moment too late that it wasn't his business to appear on the porch of a house that was still half Henry's with a woman who was still, technically, his wife.

"Those flowers are incredible," Julie called out. "Please don't tell me you grew all of them."

"They're mostly perennials," Carol said. "And half of them were already there when I moved into the house. All I have to do is weed. I brought something to put them in, but if you don't like it, I promise I won't be insulted." She produced an innocuous clear blue vase from the car. "I thought the color went well with the harvest bells and agapanthus."

"Oh, yes," Julie said.

Carol had a high, girlish voice. She took superb care of herself—her skin appeared to be polished—but she had the hard face of someone who could stand to eat a cupcake once or twice a year. The bones were too prominent, and the muscles around her jaw flexed visibly when she spoke. As was to be expected, she was pretty. But it was the flat prettiness of a sorority sister who wears pastels, subscribes to *Self* magazine, and actually reads the articles. She punctuated her comments with a dry, nervous laugh that reminded David of the panting of a dog eager to be petted.

Julie made the requisite introduction, and, as instructed, David complimented the flowers in detail, looking down at the bouquet as one looks at an infant in a stroller, desperately searching for things to praise.

"Doesn't David remind you of my brother?" Carol asked Henry.

"Your brother's thirty-five," Henry said.

"No, but I mean his manner."

From this, David gathered that Carol had a gay brother, a suspicion confirmed later when the brother came up in conversation again and his profession (set designer), real estate (adorable studio in the West Village), and love life (dating Eric) were revealed.

If Carol was making an exhausting effort to please, Henry was aiming for a stern demeanor that gave away nothing. David had noted this deportment in strong-willed men overcompensating for the fact that their lives are controlled by their wives or girlfriends.

He had a dark suntan, an attractive affectation, but one that these days looked somehow vintage, like a dial telephone or an electric carving knife.

Henry sidled up next to David as Carol and Julie were walking into the house, still cooing about the bouquet. "I see," he said, "you've made some improvements."

"There were a few loose brackets that needed to be tightened," David said. "Nothing very complicated." And then, first step on the guilt trip he was planning to use to purchase more time, he added, "You know how important this house is to Julie."

Henry didn't respond to the comment, nor did he say anything when David mentioned that he'd also cleaned out the gutters. He foresaw awkwardness about who would open the door for whom, so he told Henry he needed to get something out of the back of Julie's car and would be in in a few minutes.

When he entered the living room, everyone was perched on the edges of sofas and chairs, engaged on multiple fronts in a shoving match with the new toss pillows. Julie was explaining that David had cleared out a lot of the excess furniture.

"I'll bet that was hard for you, Julie," Carol said. She spoke in a sympathetic tone, but the implied criticism was clear. David wondered if Julie had noticed it. "It must be interesting meeting all the people who stay here," she went on. She was fiddling with her pink T-shirt, which had become tangled in the fight with the pillows. "Are there, what, dozens a month?"

"We only have a few rooms," David said.

"Have you?" Henry said.

"And of course, I'm taking up one of them."

"Mandy told me you had someone die here the other day," Henry said. "She seemed upset by it. It must have been traumatic for her."

"She was exaggerating," Julie said. "Someone had a stroke."

"Aw, a mini-stroke?" Carol asked. She said it the way you'd say "mini-marshmallow," as if there was something inherently cute in it.

"Minor," David said. "Julie told me you manage a doctor's office. What kind of practice?"

"Family medicine," she said. "We see a lot of teenagers and their parents. A great deal of what we do is a form of family therapy. I suppose it is for you, too, David."

"Sometimes," he said. "If each parent wants their child to go to the school they went to, it gets tricky. It usually has less to do with what's best for the child than with the parent's desire to relive their youth."

"I suppose there are many ways to do that," Henry said. "Attempt to relive your youth, that is. Speaking of which, where's Mandy?"

"Upstairs getting Opal settled," Julie said. "At least as settled as possible."

David had been told that Opal could tolerate Henry at Carol's house but she'd turned "confrontational" with him here in recent months.

"You know a lot of people have had success giving their troubled dogs antidepressants," Carol said. "We hear tons about dogs at the office."

"If anyone's taking antidepressants in this house," Julie said, "it's not going to be Opal."

David excused himself and went to check on dinner. He'd made a baked pasta casserole with penne and chicken that was based on a dish he'd been served at someone's house years earlier. He'd chosen it almost solely for carbohydrates, which he'd been depriving himself of for weeks now and was craving with salacious urgency. There was such an undercurrent of tension in the living room, he took the casserole out of the oven and reached a fork into it. He gobbled down a tube of pasta as if it were medicine. It tasted similar to everything he cooked, mostly because he was hostile to the idea of using recipes—which he saw as similar to tracing a picture instead of drawing it—and always used the same basic spice combination: two kinds of salt.

As he was about to return to the living room, he heard Mandy's footsteps on the back staircase. She strolled into the kitchen, sat at the table, and began playing with an empty wineglass. She had the slightly confused look he'd noticed in her eyes lately, and he wondered if he'd been too harsh with her about her essay.

"Opal's all set?" he asked.

"I propped the door open so she'd get a breeze. She went right to sleep." She laid her cheek down on the table as if she was too exhausted to hold up her head. "What would you say if I told you I'd like a glass of wine?"

"I'd have to ask for an ID."

"I'm seventeen, have only had alcohol twice, and hated it both times."

"In that case, I'd ask why you'd like it now."

"Because I'm about to have dinner with my divorcing parents and my father's new girlfriend and my mother's new whatever and we're all going to talk about my future."

"You make a strong case," he said. He poured half a glass of wine and handed it to her. "It's on the cheap side, so don't judge all wine by the taste of this. If it makes you feel any better, I'm planning to take control of the college conversation. You're free to disagree, but that could also be done afterward, in private."

Mandy sipped the wine slowly, as if she was trying to get used to the bitterness. In the past week or so, David had seen that there was something different about her, more mature than when he'd arrived, even though it had been only six weeks earlier. Though he'd tried, he'd been unable to put his finger on precisely what it was, just as it was often impossible to locate the source of a bad odor. But now, as she set down the wineglass and brushed her hair behind her ears, something clicked into place. This was a gesture he'd seen her make many times before, but tonight there was an element of sensuality in it and in the way she tilted her head and looked up knowingly. Too knowingly for someone who had, on some level, seemed entirely innocent a few weeks earlier.

"Mandy," he said. "I went to Beachy Keen the other day."

She looked up, wary and clearly unsure how to respond.

"Why did you go there?"

"The point is, why didn't you tell us you got fired?"

She eyed the wine in her glass. "I don't know. I guess I was ashamed that I'd screwed up even the world's worst job."

She got off her chair and went to hug David, once again child-like. "You aren't going to bring that up tonight, are you?"

"Where do you go when you claim to be working?"

She was silent for a moment, and then carefully she said, "There's a guy who has a little computer company. He works at the high school sometimes. I'm one of the people who answers the phone and some other stuff for him at his office. In Hammond."

This information should have been reassuring, even welcome, and yet it was not. There was something inherently unwholesome in David's mind about people who work in a vague way with com-puters. They were like men who ran vacuum cleaner stores—yes, they knew what they were doing and they provided a service, but there was often something off, even if it was hard to pinpoint what.

As if she understood his doubts, she said, "I'm learning more than I was at Beachy Keen."

"That's a low bar," David said.

She hugged David again, not with affection exactly, but with a need for comfort.

Henry walked through the swinging door carrying his glass. He took in the scene and went to the counter, where the wine bottle was. "So," he said as he poured. "This is where you've been hiding out, Mandy. Do I get a hug, too?"

"I'll leave you two," David said.

In the living room, Carol was explaining to Julie the particu-lars of her Fitbit. It calculated steps and calories and heartbeats and other statistical information that was essentially meaning-less to anyone, even Carol. Americans were increasingly addicted to information, especially when it could be used in support of opinions that were inaccurately described as facts. David supposed that the numbers spit out by the device on Carol's wrist supported her obsessive need for exercise, a neurosis masked as a virtue. Julie was listening with rapt fascination, not, David knew, because she was interested in the details but because she was astonished that Carol was.

"Carol is a serious athlete," she announced.

"Only when I find the time," Carol apologized.

Henry came back into the living room with his arm around Mandy, and David was relieved to see they'd made up.

"And she always finds the time," Henry said. There was a dismissive note in his voice, despite the fact that he obviously enjoyed the benefits of her unyielding regimen. Those firm, shapely legs.

"Come here and sit with me, you two," Carol said. Her voice had developed the friendly warmth that explains the popularity of wine at awkward social functions.

Mandy did as requested and sat on the sofa between Henry and Carol. David could imagine Carol as a strict-but-loving stepmom who'd treat Mandy like a younger sister with whom she was vying for Daddy's attention. There were worse arrangements.

Now that Carol was slightly lubricated, she seemed to have assumed the job of keeping the conversation rolling. "I guess there must be all kinds of exes," she said, wagging a finger between David and Julie. "I haven't talked with mine in years, and I can't imagine even having dinner with him, let alone an extended visit."

"Did things end badly?" Julie asked. "I guess they always do, in one way or another."

"Not exactly badly," she said. "I moved to Tucson to be with him, and we discovered we didn't have anything in common. So that ended it."

This complaint, which often referred to divergent careers and hobbies, had always baffled David. The only thing relationships needed in common was love—of some kind—and true love was rarely the result of a shared fondness for quilting.

Henry pointedly announced that he was beginning renovations on the restaurant at the end of September, after the height of the summer season. The contractors had been lined up and the time blocked. "As soon as we close on the house," he said, "I'll send in the deposits. That's in ten days, I believe."

"I'd have thought you'd wait until November," David said. "There must be a lot of tourism here right through October. Foliage season and all."

"Some," he said, "but it drops off sharply after Labor Day. You'd see for yourself if you were going to be around."

"He might be," Mandy said.

Henry nodded, as if, on some level, he'd known this was coming. "I wouldn't think there was much for you here," he said.

David commented that a lot of his work could be done online, even though he doubted Henry had been referring to career opportunities.

The subject of Mandy's plans did not come up until they were seated at the dinner table and David was serving his casserole. He'd left it in the oven perhaps fifteen minutes too long, and it had the texture of oatmeal and not much more flavor. To try to salvage it, he'd resorted to the standard culinary Band-Aid—he added cheese, lots of cheese, and stuck it under the broiler. This created a crust and aroma that fooled everyone except Carol, who, with the bloodhound instincts of all people with mild eating disorders, saw through the ruse immediately. Her Fitbit was probably sending her electric shocks. When Henry indulged in a second helping, she shot him a smile that reeked of disapproval. She talked in a cheerful way about a doctor she'd worked for who'd moved to San Francisco and the astonishing real estate prices there, all while carefully extracting vegetables from the pasta with the skill of a brain surgeon and then creasing and folding them with her knife and fork as if she were practicing a culinary form of origami.

After he'd cleared the plates, David brought out four identical binders into which he'd slipped copies of Mandy's dossier, including a list of a dozen schools he saw as possibilities worth pursuing. He'd started off the list with the most impressive schools, even if they weren't the most likely. In this case, Wellesley, Smith, Johns Hopkins, Barnard, and Williams. He'd noted that parents were inevitably flattered by the inclusion of schools of this caliber, even if they knew they were long shots for their kids and weren't happy to pay for them if they did get in. It was a facile, mandatory compliment he paid to the family DNA.

"Why so many women's colleges?" Henry asked.

David had an opinion that Mandy would do better surrounded by smart, serious women who were not, at least on the surface, vying for the attention of men in the same school. Or perhaps his feelings about her best interests had been formed that first day when he saw her talking with the guy in the van and discussed library steps with Amira. Her grades made any of these schools a reach, but her test scores were strong enough that it was possible to make a case for her, especially if she could pull off an eye-catching essay.

"We've chosen these schools because they have outstanding programs in psychology," he said.

"I'm not sure that's a very practical thing to focus on," Henry said. "What about business?"

"It's not like that always works out either," Julie said. The meaning of this was unmistakable.

Although Henry and Carol were seated on one side of the table, there was a palpable intimacy between Julie and Henry born of having lived together for decades and therefore knowing precisely where to stick the daggers. As the coded discussion went on, it seemed as if they were the real couple and Carol and David the mere backup singers, almost an item themselves.

Finally, Mandy spoke up. "I ought to get an opinion here, don't you think? We all know I'm not getting into any of these first schools, so there's no point in discussing. And I'm sorry, Dad, but if you think I'm a good candidate for studying business, you haven't been looking closely. David's right—I'm more suited to psychology. If I never brought it up before, it's because I needed his help figuring it out, or at least admitting it to myself. I can see it as a real direction, which I've never had before. And I'd probably be better off at a state school anyway."

There was nothing hesitant in her delivery, nothing unsure. Maybe it was the few sips of wine she'd had in the kitchen. Whatever it was, David was proud of her: she'd made a stand for herself;

and Henry, no doubt both pleased and disappointed at her new-found conviction, merely shrugged and said, "I'm glad you have a direction, Mandy."

Later, when David was standing at the kitchen sink scraping food off the plates into a scrap bucket, Henry came in and placed a bowl of salad remains on the counter. He looked around the room as if he was seeing it for the first time. "Something's different in here," he said. "The lighting?"

"Good call," David said. "I had some of the old fluorescent ceiling lights replaced. It warms things up. A simple fix."

Henry nodded. "Thanks for the meal. Comfort food. I don't get much of that at home."

David saw this confession as an attempt at male bonding. "Carol have you on a short leash?" he asked.

"She and some others. I had a scare last winter, so it's all for the best. As is an indulgence like this every once in a while."

"What kind of scare?"

Henry gestured toward his chest. "Heart. Nothing major, but then again, in that area, there's nothing minor, either. I don't think the stress of the restaurant and the divorce helped much. It will be good for all of us to have it over."

David was sorry to hear about the scare. It put the food and the fitness into a new category—a matter of necessity rather than vanity. Even Carol's nervousness and Henry's urgency about selling the house looked different in this context, although he was going to have to raise the issue anyway.

"Julie doesn't know anything about this," Henry added, "so I'd appreciate it if you wouldn't mention it."

"Of course. And I did want to ask something of you, too, Henry."

He couldn't falter or be sheepish about it. He had to ask as if it was not a big deal, as if it was a completely reasonable request. He mentioned his plans for turning the barn into a unit for himself and thereby helping Julie purchase the property. "There is one problem," he said. "We're going to need a little more time."

Henry looked around the room and then back at David. "Define 'a little,' please."

"I'm not sure exactly. A few more months. Not much beyond that."

"I appreciate the work you've been doing around here, David. Now it's obvious why you've bothered, but I'm still grateful. It will help bring a better price. If Amira's husband backs out, we can put it on the market next week. Julie has wasted enough of my time. I originally wanted to sell a year ago. As for you, I don't get what your game is here, but maybe it's not my business."

"Game," David said. "I'm not sure how any of this qualifies as a game. It's a friendship and a living arrangement. I don't imagine it's perfect, and I doubt Julie does either. Then again, I don't believe much in perfection when it comes to relationships and human behavior."

Henry took this in without expression and then said, "You're not Mandy's stepfather, and I hope you don't forget that, but she seems to like you, and if you help her find a direction, even if it's one I don't necessarily agree with, I can't complain. If it fits her, it fits her." He opened and closed a few cabinets, looking for a place to put the vinegar and oil. "You've changed everything."

David pointed to a shelf on the opposite side of the sink. "A little reorganizing. I think it's more efficient this way."

Henry put the bottles on the counter, apparently resisting the new order, efficient or not. "On top of everything," he said, "I've always felt bad about what happened with you and Julie. I mean that sincerely, but it's not enough to make me put my life on hold any longer."

"It was a long time ago," David said. "As you know, I'm sure, a lot of it related to my own issues and behavior. I don't spend time dwelling on the past, but it's been nice reconnecting with Julie on different terms." And then, as if he was talking with the father of his beloved, he added, "She's dear to me."

"I meant about the baby," Henry said.

David looked at him more closely in the atmospheric lighting of the kitchen. There was sweat on his forehead, and although he'd said the words with a tinge of tenderness, his eyes were hard. It was a shock to hear this mentioned, since it was, in David's view, one of those topics that was off-limits by unspoken consensus. It was hard to know if Henry was expressing genuine empathy or was trying to open old wounds.

"Julie's always felt bad about it," he went on. "In an essential way, I think it was the cause of a lot of floundering and mistakes in the years that followed. Guilt, whatever that concept means."

"Different things to different people," David said. "I've always felt somehow responsible myself."

There was a crash from upstairs and the scratching and scrambling of paws on wood. Opal had obviously woken up and freed herself from Mandy's bedroom. He hoped she wouldn't cause any trouble with the guests.

"Yes," Henry said, "but she's the one who made the decision, not you. She's the one who's had to carry that around all these years."

David turned off the water he'd been running in the sink and gripped the counter. He felt a strange chill enter his body as he replayed and absorbed Henry's words. Then, immediately, the assumptions he'd made about a few of the most significant events of his life began to rearrange themselves in his head. It took a moment or two for them to form a coherent narrative. He gazed at Henry, trying to figure out if he assumed that David already knew this or had said it out of spite, revenge for his relationship with Julie, with Mandy, and even with the house itself. It was easier to think about this than the information he'd imparted.

Opal clattered down the back staircase and began pawing at the door to the kitchen and whimpering. David walked across the room and let her in, and with a burst of pent-up energy, she slid across the floor with her tongue hanging out and her one hind leg splayed behind her. Mandy had probably forgotten to leave out water, David thought, concentrating on something it was easy to focus on. Opal went to David and sniffed, then hobbled to Henry. He reached down to pat her head, and she sank her teeth into his hand.

40

Something was wrong. Probably more than one thing, if she had to guess. For two days after the dinner, Julie saw David infrequently. Twice she'd made him his morning tea and twice the big white mug had sat on the table in the kitchen until it turned cold and she had to dump it down the sink. He hadn't cooked dinner or eaten with them, and there had been no reading, no walks, and no explanations. When she passed him in the hall, he smiled in a benign way that was warm enough to lack hostility but remote enough to be confusing. It was as if he was one of the paying guests and was trying to be as politely unobtrusive as possible. The dinner with Henry had not been a massive success, but aside from the incident with Opal, it hadn't been a disaster. Mandy hadn't done all that Henry wanted, but Julie could tell that he'd been mollified, at least for the moment. There had been no mention of Mandy's living anywhere but there.

The "there," however, was beginning to look unlikely.

The closing was next week, and although the benefits office at Crawford was ready to send her a portion of the funds she needed from her retirement account, the approaching event had begun to take on the surreal atmosphere of a recurring nightmare in which she was about to step onstage to give a lecture without notes or any knowledge of the subject. David was not going to come through. She knew, on some level, that she was headed toward disaster, but she was moving toward it inexorably. No one had made the announcement that the plane was crashing, the flight attendants weren't screaming, and so she didn't see any alternatives except to fasten her seat belt and stay the course. Maybe by some miracle, they'd pull out of the nosedive at the last moment.

This morning, she'd asked David, as he passed in the kitchen, if he'd been seeing more of Kenneth, one other possible explanation for his absence.

"No," he said. "I don't think I'll be seeing any more of him. He isn't quite who I thought he was."

Again, the mysteriously remote smile, and then an escape to his room. The whole mood of the house filled her with melancholy regret. They were having one of those spells of deceptively autumnal weather that frequently occurs in mid-August. The mornings were chilly and crisp with what felt like heartbreaking clarity in the light. Somehow, this contributed to unease. *Ask him*, she kept telling herself, but some unnamed instinct prevented her from doing so.

Around noon, Henry called as she was changing the sheets for a tenant who was coming into the Window Seat Room later that afternoon.

"I've just come back from the doctor," Henry said.

Julie sat down on the feature for which the room was named, pulled her knees to her chest, and tried to focus on the view of the pine tree and the barn.

"Oh? Anything wrong?"

"As a matter of fact, yes. I was bitten by a dog recently."

Opal, who seemed to know that she'd done something bad, had been unusually passive since the incident. That was for the good, but it still troubled Julie that if she'd done it once, there was no guarantee she wouldn't do it again. She was lying on the floor beside the bed Julie had been making, a three-legged angel of a dog. When she'd asked David if Henry had provoked Opal in any way, he'd said no, but then mysteriously added, "I suppose I was the one he was trying to provoke."

"Obviously," she said now, "you didn't need stitches." It was a safe assumption. Henry had tricky gums and she'd seen him bleed more when he'd brushed his teeth too vigorously than he had after Opal had nipped him.

"I did not," he said. "What I need is the paperwork showing the dog is up-to-date on shots. Just fax them over to me. She *has* had her shots, hasn't she?"

"Of course she has. I'll send the papers over later today."

Although she'd been expecting him to demand them right away, he said, "That's fine. It's standard procedure. I'm not asking for them to harass you. If it had been up to me, I wouldn't have bothered going to the doctor. It's healing anyway."

She suspected he took pleasure in this demand, even if it had been mandated by someone else. "Is that all?" she asked.

"Don't be so cold, Julie. We don't have to hate each other."

She couldn't respond to this. When she thought back to how she'd felt about him when they first met, about the hopes she'd had for their future together, about how thrilled they'd both been about the house, about the contentment and joy in the first few years after Mandy was born, the comment was like a slap across the face. After all the proclamations of love they'd made to each other decades earlier, this was where they'd ended up. Not hating each other.

"No," she said. "We don't."

"Carol cleaned and bandaged my hand again as soon as we got home that night. She has a medical kit in the bathroom. I'm guessing that fact doesn't come as a surprise to you. She made the appointment. When I went to the clinic today, they took one look at it and were convinced I'd gone to the ER when it happened. It was that professionally done."

Pretty and toned and—yes, all right—youngish as she was, it was hard to imagine someone as carefully controlled and meticulous as Carol in the throes of passion. The way Julie had been with Raymond, even if briefly. Raymond, who still appeared in her dreams more often than she liked, but less frequently than he had a few weeks ago. With Carol, there would probably be a long shower afterward and sanitizer, possibly from the medical kit.

"You need someone like that," Julie said quietly. "I'm sure she makes your life easier."

"Yes, she does. But when I was in the house with you and David, I realized she makes my life a little less interesting, too."

It was late in the game for him to tell her this. No doubt there was some calculation behind it.

"Life is full of trade-offs," she said.

"If you want to know the truth, I was jealous that he was living in my house with my wife and my daughter and that you all seemed to get along so well together. Call me petty. I love the stability of what I have now. I'm too old for anything else. But it made me realize, there were a lot of ways in which the things that drove me crazy about our relationship made me happy, too."

Give me information I can use was what she wanted to say, but she was curious about where this was coming from and where it was headed. "Why tell me this now, Henry? What's the point?"

"I just thought you should know. I thought you'd want to know. I figured you'd enjoy hearing that I have a few faint regrets about the divorce."

"I'm not that small-minded," she said. And then, after a moment, "On second thought, maybe I am. Thank you."

"There's something else," he said. "Some of those feelings might have led me to say things to David I shouldn't have said. I apologize."

Maybe that answered some of her concerns about David's behavior. "To me?" she said. "Why not apologize to him?"

He said nothing, and she told him she'd get him the papers as soon as possible.

There was a pause and then he said, "Are you two sleeping together?"

She almost put down the phone. "How could that possibly be relevant to you?"

"I'm curious."

"You haven't earned an answer from me, Henry. I'm sorry. I'm sure you can figure it out on your own if you take all the facts into consideration."

"I'll see you next week at the closing?" It shouldn't have been a question.

He knew, she could tell, that it wasn't going to happen, but he was playing along. Either to appease her or to make his final triumph all that much more triumphant.

"We'll talk," she said.

Later in the afternoon, she started looking for Opal's papers in all the usual places but couldn't come up with anything. She'd have to call the vet, but it felt like one extra step she didn't want to take. She was in the hall, going through the drawers of a bureau that was the refuge of last resort for things like warranties on air conditioners and instruction booklets on the washing machine, when David came into the house. She wanted to ask where he'd been, but what right did she have, and on top of that, he looked uncharacteristically grave.

"Looking for something?" he asked.

"Opal's papers," she said. "I need to send them to Henry. The doctor has to have them. By law, I gather. You didn't see anything like that in your cleaning, did you?"

"No, I didn't. I'm sure they'll turn up. Things like that usually do."

His voice wasn't cold, but it sounded like he was talking to a stranger. Did she want to hear what was wrong or did she already know?

She put her hand on his arm as he was turning to go. "David, what is it? I've only seen you in passing for the last couple of days. We've barely spoken. I haven't even had a chance to thank you for the dinner and the work with Mandy."

"You don't need to thank me. It's what I came for."

"You're angry with me but you're not saying why. I don't think I can stand it much longer. We have plans, but if the money isn't going to come through, we can figure out something else."

He took a seat on the staircase. At least he wasn't running away. She sat on the step below him, looking up. He put his hand on her hair gently. It was such a relief to be touched after all the silence, she started to cry. "I'm sorry," he said. "I'm not getting the money I thought I would. It was probably too much to hope for, a nice fantasy while it lasted. I thought I could make up for the ways I failed you in the past, but I'm afraid it's turning out to be another disappointment. You'll end up with enough from the sale to get something for you and Mandy. Something nice."

She rested her head against his leg. It wasn't right to make him do all the work. "I know the money is only part of it," she said. "It's about the baby." She'd said the last words so quietly, she wasn't sure he'd heard her.

"You should have told me," he said, still stroking her hair. "It's not as if I wouldn't have understood. It's not as if I would have stopped you, if it was something you were sure about."

"I wasn't sure." One of the guests was taking a shower in the bathroom at the top of the stairs, but the sounds of water running through the pipes seemed to be coming from miles away, from someone else's house. "I was panicked."

"I know, and I know why. I've tried to imagine what I would have done if I'd been in your place, and probably I would have done the same thing. It wasn't right, it wasn't wrong. If we're halfway decent people, we do the best we can with what we've got at the time. And you're more than decent, Julie." The shower was turned off; she heard footsteps. "But you should have told me, if not then, then now. It would have been good for both of us."

He made it sound so simple and clear, so easy, especially at this distance. Maybe this moment would fall into perspective, too, at some later date.

"You can forgive me after all this time, can't you? I don't want you to leave."

He kissed the top of her head, as he had the day he'd first arrived.

"I don't have anything to forgive you for. I've been happier here these past weeks than I've been in a long time. I just made some miscalculations about belonging here. I'm going back to San Francisco in four days. I made the reservation this morning."

41

In her senior year of college, Julie had started dating a boy named Dennis Schaeffer. She remembered him now as leggy and long-faced, but in her memory, all the boys she dated back then, all the boys she knew, were leggy and long-faced.

Julie was in over her head at Sarah Lawrence, and Dennis was in his element at Columbia, studying political science. He was a passionate, intellectually intense student with plans to go to law school and then run for office. He was, like a lot of ambitious people, manic depressive, although Julie hadn't known that for the first six months they were going out. She thought he was just energetic. Intellectually, they were in different leagues. Her own mother—always ready with a harsh opinion—had confirmed this after her parents had taken them out to dinner in the city. "He'll do great things," her mother had said, "assuming he doesn't become a drug addict and/or commit suicide. It won't last, darling, but maybe it will be educational for you."

When, after a year and a half of dating, they broke up and Julie got enough distance to look at the realities of the relationship, she was struck primarily by how little fun they'd had. Everything had been a battle of wills, an opportunity for him to lecture her, another reason for him to correct her faulty logic or lack of information. Ah yes, reenacting the family dynamics. No wonder her mother had approved.

In retrospect, she was plagued by two questions: Why had he been interested in her and, perhaps more important, Why had she put up with him? "The answer to both questions is the same," her mother had said when she'd made the mistake of discussing her feelings over Thanksgiving dinner. "Low self-esteem."

It was a brilliant response. It was accurate and explained, by its wounding nature, everything Julie needed to know about her insecurities and their source.

Sexually, Dennis had been insatiable, a fact that Julie took to be evidence of his attraction to her but was probably just another manifestation of his mental illness. Whatever it was, that hadn't been fun, either. Dennis had been so completely focused on the demands and sensations of his own body, sex with him had been like sitting in a busy restaurant and being ignored by the waiter. *Hello? I'd like to place my order?* Julie often ended up wondering what had just happened and if she'd actually been in the room when it did.

She sometimes pondered how she would have felt about David Hedges if they hadn't met when Dennis Schaeffer was still a shape on the horizon in her rearview mirror. Would she have been so overjoyed that he supported all her creative aspirations and never criticized her addled tendency to leap from one project to the next? Would she have been so taken with his calm, steady demeanor? Would their playful, tender sex life have seemed so completely satisfying to her even when she was aware that David seemed more attentive to her needs than to his own? Would she have wondered more about what his needs were?

Very possibly, yes, but she would never know now.

They were happy together, laughed a lot, had their books and the music he loved introducing her to. In the midst of their light-hearted domesticity, it had been easy for Julie to overlook a few qualities that she should have questioned. It had never occurred to her to wonder why they never discussed the future.

When they'd been living together for a year and a half, when David was talking vaguely about a move to Boston for a doctoral program in education, a move that might or might not involve her (it had never been clear), she discovered she was pregnant. She'd cried and apologized when she'd told him. There was a prescription she hadn't gotten around to filling for longer than she cared to admit.

"It's not as if I'm not equally responsible," David had said.

None of the options was especially appealing, but in the end, they made one of their giddy, impetuous decisions to marry quietly and make announcements after the fact.

Her mother, in particular, was not amused. "I can't believe you think he's the marrying kind," she'd said.

Antrim, a history teacher at the school where David was on the faculty, was introduced into their lives as a minor offstage character a couple of months before the pregnancy. He'd come to the school in the middle of the year. He and his wife lived in what was then an unfashionable neighborhood in Brooklyn. Based on David's descriptions of their conversations, Julie had developed a crush, which, at some point, she realized she'd contracted from David. It was she who insisted they invite Antrim and his wife for dinner, and they arrived one early-spring night bearing flowers and wine. The four of them had an instant rapport, and Julie had fallen in love with both of them while, at the same time, feeling even closer to David in their presence. When they were trying to decide what to do about her pregnancy, Julie had mentioned how happy Antrim and his wife, about the same age as they were, always seemed.

And then, one night, after they had married, Julie had walked into the kitchen and seen David and Antrim laughing together about something that had happened at school, and all the suppressed suspicions she'd had, all the fleeting doubts, all the unspoken concern about the amount of time he spent with Antrim gelled into conviction. She felt she had a right, even an obligation, to leaf through books and rummage through desk drawers. Within a few hours, she'd found a note from Antrim to David tucked into a folder, the very thing she'd been looking for and simultaneously hoping she wouldn't find.

Panicked, she'd called the one person she knew who had never given her sympathy, comfort, or solace, but who was unyielding and often right in her convictions and opinions. Her mother came to the city and took Julie out for dinner.

"It was ridiculous to get married," she said. "If you'd told me what you were planning, I would have talked you out of it. There was a much simpler solution. I knew this as soon as I met him. You think David will change, but he won't. A baby will be a brief distraction, at most. This is about who he is, not what he's doing. If you're upset about it now, you'll feel worse in a year, except then you'll have a baby. You're not capable of raising a child on your own, Julie. I'm not saying it to be unkind; it's the unfortunate truth. Period. You're too young, too unfocused, and too poor. Life has to be lived one step at a time, and this is not the step you need to take now. I'll make the arrangements for you. You're lucky you found out while there's still time to change course."

Julie had chosen a week when David and Antrim had gone off to Washington, D.C., as chaperones for a school trip. When he returned, she couldn't stop crying. She said she was no longer pregnant, they'd lost the baby. *Lost.*

"Why didn't you call me?" he asked. "I would have come back."

"It wouldn't have changed anything," she said.

A few days later, she said, "You do see, don't you, that I wouldn't be capable of being a single mother? You do see that, don't you?"

"What does that have to do with anything?" he asked. "You're not single."

"Oh, David," she said. "We both know I am."

He had no answer to that, which told her, with some relief, that she hadn't made a mistake. The rest of his story came out in fragments, and six months later, they went their separate ways.

42

For days following the dinner with Henry, David had spent most of his time walking around Beauport, trying to piece together his thoughts and organize his feelings. How could he criticize Julie for having kept a secret from him when the whole basis for it had been his own secrecy? Maybe, even after all these years, she was in denial about the facts of what she'd done as he had been in denial about himself then.

Had Julie acted out of despair or anger toward him or simple practicality? Undoubtedly a combination of all three. Maybe, in the end, it didn't matter. He had lived his life as he needed to, she had gone on and lived hers and remarried. For a while, she'd been happy. She had Mandy. If he could go back, would he change anything, ask her to do anything differently? It was impossible to know. He'd spent a lifetime training himself to short-circuit regret, and there was no point in trying to undo all that work now. As for blame, that was as unproductive as regret.

All of it coming to light—and thanks to Henry, too—had pointed out the flimsiness of the foundation on which he'd built this feeling of home. It was time to go back to his interrupted life in San Francisco and try to restart that stalled engine.

There were questions about Mandy's job and her boyfriend, but that was a problem he would have to leave to her parents. He saw that Henry had been right—he was not a stepparent, and perhaps his interference was more of a problem than a solution to one.

After his talk on the stairs with Julie he left the house and called Renata. He was shocked that she actually took his call.

"Is this you or your lawyer?" she asked.

"For better or worse," he said, "it's me."

"How sweet of you to return my call after, how many weeks? Seven? *Eight?* What can I do for you?"

It was important to swallow his pride and get the job done. "My plans have finally come together. I'm heading back to San Francisco. Michael said you'd begun looking for something for me, and I was wondering if you have any leads in my range."

"As a matter of fact, I do have a place, but we're up against a deadline. If you want it, you'll have to take the twenty-five thousand and move out of the carriage house by September first."

"I'm ready to do that," David said. "And since I didn't want the money for myself anyway, I'm ready to forgo the buyout."

"Noble on top of everything else."

She described a small, sunny apartment on the top floor of a house in Noe Valley, a neighborhood David had always loved. There was a small master bedroom and a tiny second room that could be used as an office. "The kitchen is completely outdated and the bathroom is absurd, but someone like you might be able to talk himself into believing they have charm." She named a rent that was shockingly low by the standards of San Francisco real estate.

"There must be a catch," David said.

"Of course there is. This is life, David. There are several catches. The bathroom is one, the kitchen another. The owners on the floor beneath you are a couple of older gay men. Lovely, in their eccentric ways, those eccentricities being catches three, four, and five."

He asked for clarification, knowing ahead of time that, whatever they were, he'd have to accept them. He wasn't in a position to be choosy.

"They had a young couple renting from them for a fortune for a year or two. They had parties, loud friends, and worst of all, were noisily fucking all the time."

"Heterosexuals?"

"Apparently. They ended up having a baby."

"That'll teach them."

"The boys didn't renew the lease and now they want a new tenant, but they're willing to take a fraction of what they could get on the open market provided I find them someone who's clean and 'quiet,' if you see what I mean. Their ideal renter is a sixty-five-year-old woman with a cat, but there are the stairs to consider.

You'd offer the same benefits, and they wouldn't have to worry about a litter box."

"Can you explain 'quiet'?" He had an idea where this was headed, but he wanted confirmation.

"No renovations, for one thing. Everything has to remain as it is. Intolerable for me, but probably less problematic for you. They also don't want to have to deal with the particular noise problem they had with the couple."

There was an echo of Sandra's rant in this from her drunken consultation the day of his arrival. It saddened him to think about it.

"Am I expected to sign a celibacy agreement?"

"I doubt that would be legal. Or necessary."

He wasn't clear if she was reassuring him or making an assumption about the prospects for his sex life.

"Believe me, David, you're not going to land a fluky deal like this anytime soon. You do seem to have decent real estate karma, but even that must have its limits. I told a sad little academic I met—with *braids,* if you can picture it—she could look at it next week, but if you get here right away, and the boys approve of you, we can sign the lease immediately."

"Can you hold it until Friday?"

"Believe me," she said, "you won't regret it. I know you think I'm a heartless bitch, which I do not necessarily consider an insult, but this still pleases me. I could have been a better friend and now the slate is wiped clean. Send me your flight information. I'll pick you up at the airport and we can head straight to Noe Valley. If you have sneakers, wear them. Or better yet, I'll bring slippers for you. Did I mention they prefer you not wear shoes upstairs?"

"Do they have a preference as to boxers or briefs?"

"No, but I do. We can discuss that driving from the airport. Thank god you decided to grow up."

43

Amira appeared stunned when Julie told her that David was leaving for good the following day. Julie had come to think of her as being above genuine emotion or at least above the expression of genuine emotion. But sitting in a molded plastic chaise longue on the roof deck of Amira's house, Julie watched as her neighbor gasped and brought her hand to her pretty bow of a mouth.

"But this is terrible news," she said. "You're being abandoned again."

The words, which should have stung, passed over her.

It was a sunny day and the water was sparkling in the harbor below. About ten minutes earlier, Amira had lit up a joint. "I won't ask if you want any," Amira had said, "because I know you are now one of the eighteen people in the country who don't smoke."

"Try me," Julie had said, and when Amira had passed her the

joint, she'd inhaled eagerly. *Hello, old friend,* she'd thought as a wave of forgetfulness rolled in. *Where have you been hiding?*

There was too much to take in, too much disappointment and sadness and deep regret about things she couldn't change. She supposed that one day she'd be angry at Henry about this, but for the moment she was almost relieved. He had told David the one thing that she had been trying to tell him for years but had lacked the courage to mention. Now she was back to a welcome state of bleary, false, fleeting peace. Someone in the neighborhood was practicing the piano again, and from up here, the soft music was blending with the reassuring sounds of children playing on the baseball field many blocks away. It was nice, in her current frame of mind, to be able to pretend it was a perfect late-summer afternoon.

"I'd rather not think of it as abandonment," Julie said. "I'd rather think of it as the inevitable end of David's summer vacation."

"But now you can't buy the house," Amira said.

"No," Julie said. It was so much easier to say now that she was stoned. "I can't. You'd better let Richard contact the pool people so they can start digging."

Amira pondered this for a moment as she tapped ash off the end of the joint. "I'm not going to let you smoke any more pot," she said. "I don't want to be a bad influence, and you were more alert when you were sober. I'm going to try to give it up, too. I can join a twelve-step group and tell my life story and find damaged boyfriends." She flicked the joint off the edge of the roof with surprising vigor. "I'm also not going to let Richard buy the house unless he lets you stay there. He will do whatever I say."

Julie was touched by this, the most considerate thing Amira had ever said. But the truth was, she had infinitely less control over Richard than she had over her various lovers. Julie suspected that Amira, who knew she needed order in her life, had married him for this very reason: he couldn't be bullied or manipulated.

"Even if you could make him, I wouldn't want that. I'll be renting something for a year so Mandy can finish school here, and then I'll buy a place in another town, one closer to work. I don't want to have my old house looming above me every time I walk out the door. Or, even worse, watch it being knocked down."

"But David was supposed to rescue Mandy," Amira said. "Now he can't."

Amira's English was flawless but occasionally fanciful. "Rescue" was a dramatic word, and in this case, Julie didn't see the relevance.

"He was supposed to help with her college applications, and he did. He's promised he'll do more of it from San Francisco. I can't complain."

Amira lifted her round sunglasses from her lovely eyes, surveyed the horizon, and then put them back on. "If I see her on the steps of the library, I will let you know."

Mandy preferred to read her way through the books tucked into boxes and shelves around the house. As far as Julie knew, she hadn't used her library card in ages. She mentioned this to Amira, but she ignored Julie's comment. "And what about the clarinetist?" Amira asked. "Is he coming back anytime soon?"

Julie had not explained the whole story of Raymond Cross's wife to Amira, mostly because she feared that anything Amira would say about the situation would only make Julie feel worse—that she would be doing Raymond's wife a favor by having sex with her husband or that once she was out of the picture, she could move in on Raymond. Julie had simply told Amira that it was over and had even stopped correcting her about the clarinet. At this point, it didn't matter.

"No," Julie said. "My clarinetist is not coming back. We're all just moving on."

Last week, he'd sent her an email with a file attached, which, when she downloaded it, turned out to be a piece of orchestral music she had never heard before—a little jazzy, a little cinematic. Perhaps it was something he'd written himself. She thought she recognized in it a melodic line that recalled the one he'd played for her that first night at the concert in Beauport. But she couldn't be sure. He'd written nothing in the email, as if the sad, haunting piece of music said everything he needed to say. Maybe, when she thought about it, it said everything she needed to hear.

44

David had booked himself on a late-afternoon flight and had rented a car he planned to return at the airport. Julie had offered to drive him, but he preferred to say goodbye to her as he'd said hello two months earlier—at the house. She'd gone to school in the morning for a preliminary faculty meeting but promised him she'd be back before he left. He wondered if it might not be better for everyone if she got held up at school; they'd already said more than enough goodbyes over the years. His rented car was packed. All he needed to do was make sure he hadn't forgotten anything.

He checked his watch and decided to walk through the village. Despite everything that had happened, he'd grown attached to it and was already feeling an ache at the thought of leaving it behind. It was easy to imagine that over time, his feelings about the past would change, and he'd come back here for a visit, perhaps an extended one, but it was equally easy to imagine he never would.

He set off down the hill toward town. It was hot again, but the heat at this late point in the summer had lost its edge; like a snowstorm in springtime, it wasn't a harbinger of the season ahead, more of an aberration. He'd been looking forward to autumn in New England, but now he thought he might be better off missing it. Given his age, that particular season had too much metaphoric significance.

Renata had sent him a series of photos of the apartment in Noe Valley, and it was just as she'd described it—brightly lit and outdated. It was indeed small. He could tell that right away because in the photos it looked large. Real estate photos emphasized the intimacy of sprawling rooms and exaggerated the size of small ones. Renata had also sent a photo of the couple renting the apartment, a dour pair that were a cross between an urban, homosexual *American Gothic* type and a couple of elderly priests impatiently waiting for cocktail hour. It was not going to be a rollicking life, he could see that, but then, rollicking had never been his forte. He was resigning himself to a quiet life, which he hoped would not turn out to be a life of quiet desperation.

As he got close to Kenneth's Kitchen, he decided to cross the street and avoid any possible confrontation. He stepped onto the crosswalk, but before he had a chance to cross, Kenneth called out to him: "You're just going to avoid me altogether? Is that the plan?"

David stopped, defeated, and turned around. Kenneth was standing in the doorway of his store, dwarfed by the shingled building around him, and, although dressed with characteristic care, somehow looking a little more worn than usual.

"I'm afraid I was," David said, approaching him. "I'm a bit pressed for time this morning."

"I know Elaine told you about the petition."

"Yes, she did."

"And you chose to take it personally? Like I'd done all that work to hurt you and your ex-wife specifically? Isn't that a little egotistical?"

He had his arms folded across his chest in battle mode, but his voice revealed genuine disappointment, and David had to admit that he had hurt Kenneth after all, despite his promise not to.

"Things got busy and complicated up at the house."

"Something always comes up, doesn't it?" Kenneth said with the touchingly forced dignity of a short man trying to make a stand for himself. "You should know that I've resigned from the committee and taken my name off the petition."

There was something gratifying in this, even if it was coming a little too late to mean much to David. "What made you change your mind?" he asked.

"I suppose you'll try to take that personally, too, but it didn't have anything to do with you. It turns out that a third of the storeowners in the group had rooms listed on Airbnb. I'm not interested in hypocrisy. I've dealt with enough of it in my life already."

This reminded David again of the struggles that Kenneth seemed to have risen above, and he was touched once more by that most sympathetic quality of his, the very one he did his best to keep hidden—his vulnerability.

"I apologize for not telling you this sooner, but I have to move back to San Francisco. I'm leaving for the airport soon. Once I get settled back into my life, I'll call and explain what happened."

Kenneth eyed David closely, probably trying to figure out whether or not to believe him. "No you won't," he said. "You're a tourist. Once a tourist leaves a tourist town it becomes a postcard in his mind and all the inhabitants become props. I'll save us both a lot of trouble and block you on my phone. But just so you'll know, I did have a nice time with you."

David started to tell him that he felt the same way, but Kenneth turned and entered his store before he had a chance.

He checked his watch again as he was trudging up the hill. He had enough time to make one more sweep through the rooms of the house before driving off. Cars were coming down the street at a crawl as they usually did: visitors were desperate to make the most of the scenic vista of harbor and open ocean and sailing boats that was now at his back. A van was taking up the rear in the line of cars, honking impatiently, a discordant note. Having reached the limits of his patience, the driver swerved into the wrong lane and sped past the other cars. As if there was anyplace to hurry to in this town.

As the van passed, David recognized it as the one Mandy had been leaning into that day after his arrival. There were faded letters on the side partly hidden by grime. Once, they'd probably said something about computers, but now all that was visible was "MPUT." The driver was flushed and scowling as he raced past. If this was the not-really boyfriend Mandy was working for in Hammond, it was not a good sign. As he continued up the hill, David guiltily felt relieved that all this was no longer his responsibility, not that it ever had been.

"It's not my problem," he said aloud. He didn't know why he needed to explain himself to himself, and then he recognized that he was excusing himself to that specific but nameless imaginary other who visited him from time to time. "I'm sorry if I'm disappointing you," he said, "but I did the best for them I could."

As he was turning into the drive at Julie's house, Amira stepped out from her own property, dressed for the beach in what appeared to be a close relative of the white bathing suit Elizabeth Taylor had worn in *Suddenly, Last Summer*. She had a colorful cloth wrapped around her waist, a surprising nod toward modesty. She looked more harried than usual, but announced, in her typically ironic tones, that she'd heard David talking to himself.

"Really?" he said. "Was I saying anything interesting?"

"I have no idea. I don't usually listen to other people, especially when they're about to move away to a place that I wish I was moving to instead of staying here in hell."

"I've come to the conclusion, Amira, that you like Beauport about as well as you'd like anyplace. Which is to say, a lot more than you like to admit."

"Yes, the sad truth," she said. "I'm easy to please. So humiliating." She hugged him goodbye and waved as she walked off.

"And that," David said aloud as he turned into the drive, "is the best I can do for her."

He paused on the lawn and looked at the house one last time.

There under the eaves was Mandy's room, one window open with the curtains blowing out, the other stuffed with an air conditioner. He headed up the stairs and then went back to the lawn and looked up. It was a new air conditioner in Mandy's window, spotlessly clean and installed with professional brackets to keep it in place. She'd complained that her air conditioner was noisy, but when had this come into the house and how had she paid for it? More to the point, why hadn't she mentioned it?

He jogged back to the sidewalk. By the time he reached Amira, he was winded.

"Can I ask you one thing?" he said, puffing.

"You can ask me anything as long as you do not require a serious answer."

He paused until he'd caught his breath. "Were you having computer problems today?"

She raised her thin, pretty eyebrows and said, "You must be psychic. I am impressed."

"I saw a van leaving, and I thought maybe he'd been at your house."

"Yes, a handsome man with eyes out of a lunatic asylum. Just my type usually, but I'm afraid too stupid to fix my problems. I can't give my lessons, so I am going to the beach instead."

Lessons? The idea that Amira was working was so distracting, David forgot the urgency he'd felt a minute earlier. "What kind of lessons?"

"On Skype. Language lessons for international refugees. And do not look so shocked. I am not as stupid and vain as I like people to think. I have convictions and a desire to help. Mainly help myself, but sometimes others as well. But please don't tell anyone. I prefer they think I am just a courtesan. You get more respect if people think you are doing your best with what you have instead of choosing not to use most of what you were given."

"So he wasn't able to help you?"

"No, and on top of that he insulted me terribly, David. He made an ugly, filthy suggestion." She adjusted her sunhat and the shadow across her face moved. David saw that she was genuinely upset. "He asked me, if you can imagine, if I wanted a *job*! Someone who looks like me and lives in a house like mine is seeking employment? I threw him out."

"Yes, it's outrageous," he said, trying to make sense of these pieces. "What kind of job?"

"He has models in his basement showing their bodies and talking dirty to a bunch of pathetic old men. He told me I could make a hundred dollars an hour doing it. The nerve. To be honest, it is something I could imagine doing, but at that price? If Richard is worth a quarter of what he claims, I will have made more than that a minute once he dies, even if he lives until ninety."

"I don't suppose he gave you his business card?"

She burst out laughing at the suggestion. "Do you think he would have one? Look him up on your phone. 'Craig's Computers' in Hammond. Even the name has no imagination."

He thanked her and kissed her goodbye. "I should hurry," he said, although he realized as he was saying it that he was probably already too late.

The look Mandy had given him the night of the dinner and the seductive way she'd touched her hair came back to him as he drove into Hammond. It's always the small gestures that give people away as they're occupied with carefully trying to hide the bigger ones. According to what Julie had told him, he'd given himself away merely by laughing with Antrim in the kitchen of their apartment.

The traffic into Hammond was slow with sightseers and lines of cars waiting to get to the beach. He decided he had to call Renata to tell her. Changing his plans yet again would probably infuriate her, but at least he could make sure she wasn't waiting for him at the airport.

"I hope you're driving to Logan," she said. "That airport is hopeless. Leonard and I missed our flight out last time we went for a parents' weekend. Thank god Teddy is graduating next year."

"I'm driving," he said, "but not to the airport. Unfortunately, something came up, and I had to cancel my reservation."

There was silence on the other end of the line, a rarity when talking to Renata.

"Are you there?" he asked.

"Oh, yes, I'm here. Were you expecting some explosive overreaction? I'm not about to give you the satisfaction, David. For once in my life, I'm going to maintain my composure. The braided academic will take the apartment, so it's irrelevant. As an added bonus: no need for me to drive to the airport in Friday traffic. It all works out for the best."

"There's a situation here, I'm afraid, and I have to attend to it. I'll let you know when I'm coming back."

"Do that. Of course, if you want me to hire movers to clear out the carriage house and put your treasure in storage, I'd be delighted."

"I should go," he said, but Renata had already hung up.

David pulled into a dark little neighborhood of small, fenced houses behind the downtown center of Hammond. According to his phone, he was 120 feet from Craig's Computers.

45

There were certain periods in the day when business spiked and other moments when it went into a lull. Mandy figured this was probably an indicator of human nature on one hand and office productivity in general on the other.

For instance, she'd noted that on Fridays, business started to go up around noon, a sign that people were beginning to act as if their weekends were officially under way. Casual Fridays, indeed. She supposed it also meant that the men who visited the site were preparing for the weekends they'd spend with their wives and kids by first chatting with her. Some of them even referred to plans to go away for the weekend or on a family camping trip and then told her what they'd do if they could spend the weekend in a tent with her instead. It was lucrative once she got them talking, but there was something basically sad in it. Sad for the wives and kids, and sad for the men who were stuck in a life they weren't truly committed to and didn't appear to like all that much. More recently, she'd begun to realize that all of it said something sad about her, too, but why bother going there?

The most depressing time of the week was now—late Friday afternoon. This was when the number of men online began to slowly drop as people turned off their computers. It made her feel as if she was being left in this dank basement. The men had places to go, even if they didn't like where they were headed.

That was why, ordinarily, she made sure she was home by now. But since David was leaving, she didn't want to be around for the big goodbye. She was too angry with him, even if she knew the anger didn't make a lot of sense. She'd asked him to come to Beauport, and he'd come. He'd helped get her father less worried about the college thing, had helped her mother tidy up the house, and now he was leaving. That had been the deal all along, so what right did she have to complain if he'd changed his mind about staying?

She couldn't completely put her finger on it, but if she had to guess, she'd guess that she was upset that he, like the creepy men she talked to, had somewhere else to go and was going, while she was stuck. Even though she often found the men she talked to awful in different ways—they probably all hated women, and a few had made racist comments about singers or the Obamas—she sometimes felt a flicker of jealousy when they signed off. As if they were abandoning her. The way David was abandoning her and her mother.

She was, at the moment, making zero money, not a huge surprise since she was basically sitting there staring off into space. Who'd pay to see that?

The worst of all her inconsistent and contradictory feelings was that she'd tried to hide what she'd been doing from David, billing it as a receptionist job or whatever he got from her vague comments, and now she resented him for not challenging her on it, for not realizing that she had been lying. For not—why try to kid herself?—rescuing her.

According to the time on the computer, David would have left the house by now, would be on his way to the airport, or maybe was already there. It would be painful to walk into the house and walk past his tiny room and see it empty. He was so OCD about making everything tidy, she knew that the room would be spotless and the bed made and all his clean towels back in the locked linen closet.

What she really hated to picture was him getting on the plane and putting on his seat belt and sitting back as the plane lifted off and all of this summer, including her and her mother and Opal, fell off into the insignificant distance.

In the weeks she'd been coming to this house, she'd felt as if she was coming to an isolated island. This despite the fact that it was surrounded by houses on all sides. Craig liked to keep the shades down and the curtains pulled. Once, when she'd been in the kitchen getting water, she'd opened a shade to look out. He'd come in from the other room and pulled it down.

"What's wrong with a little sunlight?" she'd asked. "It's good for you."

"I guess you haven't heard that it causes skin cancer plus destroys your immune system."

Whatever.

After all this time thinking about this house as its own isolated world, it was so strange to hear loud knocking, she at first didn't realize what it was. She thought it was a sound coming from one of the neighboring houses. She'd heard the couple in the house behind fighting one day and had heard a pizza being delivered somewhere else.

When she realized it was coming from upstairs, she froze in front of the computer. What was she supposed to do now? What if it was the police? Craig was constantly bragging that what he was doing (or more accurately, what she was doing) was perfectly legal, but who knew if that was true.

The knocking stopped. Just as well. Probably a religious nut with pamphlets.

Then she heard rapping, this time at the back door. It was amazing how much personality a sound could have. This wasn't the police—it wasn't forceful enough—but it was too loud and insistent to be the Seventh-Day Adventist people. Craig was due home soon, but he wouldn't be knocking.

Her instinct was to ignore it, but somehow she could tell it wasn't going to stop.

She went up to the kitchen quietly, or as quietly as she could on the old stairs. The person outside must have heard her, for there was a pause.

She walked halfway to the door and called out, "Who's there?"

"Mandy? Open the door, please."

The red-and-blue warning signal started flashing and then stopped. He'd never been a threat to her. "David?"

"Open the door, Mandy. I want to talk to you."

Craig had said he'd be back by now, but he was always later than he said he'd be. And more important, David ought to be long gone.

She pulled back the curtain on the door and looked out. He was staring straight at her through a pair of aviator sunglasses. Not angrily, but with determination.

"I thought you left a long time ago," she said.

"Obviously not. Open the door, Mandy."

There was something so disorienting about seeing David, someone she thought of as a part of her real life, standing outside this house, that she realized all of this—coming here, chatting in the basement, doing what she'd done with Craig—had felt like it was happening to someone else, or maybe wasn't happening at all.

She swung the door open, and a hot breeze from the ocean blew in, dispersing the smell of grease and ancient cigarettes that she'd become so used to by now, she barely noticed it anymore. He hesitated for a moment and then took off the glasses and walked in.

"Why are you here?" he asked her.

"I told you. I'm working at this guy's computer company."

His eyes scanned the kitchen and the living room beyond, and she saw what he was seeing—a dirty kitchen in a shabby house, a dining room cluttered with salvaged computer parts that might as well have been recovered from a building collapsed by an earthquake. Altogether, the least plausible computer company on planet Earth.

"I never said it was Microsoft. And I thought you were leaving for the airport."

He was wearing worn green corduroys and a dress shirt, and he looked tall and authoritative in this little kitchen. Also, like a completely different man from the one she'd met in June.

"I had a change of plans," he said. He pulled out one of the yellow vinyl kitchen chairs, the one patched with red duct tape. "Why are you here, Mandy?" he asked again. He sat down at the table calmly, making it clear he wasn't leaving until she answered. The question had a bigger meaning to it, one that couldn't be answered by insisting she had a job. Why *was* she here? To answer that, she'd have to tell him so many things.

"Why did you change your plans?" she asked.

"That's not an answer."

"I know. It's a distraction."

He started to tap his fingers on the table, waiting.

"Craig will be back any minute," she said.

"Good. I'm dying to meet him. We have a lot to talk about."

"He's not a big talker."

He stopped tapping and folded his hands on the table. "You don't have to be doing this, Mandy. You do realize that, don't you? You're too smart and too young and too full of other possibilities."

She heard his disappointment in her, and it sparked her own disappointment in herself. It was building up behind her eyes.

"Everyone does stupid things in their life," he said. "I've done more than my share. You can't undo this any more than I can undo my marriage to your mother. But you can stop right now. I'm not going to ask you for details, because honestly, I'd rather not know. But I want you to understand that you don't need to be doing this."

"What if I do?" she said. "What if I'm not good at anything else?"

"You're not listening to me. I'm telling you something, and I'm not wrong."

"Don't look at me like that," she said. He was staring at her without blinking, as if he was looking into her head. She felt exposed and frightened, mostly because she was almost certain she was going to burst into tears, and she wouldn't let that happen. Still, she heard it in her voice when she asked, "Why didn't you leave like you planned?"

"Because I found out about this."

"How?"

"That's the least important part of this. If you have a backpack or something, I want you to go get it. We're leaving."

There was something about the way he'd said "we" that felt like a piece of tin foil on an exposed nerve in a tooth. It shot through her, and she felt tears start rolling down her face. She hadn't been alone in all this, which at times had felt like the worst part of it. "Are you going to tell my mother?"

"No," he said. "I'm not. You are."

"She'll kill me," she said. And then she realized this wasn't what she was worried about at all. "It will kill her," she said.

"It will be extremely painful, but it won't kill her. We'll figure out a way to tell her."

"And then you leave."

"I'll leave when the dust has settled."

"That could take years."

"I'm not an especially busy man."

She went to the basement and got her backpack and signed off the computer. As she did so, she felt a stab of sadness, not for herself but for the men she was now abandoning. Maybe some of them would wonder what had happened to her. Maybe they'd miss her. But she'd be completely out of reach and long gone. That, somehow, was sad, too. It seemed that life was going to be a series of sad moments that you couldn't escape from. Sad because you were abandoned, sad because you were the one leaving.

She walked into the kitchen, and David stood up. That's when she heard Craig unlocking the door. It swung open and he was standing in the doorway, framed by the light, looking from her to David, assessing the situation. She saw two things right away—how short Craig really was, especially compared with David, and how young he was. He was decades closer to her age than David's. How had he ever seemed so mature and important? He looked for a moment as if he was going to turn and run, and in that moment she saw what she should have seen all along—he had at least as much to lose as she did, maybe more.

"Who's this?" he said.

"I'm Mandy's uncle," David said.

He went toward Craig and held out his hand, and Mandy saw that Craig had no option but to shake it, and that having done so, everything shifted, and he lost his power. "I came to get Mandy," David said. "She's not going to be working here anymore."

Craig moved his gaze to Mandy. She wanted to think he was upset that she was leaving, that she wouldn't be coming back, but probably it was simple worry about having been found out.

"Fine," he said. "Anything else? You want a letter of recommendation?"

"I'll let you know if we do," David said.

She didn't look back as she led David out of the house.

As they drove out of the neighborhood and toward downtown Hammond, David said nothing. She couldn't stand the suspense and the feeling that he must hate her. Finally, he said, "It would help to have a hobby. Anything to take up the extra time you're going to have."

"I know. But I can't do anything. I wish I could."

"What would you like to do?"

"There's a ukulele in the window of the music store over there. I almost bought it a few times."

"Why didn't you?"

"I don't know how to play it."

David swerved and pulled the car into a parking space abruptly. "You can learn," he said. "You can learn anything if you put your mind to it."

She saw the muscles in his jaw flexing, as if he was chewing gum. Except he wasn't.

"Where's the store?" he asked.

"Just up there. But I don't have any money on me."

He turned off the car and opened his door.

"It's all right," he said. "I do. Come along."

46

Julie checked the time as she drove home from the appointment with the rental agent. David's flight was scheduled to be taking off now. He would be in his seat, putting a book into the pocket in front of him and securing his seat belt. It was safe to go home. No goodbyes.

She was determined to be practical and adult about the whole situation and, most of all, to avoid self-pity. She'd tried everything she could think of to get the house, and she'd failed. So be it. Maybe if she tried really hard, she could talk herself into believing it was all for the best. Unfortunately, she wasn't there yet. Whenever she looked around the house, at all the furniture and Aggressively Acquired items she'd bought from probably hundreds of sales over the years, she had trouble believing she was really going to have to move. As if *stuff* could save her. Probably as people were dying, they clung unrealistically to the belief that they couldn't go while there was still food in the fridge far from its expiration date and newspapers that were being delivered.

She'd left a message for Henry this morning, telling him the closing was off. He'd won. They could proceed with the sale and then they'd finalize the divorce. By October, it would all be over.

The rental agent had been kind and understanding when she spoke with her on the phone. Within seconds, she understood that Julie was on the verge of being single again. "I help a lot of women in your situation," she'd said.

It had been such a short trip from wife, mother, and enthusiastic homeowner to "woman in a situation."

"We'll have no trouble finding you something," she'd said. "There are three lovely places we can see immediately."

And so, Julie had gone this afternoon. Two of the lovely places were in what had formerly been a motel near a new industrial park. ("No one wants to stay in motels anymore," the agent had said. "They rent houses or rooms in someone else's house.") The third was a "townhome" in a development called Mill Stream Meadow Estates. A strange name considering there was no mill, meadow, stream, or estates. It was a collection of stripped-down boxes behind a shopping center with a Super Stop and Shop, a Five Guys burger joint, and a few other stores that could be anywhere at all. For decades, Beauport had managed to keep out chains, but the efforts had been swamped by the influence of money and promises of jobs that rarely materialized.

The inside of the townhome was so blank and featureless, Julie had felt herself slipping into an existential malaise, mainly at the thought that there were people who actually liked living in places like this.

"Isn't there something with a little more age and character?" she'd asked. "It doesn't have to be large, but some personality would help. Maybe closer to the center of the town?"

"I'm afraid not," the agent had said. "The year-round-rental market is practically dead. Anything with the kind of character you're looking for and in a decent location is being rented on Airbnb for more per week than the owners could charge for a month."

Karma. There was some consolation in knowing she partly deserved this. Even so, she'd had to excuse herself and go into the townhome bathroom to splash water on her face to stave off a townhome panic attack. As she was shaking her hands dry, she looked out the window and saw the massive parking lot of the shopping center, baking under the sun and shimmering with heat waves. It was so awful, it almost crossed into beauty. She composed herself and went out to tell the agent she'd take it. It was just for a year.

When she pulled into the driveway of her house, she saw that David's rental car was still there. Maybe she'd confused the time of his departure just as she'd confused the time of his arrival. She had a moment of fleeting happiness and then felt a confused flutter in her chest, a premonition that something was amiss.

She sat in the car for another moment, and then, following instinct or perhaps a desire to delay, she walked around the perimeter of the yard to the front of the house. David and Mandy were sitting there on the porch, side by side in the rockers. David was reading to her from one of the Lucia novels, as if it was the most normal, expected thing in the world. Opal was lying quietly at their feet, completely content. David looked at her and smiled, as if he was surprised to see her, but Mandy was averting her eyes. Opal hopped down to her and barked. *You're home, you're home, you're home.*

"I don't understand," she said, picking up her dog and hugging her to her chest. "Was your flight canceled?"

He stood and put down the book. "No," he said. "It wasn't. Mandy wants to talk with you about something, but before she does, I want you to know that I'm going to stay with you until everything gets settled and we figure out a plan for her. Will that be okay?"

A strange calm came over her and her whole body went slack. Supposedly, this was the best way to prevent injury if you had a fall—go limp. She was, she knew, about to have a fall. When Mandy looked up, Julie smiled at her, trying to mimic David's calm. She looked especially young and guileless sitting on the porch, especially pretty in the soft light of the August afternoon. Julie studied her for a minute, her kind, round eyes and sweet face. As she went up to the porch, she tried to take it all in. She had a terrible feeling she'd never be able to see her quite this way again.

47

Renata looked out the window of her Uber and shook her head. Boston.

As she saw it, there were certain cities in the country that were pointless. Yes, they had their fleeting beauty, their esteemed institutions, but on the whole, looked at objectively, they were inessential and pointless. Boston was one of those places. The city made sense only if you thought of it as a sprawling college campus decorated with historic sites and with a few hospitals tossed in for the convenience of Saudi princes in need of cancer treatment.

The college campus aspect of the place explained why Teddy had decided to go to school here. That's what she kept telling herself, but she'd never been able to completely shrug off the suspicion that going to college three thousand miles from home had something to do with his desire to get away from Leonard. Oh, and all right, probably her as well.

If she had it to do over again, she wouldn't marry Leonard. She'd have him impregnate her so she could still have Teddy, and then dump him. For all the financial advantages of the marriage, it was just too contentious, too distant, too abrasive. The marriage had made her a harder, more cynical person. At this point, though, there was no doing it over. She had some happy memories to live on, although those had nothing to do with Leonard. How weird to count as the best and most memorable moments of your life the few hours—which, all totaled, probably didn't amount to twenty-four—she'd spent in hotel rooms with someone she barely knew. Paolo. Mr. Alitalia. Who knew what had happened to him? Their affair had come at the last possible second she could attract such a man. If he suddenly called again, would she take the bait and agree to see him? Absolutely not. Too much had changed in the past fifteen years—a loss of muscle tone in her legs, a pad of fat around her abdomen, an eyelift that hadn't disguised her actual age but instead had made her look perpetually startled by the reality of being in her sixties.

Oh, not that she was going to get any second chances, but what the hell, if she did, maybe she would marry Leonard after all. He had been a good father to Teddy, at least in the sense that he'd had the decency to let her raise him. And the truth was, since they'd taken sex off the table altogether, they were becoming mildly affectionate with each other. She could snuggle into his warm, pudgy body without having to worry that anyone was going to remove clothing. Secretly, she was more physically attracted to him than she'd been in her forties, although she suspected it was similar to the attraction she felt for Mumbai now that she knew she'd never have to visit that hellishly humid and crowded city again. In a marriage, you either kept at it on a weekly basis or you kept to different sides of a bed wide enough to count as separate rooms. The middle ground of fucking twice a year was grotesque.

She liked seeing life in stages. Very Eric Erikson. The current stage (the Yes-to-Mirrors-No-to-Photos Stage) would lead to the It's-Not-Cancer Stage (although in Leonard's case, it might be) and then, the inevitable next stage—the Bedpan Stage. It was important to have someone there for the final stages. And by "there" she meant in the distance signing the checks.

When she first moved to San Francisco, she'd thought it was one of the pointless cities. The prettiness was iconic, but somehow counted against it. Yes, it was constantly on the edge of disaster—earthquakes, drought, AIDS, massive economic inequality—but even those didn't give it the gravitas of New York or Los Angeles or even lesser lights like Miami and Chicago. She had conquered the city. She'd made a name for herself, in an insignificant way. She'd never have been able to do that in Los Angeles or New York—not in acting, naturally, and not even in real estate.

The Boston sky was gray. She certainly could have conquered this city, or at least made a name for herself in it. It was that minor. The air was heavy and humid. September 4 and still summer here on the East Coast.

"How long is the ride to Beauport?" she asked the driver.

"Probably an hour," he said.

"An hour? How much is this going to cost?"

"It should have come up on your app."

"Oh, right." Her app.

The driver was attractive in an awkward way, one of those clumsy young men who might turn out to be an ardent and unexpectedly unselfish lover with an older woman, if only because he believed in showing his mother respect. He was wearing a white shirt and a tie and a pair of red suspenders. The outfit commented on the role he was playing. Seduction was, thank god, out of the question, but flirtation was still on the table. If she could no longer get someone like this to want her, she could get him to be intimidated by her, which was, in its way, the bigger thrill. All you had to do was act a little languid and this type backed off, terrified you were going to make an advance that would be impossible to accept and embarrassing to reject, like an inappropriate kiss from a drunken, aging aunt.

"What's your name?"

"Clarke."

"Have you been to Beauport, Clarke?"

"Once."

"Did you like it?"

He looked at her in the rearview. "It's all right, especially if you're into the ocean. Otherwise, I'm not sure I see the point."

"We think alike, Clarke. I'm going to make a surprise visit to a friend. I was coming to Boston to visit my son—another surprise visit, but irrelevant to this conversation—and I thought I might as well drop in on David. He was supposed to return to San Francisco two weeks ago and he canceled at the last minute."

"Will he be happy to see you?"

"Very few people are happy to see me these days, Clarke, but he'll be overjoyed once I hand him the envelope I have in my bag."

"Money?"

"Is there another option?"

"What if he's not home?"

"I was under the impression Beauport was the kind of place where there's nowhere else to go but home."

"There are a lot of seafood restaurants," he said.

"Any you'd recommend? I wouldn't mind a lobster roll."

"I'm vegan."

This word had become ubiquitous and absurdly trendy. She supposed there were a few young women with anorexia who kept to this diet, but otherwise it had to be lip service.

"I have a theory, Clarke. Want to hear it? There are no male vegans. There are men who say they are to appear more sensitive to their girlfriends or anyone else they're hoping to lure into bed with them. Once they're on their own, they're in a drive-through line at Burger King."

"McDonald's," he said.

"I'm famous for my burgers, Clarke. We didn't have vegans when I was your age, dear. We had macrobiotics. I don't know where they all went. We didn't have gluten intolerance, either. We had hypoglycemia. I'll bet you've never heard of that."

She didn't care what she sounded like. They still had a long way to go, and she was enjoying herself.

"We had aerobics, not Pilates. We didn't have different layers of gender. We had Martina Navratilova and no one thought anything of it."

"You didn't have Uber."

"No, of course not. We had jobs."

She closed her eyes and leaned back against the seat. The flight had been long and at times bumpy. Once upon a time, she'd been a nervous flyer, but now that the best years of her life were, by almost any measure, behind her, the idea of dying in a crash was unpleasant but not tragic. She took off her shoes and folded her feet under her.

Teddy had refused to come home for the summer, claiming he had an internship with a public relations firm. Internships. Please! Classes started later in the week, so she decided to pop in for a visit before he got too busy. And then the plan to surprise David. She needed to find out what the hell had been going on. He'd actually taken her up on the offer to have everything moved out of the carriage house and into storage so Porter and Soren—bless their rich hearts—could get the house. He'd be back "later in the fall," whatever that meant. She'd pressed Michael Taylor for details. Lovely Michael. Essentially dull in that Midwestern way she knew from her childhood, but endlessly interested in her salacious tales of Paolo. When he told her of David's plans to help out his ex-wife and stay in Beauport, she'd actually been touched. It undoubtedly wasn't selfless, but it seemed to be. She'd been even more horrible to him than she'd admitted. She'd sought out the listing for the property he'd been living on by calling the landlady for months and promising her she'd have a buyer without any inconvenience to her. Then she'd contacted Porter. (If Leonard needed to have his chest sawed open at some point, Porter was getting a call.) Worst of all, she didn't need the commission. She had more than enough money already. She'd just been trying to show the young agents in her office she still had it. The envelope contained a check equal to the commission she'd earn—found money or ill-gotten gains, dispensable either way—a nice fat profit for David, and, she hoped, a new beginning for her. She was going to become a kinder, gentler person, less selfish, less greedy. That would deflect attention from her harder, less expressive face.

Thoughts of her new beneficence lulled her, and she drifted off.

When she woke up, the temperature had dropped and Clarke was turning into the driveway of a monstrous house somewhere on the early end of the Grey Gardens trajectory. It was late afternoon and a pretty sunset was lighting up the side of the house and the impressive privet hedge surrounding the property. If she was listing this dump in San Francisco, she'd put it on the market for mid-seven figures and set off a nuclear bidding war. Here? Lunch money.

"Pull over behind those cars, Clarke. I want to attempt an entrance. Once we make sure they're home, you can go for a fried clam plate for a couple of hours until I'm ready to leave. Mama's treat."

The moment to start wearing flats was approaching (according to her doctor, it had arrived five years earlier), but she was still going to work her advantage. The lawn was a bumpy, pitted mess, but she was not going to be seen wobbling and stumbling across it. Who needed good balance and arthritis-free feet as long as you had determination?

David was sitting at the dining room table, working on his computer, when he heard the car pull into the drive. Probably someone who'd made a wrong turn. In the aftermath of the tears and meetings that came with the Mandy crisis, they'd decided to suspend renting rooms for a few weeks, at least until she got settled back in school. Amira's husband was not buying the house, so Julie had a little more time to get out. He'd stay, as promised, until everything was settled, and then make his own plans.

He listened for the car to back out, but after a few minutes, he went to the stairs and called up to Julie, "Someone pulled into the drive. Are you expecting anyone?"

"No, unless it's someone coming to look at the house. In which case, I'm going for a walk."

"I'll go out and check."

The hardest part for Julie had been trying to remember that Mandy was, fundamentally, the same person she'd been before Julie learned the whole horrifying story. She didn't want to make the mistake of looking at her as if she was a stranger and alienating her further, but that was easier said than done. That had been an afternoon she had no desire to relive. In the two weeks since, Mandy had spent most of her time in her room playing the ukulele with a commitment that was impressive even if her musical skills were . . . well, developing. Every once in a while, she heard Mandy singing and fumbling her way through something like "Blue Moon" or "Blue Skies" and her heart broke all over again. She just wanted everything to be the way it had been two months earlier, when helping her navigate her way through college applications had been her big challenge. And on top of everything, David had started to help her pack up the house. One box at a time.

When David didn't report back about the car in the drive, she decided to go and investigate with him. One way or another, she was going to have to face prospective buyers eventually.

As Renata was halfway to the house, a trim, attractive man stepped out onto the deck. Probably one of the guests or whatever they were called in this kind of establishment. When she got a little closer, she realized it was David. He was shielding his eyes against the sun. He had a tan, and he'd lost at least twenty pounds. That was a horrible disappointment. It robbed her of an advantage. On the other hand, it probably indicated he was happy, and if she was really going to be a nicer person, she had to start approving of things like that. A woman stepped out and stood beside him. Good-looking in the New England, I've-never-worn-makeup mode. No doubt the ex-wife. David put his arm around her waist as they discussed something. Oddly, they did look like a couple, although a couple of what wasn't entirely clear.

"Well, you could at least say hello," she called out.

David scrutinized her and said, "Renata? What the fuck are you doing here?"

"I've come to check in for a week. And I hope that's how you greet all of your guests."

48

By the first of October, the daytime temperatures had become completely erratic, in the high forties one day and soaring into the high eighties the next. Environmental mood swings. The nights were mostly cool and clear, and with the leaves starting to thin, Mandy could hear the ocean from her bedroom if she slept with the windows open and if the wind was blowing onshore. It was the sound of her childhood, the waves washing against the rocks in the harbor below as she tried to go to sleep, that and the house creaking as it embraced her. She would miss those sounds. She would miss Beauport, the morning sun on the water, and the mathematically predicable rhythm of the tides. She had started to miss everything and everyone else she thought she hated: Beachy Keen, Elaine Guild, Lindsay. She even missed Craig sometimes, but only in the way she missed the lazy dopiness of having the flu once she was over it.

Her father was arriving any minute, and she still hadn't finished packing. It wasn't that she had trouble deciding what to bring, it was more that she couldn't decide what to leave behind. She'd started out packing the six pairs of overalls she owned, but little by little, over the course of a few hours, had pruned down to two. Now as she sat on the edge of her bed looking into the duffel bag where everything was neatly rolled—as David had suggested—she wondered if it might not be a good idea to take them out, too. She and Sheila (aka Dr. Pierson) had spent most of their time together talking about letting go. She'd seen Sheila twice a week for the past five weeks, and even though she hadn't trusted her at first and had never grown to like her, she knew she'd miss her, too. Her quiet little office with the ugly framed posters and the ticking clock and the slight menace in Sheila's smile when she told Mandy that forgiving herself was the first step toward putting everything in perspective.

"What about my mother forgiving me?" Mandy had asked her. "How do I know when that's happened?"

Sheila, with her maddening tendency to answer questions with a question, said, "You tell me. How *will* you know?"

She hadn't had to give it much thought. "I guess when she looks at me and I can tell that what I did isn't the first thing she thinks about."

She was still waiting on that, and time was running out.

The house was officially her mother's. That was a relief. David's, too, apparently, since they'd used some of his money to buy it. Some big check had been delivered by his weird friend from San Francisco who—one thing in her favor—had kept calling her "Amanda," even after she explained that that wasn't her name.

Supposedly they were going to start to convert the barn for David before winter, but she'd believe that when she saw it.

She zipped up the duffel bag and slung it over her shoulder. It was so heavy, it threw her off balance and she fell back on the bed. It was embarrassing to think about arriving at school with, literally, so much baggage. She unzipped the bag, took out both remaining pairs of overalls, and tossed them into the far reaches of her closet. It was amazing how much lighter it felt.

David had used his connections to persuade a school in western Massachusetts to take her now, three weeks after the official start of classes. It wasn't as if she was looking forward to it, but it was a lot better than going to Beauport High or moving in with her father and Carol. She was supposedly too traumatized to go back to her old school, where rumors were circulating. If you could believe the hype on this new school's website, it emphasized life experience and got students out into the community to do actual good in the real world. They had lined up an internship for her at a food bank. At first, it sounded like a sentence you'd get from a judge after vandalizing the school cafeteria, but the more she read about it, the more interesting it sounded, and in her own private way, she had been a vandal of some kind. She'd talked to her roommate already. Three times. The roommate's name was "D" and wanted to be called "they" instead of "she." Mandy had a feeling she was not going to be the only person at the school with a complicated story.

"Mandy," David called. "You'd better hurry, your father just arrived."

"Be right there."

She dropped her bag one more time and went into her mother's bedroom. She lay down on the bed for a minute and buried her face in her pillow, breathing in the familiar smell of her mother's shampoo and whatever else it was that gave people distinctive scents aside from perfumes and cosmetics. It might be nice to steal the pillowcase and take it with her, but that would be too weird and doglike. She'd leave it for Opal. She took the college essay she'd finally completed and printed out and slipped it under her pillow. She imagined her mother reading it that night when she got into bed. She thought probably she should say all this to her face, but her mother was so hurt and disappointed, it was hard to say anything to her. And sometimes it was good to commit things to paper.

What Is Square One and Can You Really Go Back to It?

When I was ten years old, my mother and father and I went to the Catskills. We rented a cottage along a rocky stream and went hiking in the mountains most days. Late in the afternoon, we'd go swimming. To get to the lake from our cottage, we had to drive up a steep, twisting, seasonal road that hugged the side of a mountain. It had no railings and sheer drops on one side into the ravine below. My father couldn't believe the State of New York allowed this road to be open when it was so dangerous. I liked the roller-coaster thrill of the drive and never believed there was any real danger.

One afternoon when we were swimming, dark clouds rolled in, and we packed everything up and started to head back to the cottage. By the time we were on the steep, twisting road, the sky was black and there was lightning ripping up the sky and so much rain, my father decided it was better to not even try using the windshield wipers. The three of us sat silent as we slowly wound down the mountain. When branches blowing off the trees started to hit the roof of the car, my mother asked my father if it wouldn't be a better idea to head back and wait at the top until the storm passed. But we couldn't. We were halfway down, there was nowhere to turn around, and going up was no safer than going down. We just had to drive through to the end.

I spent most of my summer in a dark place, wanting to undo my mistakes, looking behind me to find a place to turn around and go back where everything was brighter and none of my bad decisions had been made. Where I hadn't disappointed the people I care about the most. But I couldn't, I had to drive through to the end. I'm not there yet, but I can see now that if there is a Square One, it's on the road ahead, and the only thing that will prevent me from getting there is looking back. And when I get there, Mom, I promise you'll be the first person I call.

Her parents and David were sitting in the living room, talking like normal human beings, and when she walked in, they all stood at once. Except that her mother still had that look on her face—not cold, not angry, but as if it hurt her muscles to produce her tight, forced smile. It made Mandy's stomach ache to be seen the way she knew her mother was seeing her. Not as the girl she wanted to hold and praise—even when she didn't deserve it—or tuck in at night—even though she was too old for that—but as the girl in the basement, talking with predators. But there was nothing she could do to change it now. She had to keep putting one foot in front of the other and hope that somewhere along the road, her mother would meet her, and see that she was, despite everything, still her daughter.

"I told them we'd be there by two," her father said, "so we'd better get going."

They all went out to the lawn, and Opal, who seemed to know what was going on, hopped around the pine tree in crazy circles, barking and growling. Mandy hugged David goodbye and thanked him. "For showing up," she said, but she didn't know if she meant in Beauport or at Craig's.

"But you're the one who invited me," he said. "So let's call it even. Look what I ended up with." He gestured toward the barn and the yard and then Julie, who was standing beside him.

She looked at her mother, not sure if it was okay to put her arms around her.

"I feel like I'm forgetting something," her mother said sadly, "but I can't remember what. Text me when you get there, okay?" She hugged her tightly, but Mandy had the feeling it took some effort.

"I will," she said.

Once she and her father had loaded everything into the back of his car, she had a fantasy that the engine would be dead, and the whole move would be put off for another day or another week, but the engine ran smoothly, and by the time she had her seat belt buckled, her father was releasing the emergency brake.

As her father backed up the car, she had a view of her mother and David on the lawn with Opal, waving goodbye with the pine tree and the house behind them and the hedge turning yellow. Her father turned the car around, and she looked in the rearview mirror for a second, hoping to see some sign on her mother's face that it was all right. But there was no one on the lawn now, and the screen door into the house was swinging closed.

Even her father sensed that something was wrong. "You'll be back for Thanksgiving break before you know it," he said.

She nodded, unable to reassure him that everything was all right.

They turned out of the drive and started down the road to town. But then, just past the front of the house, her father braked the car. Mandy looked up hopefully. And yes, there was her mother hurrying down the sidewalk, waving at them with a bag tucked under her arm. As she came up to the car, Mandy lowered her window. Her mother's hair, loose and graying, was blowing in her face.

"I knew there was something," her mother said. "I meant to give you this inside." She was smiling, a real smile this time, and she handed Mandy the plastic bag with a little piece of red ribbon holding it closed. "Go ahead and look," she said.

It was a blue sweater of Mandy's that she'd worn almost daily all of last year and had abandoned in the bottom of a drawer when the weather had turned warm.

"This used to be your favorite," her mother said. "I thought you might like to have it with you, even if you don't wear it."

And then she leaned in the window and kissed her and walked back toward the house.

Her father was watching her closely; she felt his eyes on her.

He put his hand on her knee. "You tell me when you're ready to go," he said.

It was a warm, clear afternoon, and down in the harbor, a lone sailboat was heading out past the jetty. Mandy took the sweater out of the bag and folded it. She put it on her lap and gently fingered a moth hole in the wool. Even if she didn't wear it, it might become her favorite again.

"Okay, Dad," she said. "I'm ready."

David watched Julie walk up the sidewalk toward the house, her hair blowing in the warm breeze.

In that other, earlier life they'd had together, their ex-life, they'd imagined a future ahead of them full of limitless possibilities. Oh, he'd known even then that everything has its limits, but it appeared there was an immense, glittering expanse of time rolling out before them with a bright end point so far in the distance it was unknowable, but easy to picture being as splendid as Oz.

That stretch of time hadn't been nearly as long or as carefully ordered as they'd thought it would be. Really, it had been a jumble of years that had passed more quickly and chaotically than either of them could have predicted. And, for the most part, they'd traveled through it separately. Most surprising of all, it turned out there was no predetermined destination in the hazy distance they'd been headed toward, Emerald City or otherwise.

Julie came up to the porch and stood beside him, and they looked out at the water and the sailboat heading toward the horizon. After a few minutes, he took her hand, and they went into the house.

There's just the place, David thought, *where you're happiest and most at ease and unpack your bags once and for all.* The pretty, imperfect, unimagined place you decide to call home.

Acknowledgments

Many thanks to the Ragdale Foundation, the Corporation of Yaddo, the Virginia Center for the Creative Arts, and Katherine Sherbooke's Hemingway House. Also to public libraries in Cambridge, Northampton, and Provincetown, Massachusetts; Woodstock and Saugerties, New York; and Montpelier and Burlington, Vermont. Also to Genevieve and Henry Lee and to Paul and Gary Hickox. Also to Peter and Rose.

Also to Larry Rosenberg and Joanne Greenfield.

Also to Christopher Castellani and Michael Borum. Also to Elizabeth Benedict. Also to Brice Cauvin and Franck Crombet. Also to Anita and Amy. Also to Lisa Pannella.

Many, many thanks to Amy Einhorn for making this a much better novel and to Conor Mintzer for making it a more grammatically coherent one.

Many thanks and much love to Sebastian and Chuck and Patti and Matt and Rob and Danielle and Jack.

My Ex-Life
by Stephen McCauley

PLEASE NOTE: In order to provide reading groups with the most informed and thought-provoking questions possible, it is necessary to reveal important aspects of the plot of this novel— as well as the ending. If you have not finished reading *My Ex-Life*, we respectfully suggest that you may want to wait before reviewing this guide.

1. Did you read the book in print or on an e-reader? Did you listen to the audiobook? How might the experience of this novel have been different if you had chosen otherwise?

2. Which character was your favorite? Least favorite? Which character changed the most?

3. Who does "my" refer to in the title *My Ex-Life*?

4. In chapter 4, Mandy says, "This was a bad idea and she knew it, but...she was pulled into it by an urge to find out what would happen that was stronger than the urge to listen to the voice telling her not to." At times, Mandy and other characters seem to be acting out of step with their truest selves. Can you think of examples from the novel? What, if anything, sets them right? Do you see any parallels to your own life?

5. Julie's neighbor Amira doesn't hide her husband's aim to take over the Fiske house to make a pool, while David's flame, Kenneth, isn't completely forthcoming about the Airbnb petition. And then there's Renata and Mandy's friend Lindsay. Would you rather have an honestly disloyal friend or a dishonestly loyal one? Who's the best friend in the novel? Who is the worst?

6. McCauley has been praised for his characters' sometimes caustic witticisms, such as "Leonard doesn't have friends. He has financial opportunities wearing socks." Did you have a favorite one-liner in this novel?

7. David reads E. F. Benson's Mapp and Lucia novels aloud to Julie both in their past life and their current one, and the book means different things then and now, but illuminates

both times equally. Are there any books that provide such a touchstone for you?

8. David seems to object to his student Nancy's stretching of the truth for her college application essay, but Nancy's mom, Janine, shrugs it off. Should the truth ever get in the way of a good story?

9. In chapter 18, David presents Mandy with three essay prompts to sharpen her college application:

   - Tell us about the relationship between you and your arch-nemesis, real or imagined.

   - Dog and cat. Coffee and tea. Everyone knows there are two types of people in the world. What are they?

   - What is Square One and can you really go back to it? Pick one and answer it from your own experience. What do you think the novel's answer to each question is?

10. Do you agree with Julie's decision not to tell David she was going to have an abortion? Did he have a right to know? Or did David cede that right by hiding his own secret from Julie?

11. Toward the end of the novel, in chapter 40, David and Julie have a long-deferred reckoning on the stairs. What do you think has greater power, the said or the unsaid? Does timing matter?

12. How has Mandy's life changed as a result of what happened with Craig Crespo? Will she be able to get beyond it?

13. Does David save Julie or does Julie save David? Neither? Both?

14. "All couples start off as Romeo and Juliet and end up as Laurel and Hardy." True?

15. We can always deceive ourselves better than others can deceive us. Do you agree? What might the novel argue? (Consider: David's sexual orientation, Julie's marijuana habit, etc.)

16. In the past, McCauley has said he's fascinated by the idea of chosen (as opposed to born) families. Which family in the novel strikes you as most true? What might your answer say about "family" in our times?